Georg Ebers, Mary Joanna Safford

The Burgomaster's Wife

Georg Ebers, Mary Joanna Safford

The Burgomaster's Wife

ISBN/EAN: 9783744782265

Printed in Europe, USA, Canada, Australia, Japan

Cover: Foto ©Andreas Hilbeck / pixelio.de

More available books at **www.hansebooks.com**

BARONESS ·SOPHIE VON BRANDENSTEIN,

née EBERS.

My reason for dedicating a book, and particularly this book, to you, the only sister of my dead father, needs no word of explanation between us. From early childhood you have been a dear and faithful friend to me, and certainly have not forgotten how industriously I labored, while your guest seventeen years ago, in arranging the material which constitutes the foundation of the " Burgomaster's Wife." You then took a friendly interest in many a note of facts, that had seemed to me extraordinary, admirable, or amusing, and when the claims of an arduous profession prevented me from pursuing my favorite occupation of studying the history of Holland, my mother's home, in the old way, never wearied of reminding me of the fallow material, that had previously awakened your sympathy.

At last I have been permitted to give the matter so long laid aside its just dues. A beautiful portion of Holland's glorious history affords the espalier, around which the tendrils of my narrative entwine. You have watched them grow, and therefore will view them kindly and indulgently.

In love and friendship,

Ever the same,

GEORG EBERS

Leipsic, Oct. 30th, 1881.

THE BURGOMASTER'S WIFE.

CHAPTER I.

In the year 1574 A. D. spring made its joyous entry into the Netherlands at an unusually early date.

The sky was blue, gnats sported in the sunshine, white butterflies alighted on the newly-opened yellow flowers, and beside one of the numerous ditches inter-secting the wide plain stood a stork, snapping at a fine frog; the poor fellow soon writhed in its enemy's red beak. One gulp—the merry jumper vanished, and its murderer, flapping its wings, soared high into the air. On flew the bird over gardens filled with blossoming fruit-trees, trimly laid-out flower-beds, and gaily-painted arbors, across the frowning circlet of walls and towers that girdled the city, over narrow houses with high, pointed gables, and neat streets bordered with elm, poplar, linden and willow-trees, decked with the first green leaves of spring. At last it alighted on a lofty gable-roof, on whose ridge was its firmly-fastened nest. After generously giving up its prey to the little wife brooding over the eggs, it stood on one leg and gazed thoughtfully down upon the city, whose shining red tiles gleamed spick and span from the green velvet carpet of the meadows. The bird had known beautiful Leyden, the gem of Holland, for many a year, and was familiar with all the branches of the Rhine that divided the stately city into numerous islands, and over which arched as many stone bridges as there are days in five months of the year; but surely many changes had occurred here since the stork's last departure for the south.

Where were the citizens' gay summer-houses and orchards, where the wooden frames on which the weavers used to stretch their dark and colored cloths?

Whatever plant or work of human hands had risen, outside the city walls and towers to the height of a man's breast, thus interrupting the uniformity of the plain, had vanished from the earth, and beyond, on the bird's best hunting-grounds, brownish spots sown with black circles appeared among the green of the meadows.

Late in October of the preceding year, just after the storks left the country, a Spanish army had encamped here, and a few hours before the return of the winged wanderers in the first opening days of spring, the besiegers retired without having accomplished their purpose.

Barren spots amid the luxuriant growth of vegetation marked the places where they had pitched their tents, the black cinders of the burnt coals their camp-fires.

The sorely-threatened inhabitants of the rescued city, with thankful hearts, uttered sighs of relief. The industrious, volatile populace had speedily forgotten the sufferings endured, for early spring is so beautiful, and never does a rescued life seem so delicious as when we are surrounded by the joys of spring.

A new and happier time appeared to have dawned, not only for Nature but for human beings. The troops quartered in the besieged city, which had the day before committed many an annoyance, had been dismissed with song and music. The carpenter's axe flashed in the spring sunlight before the red walls, towers and gates, and cut sharply into the beams from which new scaffolds and frames were to be erected; noble cattle grazed peacefully undisturbed around the city, whose desolated gardens were being dug, sowed and planted afresh. In the streets and houses a thousand hands, which but a short time before had guided spears and arquebuses on the walls and towers, were busy at useful work, and old people sat quietly before their doors to let the warm spring sun shine on their backs.

Few discontented faces were to be seen in Leyden on this eighteenth of April. True, there was no lack of impatient ones, and whoever wanted to seek them need only go to the principal school, where noon was approaching and many boys gazed far more eagerly through the open windows of the school-room, than at the teacher's lips.

But in that part of the spacious hall where the older lads received instruction, no restlessness prevailed. True, the spring sun shone on their books and exercises too, the spring called them into the open air, but even more powerful than its alluring voice seemed the influence exerted on their young minds by what they were now hearing.

Forty sparkling eyes were turned towards the bearded man, who addressed them in his deep voice.

Even wild Jan Mulder had dropped the knife with which he had begun to cut on his desk a well-executed figure of a ham, and was listening attentively.

The noon bell now rang from the neighboring church, and soon after was heard from the tower of the town-hall, the little boys noisily left the room, but—strange—the patience of the older ones still held out;

they were surely hearing things that did not exactly belong to their lessons.

The man who stood before them was no teacher in the school, but the city clerk, Van Hout, who, to-day filled the place of his sick friend, Verstroot, master of arts and preacher. During the ringing of the bells he had closed the book, and now said :

" *Suspendo lectionem.* Jan Mulder, how would you translate my ' *suspendere*' ? "

" Hang," replied the boy.

" Hang !" laughed Van Hout. " You might be hung from a hook perhaps, but where should we hang a lesson ? Adrian Van der Werff."

The lad called rose quickly, saying :

" ' *Suspendere lectionem* ' means to break off the lesson."

" Very well; and if we wanted to hang up Jan Mulder, what should we say ?"

" *Patibulare—ad patibulum !*" cried the scholars.

Van Hout, who had just been smiling, grew very grave. Drawing a long breath, he said :

" *Patibulo* is a bad Latin word, and your fathers, who formerly sat here, understood its meaning far less thoroughly than you. Now, every child in the Netherlands knows it, Alva has impressed it on our minds. More than eighteen thousand worthy citizens have come to the gallows through his ' *ad patibulum.*' "

With these words he pulled his short black doublet through his girdle, advanced nearer the first desk, and bending his muscular body forward, said with constantly increasing emotion :

" This shall be enough for to-day, boys. It will do no great harm, if you afterwards forget the names learned here. But always remember one thing: your country first of all. Leonidas and his three hundred Spartans did not die in vain, so long as there are men ready to follow their example. Your turn will come too. It is not my business to boast, but truth is truth. We Hollanders have furnished fifty times three hundred men for the freedom of our native soil. In such stormy times there are steadfast men; even boys have shown themselves great. Ulrich yonder, at your head, can bear his nickname of Löwing with honor. 'Hither Persians—hither Greeks!' was said in ancient times, but we cry: 'Hither Netherlands, hither Spain!' And indeed, the proud Darius never ravaged Greece as King Philip has devastated Holland. Ay, my lads, many flowers bloom in the breasts of men. Among them is hatred of the poisonous hemlock. Spain has sowed it in our gardens. I feel it growing within me, and you too feel and ought to feel it. But don't misunderstand me! 'Hither Spain—hither Netherlands!' is the cry, and not: 'Hither Catholics and hither Protestants.' Every faith may be right in the Lord's eyes, if only the man strives earnestly to walk in Christ's ways. At the throne of Heaven, it will not be asked: Are you Papist, Calvinist, or Lutheran? but: What were your intentions and acts? Respect every man's belief; but despise him who makes common cause with the tyrant against the liberty of our native land. Now pray silently, then you may go home."

The scholars rose; Van Hout wiped the perspiration from his high forehead, and while the boys were collecting books, pencils, and pens, said slowly, as if apologizing to himself for the words already uttered:

"What I have told you perhaps does not belong to

the school-room; but, my lads, this battle is still far from being ended, and though you must occupy the school-benches for a while, you are the future soldiers. Löwing, remain behind, I have something to say to you."

He slowly turned his back to the boys, who rushed out of doors. *In a corner of the yard of St. Peter's church, which was behind the building and entered by few of the passers-by, they stood still, and from amid the wild confusion of exclamations arose a sort of consultation, to which the organ-notes echoing from the church formed a strange accompaniment.

They were trying to decide upon the game to be played in the afternoon.

It was a matter of course, after what Van Hout had said, that there should be a battle; it had not even been proposed by anybody, but the discussion that now arose proceeded from the supposition.

It was soon decided that patriots and Spaniards, not Greeks and Persians, were to appear in the lists against each other; but when the burgomaster's son, Adrian Van der Werff, a lad of fourteen, proposed to form the two parties, and in the imperious way peculiar to him attempted to make Paul Van Swieten and Claus Dirkson Spaniards, he encountered violent opposition, and the troublesome circumstance was discovered that no one was willing to represent a foreign soldier.

Each boy wanted to make somebody else a Castilian, and fight himself under the banner of the Netherlands. But friends and foes are necessary for a war, and Holland's heroic courage required Spaniards to prove it. The youngsters grew excited, the cheeks of the disputants began to flush, here and there clenched fists were raised, and everything indicated that a horrible civil war would precede the battle to be given the foes of the country.

In truth, these lively boys were ill-suited to play the part of King Philip's gloomy, stiff-necked soldiers. Amid the many fair heads, few lads were seen with brown locks, and only one with black hair and dark eyes. This was Adam Baersdorp, whose father, like Van der Werff's, was one of the leaders of the citizens. When he too refused to act a Spaniard, one of the boys exclaimed:

"You won't? Yet my father says your father is half a Glipper,* and a whole Papist to boot."

At these words young Baersdorp threw his books on the ground, and was rushing with upraised fist upon his enemy—but Adrian Van der Werff hastily interposed, crying:

"For shame, Cornelius.—I'll stop the mouth of anybody who utters such an insult again. Catholics are Christians, as well as we. You heard it from Van Hout, and my father says so too. Will you be a Spaniard, Adam, yes or no?"

"No!" cried the latter firmly. "And if anybody else—"

"You can quarrel afterward," said Adrian Van der Werff, interrupting his excited companions, then good-naturedly picking up the books Baersdorp had flung down, and handing them to him, continued resolutely: "I'll be a Spaniard to-day. Who else?"

"I, I, I too, for aught I care," shouted several of the scholars, and the forming of the two parties would

---

* The name given in Holland to those who sympathized with Spain.

have been carried on in the best order to the end, if the boys' attention had not been diverted by a fresh incident.

A young gentleman, followed by a black servant, came up the street directly towards them. He too was a Netherlander, but had little in common with the school-boys except his age, a red and white complexion, fair hair, and clear blue eyes, eyes that looked arrogantly out upon the world. Every step showed that he considered himself an important personage, and the gaily-costumed negro, who carried a few recently purchased articles behind him, imitated this bearing in a most comical way. The negro's head was held still farther back than the young noble's, whose stiff Spanish ruff prevented him from moving his handsome head as freely as other mortals.

"That ape, Wibisma," said one of the school-boys, pointing to the approaching nobleman.

All eyes turned towards him, scornfully scanning his little velvet hat decked with a long plume, the quilted red satin garment padded in the breast and sleeves, the huge puffs of his short brown breeches, and the brilliant scarlet silk stockings that closely fitted his well-formed limbs.

"The ape," repeated Paul Van Swieten. "He wants to be a cardinal, that's why he wears so much red."

"And looks as Spanish as if he came straight from Madrid," cried another lad, while a third added:

"The Wibismas certainly were not to be found here, so long as bread was short with us."

The Wibismas are all Glippers.

"And he struts about on week-days, dressed in velvet and silk," said Adrian. "Just look at the black boy the red-legged stork has brought with him to Leyden."

The scholars burst into a loud laugh, and as soon as the youth had reached them, Paul Van Swieten snarled in a nasal tone:

"How did deserting suit you? How are affairs in Spain, master Glipper?"

The young noble raised his head still higher, the negro did the same, and both walked quietly on, even when Adrian shouted in his ear:

"Little Glipper, tell me, for how many pieces of silver did Judas sell the Saviour?"

Young Matanesse Van Wibisma made an indignant gesture, but controlled himself until Jan Mulder stepped in front of him, holding his little cloth cap, into which he had thrust a hen's feather, under his chin like a beggar, and saying humbly:

"Give me a little shrove-money for our tom-cat, Sir Grandee; he stole a leg of veal from the butcher yesterday."

"Out of my way!" said the youth in a haughty, resolute tone, trying to push Mulder aside with the back of his hand.

"Hands off, Glipper!" cried the school-boys, raising their clenched hands threateningly.

"Then let me alone," replied Wibisma, "I want no quarrel, least of all with you."

"Why not with us?" asked Adrian Van der Werff, irritated by the supercilious, arrogant tone of the last words.

The youth shrugged his shoulders, but Adrian cried:

"Because you like your Spanish costume better than our doublets of Leyden cloth."

Here he paused, for Jan Mulder stole behind Wibisma, struck his hat down on his head with a book, and while Nicolas Van Wibisma was trying to free his eyes from the covering that shaded them, exclaimed:

"There, Sir Grandee, now the little hat sits firm! You can keep it on, even before the king."

The negro could not go to his master's assistance, for his arms were filled with parcels, but the young noble did not call him, knowing how cowardly his black servant was, and feeling strong enough to help himself.

A costly clasp, which he had just received as a gift on his seventeenth birthday, confined the plume in his hat; but without a thought he flung it aside, stretched out his arms as if for a wrestling-match, and with flushed cheeks, asked in a loud, resolute tone: "Who did that?"

Jan Mulder had hastily retreated among his companions, and instead of coming forward and giving his name, called:

"Look for the hat-fuller, Glipper! We'll play blind-man's buff."

The youth, frantic with rage, repeated his question.

When, instead of any other answer, the boys entered into Jan Mulder's jest, shouting gaily: "Yes, play blind-man's buff! Look for the hat-fuller. Come, little Glipper, begin." Nicolas could contain himself no longer, but shouted furiously to the laughing throng:

"Cowardly rabble!"

Scarcely had the words been uttered, when Paul Van Swieten raised his grammar, bound in hog-skin, and hurled it at Wibisma's breast.

Other books followed, amid loud outcries, striking

him on the legs and shoulders. Bewildered, he shielded his face with his hands and retreated to the church-yard wall, where he stood still and prepared to rush upon his foes.

The stiff, fashionable high Spanish ruff no longer confined his handsome head with its floating golden locks. Freely and boldly he looked his enemies in the face, stretched the young limbs hardened by many a knightly exercise, and with a true Netherland oath sprang upon Adrian Van der Werff, who stood nearest.

After a short struggle, the burgomaster's son, inferior in strength and age to his opponent, lay extended on the ground; but the other lads, who had not ceased shouting, "Glipper, Glipper," seized the young noble, who was kneeling on his vanquished foe.

Nicolas struggled bravely, but his enemies' superior power was too great.

Frantic with fury, wild with rage and shame, he snatched the dagger from his belt.

The boys now raised a frightful yell, and two of them rushed upon Nicolas to wrest the weapon from him. This was quickly accomplished; the dagger flew on the pavement, but Van Swieten sprang back with a low cry, for the sharp blade had struck his arm, and the bright blood streamed on the ground.

For several minutes the shouts of the lads and the piteous cries of the black page drowned the beautiful melody of the organ, pouring from the windows of the church. Suddenly the music ceased; instead of the intricate harmony the slowly-dying note of a single pipe was heard, and a young man rushed out of the door of the sacristy of the House of God. He quickly perceived the cause of the wild uproar that had interrupted his practising, and a smile flitted over the handsome face which, framed by a closely-cut beard, had just looked startled enough, though the reproving words and pushes with which he separated the enraged lads were earnest enough, and by no means failed to produce their effect.

The boys knew the musician, Wilhelm Corneliussohn, and offered no resistance, for they liked him, and his dozen years of seniority gave him an undisputed authority among them. Not a hand was again raised against Wibisma, but the boys, all shouting and talking together, crowded around the organist to accuse Nicolas and defend themselves.

Paul Van Swieten's wound was slight. He stood outside the circle of his companions, supporting the injured left arm with his right hand. He frequently blew upon the burning spot in his flesh, over which a bit of cloth was wrapped, but curiosity concerning the result of this entertaining brawl was stronger than the wish to have it bandaged and healed.

As the peace-maker's work was already drawing to a close, the wounded lad, pointing with his sound hand in the direction of the school, suddenly called warningly:

"There comes Herr von Nordwyk. Let the Glipper go, or there will be trouble."

Paul Van Swieten again clasped his wounded arm with his right hand and ran swiftly around the church. Several other boys followed, but the new-comer of whom they were afraid, a man scarcely thirty years old, had legs of considerable length, and knew how to use them bravely.

"Stop, boys!" he shouted in an echoing voice of command. "Stop! What has happened here?"

Every one in Leyden respected the learned and brave young nobleman, so all the lads who had not instantly obeyed Van Swieten's warning shout, stood still until Herr von Nordwyk reached them.

A strange, eager light sparkled in this man's clever eyes, and a subtle smile hovered around his moustached lip, as he called to the musician:

"What has happened here, Meister Wilhelm? Didn't the clamor of Minerva's apprentices harmonize with your organ-playing, or did — but by all the colors of Iris, that's surely Nico Matanesse, young Wibisma! And how he looks! Brawling in the shadow of the church — and you here too, Adrian, and you, Meister Wilhelm?"

"I separated them," replied the other quietly, smoothing his rumpled cuffs.

"With perfect calmness, but impressively — like your organ-music," said the commander, laughing. "Who began the fight? You, young sir? or the others?"

Nicolas, in his excitement, shame, and indignation, could find no coherent words, but Adrian came forward saying: "We wrestled together. Don't be too much vexed with us, Herr Janus."

Nicolas cast a friendly glance at his foe.

Herr von Nordwyk, Jan Van der Does, or as a learned man he preferred to call himself, Janus Dousa, was by no means satisfied with this information, but exclaimed:

"Patience, patience! You look suspicious enough, Meister Adrian; come here and tell me, '*atrekeos*,' according to the truth, what has been going on."

The boy obeyed the command and told his story

honestly, without concealing or palliating anything that had occurred.

"Hm," said Dousa, after the lad had finished his report. "A difficult case. No one is to be acquitted. Your cause would be the better one, had it not been for the knife, my fine young nobleman, but you, Adrian, and you, you chubby-cheeked rascals, who—There comes the rector—If he catches you, you'll certainly see nothing but four walls the rest of this beautiful day. I should be sorry for that."

The chubby-cheeked rascals, and Adrian also, understood this hint, and without stopping to take leave scampered around the corner of the church like a flock of doves pursued by a hawk.

As soon as they had vanished, the commander approached young Nicolas, saying:

"Vexatious business! What was right to them is just to you. Go to your home. Are you visiting your aunt?"

"Yes, my lord," replied the young noble.

"Is your father in the city too?"

Nicolas was silent.

"He doesn't wish to be seen?"

Nicolas nodded assent, and Dousa continued:

"Leyden stands open to every Netherlander, even to you. To be sure, if you go about like King Philip's page, and show contempt to your equals, you must endure the consequences yourself. There lies the dagger, my young friend, and there is your hat. Pick them up, and remember that such a weapon is no toy. Many a man has spoiled his whole life, by thoughtlessly using one a single moment. The superior numbers that pressed upon you may excuse you. But how will you get to your aunt's house in that tattered doublet ?"

" My cloak is in the church," said the musician, " I'll give it to the young gentleman."

" Bravo, Meister Wilhelm !" replied Dousa.   " Wait here, my little master, and then go home.   I wish the time, when your father would value my greeting, might come again.   Do you know why it is no longer pleasant to him ?"

" No, my lord."

" Then I'll tell you.   Because he is fond of Spain, and I cling to the Netherlands."

" We are Netherlanders as well as you," replied Nicolas with glowing cheeks.

" Scarcely," answered Dousa calmly, putting his hand up to his thin chin, and intending to add a kinder word to the sharp one, when the youth vehemently exclaimed :

"Take back that 'scarcely,' Herr von Nordwyk."

Dousa gazed at the bold lad in surprise, and again an expression of amusement hovered about his lips. Then he said kindly :

" I like you, Herr Nicolas; and shall rejoice if you wish to become a true Hollander. There comes Meister Wilhelm with his cloak. Give me your hand. No, not this one, the other."

Nicolas hesitated, but Janus grasped the boy's right hand in both of his, bent his tall figure to the latter's ear, and said in so low a tone that the musician could not understand :

" Ere we part, take with you this word of counsel from one who means kindly. Chains, even golden ones, drag us down, but liberty gives wings. You shine in the glittering splendor, but we strike the Spanish chains with the sword, and I devote myself to our work. Remember these words, and if you choose repeat them to your father."

Janus Dousa turned his back on the boy, waved a farewell to the musician, and went away.

CHAPTER II.

YOUNG Adrian hurried down the Werffsteg, which had given his family its name. He heeded neither the lindens on both sides, amid whose tops the first tiny green leaves were forcing their way out of the pointed buds, nor the birds that flew hither and thither among the hospitable boughs of the stately trees, building their nests and twittering to each other, for he had no thought in his mind except to reach home as quickly as possible.

Beyond the bridge spanning the Achtergracht, he paused irresolutely before a large building.

The knocker hung on the central door, but he did not venture to lift it and let it fall on the shining plate beneath, for he could expect no pleasant reception from his family.

His doublet had fared ill during his struggle with his stronger enemy. The torn neck-ruffles had been removed from their proper place and thrust into his pocket, and the new violet stocking on his right leg, luckless thing, had been so frayed by rubbing on the pavement, that a large yawning rent showed far more of Adrian's white knee than was agreeable to him.

The peacock feather in his little velvet cap could

easily be replaced, but the doublet was torn, not ripped, and the stocking scarcely capable of being mended.

The boy was sincerely sorry, for his father had bade him take good care of the stuff to save money; during these times there were hard shifts in the big house, which with its three doors, triple gables adorned with beautifully-arched volutes, and six windows in the upper and lower stories, fronted the Werffsteg in a very proud, stately guise.

The burgomaster's office did not bring in a large income, and Adrian's grandfather's trade of preparing chamois leather, as well as the business in skins, was falling off; his father had other matters in his head, matters that claimed not only his intellect, strength and time, but also every superfluous farthing.

Adrian had nothing pleasant to expect at home—certainly not from his father, far less from his aunt Barbara. Yet the boy dreaded the anger of these two far less, than a single disapproving glance from the eyes of the young wife, whom he had called " mother " scarcely a twelve month, and who was only six years his senior.

She never said an unkind word to him, but his defiance and wildness melted before her beauty, her quiet, aristocratic manner. He scarcely knew himself whether he loved her or not, but she appeared like the good fairy of whom the fairy tales spoke, and it often seemed as if she were far too delicate, dainty and charming for her simple, unpretending home. To see her smile rendered the boy happy, and when she looked sad—a thing that often happened—it made his heart ache. Merciful Heavens! She certainly could not receive him kindly when she saw his doublet, the ruffles thrust into his pocket, and his unlucky stockings.

And then!

There were the bells ringing again!

The dinner hour had long since passed, and his father waited for no one. Whoever came too late must go without, unless Aunt Barbara took compassion on him in the kitchen.

But what was the use of pondering and hesitating?

Adrian summoned up all his courage, clenched his teeth, clasped his right hand still closer around the torn ruffles in his pocket, and struck the knocker loudly on the steel plate beneath.

Trautchen, the old maid-servant, opened the door, and in the spacious, dusky entrance-hall, where the bales of leather were packed closely together, did not notice the dilapidation of his outer man.

He hurried swiftly up the stairs.

The dining-room door was open, and—marvellous —the table was still untouched, his father must have remained at the town-hall longer than usual.

Adrian rushed with long leaps to his little attic room, dressed himself neatly, and entered the presence of his family before the master of the house had asked the blessing.

The doublet and stocking could be confided to the hands of Aunt Barbara or Trautchen, at some opportune hour.

Adrian sturdily attacked the smoking dishes; but his heart soon grew heavy, for his father did not utter a word, and gazed into vacancy as gravely and anxiously as at the time when misery entered the beleagured city.

The boy's young step-mother sat opposite her husband, and often glanced at Peter Van der Werff's grave face to win a loving glance from him.

Whenever she did so in vain, she pushed her soft, golden hair back from her forehead, raised her beautiful head higher, or bit her lips and gazed silently into her plate.

In reply to Aunt Barbara's questions: " What happened at the council? Has the money for the new bell been collected? Will Jacob Van Sloten rent you the meadow?" he made curt, evasive replies.

The steadfast man, who sat so silently with frowning brow among his family, sometimes attacking the viands on his plate, then leaving them untouched, did not look like one who yields to idle whims.

All present, even the men and maid-servants, were still devoting themselves to the food, when the master of the house rose, and pressing both hands over the back of his head, which was very prominently developed, exclaimed groaning:

" I can hold out no longer. Do you give thanks, Maria. Go to the town-hall, Janche, and ask if no messenger has yet arrived."

The man-servant wiped his mouth and instantly obeyed. He was a tall, broad-shouldered Frieselander, but only reached to his master's forehead.

Peter Van der Werff, without any form of salutation, turned his back on his family, opened the door leading into his study, and after crossing the threshold, closed it with a bang, approached the big oak writing-desk, on which papers and letters lay piled in heaps, secured by rough leaden weights, and began to rummage among the newly-arrived documents. For fifteen minutes he vainly strove to fix the necessary attention upon his task, then grasped his study-chair to rest his folded arms on the high, perforated back, adorned with simple carving, and gazed thoughtfully at the wooden wainscoting of the ceiling. After a few minutes he pushed the chair aside with his foot, raised his hand to his mouth, separated his moustache from his thick brown beard, and went to the window. The small, round, leaden-cased panes, however brightly they might be polished, permitted only a narrow portion of the street to be seen, but the burgomaster seemed to have found the object for which he had been looking. Hastily opening the window, he called to his servant, who was hurriedly approaching the house:

"Is he in, Janche?"

The Frieselander shook his head, the window again closed, and a few minutes after the burgomaster seized his hat, which hung, between some cavalry pistols and a plain, substantial sword, on the only wall of his room not perfectly bare.

The torturing anxiety that filled his mind, would no longer allow him to remain in the house.

He would have his horse saddled, and ride to meet the expected messenger.

Ere leaving the room, he paused a moment lost in thought, then approached the writing-table to sign some papers intended for the town-hall; for his return might be delayed till night.

Still standing, he looked over the two sheets he had spread out before him, and seized the pen. Just at that moment the door of the room gently opened, and the fresh sand strewn over the white boards creaked under a light foot. He doubtless heard it, but did not allow himself to be interrupted.

His wife was now standing close behind him. Four and twenty years his junior, she seemed like a timid girl, as she raised her arm, yet did not venture to divert her husband's attention from his business.

She waited quietly till he had signed the first paper, then turned her pretty head aside, and blushing faintly, exclaimed with downcast eyes:

"It is I, Peter!"

"Very well, my child," he answered curtly, raising the second paper nearer his eyes.

"Peter!" she exclaimed a second time, still more eagerly, but with timidity. "I have something to tell you."

Van der Werff turned his head, cast a hasty, affectionate glance at her, and said:

"Now, child? You see I am busy, and there is my hat."

"But Peter!" she replied, a flash of something like indignation sparkling in her eyes, as she continued in a voice pervaded with a slightly perceptible tone of complaint: "We haven't said anything to each other to-day. My heart is so full, and what I would fain say to you is, must surely—"

"When I come home Maria, not now," he interrupted, his deep voice sounding half impatient, half beseeching. "First the city and the country—then love-making."

At these words, Maria raised her head proudly, and answered with quivering lips:

"That is what you have said ever since the first day of our marriage."

"And unhappily—unhappily—I must continue to say so until we reach the goal," he answered firmly.

The blood mounted into the young wife's delicate

cheeks, and with quickened breathing, she answered in a hasty, resolute tone:

"Yes, indeed, I have known these words ever since your courtship, and as I am my father's daughter never opposed them, but now they are no longer suited to us, and should be: 'Everything for the country, and nothing at all for the wife.'"

Van der Werff laid down his pen and turned full towards her.

Maria's slender figure seemed to have grown taller, and the blue eyes, swimming in tears, flashed proudly. This life-companion seemed to have been created by God especially for him. His heart opened to her, and frankly stretching out both hands, he said tenderly:

"You know how matters are! This heart is changeless, and other days will come."

"When?" asked Maria, in a tone as mournful as if she believed in no happier future.

"Soon," replied her husband firmly. "Soon, if only each one gives willingly what our native land demands."

At these words the young wife loosed her hands from her husband's, for the door had opened and Barbara called to her brother from the threshold.

"Herr Matanesse Van Wibisma, the Glipper, is in the entry and wants to speak to you."

"Show him up," said the burgomaster reluctantly.

When again alone with his wife, he asked hastily:

"Will you be indulgent and help me?"

She nodded assent, trying to smile.

He saw that she was sad and, as this grieved him, held out his hand to her again, saying:

"Better days will come, when I shall be permitted

to be more to you than to-day.   What were you going to say just now?"

" Whether you know it or not—is of no importance to the state."

" But to you.   Then lift up your head again, and look at me.   Quick, love, for they are already on the stairs."

" It isn't worth mentioning—a year ago to-day— we might celebrate the anniversary of our wedding to-day."

" The anniversary of our wedding-day!" he cried, striking his hands loudly together.   " Yes, this is the seventeenth of April, and I. have forgotten it."

He drew her tenderly towards him, but just at that moment the door opened, and Adrian ushered the baron into the room.

Van der Werff bowed courteously to the infrequent guest, then called to his blushing wife, who was retiring:

" My congratulations! I'll come later.   Adrian, we are to celebrate a beautiful festival to-day, the anniversary of our marriage."

The boy glided swiftly out of the door, which he still held in his hand, for he suspected the aristocratic visitor boded him no good.

In the entry he paused to think, then hurried up the stairs, seized his plumeless cap, and rushed out of doors.

He saw his school-mates, armed with sticks and poles, ranging themselves in battle array, and would have liked to join the game of war, but for that very reason preferred not to listen to the shouts of the combatants at that moment, and ran towards the Zylhof until beyond the sound of their voices.

He now checked his steps, and in a stooping posture,

often on his knees, followed the windings of a narrow canal that emptied into the Rhine.

As soon as his cap was overflowing with the white, blue, and yellow spring flowers he had gathered, he sat down' on a boundary stone, and with sparkling eyes bound them into a beautiful bouquet, with which he ran home.

On the bench beside the gate sat the old maid-servant with his little sister, a child six years old. Handing the flowers, which he had kept hidden behind his back, to her, he said:

"Take them and carry them to mother, Bessie; this is the anniversary of her wedding-day. Give her warm congratulations too, from us both."

The child rose, and the old servant said:

"You are a good boy, Adrian."

"Do you think so?" he asked, all the sins of the forenoon returning to his mind.

But unluckily they caused him no repentance; on the contrary, his eyes began to sparkle mischievously, and a smile hovered around his lips, as he patted the old woman's shoulder, whispering softly in her ear:

"The hair flew to-day, Trautchen. My doublet and new stockings are lying up in my room under the bed. Nobody can mend as well as you."

Trautchen shook her finger at him, but he turned hastily back and ran towards the Zyl-gate, this time to lead the Spaniards against the Netherlanders.

CHAPTER III.

THE burgomaster had pressed the nobleman to sit down in the study-chair, while he himself leaned in a half-sitting attitude on the writing-table, listening somewhat impatiently to his distinguished guest.

"Before speaking of more important things," Herr Matanesse Van Wibisma had begun, "I should like to appeal to you, as a just man, for some punishment for the injury my son has sustained in this city."

"Speak," said the burgomaster, and the nobleman now briefly, and with unconcealed indignation, related the story of the attack upon his son at the church.

"I'll inform the rector of the annoying incident," replied Van der Werff, "and the culprits will receive their just dues; but pardon me, noble sir, if I ask whether any inquiry has been made concerning the cause of the quarrel?"

Herr Matanesse Van Wibisma looked at the burgomaster in surprise and answered proudly:

"You know my son's report."

"Both sides must be fairly heard," replied Van der Werff calmly. "That has been the custom of the Netherlands from ancient times."

"My son bears my name and speaks the truth."

"Our boys are called simply Leendert or Adrian or Gerrit, but they do the same, so I must beg you to send the young gentleman to the examination at the school."

"By no means," answered the knight resolutely. "If I had thought the matter belonged to the rector's department, I should have sought him and not you, Herr Peter. My son has his own tutor, and was not attacked in your school, which in any case he has outgrown, for he is seventeen, but in the public street, whose security it is the burgomaster's duty to guard."

"Very well then, make your complaint, take the youth before the judges, summon witnesses and let the law follow its course. But, sir," continued Van der Werff, softening the impatience in his voice, "were you not young yourself once? Have you entirely forgotten the fights under the citadel? What pleasure will it afford you, if we lock up a few thoughtless lads for two days this sunny weather? The scamps will find something amusing to do indoors, as well as out, and only the parents will be punished."

The last words were uttered so cordially and pleasantly, that they could not fail to have their effect upon the baron. He was a handsome man, whose refined, agreeable features, of the true Netherland type, expressed anything rather than severity.

"If you speak to me in this tone, we shall come to an agreement more easily," he answered, smiling. "I will only say this. Had the brawl arisen in sport, or from some boyish quarrel, I wouldn't have wasted a word on the matter—but that children already venture to assail with jeers and violence those who hold different opinions, ought not to be permitted to pass without reproof. The boys shouted after my son the absurd word—"

"It is certainly an insult," interrupted Van der Werff, "a very disagreeable name, that our people bestow on the enemies of their liberty."

The baron rose, angrily confronting the other.

"Who tells you," he cried, striking his broad breast, padded with silken puffs, "who tells you that we grudge Holland her liberty?   We desire, just as earnestly as you, to win it back to the States, but by other, straighter paths than Orange—"

"I cannot test here whether your paths are crooked or straight," retorted Van der Werff; "but I do know this—they are labyrinths."

"They will lead to the heart of Philip, our king and yours."

"Yes, if he only had what we in Holland call a heart," replied the other, smiling bitterly; but Wibisma threw his head back vehemently, exclaiming reproachfully:

"Sir Burgomaster, you are speaking of the anointed Prince to whom I have sworn fealty."

"Baron Matanesse," replied Van der Werff, in a tone of deep earnestness, as he drew himself up to his full height, folded his arms, and looked the nobleman sharply in the eye, "I speak rather of the tyrant, whose bloody council declared all who bore the Netherland name, and you among us, criminals worthy of death; who, through his destroying devil, Alva, burned, beheaded, and hung thousands of honest men, robbed and exiled from the country thousands of others, I speak of the profligate—"

"Enough!" cried the knight, clenching the hilt of his sword. "Who gives you the right—"

"Who gives me the right to speak so bitterly, you would ask?" interrupted Peter Van der Werff, meeting the nobleman's eyes with a gloomy glance. "Who gives me this right?   I need not conceal it.   It was bestowed by the silent lips of my valiant father, beheaded for the sake of his faith, by the arbitrary decree, that without form of law, banished my brother and myself from the country—by the Spaniards' broken vows, the torn charters of this land, the suffering of the poor, ill-treated, worthy people that will perish if we do not save them."

"You will not save them," replied Wibisma in a calmer tone. "You will push those tottering on the verge of the abyss completely over the precipice, and go to destruction with them."

"We are pilots. Perhaps we shall bring deliverance, perhaps we shall go to ruin with those for whom we are ready to die."

"You say that, and yet a young, blooming wife binds you to life."

"Baron, you have crossed this threshold as complainant to the burgomaster, not as guest or friend."

"Quite true, but I came with kind intentions, as monitor to the guiding head of this beautiful, hapless city. You have escaped the storm once, but new and far heavier ones are gathering above your heads."

"We do not fear them."

"Not even now?"

"Now, with good reason, far less than ever."

"Then you don't know the Prince's brother—"

"Louis of Nassau was close upon the Spaniards on the 14th, and our cause is doing well—"

"It certainly did not fare ill at first."

"The messenger, who yesterday evening—"

"Ours came this morning."

"This morning, you say? And what more—"

"The Prince's army was defeated and utterly destroyed on Mook Heath. Louis of Nassau himself was slain."

Van der Werff pressed his fingers firmly on the wood

of the writing-table. The fresh color of his cheeks and lips had yielded to a livid pallor, and his mouth quivered painfully as he asked in a low, hollow tone, "Louis dead, really dead?"

"Dead," replied the baron firmly, though sorrowfully. "We were enemies, but Louis was a noble youth. I mourn him with you."

"Dead, William's favorite dead!" murmured the burgomaster as if in a dream. Then, controlling himself by a violent effort, he said, firmly:

"Pardon me, noble sir. Time is flying. I must go to the town-hall."

"And spite of my message, you will continue to uphold rebellion?"

"Yes, my lord, as surely as I am a Hollander."

"Do you remember the fate of Haarlem?"

"I remember her citizens' resistance, and the rescued Alkmaar."

"Man, man!" cried the baron. "By all that is sacred, I implore you to be circumspect."

"Enough, baron, I must go to the town-hall."

"No, only this one more word, this one word. I know you upbraid us as 'Glippers,' deserters, but as truly as I hope for God's mercy, you misjudge us. No, Herr Peter, no, I am no traitor! I love this country and this brave, industrious people with the same love as yourself, for its blood flows in my veins also. I signed the compromise. Here I stand, sir. Look at me. Do I look like a Judas? Do I look like a Spaniard? Can you blame me for faithfully keeping the oath I gave the king? When did we of the Netherlands ever trifle with vows? You, the friend of Orange, have just declared that you did not grudge any man the faith to which he clung, and I will not doubt it. Well, I hold firmly to the old church, I am a Catholic and shall remain one. But in this hour I frankly confess, that I hate the inquisition and Alva's bloody deeds as much as you do. They have as little connection with our religion as iconoclasm had with yours Like you, I love the freedom of our home. To win it back is my endeavor, as well as yours. But how can a little handful like us ever succeed in finally resisting the most powerful kingdom in the world? Though we conquer once, twice, thrice, two stronger armies will follow each defeated one. We shall accomplish nothing by force, but may do much by wise concession and prudent deeds. Philip's coffers are empty; he needs his armies too in other countries. Well then, let us profit by his difficulties, and force him to ratify some lost liberty for every revolted city that returns to him. Let us buy from his hands, with what remains of our old wealth, the rights he has wrested from us while fighting against the rebels. You will find open hands with me and those who share my opinions. Your voice weighs heavily in the council of this city. You are the friend of Orange, and if you could induce him—"

"To do what, noble sir?"

"To enter into an alliance with us. We know that those in Madrid understand how to estimate his importance and fear him. Let us stipulate, as the first condition, a full pardon for him and his faithful followers. King Philip, I know, will receive him into favor again—"

"In his arms to strangle him," replied the burgomaster resolutely. "Have you forgotten the false promises of pardon made in former times, the fate of Egmont and Horn, the noble Montigney and other lords? They ventured it and entered the tiger's den.

What we buy to-day will surely be taken from us to-morrow, for what oath would be sacred to Philip? I am no statesman, but I know this—if he would restore all our liberties, he will never grant the one thing, without which life is valueless."

"What is that, Herr Peter?"

"The privilege of believing according to the dictates of our hearts. You mean fairly, noble sir;—but you trust the Spaniard, we do not; if we did, we should be deceived children. You have nothing to fear for your religion, we everything; you believe that the number of troops and power of gold will turn the scales in our conflict, we comfort ourselves with the hope, that God will give victory to the good cause of a brave people, ready to suffer a thousand deaths for liberty. This is my opinion, and I shall defend it in the town-hall."

"No, Meister Peter, no! You cannot, ought not."

"What I can do is little, what I ought to do is written within, and I shall act accordingly."

"And thus obey the sorrowing heart rather than the prudent head, and be able to give naught save evil counsel. Consider, man, Orange's last army was destroyed on Mook Heath."

"True, my lord, and for that very reason we will not use the moments for words, but deeds."

"I'll take the hint myself, Herr Van der Werff, for many friends of the king still dwell in Leyden, who must be taught not to follow you blindly to the shambles."

At these words Van der Werff retreated from the nobleman, clenched his moustache firmly in his right hand, and raising his deep voice to a louder tone, said coldly and imperiously:

"Then, as guardian of the safety of this city, I command you to quit Leyden instantly.   If you are found within these walls after noon to-morrow, I will have you taken across the frontiers by the city-guard."

The baron withdrew without any form of leave-taking.

As soon as the door had closed behind him, Van der Werff, threw himself into his arm-chair and covered his face with his hands. When he again sat erect, two large tear-drops sparkled on the paper which had lain under his fingers. Smiling bitterly, he wiped them from the page with the back of his hand.

"Dead, dead," he murmured, and the image of the gallant youth, the clever mediator, the favorite of William of Orange, rose before his mind—he asked himself how this fresh stroke of fate would affect the Prince, whom he revered as the providence of the country, admired and loved as the wisest, most unselfish of men.

William's affliction grieved him as sorely as if it had fallen upon himself, and the blow that had struck the cause of freedom was a heavy one, perhaps never to be overcome.

Yet he only granted himself a short time to indulge in grief, for the point in question now was to summon all the nation's strength to repair what was lost, avert by vigorous acts the serious consequences which threatened to follow Louis's defeat, and devise fresh means to carry on the war.

He paced up and down the room with frowning brow, inventing measures and pondering over plans.

His wife had opened the door, and now remained standing on the threshold, but he did not notice her until she called his name and advanced towards him.

In her hand she held part of the flowers the boy had brought, another portion adorned her bosom.

"Take it," she said, offering him the bouquet. "Adrian, dear boy, gathered them, and you surely know what they mean."

He willingly took the messengers of spring, raised them to his face, drew Maria to his breast, pressed a long kiss upon her brow, and then said gloomily:

"So this is the celebration of the first anniversary of our wedding-day. Poor wife! The Glipper was not so far wrong; perhaps it would have been wiser and better for me not to bind your fate to mine."

"How can such thoughts enter your mind, Peter!" she exclaimed reproachfully.

"Louis of Nassau has fallen," he murmured in a hollow tone, "his army is scattered."

"Oh—oh!" cried Maria, clasping her hands in horror, but he continued:

"It was our last body of troops. The coffers are empty, and where we are to obtain new means, and what will happen now—this, this—Leave me, Maria, I beg you. If we don't profit by the time now, if we don't find the right paths now, we shall not, cannot prosper."

With these words he threw the bouquet on the table, hastily seized a paper, looked into it, and, without glancing at her, waved his right hand.

The young wife's heart had been full, wide open, when she entered the room. She had expected so much that was beautiful from this hour, and now stood alone in the apartment he still shared with her. Her arms had fallen by her side; helpless, mortified, wounded, she gazed at him in silence.

Maria had grown up amid the battle for freedom, and knew how to estimate the grave importance of the tidings her husband had received. During his wooing he had told her that, by his side, she must expect a life full of anxiety and peril, yet she had joyously gone to the altar with the brave champion of the good cause, which had been her father's, for she had hoped to become the sharer of his cares and struggles. And now? What was she permitted to be to him? What did he receive from her? What had he consented to share with her, who could not feel herself a feeble woman, on this, the anniversary of their wedding-day.

There she stood, her open heart slowly closing and struggling against her longing to cry out to him, and say that she would as gladly bear his cares with him and share every danger, as happiness and honor.

The burgomaster, having now found what he sought, seized his hat and again looked at his wife.

How pale and disappointed she was!

His heart ached; he would so gladly have given expression in words to the great, warm love he felt for her, offered her joyous congratulations; but in this hour, amid his grief, with such anxieties burdening his breast, he could not do it, so he only held out both hands, saying tenderly:

"You surely know what you are to me, Maria, if you do not, I will tell you this evening. I must meet the members of the council at the town-hall, or a whole day will be lost, and at this time we must be avaricious even of the moments. Well, Maria?"

The young wife was gazing at the floor. She would gladly have flown to his breast, but offended pride would not suffer her to do so, and some mysterious power bound her hands and did not permit her to lay them in his.

"Farewell," she said in a hollow tone.

"Maria!" he exclaimed reproachfully. "To-day is no well-chosen time for pouting. Come and be my sensible wife."

She did not move instantly; but he heard the bell ring for the fourth hour, the time when the session of the council ended, and left the room without looking back at her.

The little bouquet still lay on the writing-table; the young wife saw it, and with difficulty restrained her tears.

CHAPTER IV.

COUNTLESS citizens had flocked to the stately town-hall. News of Louis of Nassau's defeat had spread quickly through all the eighteen wards of the city, and each wanted to learn farther particulars, express his grief and fears to those who held the same views, and hear what measures the council intended to adopt for the immediate future.

Two messengers had only too thoroughly confirmed Baron Matanesse Van Wibisma's communication. Louis was dead, his brother Henry missing, and his army completely destroyed.

Jan Van Hout, who had taught the boys that morning, now came to a window, informed the citizens what a severe blow the liberty of the country had received, and in vigorous words exhorted them to support the good cause with body and soul.

Loud cheers followed this speech. Gay caps and plumed hats were tossed in the air, canes and swords were waved, and the women and children, who had crowded among the men, fluttered their handkerchiefs, and with their shriller voices drowned the shouts of the citizens.

The members of the valiant city-guard assembled, to charge their captain to give the council the assurance, that the "Schutterij" was ready to support William of Orange to the last penny and drop of their blood, and would rather die for the cause of Holland, than live under Spanish tyranny. Among them was seen many a grave, deeply-troubled face, for these men, who filled its ranks by their own choice, all loved William of Orange: his sorrow hurt them — and their country's distress pierced their hearts. As soon as the four burgomasters, the eight magistrates of the city, and the members of the common council appeared at the windows, hundreds of voices joined in the Geusenlied,* which had long before been struck up by individuals, and when at sunset the volatile populace scattered and, still singing, turned, either singly or by twos or threes, towards the taverns, to strengthen their confidence in better days and dispel many a well-justified anxiety by drink, the market-place of Leyden and its adjoining streets presented no different aspect, than if a message of victory had been read from the town-hall.

The cheers and Beggars' Song had sounded very powerful — but so many hundreds of Dutch throats would doubtless have been capable of shaking the air with far mightier tones.

---

* Beggars' Song or Hymn. Beggar was the name given to the patriots by those who sympathized with Spain.

This very remark had been made by the three well-dressed citizens, who were walking through the wide street, past the blue stone, and the eldest said to his companions:

"They boast and shout and seem large to themselves now, but we shall see that things will soon be very different."

"May God avert the worst!" replied the other, "but the Spaniards will surely advance again, and I know many in my ward who won't vote for resistance this time."

"They are right, a thousand times right. Requesens is not Alva, and if we voluntarily seek the king's pardon—"

"There would be no blood shed and everything would take the best course."

"I have more love for Holland than for Spain," said the third. "But, after Mook-Heath, resistance is a thing of the past. Orange may be an excellent prince, but the shirt is closer than the coat."

"And in fact we risk our lives and fortunes merely for him."

"My wife said so yesterday."

"He'll be the last man to help trade. Believe me, many think as we do, if it were not so, the Beggars' Song would have sounded louder."

"There will always be five fools to three wise men," said the older citizen. "I took good care not to split my mouth."

"And after all, what great thing is there behind this outcry for freedom? Alva burnt the Bible-readers, De la Marck hangs the priests. My wife likes to go to

Mass, but always does so secretly, as if she were committing a crime."

"We, too, cling to the good old faith."

"Never mind faith," said the third.   "We are Calvinists, but I take no pleasure in throwing my pennies into Orange's maw, nor can it gratify me to again tear up the poles before the Cow-gate, ere the wind dries the yarn."

"Only let us hold together," advised the older man. "People don't express their real opinions, and any poor ragged devil might play the hero.   But I tell you there will be sensible men enough in every ward, every guild, nay, even in the council, and among the burgomasters."

"Hush," whispered the second citizen, "there comes Van der Werff with the city clerk and young Van der Does; they are the worst of all."

The three persons named came down the broad street, talking eagerly together, but in low tones.

"My uncle is right, Meister Peter," said Jan Van der Does, the same tall young noble, who, on the morning of that day, had sent Nicolas Van Wibisma home with a kindly warning. "It's no use, you must seek the Prince and consult with him."

"I suppose I must," replied the burgomaster. "I'll go to-morrow morning."

"Not to-morrow," replied Van Hout.   "The Prince rides fast, and if you don't find him in Delft—"

"Do you go first," urged the burgomaster, "you have the record of our session."

"I cannot; but to-day you, the Prince's friend, for the first time lack good-will."

"You are right, Jan," exclaimed the burgomaster, "and you shall know what holds me back."

" If it is anything a friend can do for you, here he stands," said von Nordwyk.

Van der Werff grasped the hand the young nobleman extended, and answered, smiling: " No, my lord, no. You know my young wife. To-day we should have celebrated the first anniversary of our marriage, and amid all these anxieties I disgracefully forgot it."

" Hard, hard," said Van Hout, softly. Then he drew himself up to his full height, and added resolutely: "And yet, were I in your place, I would go, in spite of her."

" Would you go *to-day ?*"

"To-day, for to-morrow it may be too late. Who knows how soon egress from the city may be stopped and, before again venturing the utmost, we must know the Prince's opinion. You possess more of his confidence than any of us."

"And God knows how gladly I would bring him a cheering word in these sorrowful hours; but it must not be to-day. The messenger has ridden off on my bay."

"'Then take my chestnut, he is faster too," said Janus Dousa and Van der Werff answered hastily:

" Thanks, my lord. I'll send for him early to-morrow morning."

The blood mounted to Van Hout's head and, thrusting his hand angrily between his girdle and doublet, he exclaimed: "Send *me* the chestnut, if the burgomaster will give me leave of absence."

"No, send him to me," replied Peter calmly. "What must be, must be; I'll go to-day."

Van Hout's manly features quickly smoothed and,

clasping the burgomaster's right hand in both his, he said joyously :

"Thanks, Herr Peter. And no offence; you know my hot temper. If the time seems long to your young wife, send her to mine."

"And mine," added Dousa. "It's a strange thing about those two little words 'wish' and 'ought.' The freer and better a man becomes, the more surely the first becomes the slave of the second.

"And yet, Herr Peter, I'll wager that your wife will confound the two words to-day, and think you have sorely transgressed against the 'ought.' These are bad times for the 'wish.'"

Van der Werff nodded assent, then briefly and firmly explained to his friends what he intended to disclose to the Prince.

The three men separated before the burgomaster's house.

"Tell the Prince," said Van Hout, on parting, "that we are prepared for the worst, will endure and dare it."

At these words Janus Dousa measured both his companions with his eyes, his lips quivered as they always did when any strong emotion filled his heart, and while his shrewd face beamed with joy and confidence, he exclaimed: "We three will hold out, we three will stand firm, the tyrant may break our necks, but he shall not bend them. Life, fortune, all that is dear and precious and useful to man, we will resign for the highest of blessings."

"Ay," said Van der Werff, loudly and earnestly, while Van Hout impetuously repeated: "Yes, yes, thrice yes."

The three men, so united in feeling, grasped each other's hands firmly for a moment. A silent vow bound them in this hour, and when Herr von Nordwyk and Van Hout turned in opposite directions, the citizens who met them thought their tall figures had grown taller still within the last few hours.

The burgomaster went to his wife's room without delay, but did not find her there.

She had gone out of the gate with his sister.

The maid-servant carried a light into his chamber; he followed her, examined the huge locks of his pistols, buckled on his old sword, put what he needed into his saddle-bags, then, with his tall figure drawn up to its full height, paced up and down the room, entirely absorbed in his task.

Herr von Nordwyk's chestnut horse was stamping on the pavement before the door, and Hesperus was rising above the roofs.

The door of the house now opened.

He went into the entry and found, not his wife, but Adrian, who had just returned home, told the boy to give his most loving remembrances to his mother, and say that he was obliged to seek the Prince on important business.

Old Trautchen had already washed and undressed little Elizabeth, and now brought him the child wrapped in a coverlet. He kissed the dear little face, which smiled at him out of its queer disguise, pressed his lips to Adrian's forehead, again told him to give his love to his mother, and then rode down Marendorpstrasse.

Two women coming from the Rheinsburger gate, met him just as he reached St. Stephen's cloister. He did not notice them, but the younger one pushed the kerchief back from her head, hastily grasped her companion's wrist, and exclaimed in a low tone:

"That was Peter!"

Barbara raised her head higher.

"It's lucky I'm not timid. Let go of my arm. Do you mean the horseman trotting past St. Ursula alley?"

"Yes, it is Peter."

"Nonsense, child! The bay has shorter legs than that tall camel; and Peter never rides out at this hour."

"But it was he."

"God forbid! At night a linden looks like a beech-tree. It would be a pretty piece of business, if he didn't come home to-day."

The last words had escaped Barbara's lips against her will; for until then she had prudently feigned not to suspect that everything between Maria and her husband was not exactly as it ought to be, though she plainly perceived what was passing in the mind of her young sister-in-law.

She was a shrewd woman, with much experience of the world, who certainly did not undervalue her brother and his importance to the cause of their native land; nay, she went so far as to believe that, with the exception of the Prince of Orange, no man on earth would be more skilful than Peter in guiding the cause of freedom to a successful end; but she felt that her brother was not treating Maria justly, and being a fair-minded woman, silently took sides against the husband who neglected his wife.

Both walked side by side for a time in silence.

At last the widow paused, saying:

"Perhaps the Prince has sent a messenger for Peter.

In such times, after such blows, everything is possible. You might have seen correctly."

"It was surely he," replied Maria positively.

"Poor fellow!" said the other. "It must be a sad ride for him! Much honor, much hardship! You've no reason to despond, for your husband will return to-morrow or the day after; while I—look at me, Maria! I go through life stiff and straight, do my duty cheerfully; my cheeks are rosy, my food has a relish, yet I've been obliged to resign what was dearest to me. I have endured my widowhood ten years; my daughter Gretchen has married, and I sent Cornelius myself to the Beggars of the Sea. Any hour may rob me of him, for his life is one of constant peril. What has a widow except her only son? And I gave him up for our country's cause! That is harder than to see a husband ride away for a few hours on the anniversary of his wedding-day. He certainly doesn't do it for his own pleasure!"

"Here we are at home," said Maria, raising the knocker.

Trautchen opened the door and, even before crossing the threshold, Barbara exclaimed:

"Is your master at home?"

The reply was in the negative, as she too now expected.

Adrian gave his message; Trautchen brought up the supper, but the conversation would not extend beyond "yes" and "no."

After Maria had hastily asked the blessing, she rose, and turning to Barbara, said:

"My head aches, I should like to go to bed."

"Then go to rest," replied the widow. "I'll sleep

in the next room and leave the door open. In darkness and silence—whims come."

Maria kissed her sister-in-law with sincere affection, and lay down in bed; but she found no sleep, and tossed restlessly to and fro until near midnight.

Hearing Barbara cough in the next room, she sat up and asked:

"Sister-in-law, are you asleep?"

"No, child. Do you feel ill?"

"Not exactly; but I'm so anxious—horrible thoughts torment me."

Barbara instantly lighted a candle at the night-lamp, entered the chamber with it, and sat down on the edge of the bed.

Her heart ached as she gazed at the pretty young creature lying alone, full of sorrow, in the wide bed, unable to sleep from bitter grief..

Maria had never seemed to her so beautiful; resting in her white night-robes on the snowy pillow, she looked like a sorrowing angel.

Barbara could not refrain from smoothing the hair back from the narrow forehead and kissing the flushed cheeks.

Maria gazed gratefully into her small, light-blue eyes and said beseechingly:

"I should like to ask you something."

"Well?"

"But you must honestly tell me the truth."

"That is asking a great deal!"

"I know you are sincere, but it is—"

"Speak freely."

"Was Peter happy with his first wife?"

"Yes, child, yes."

"And do you know this not only from him, but also from his dead wife, Eva?"

"Yes, sister-in-law, yes."

"And you can't be mistaken?"

"Not in this case certainly! But what puts such thoughts into your head? The Bible says: 'Let the dead bury their dead.' Now turn over and try to sleep."

Barbara went back to her room, but hours elapsed ere Maria found the slumber she sought.

CHAPTER V.

THE next morning two horsemen, dressed in neat livery, were waiting before the door of a handsome house in Nobelstrasse, near the market-place. A third was leading two sturdy roan steeds up and down, and a stable-boy held by the bridle a gaily-bedizened, long-maned pony. This was intended for the young negro lad, who stood in the door-way of the house and kept off the street-boys, who ventured to approach, by rolling his eyes and gnashing his white teeth at them.

"Where can they be?" said one of the mounted men. "The rain won't keep off long to-day."

"Certainly not," replied the other. "The sky is as grey as my old felt-hat, and, by the time we reach the forest, it will be pouring."

"It's misting already."

"Such cold, damp weather is particularly disagreeable to me."

"It was pleasant yesterday."

"Button the flaps tighter over the pistol-holsters! The portmanteau behind the young master's saddle isn't exactly even. There! Did the cook fill the flask for you?"

"With brown Spanish wine. There it is."

"Then let it pour. When a fellow is wet inside, he can bear a great deal of moisture without."

"Lead the horses up to the door; I hear the gentlemen."

The man was not mistaken; for before his companion had succeeded in stopping the larger roan, the voices of his master, Herr Matanesse Van Wibisma, and his son, Nicolas, were heard in the wide entry.

Both were exchanging affectionate farewells with a young girl, whose voice sounded deeper than the half-grown boy's.

As the older gentleman thrust his hand through the roan's mane and was already lifting his foot to put it in the stirrup, the young girl, who had remained in the entry, came out into the street, laid her hand on Wibisma's arm, and said:

"One word more, uncle, but to you alone."

The baron still held his horse's mane in his hand, exclaiming with a cordial smile:

"If only it isn't too heavy for the roan. A secret from beautiful lips has its weight."

While speaking, he bent his ear towards his niece, but she did not seem to have intended to whisper, for she approached no nearer and merely lowered her tone, saying in the Italian language:

"Please tell my father, that I won't stay here."

"Why, Henrica!"

"Tell him I won't do so under any circumstances."

"Your aunt won't let you go."

"In short, I won't stay."

"I'll deliver the message, but in somewhat milder terms, if agreeable to you."

"As you choose. Tell him, too, that I beg him to send for me. If he doesn't wish to enter this heretic's nest himself, for which I don't blame him in the least, he need only send horses or the carriage for me."

"And your reasons?"

"I won't weight your baggage still more heavily. Go, or the saddle will be wet before you ride off."

"Then I'm to tell Hoogstraten to expect a letter."

"No. Such things can't be written. Besides, it won't be necessary. Tell my father I won't stay with aunt, and want to go home. Good-bye, Nico. Your riding-boots and green cloth doublet are much more becoming than those silk fal-lals."

The young lady kissed her hand to the youth, who had already swung himself into the saddle, and hurried back to the house. Her uncle shrugged his shoulders, mounted the roan, wrapped the dark cloak closer around him, beckoned Nicolas to his side, and rode on with him in advance of the servants.

No word was exchanged between them, so long as their way led through the city, but outside the gate, Wibisma said:

"Henrica finds the time long in Leyden; she would like to go back to her father."

"It can't be very pleasant to stay with aunt," replied the youth.

"She is old and sick, and her life has been a joyless one."

"Yet she was beautiful. Few traces of it are visible,

but her eyes are still like those in the portrait, and besides she is so rich."

" That doesn't give happiness."

" But why has she remained unmarried ?"

The baron shrugged his shoulders, and replied :

" It certainly didn't suit the men."

" Then why didn't she go into a convent ?"

" Who knows ?   Women's hearts are harder to understand than your Greek books. You'll learn that later. What were you saying to your aunt as I came up ?"

" Why, just see," replied the boy, putting the bridle in his mouth, and drawing the glove from his left hand, " she slipped this ring on my finger."

" A splendid emerald !   She doesn't usually like to part with such things."

" She first offered me another, saying she would give it to me to make amends for the thumps I received yesterday as a faithful follower of the king.   Isn't it comical ?"

" More than that, I should think."

" It was contrary to my nature to accept gifts for my bruises, and I hastily drew my hand back, saying the burgher lads had taken some home from me, and I wouldn't have the ring as a reward for *that*."

" Right, Nico, right."

" So she said too, put the little ring back in the box, found this one, and here it is."

" A valuable gem !" murmured the baron, thinking : " This gift is a good omen.   The Hoogstratens and he are her nearest heirs; and if the silly girl doesn't stay with her, it might happen—"

But he found no time to finish these reflections, Nicolas interrupted them by saying :

" It's beginning to rain already.   Don't the fogs on the meadows look like clouds fallen from the skies ?   I am cold."

" Draw your cloak closer."

" How it rains and hails !   One would think it was winter.   The water in the canals looks black, and yonder—see—what is that ?"

A tavern stood beside the road, and just in front of it a single lofty elm towered towards the sky. Its trunk, bare as a mast, had grown straight up without separating into branches until it attained the height of a house.   Spring had as yet lured no leaves from the boughs, but there were many objects to be seen in the bare top of the tree.   A small flag, bearing the colors of the House of Orange, was fastened to one branch, from another hung a large doll, which at a distance strongly resembled a man dressed in black, an old hat dangled from a third, and a fourth supported a piece of white pasteboard, on which might be read in large black letters, which the rain was already beginning to efface:

"Good luck to Orange, to the Spaniard death.
So Peter Quatgelat welcomes his guests."

This tree, with its motley adornments, offered a by no means pleasant spectacle, seen in the grey, cold, misty atmosphere of the rainy April morning.

Ravens had alighted beside the doll swaying to and fro in the wind, probably mistaking it for a man. They must have been by no means teachable birds, for during the years the Spaniards had ruled in Holland, the places of execution were never empty.   They were screeching as if in anger, but still remained perched on the tree, which they probably mistook for a gibbet.   The rest of the comical ornaments and the thought of the nimble adventurer, who must have climbed up to fasten them, formed a glaring and offensive contrast to the caricature of the gallows.

Yet Nicolas laughed loudly, as he perceived the queer objects in the top of the elm, and pointing upward, said:

"What kind of fruits are hanging there?"

But the next instant a chill ran down his back, for a raven perched on the black doll and pecked so fiercely at it with its hard beak, that bird and image swayed to and fro like a pendulum.

"What does this nonsense mean?" asked the baron, turning to the servant, a bold-looking fellow, who rode behind him.

"It's something like a tavern-sign," replied the latter. "Yesterday, when the sun was shining, it looked funny enough—but to-day—b-r-r-r—it's horrible."

The nobleman's eyes were not keen enough to read the inscription on the placard. When Nicolas read it aloud to him, he muttered an oath, then turned again to the servant, saying:

"And does this nonsense bring guests to the rascally host's tavern?"

"Yes, my lord, and 'pon my soul, it looked very comical yesterday, when the ravens were not to be seen; a fellow couldn't look at it without laughing. Half Leyden was there, and we went with the crowd. There was such an uproar on the grass-plot yonder. Dudeldum—Hübütt, Hubütt—Dudeldum—fiddles squeaking and bag-pipes droning as if they never would stop. The crazy throng shouted amidst the din; the noise still rings in my ears. There was no end to the games and dancing. The lads tossed their brown, blue and red-stockinged legs in the air, just as the fiddle played— the coat-tails flew and, holding a girl clasped in the right arm and a mug of beer high over their heads till the foam spattered, the throng of men whirled round and round. There was as much screaming and rejoicing as if every butter-cup in the grass had been changed into a gold florin. But to-day—holy Florian—this *is* a rain!"

"It will do the things up there good," exclaimed the baron. "The tinder grows damp in such a torrent, or I'd take out my pistols and shoot the shabby liberty hat and motley tatters off the tree."

"That was the dancing ground," said the man, pointing to a patch of trampled grass.

"The people are possessed, perfectly possessed," cried the baron, "dancing and rejoicing to-day, and to-morrow the wind will blow the felt-hat and flag from the tree, and instead of the black puppet they them-selves will come to the gallows. Steady roan, steady! The hail frightens the beasts. Unbuckle the portman-teau, Gerrit, and give your young master a blanket."

"Yes, my lord. But wouldn't it be better for you to go in here until the shower is over? Holy Florian! Just see that piece of ice in your horse's mane! It's as large as a pigeon's egg. Two horses are already stand-ing under the shed, and Quatgelat's beer isn't bad."

The baron glanced inquiringly at his son.

"Let us go in," replied Nicolas; "we shall get to the Hague early enough. See how poor Balthasar is shiver-ing! Henrica says he's a white boy painted; but if she could see how well he keeps his color in this weather, she would take it back."

Herr Van Wibisma turned his dripping, smoking steed, frightened by the hail-stones, towards the house, and in a few minutes crossed the threshold of the inn with his son.

CHAPTER VI.

A CURRENT of warm air, redolent of beer and food, met the travellers as they entered the large, low room, dimly lighted by the tiny windows, scarcely more than loop-holes, pierced in two sides. The tap-room itself looked like the cabin of a ship. Ceiling and floor, chairs and tables, were made of the same dark-brown wood that covered the walls, along which beds were ranged like berths.

The host, with many bows, came forward to receive the aristocratic guests, and led them to the fire-place, where huge pieces of peat were glimmering. The heat they sent forth answered several purposes at the same time. It warmed the air, lighted a portion of the room, which was very dark in rainy weather, and served to cook three fowl that, suspended from a thin iron bar over the fire, were already beginning to brown.

As the new guests approached the hearth, an old woman, who had been turning the spit, pushed a white cat from her lap and rose.

The landlord tossed on a bench several garments spread over the backs of two chairs to dry, and hung in their place the dripping cloaks of the baron and his son.

While the elder Wibisma was ordering something

hot to drink for himself and servants, Nicolas led the black page to the fire.

The shivering boy crouched on the floor beside the ashes, and stretched now his soaked feet, shod in red morocco, and now his stiffened fingers to the blaze.

The father and son took their seats at a table, over which the maid-servant had spread a cloth. The baron was inclined to enter into conversation about the decorated tree with the landlord, an over-civil, pock-marked dwarf, whose clothes were precisely the same shade of brown as the wood in his tap-room; but refrained from doing so because two citizens of Leyden, one of whom was well known to him, sat at a short distance from his table, and he did not wish to be drawn into a quarrel in a place like this.

After Nicolas had also glanced around the tap-room, he touched his father, saying in a low tone:

"Did you notice the men yonder? The younger one—he's lifting the cover of the tankard now—is the organist who released me from the boys and gave me his cloak yesterday."

"The one yonder?" asked the nobleman. "A hand-some young fellow. He might be taken for an artist or something of that kind. Here, landlord, who is the gentleman with brown hair and large eyes, talking to Allertssohn, the fencing-master?"

"It's Herr Wilhelm, younger son of old Herr Cornelius, Receiver General, a player or musician, as they call them."

"Eh, eh," cried the baron. "His father is one of my old Leyden acquaintances. He was a worthy, excellent man before the craze for liberty turned people's heads. The youth, too, has a face pleasant to look at.

There is something pure about it—something—it's hard to say, something—what do you think, Nico? Doesn't he look like our Saint Sebastian? Shall I speak to him and thank him for his kindness?"

The baron, without waiting for his son, whom he treated as an equal, to reply, rose to give expression to his friendly feelings towards the musician, but this laudable intention met with an unexpected obstacle.

The man, whom the baron had called the fencing-master Allertssohn, had just perceived that the "Glippers" cloaks were hanging by the fire, while his friend's and his own were flung on a bench. This fact seemed to greatly irritate the Leyden burgher; for as the baron rose, he pushed his own chair violently back, bent his muscular body forward, rested both arms on the edge of the table opposite to him and, with a jerking motion, turned his soldierly face sometimes towards the baron, and sometimes towards the landlord. At last he shouted loudly :

"Peter Quatgelat—you villain, you! What ails you, you, miserable hunchback!—Who gives you a right to toss our cloaks into a corner?"

"Yours, Captain," stammered the host, "were already—"

"Hold your tongue, you fawning knave!" thundered the other in so loud a tone and such excitement, that the long grey moustache on his upper lip shook, and the thick beard on his chin trembled. "Hold your tongue! We know better. Jove's thunder! Nobleman's cloaks are favored here. They're of Spanish cut. That exactly suits the Glippers' faces. Good Dutch cloth is thrown into the corner. Ho, ho, Brother Crooklegs, we'll put you on parade."

"Pray, most noble Captain—"

"I'll blow away your most noble, you worthless scamp, you arrant rascal! First come, first served, is the rule in Holland, and has been ever since the days of Adam and Eve. Prick up your ears, Crooklegs! If my 'most noble' cloak, and Herr Wilhelm's too, are not hanging in their old places before I count twenty, something will happen here that won't suit you. One—two—three—"

The landlord cast a timid, questioning glance at the nobleman, and as the latter shrugged his shoulders and said audibly: "There is probably room for more than two cloaks at the fire," Quatgelat took the Leyden guests' wraps from the bench and hung them on two chairs, which he pushed up to the mantel-piece.

While this was being done, the fencing-master slowly continued to count. By the time he reached twenty the landlord had finished his task, yet the irate captain still gave him no peace, but said:

"Now our reckoning, man. Wind and storm are far from pleasant, but I know even worse company. There's room enough at the fire for four cloaks, and in Holland for all the animals in Noah's ark, except Spaniards and the allies of Spain. Deuce take it, all the bile in my liver is stirred. Come to the horses with me, Herr Wilhelm, or there'll be mischief."

The fencing-master, while uttering the last words, stared angrily at the nobleman with his prominent eyes, which even under ordinary circumstances, always looked as keen as if they had something marvellous to examine.

Wibisma pretended not to hear the provoking words, and, as the fencing-master left the room, walked calmly, with head erect, towards the musician, bowed courteously, and thanked him for the kindness he had shown his son the day before.

"You are not in the least indebted to me," replied Wilhelm Corneliussohn. "I helped the young nobleman, because it always has an ill look when numbers attack one."

"Then allow me to praise this opinion," replied the baron.

"Opinion," repeated the musician with a subtle smile, drawing a few notes on the table.

The baron watched his fingers silently a short time, then advanced nearer the young man, asking:

"Must everything now relate to political dissensions?"

"Yes," replied Wilhelm firmly, turning his face with a rapid movement towards the older man. "In these times 'yes,' twenty times 'yes.' You wouldn't do well to discuss opinions with me, Herr Matanesse."

"Every man," replied the nobleman, shrugging his shoulders, "every man of course believes his own opinion the right one, yet he ought to respect the views of those who think differently."

"No, my lord," cried the musician. "In these times there is but *one* opinion for us. I wish to share nothing, not even a drink at the table, with any man who has Holland blood, and feels differently. Excuse me, my lord; my travelling companion, as you have unfortunately learned, has an impatient temper and doesn't like to wait."

Wilhelm bowed distantly, waved his hand to Nicolas, approached the chimney-piece, took the half-dried cloaks on his arm, tossed a coin on the table and, holding in his hands a covered cage in which several birds were fluttering, left the room.

The baron gazed after him in silence. The simple words and the young man's departure aroused painful emotions. He believed he desired what was right, yet at this moment a feeling stole over him that a stain rested on the cause he supported.

It is more endurable to be courted than avoided, and thus an expression of deep annoyance rested on the nobleman's pleasant features as he returned to his son.

Nicolas had not lost a single word uttered by the organist, and the blood left his ruddy cheeks as he was forced to see this man, whose appearance had especially won his young heart, turn his back upon his father as if he were a dishonorable man to be avoided.

The words, with which Janus Dousa had left him the day before, returned to his mind with great force, and when the baron again seated himself opposite him, the boy raised his eyes and said hesitatingly, but with touching earnestness and sincere anxiety :

"Father, what does that mean ? Father—are they so wholly wrong, if they would rather be Hollanders than Spaniards ?"

Wibisma looked at his son with surprise and displeasure, and because he felt his own firmness wavering, and a blustering word often does good service where there is lack of possibility or inclination to contend against reasons, he exclaimed more angrily than he had spoken to his son for years :

"Are you, too, beginning to relish the bait with which Orange lures simpletons ? Another word of that kind, and I'll show you how malapert lads are treated.

Here, landlord, what's the meaning of that nonsense on yonder tree ?"

"The people, my lord, the Leyden fools are to blame for the mischief, not I. They decked the tree out in that ridiculous way, when the troops stationed in the city during the siege retired. I keep this house as a tenant of old Herr Van der Does, and dare not have any opinions of my own, for people must live, but, as truly as I hope for salvation, I'm loyal to King Philip."

"Until the Leyden burghers come out here again," replied Wibisma bitterly. "Did you keep this inn dur-- ing the siege ?"

"Yes, my lord, the Spaniards had no cause to complain of me, and if a poor man's services are not too insignificant for you, they are at your disposal."

"Ah ! ha !" muttered the baron, gazing attentively at the landlord's disagreeable face, whose little eyes glittered very craftily, then turning to Nicolas, said :

"Go and watch the blackbirds in the window yonder a little while, my son, I have something to say to the host."

The youth instantly obeyed and as, instead of looking at the birds, he gazed after the two enthusiastic supporters of Holland's liberty, who were riding along the road leading to Delft, remembered the simile of fetters that drag men down, and saw rising before his mental vision the glitter of the gold chain King Philip had sent his father, Nicolas involuntarily glanced towards him as he stood whispering eagerly with the landlord. Now he even laid his hand on his shoulder. Was it right for him to hold intercourse with a man whom he must despise at heart ? Or was he—he shuddered, for the word "traitor," which one of the school-boys had shouted in his ears during the quarrel before the church, returned to his memory.

When the rain grew less violent, the travellers left the inn. The baron allowed the hideous landlord to kiss his hand at parting, but Nicolas would not suffer him to touch his.

Few words were exchanged between father and son during the remainder of their ride to the Hague, but the musician and the fencing-master were less silent on the way to Delft.

Wilhelm had modestly, as beseemed the younger man, suggested that his companion had expressed his hostile feelings towards the nobleman too openly.

"True, perfectly true," replied Allertssohn, whom his friends called "Allerts." "Very true! Temper— oh! temper! You don't suspect, Herr Wilhelm — But we'll let it pass."

"No, speak, Meister."

"You'll think no better of me, if I do."

"Then let us talk of something else."

"No, Wilhelm. I needn't be ashamed, no one will take me for a coward."

The musician laughed, exclaiming: "You a coward! How many Spaniards has your Brescian sword killed?"

"Wounded, wounded, sir, far oftener than killed," replied the other. "If the devil challenges me I shall ask: Foils, sir, or Spanish swords? But there's one person I do fear, and that's my best and at the same time my worst friend, a Netherlander, like yourself, the man who rides here beside you. Yes, when rage seizes upon me, when my beard begins to tremble, my small share of sense flies away as fast as your doves when you let them go. You don't know me, Wilhelm."

" Don't I? How often must one see you in command and visit you in the fencing-room?"

" Pooh, pooh—there I'm as quiet as the water in yonder ditch—but when anything goes against the grain, when—how shall I explain it to you, without similes?"

" Go on."

" For instance, when I am obliged to see a sycophant treated as if he were Sir Upright—"

" So that vexes you greatly?"

" Vexes? No! Then I grow as savage as a tiger, and I ought not to be so, I ought not. Roland, my fore man, probably likes—"

" Meister, Meister, your beard is beginning to tremble already!"

" What did the Glippers think, when their aristocratic cloaks—"

" The landlord took yours and mine from the fire entirely on his own responsibility."

" I don't care! The crook-legged ape did it to honor the Spanish sycophant. It enraged me, it was intolerable."

" You didn't keep your wrath to yourself, and I was surprised to see how patiently the baron bore your insults."

" That's just it, that's it!" cried the fencing-master, while his beard began to twitch violently. " That's what drove me out of the tavern, that's why I took to my heels. That—that—Roland, my fore man."

" I don't understand you."

" Don't you, don't you? How should you; but I'll explain. When you're as old as I am, young man, you'll experience it too. There are few perfectly sound trees in the forest, few horses without a blemish, few swords without a stain, and scarcely a man who has passed his fortieth year that has not a worm in his breast. Some gnaw slightly, others torture with sharp fangs, and mine—mine.—Do you want to cast a glance in here?"

The fencing-master struck his broad chest as he uttered these words and, without waiting for his companion's reply, continued:

"You know me and my life, Herr Wilhelm. What do I do, what do I practise? Only chivalrous work. My life is based upon the sword. Do you know a better blade or surer hand than mine? Do my soldiers obey me? Have I spared my blood in fighting before the red walls and towers yonder? No, by my fore man Roland, no, no, a thousand times no."

"Who denies it, Meister Allerts? But tell me, what do you mean by your cry: Roland, my fore man?"

"Another time, Wilhelm; you mustn't interrupt me now. Hear my story about where the worm hides in me. So once more: What I do, the calling I follow, is knightly work, yet when a Wibisma, who learned how to use his sword from my father, treats me ill and stirs up my bile, if I should presume to challenge him, as would be my just right, what would he do? Laugh and ask: 'What will the passado cost, Fencing-master Allerts? Have you polished rapiers?' Perhaps he wouldn't even answer at all, and we saw just now how he acts. His glance slipped past me like an eel, and he had wax in his ears. Whether I reproach, or a cur yelps at him, is all the same to his lordship. If only a Renneberg or Brederode had been in my place just now, how quickly Wibisma's sword would have flown from its sheath, for he understands how to fight and is no coward. But I—I? Nobody would willingly allow himself to be struck in the face, yet so surely as my father was a brave man, even the worst insult could be more easily borne, than the feeling of being held in too slight esteem to be able to offer an affront. You see, Wilhelm, when the Glipper looked past me—"

" Your beard lost its calmness."

" It's all very well for you to jest, you don't know—"

" Yes, yes, Herr Allerts; I understand you perfectly."

" And do you also understand, why I took myself and my sword out of doors so quickly ?"

" Perfectly; but please stop a moment with me now. The doves are fluttering so violently; they want air."

The fencing-master stopped his steed, and while Wilhelm was removing the dripping cloth from the little cage that rested between him and his horse's neck, said:

" How can a man trouble himself about such gentle little creatures ? If you want to diminish, in behalf of feathered folk, the time given to music, tame falcons, that's a knightly craft, and I can teach you."

" Let my doves alone," replied Wilhelm. " They are not so harmless as people suppose, and have done good service in many a war, which is certainly chivalrous pastime. Remember Haarlem. There, it's beginning to pour again. If my cloak were only not so short; I would like to cover the doves with it."

" You certainly look like Goliath in David's garments."

" It's my scholar's cloak; I put my other on young Wibisma's shoulders yesterday."

"The Spanish green-finch?"

"I told you about the boys' brawl."

"Yes, yes. And the monkey kept your cloak?"

"You came for me and wouldn't wait. They probably sent it back soon after our departure."

"And their lordships expect thanks because the young nobleman accepted it!"

"No, no; the baron expressed his gratitude."

"But that doesn't make your cape any longer. Take my cloak, Wilhelm. I've no doves to shelter, and my skin is thicker than yours."

CHAPTER VII.

A SECOND and third rainy day followed the first one. White mists and grey fog hung over the meadows. The cold, damp north-west wind drove heavy clouds together and darkened the sky. Rivulets dashed into the streets from the gutters on the steep roofs of Leyden; the water in the canals and ditches grew turbid and rose towards the edges of the banks. Dripping, freezing men and women hurried past each other without any form of greeting, while the pair of storks pressed closer to each other in their nest, and thought of the warm south, lamenting their premature return to the cold, damp, Netherland plain.

In thoughtful minds the dread of what must inevitably come was increasing. The rain made anxiety grow as rapidly in the hearts of many citizens, as the young blades of grain in the fields. Conversations, that sounded anything but hopeful, took place in many taprooms—in others men were even heard declaring resistance folly, or loudly demanding the desertion of the cause of the Prince of Orange and liberty.

Whoever in these days desired to see a happy face in Leyden might have searched long in vain, and would probably have least expected to find it in the house of Burgomaster Van der Werff.

Three days had now elapsed since Peter's departure, nay the fourth was drawing towards noon, yet the burgomaster had not returned, and no message, no word of explanation, had reached his family.

Maria had put on her light-blue cloth dress with Mechlin lace in the square neck, for her husband particularly liked to see her in this gown and he must surely return to-day.

The spray of yellow wall-flowers on her breast had been cut from the blooming plant in the window of her room, and Barbara had helped arrange her thick hair.

It lacked only an hour of noon, when the young wife's delicate, slender figure, carrying a white duster in her hand, entered the burgomaster's study. Here she stationed herself at the window, from which the pouring rain streamed in numerous crooked serpentine lines, pressed her forehead against the panes, and gazed down into the quiet street.

The water was standing between the smooth red tiles of the pavement. A porter clattered by in heavy wooden shoes, a maid-servant, with a shawl wrapped around her head, hurried swiftly past, a shoemaker's boy, with a pair of boots hanging on his back, jumped from puddle to puddle, carefully avoiding the dry places;—no horseman appeared.

· It was almost unnaturally quiet in the house and

street; she heard nothing except the plashing of the rain. Maria could not expect her husband until the beat of horses' hoofs was audible; she was not even gazing into the distance—only dreamily watching the street and the ceaseless rain.

The room had been thoughtfully heated for the drenched man, whose return was expected, but Maria felt the cold air through the chinks in the windows. She shivered, and as she turned back into the dusky room, it seemed as if this twilight atmosphere must always remain, as if no more bright days could ever come.

Minutes passed before she remembered for what purpose she had entered the room and began to pass the dusting-cloth over the writing-table, the piles of papers, and the rest of the contents of the apartment. At last she approached the pistols, which Peter had not taken with him on his journey.

The portrait of her husband's first wife hung above the weapons and sadly needed dusting, for until now Maria had always shrunk from touching it.

To-day she summoned up her courage, stood opposite to it, and gazed steadily at the youthful features of the woman, with whom Peter had been happy. She felt spellbound by the brown eyes that gazed at her from the pleasant face.

Yes, the woman up there looked happy, almost insolently happy. How much more had Peter probably given to his first wife than to her?

This thought cut her to the heart, and without moving her lips she addressed a series of questions to the silent portrait, which still gazed steadily and serenely at her from its plain frame.

Once it seemed as if the full lips of the pictured face quivered, once that the eyes moved. A chill ran through her veins, she began to be afraid, yet could not leave the portrait, and stood gazing upward with dilated eyes.

She did not stir, but her breath came quicker and quicker, and her eyes seemed to grow keener.

A shadow rested on the dead Eva's high forehead.

Had the artist intended to depict some oppressive anxiety, or was what she saw only dust, that had settled on the colors?

She pushed a chair towards the portrait and put her foot on the seat, pushing her dress away in doing so. Blushing, as if other eyes than the painted ones were gazing down upon her, she drew it over the white stocking, then with a rapid movement mounted the seat.

She could now look directly into the eyes of the portrait. The cloth in Maria's trembling hand passed over Eva's brow, and wiped the shadow from the rosy flesh. She now blew the dust from the frame and canvas, and perceived the signature of the artist to whom the picture owed its origin. "Artjen of Leyden," he called himself, and his careful hand had finished even the unimportant parts of the work with minute accuracy. She well knew the silver chain with the blue turquoises, that rested on the plump neck. Peter had given it to her as a wedding present, and she had worn it to the altar; but the little diamond cross suspended from the middle she had never seen. The gold buckle at Eva's belt had belonged to her since her last birthday—it was very badly bent, and the dull points would scarcely pierce the thick ribbon.

" *She* had everything when it was new," she said to herself. "Jewels! What do I care for them! But the heart, the heart—how much love has she left in Peter's heart?"

She did not wish to do so, but constantly heard these words ringing in her ears, and was obliged to summon up all her self-control, to save herself from weeping.

"If he would only come, if he would only come!" cried a voice in her tortured soul.

The door opened, but she did not notice it.

Barbara crossed the threshold, and called her by her name in a tone of kindly reproach.

Maria started and blushing deeply, said:

"Please give me your hand; I should like to get down. I have finished. The dust was a disgrace."

When she again stood on the floor, the widow said:

"What red cheeks you have! Listen, my dear sister-in-law, listen to me, child—!"

Barbara was interrupted in the midst of her admonition, for the knocker fell heavily on the door, and Maria hurried to the window.

The widow followed, and after a hasty glance into the street, exclaimed:

"That's Wilhelm Corneliussohn, the musician. He has been to Delft. I heard it from his mother. Perhaps he brings news of Peter. I'll send him up to you, but he must first tell me below what his tidings are. If you want me, you'll find me with Bessie. She is feverish and her eyes ache; she will have some eruption or a fever."

Barbara left the room. Maria pressed her hands upon her burning cheeks, and paced slowly to and fro till the musician knocked and entered.

After the first greeting, the young wife asked eagerly:

" Did you see my husband in Delft ?"

" Yes indeed," replied Wilhelm, " the evening of the day before yesterday."

" Then tell me—"

" At once, at once.   I bring you a whole pouch full of messages.   First from your mother."

" Is she well ?"

" Well and bright.   Worthy Doctor Groot too is hale and hearty."

" And my husband ?"

" I found him with the doctor.   Herr Groot sends the kindest remembrances to you.   We had musical entertainments at his home yesterday and the day before.   He always has the latest novelties from Italy, and when we try this motet here—"

" Afterwards, Herr Wilhelm !   You must first tell me what my husband—"

" The burgomaster came to the doctor on a message from the Prince.   He was in haste, and could not wait for the singing.   It went off admirably.   If you, with your magnificent voice, will only—"

" Pray, Meister Wilhelm ?"

" No, dear lady, you ought not to refuse.   Doctor Groot says, that when a girl in Delft, no one could support the tenor like you, and if you, Frau von Nordwyk, and Herr Van Aken's oldest daughter—"

" But, my dear Meister !" exclaimed the burgomaster's wife with increasing impatience, " I'm not asking about your motets and tabulatures, but my husband."

Wilhelm gazed at the young wife's face with a half-startled, half-astonished look.   Then, smiling at his own awkwardness, he shook his head, saying in a tone of good-natured repentance :

"Pray forgive me, little things seem unduly important to us when they completely fill our own souls. One word about your absent husband must surely sound sweeter to your ears, than all my music. I ought to have thought of that sooner. So—the burgomaster is well and has transacted a great deal of business with the Prince. Before he went to Dortrecht yesterday morning, he gave me this letter and charged me to place it in your hands with the most loving greetings."

With these words the musician gave Maria a letter. She hastily took it from his hand, saying:

"No offence, Herr Wilhelm, but we'll discuss your motet to-morrow, or whenever you choose; to-day—"

"To-day your time belongs to this letter," interrupted Wilhelm. "That is only natural. The messenger has performed his commission, and the music-master will try his fortune with you another time."

As soon as the young man had gone, Maria went to her room, sat down at the window, hurriedly opened her husband's letter and read:

"My Dear and Faithful Wife!

Meister Wilhelm Corneliussohn, of Leyden, will bring you this letter. I am well, but it was hard for me to leave you on the anniversary of our wedding-day. The weather is very bad. I found the Prince in sore affliction, but we don't give up hope, and if God helps us and every man does his duty, all may yet be well. I am obliged to ride to Dortrecht to-day. I have an important object to accomplish there. Have patience, for several days must pass before my return.

"If the messenger from the council inquires, give him the papers lying on the right-hand side of the writing-

table under the smaller leaden weight.   Remember me
to Barbara and the children.   If money is needed, ask
Van Hout in my name for the rest of the sum due me;
he knows about it.   If you feel lonely, visit his wife or
Frau von Nordwyk; they would be glad to see you.
Buy as much meal, butter, cheese, and smoked meat, as
is possible.   We don't know what may happen.   Take
Barbara's advice !   Relying upon your obedience,

Your faithful husband,   .

PETER ADRIANSSOHN VAN DER WERFF."

Maria read this letter at first hastily, then slowly,
sentence by sentence, to the end.   Disappointed,
troubled, wounded, she folded it, drew the wall-flowers
from the bosom of her dress—she knew not why—and
flung them into the peat-box by the chimney-piece.
Then she opened her chest, took out a prettily-carved
box, placed it on the table, and laid her husband's letter inside.

Long after it had found a place with other papers,
Maria still stood before the casket, gazing thoughtfully
at its contents.

At last she laid her hand on the lid to close it; but
hesitated and took up a packet of letters that had lain
amid several gold and silver coins, given by godmothers
and godfathers, modest trinkets, and a withered rose.

Drawing a chair up to the table, the young wife
seated herself and began to read.   She knew these letters well enough.   A noble, promising youth had addressed them to her sister, his betrothed bride.   They
were dated from Jena, whither he had gone to complete
his studies in jurisprudence.   Every word expressed the
lover's ardent longing, every line was pervaded by the

passion that had filled the writer's heart. Often the prose of the young scholar, who as a pupil of Doctor Groot had won his bride in Delft, rose to a lofty flight.

While reading, Maria saw in imagination Jacoba's pretty face, and the handsome, enthusiastic countenance of her bridegroom. She remembered their gay wedding, her brother-in-law's impetuous friend, so lavishly endowed with every gift of nature, who had accompanied him to Holland to be his groomsman, and at parting had given her the rose which lay before her in the little casket. No voice had ever suited hers so well; she had never heard language so poetical from any other lips, never had eyes that sparkled like the young Thuringian noble's looked into hers.

After the wedding Georg von Dornberg returned home and the young couple went to Haarlem. She had heard nothing from the young foreigner, and her sister and her husband were soon silenced forever. Like most of the inhabitants of Haarlem, they were put to death by the Spanish destroyers at the capture of the noble, hapless city. Nothing was left of her beloved sister except a faithful memory of her, and her betrothed bridegroom's letters, which she now held in her hand.

They expressed *love*, the true, lofty love, that can speak with the tongues of angels and move mountains.

There lay her husband's letter. Miserable scrawl! She shrank from opening it again, as she laid the beloved mementoes back into the box, yet her breast heaved as she thought of Peter. She knew too that she loved him, and that his faithful heart belonged to her. But she was not satisfied, she was not happy, for he showed her only tender affection or paternal kindness, and she wished to be loved differently. The pupil, nay the friend of the learned Groot, the young wife who had grown up in the society of highly educated men, the enthusiastic patriot, felt that she was capable of being more, far more to her husband, than he asked. She had never expected gushing emotions or high-strung phrases from the grave man engaged in vigorous action, but believed he would understand all the lofty, noble sentiments stirring in her soul, permit her to share his struggles and become the partner of his thoughts and feelings. The meagre letter received to-day again taught her that her anticipations were not realized.

He had been a faithful friend of her father, now numbered with the dead. Her brother-in-law too had attached himself, with all the enthusiasm of youth, to the older, fully-matured champion of liberty, Van der Werff. When he had spoken of Peter to Maria, it was always with expressions of the warmest admiration and love. Peter had come to Delft soon after her father's death and the violent end of the young wedded pair, and when he expressed his sympathy and strove to comfort her, did so in strong, tender words, to which she could cling, as if to an anchor, in the misery of her heart. The valient citizen of Leyden came to Delft more and more frequently, and was always a guest at Doctor Groot's house. When the men were engaged in consultation, Maria was permitted to fill their glasses and be present at their conferences. Words flew to and fro and often seemed to her neither clear nor wise; but what Van der Werff said was always sensible, and a child could understand his plain, vigorous speech. He appeared to the young girl like an oak-tree among swaying willows. She knew of many of his journeys, undertaken at the peril of his life, in the service of the Prince and his native land, and awaited their result with a throbbing heart.

More than once in those days, the thought had entered her mind that it would be delightful to be borne through life in the strong arms of this steadfast man. Then he extended these arms, and she yielded to his wish as proudly and happily as a squire summoned by the king to be made a knight. She now remembered this by-gone time, and every hope with which she had accompanied him to Leyden rose vividly before her soul.

Her newly-wedded husband had promised her no spring, but a pleasant summer and autumn by his side. She could not help thinking of this comparison, and what entirely different things from those she had anticipated, the union with him had offered to this day. Tumult, anxiety, conflict, a perpetual alternation of hard work and excessive fatigue, this was his life, the life he had summoned her to share at his side, without even showing any desire to afford her a part in his cares and labors. Matters ought not, should not go on so. Everything that had seemed to her beautiful and pleasant in her parents' home—was being destroyed here. Music and poetry, that had elevated her soul, clever conversation, that had developed her mind, were not to be found here. Barbara's kind feelings could never supply the place of these lost possessions; for her husband's love she would have resigned them all—but what had become of this love?

With bitter emotions, she replaced the casket in the chest and obeyed the summons to dinner, but found no one at the great table except Adrian and the servants. Barbara was watching Bessie.

Never had she seemed to herself so desolate, so lonely, so useless as to-day. What could she do here? Barbara ruled in kitchen and cellar, and she—she only stood in the way of her husband's fulfilling his duties to the city and state.

Such were her thoughts, when the knocker again struck the door. She approached the window. It was the doctor. Bessie had grown worse and she, her mother, had not even inquired for the little one.

"The children, the children!" she murmured; her sorrowful features brightened, and her heart grew lighter as she said to herself:

"I promised Peter to treat them as if they were my own, and I will fulfil the duties I have undertaken."

Full of joyous excitement, she entered the sick-room, hastily closing the door behind her. Doctor Bontius looked at her with a reproving glance, and Barbara said:

"Gently, gently! Bessie is just sleeping a little."

Maria approached the bed, but the physician waved her back, saying:

"Have you had the purple-fever?"

"No."

"Then you ought not to enter this room again. No other help is needed where Frau Barbara nurses."

The burgomaster's wife made no reply, and returned to the entry. Her heart was so heavy, so unutterably heavy. She felt like a stranger in her husband's house. Some impulse urged her to go out of doors, and as she wrapped her mantle around her and went downstairs, the smell of leather rising from the bales piled in layers on the lower story, which she had scarcely noticed before, seemed unendurable. She longed for her mother,

her friends in Delft, and her quiet, cheerful home. For the first time she ventured to call herself unhappy and, while walking through the streets with downcast eyes against the wind, struggled vainly to resist some mysterious, gloomy power, that compelled her to minutely recall everything that had resulted differently from her expectations.

CHAPTER VIII.

AFTER the musician had left the burgomaster's house, he went to young Herr Matanesse Van Wibisma's aunt to get his cloak, which had not been returned to him. He did not usually give much heed to his dress, yet he was glad that the rain kept people in the house, for the outgrown wrap on his shoulders was by no means pleasing in appearance. Wilhelm must certainly have looked anything but well-clad, for as he stood in old Fraulein Van Hoogstraten's spacious, stately hall, the steward Belotti received him as patronizingly as if he were a beggar.

But the Neopolitan, in whose mouth the vigorous Dutch sounded like the rattling in the throat of a chilled singer, speedily took a different tone when Wilhelm, in excellent Italian, quietly explained the object of his visit. Nay, at the sweet accents of his native tongue, the servant's repellent demeanor melted into friendly, eager welcome. He was beginning to speak of his home to Wilhelm, but the musician made him curt replies and asked him to get his cloak.

Belotti now led him courteously into a small room at the side of the great hall, took off his cloak, and then went upstairs. As minute after minute passed, until at last a whole quarter of an hour elapsed, and neither servant nor cloak appeared, the young man lost his patience, though it was not easily disturbed, and when the door at last opened serious peril threatened the leaden panes on which he was drumming loudly with his fingers. Wilhelm doubtless heard it, yet he drummed with redoubled vehemence, to show the Italian that the time was growing long to him. But he hastily withdrew his fingers from the glass, for a girl's musical voice said behind him in excellent Dutch:

"Have you finished your war-song, sir? Belotti is bringing your cloak."

Wilhelm had turned and was gazing in silent bewilderment into the face of the young noblewoman, who stood directly in front of him. These features were not unfamiliar, and yet—years do not make even a goddess younger, and mortals increase in height and don't grow smaller; but the lady whom he thought he saw before him, whom he had known well in the eternal city and never forgotten, had been older and taller than the young girl, who so strikingly resembled her and seemed to take little pleasure in the young man's surprised yet inquiring glance. With a haughty gesture she beckoned to the steward, saying in Italian:

"Give the gentleman his cloak, Belotti, and tell him I came to beg him to pardon your forgetfulness."

With these words Henrica Van Hoogstraten turned towards the door, but Wilhelm took two hasty strides after her, exclaiming:

"Not yet, not yet, Fraulein! I am the one to apolo-

gize. But if you have ever been amazed by a resemblance—"

"Anything but looking like other people!" cried the
girl with a repellent gesture.

"Ah, Fraulein, yet—"

"Let that pass, let that pass," interrupted Henrica
in so irritated a tone that the musician looked at her in
surprise. "One sheep looks just like another, and
among a hundred peasants twenty have the same face.
All wares sold by the dozen are cheap."

As soon as Wilhelm heard reasons given, the quiet
manner peculiar to him returned, and he answered
modestly:

"But nature also forms the most beautiful things in
pairs. Think of the eyes in the Madonna's face."

"Are you a Catholic?"

"A Calvinist, Fraulein."

"And devoted to the Prince's cause?"

"Say rather, the cause of liberty."

"That accounts for the drumming of the war-song."

"It was first a gentle gavotte, but impatience quickened the time. I am a musician, Fraulein."

"But probably no drummer. The poor panes!"

"They are an instrument like any other, and in
playing we seek to express what we feel."

"Then accept my thanks for not breaking them to
pieces."

"That wouldn't have been beautiful, Fraulein, and
art ceases when ugliness begins."

"Do you think the song in your cloak—it dropped
on the ground and Nico picked it up—beautiful or
ugly?"

"This one or the other?"

"I mean the Beggar-song."

"It is fierce, but no more ugly than the roaring of the storm."

"It is repulsive, barbarous, revolting."

"I call it strong, overmastering in its power."

"And this other melody?"

"Spare me an answer; I composed it myself. Can you read notes, Fraulein?"

"A little."

"And did my attempt displease you?"

"Not at all, but I find dolorous passages in this choral, as in all the Calvinist hymns."

"It depends upon how they are sung."

"They are certainly intended for the voices of the shopkeepers' wives and washerwomen in your churches."

"Every hymn, if it is only sincerely felt, will lend wings to the souls of the simple folk who sing it; and whatever ascends to Heaven from the inmost depths of the heart, can hardly displease the dear God, to whom it is addressed. And then—"

"Well?"

"If these notes are worth being preserved, it may happen that a matchless choir—"

"Will sing them to you, you think?"

"No, Fraulein; they have fulfilled their destination if they are once nobly rendered. I would fain not be absent, but that wish is far less earnest than the other."

"How modest!"

"I think the best enjoyment in creating is had in anticipation."

Henrica gazed at the artist with a look of sympathy, and said with a softer tone in her musical voice:

"I am sorry for you, Meister. Your music pleases

me; why should I deny it? In many passages it appeals to the heart, but how it will be spoiled in your churches! Your heresy destroys every art. The works of the great artists are a horror to you, and the noble music that has unfolded here in the Netherlands will soon fare no better."

"I think I may venture to believe the contrary."

"Wrongly, Meister, wrongly, for if your cause triumphs, which may the Virgin forbid, there will soon be nothing in Holland except piles of goods, workshops, and bare churches, from which even singing and organ-playing will soon be banished."

"By no means, Fraulein. Little Athens first became the home of the arts, after she had secured her liberty in the war against the Persians."

"Athens and Leyden!" she answered scornfully. "True, there are owls on the tower of Pancratius. But where shall we find the Minerva?"

While Henrica rather laughed than spoke these words, her name was called for the third time by a shrill female voice. She now interrupted herself in the middle of a sentence, saying:

"I must go. I will keep these notes."

"You will honor me by accepting them; perhaps you will allow me to bring you others."

"Henrica!" the voice again called from the stairs, and the young lady answered hastily:

"Give Belotti whatever you choose, but soon, for I shan't stay here much longer."

Wilhelm gazed after her. She walked no less quickly and firmly through the wide hall and up the stairs, than she had spoken, and again he was vividly reminded of his friend in Rome.

The old Italian had also followed Henrica with his eyes. As she vanished at the last bend of the broad steps, he shrugged his shoulders, turned to the musician and said, with an expression of honest sympathy:

"The young lady isn't well. Always in a tumult; always like a loaded pistol, and these terrible headaches too! She was different when she came here."

"Is she ill?"

"My mistress won't see it," replied the servant. "But what the cameriera and I see, we see. Now red —now pale, no rest at night, at table she scarcely eats a chicken-wing and a leaf of salad."

"Does the doctor share your anxiety?"

"The doctor? Doctor Fleuriel isn't here. He moved to Ghent when the Spaniards came, and since then my mistress will have nobody but the barber who bleeds her. The doctors here are devoted to the Prince of Orange and are all heretics. There, she is calling again. I'll send the cloak to your house, and if you ever feel inclined to speak my language, just knock here. That calling—that everlasting calling! The young lady suffers from it too."

When Wilhelm entered the street, it was only raining very slightly. The clouds were beginning to scatter, and from a patch of blue sky the sun was shining brightly down on Nobelstrasse. A rainbow shimmered in variegated hues above the roofs, but to-day the musician had no eyes for the beautiful spectacle. The bright light in the wet street did not charm him. The hot rays of the day-star were not lasting, for "they drew rain." All that surrounded him seemed confused and restless. Beside a beautiful image which he treasured in the sanctuary of his memories, only allow-ing his mind to dwell upon it in his happiest hours, sought to intrude. His real diamond was in danger of being exchanged for a stone, whose value he did not know. With the old, pure harmony blended another similar one, but in a different key. How could he still think of Isabella, without remembering Henrica! At least he had not heard the young lady sing, so his recollection of Isabella's songs remained unclouded. He blamed himself because, obeying an emotion of vanity, he had promised to send new songs to the proud young girl, the friend of Spain. He had treated Herr Matanesse Van Wibisma rudely on account of his opinions, but sought to approach her, who laughed at what he prized most highly, because she was a woman, and it was sweet to hear his work praised by beautiful lips. " Hercules throws the club aside and sits down at the distaff, when Omphale beckons, and the beautiful Esther and the daughter of Herodias—" murmured Wilhelm indignantly. He felt sorely troubled, and longed for his quiet attic chamber beside the dove-cote.

"Something unpleasant has happened to him in Delft," thought his father.

"Why doesn't he relish his fried flounders to-day?" asked his mother, when he had left them after dinner. Each felt that something oppressed the pride and favorite of the household, but did not attempt to discover the cause; they knew the moods to which he was sometimes subject for half a day.

After Wilhelm had fed his doves, he went to his room, where he paced restlessly to and fro. Then he seized his violin and wove all the melodies he had heard from Isabella's lips into one. His music had rarely sounded so soft, and then so fierce and passionate, and his mother, who heard it in the kitchen, turned the twirling-stick faster and faster, then thrust it into the firmly-tied dough, and rubbing her hands on her apron, murmured:

"How it wails and exults! If it relieves his heart, in God's name let him do it, but cat-gut is dear and it will cost at least two strings."

Towards evening Wilhelm was obliged to go to the drill of the military corps to which he belonged. His company was ordered to mount guard at the Hoogewoort Gate. As he marched through Nobelstrasse with it, he heard the low, clear melody of a woman's voice issuing from an open window of the Hoogstraten mansion. He listened, and noticing with a shudder how much Henrica's voice — for the singer must be the young lady — resembled Isabella's, ordered the drummer to beat the drum.

The next morning a servant came from the Hoogstraten house and gave Wilhelm a note, in which he was briefly requested to come to Nobelstrasse at two o'clock in the afternoon, neither earlier nor later.

He did not wish to say "yes"—he could not say "no," and went to the house at the appointed hour.

Henrica was awaiting him in the little room adjoining the hall. She looked graver than the day before, while heavier shadows under her eyes and the deep flush on her cheeks reminded Wilhelm of Belotti's fears for her health. After returning his greeting, she said without circumlocution, and very rapidly:

"I must speak to you. Sit down. To be brief, the way you greeted me yesterday awakened strange thoughts. I must strongly resemble some other woman, and you met her in Italy. Perhaps you are reminded of some one very near to me, of whom I have lost all trace. Answer me honestly, for I do not ask from idle curiosity. Where did you meet her ?"

" In Lugano. We drove to Milan with the same vetturino, and afterwards I found her again in Rome and saw her daily for months."

" Then you know her intimately. Do you still think the resemblance surprising, after having seen me for the second time ?"

" Very surprising."

" Then I must have a double. Is she a native of this country ?"

" She called herself an Italian, but she understood Dutch, for she has often turned the pages of my books and followed the conversation I had with young artists from our home. I think she is a German lady of noble family."

"An adventuress then. And her name ?"

" Isabella—but I think no one would be justified in calling her an adventuress."

" Was she married ? "

" There was something matronly in her majestic appearance, yet she never spoke of a husband. The old Italian woman, her duenna, always called her Donna Isabella, but she possessed little more knowledge of her past than I."

" Is that good or evil ? "

" Nothing at all, Fraulein."

" And what led her to Rome ? "

" She practised the art of singing, of which she was mistress ; but did not cease studying, and made great progress in Rome. I was permitted to instruct her in counterpoint."

"And did she appear in public as a singer?"

"Yes and no.   A distinguished foreign prelate was her patron, and his recommendation opened every door, even the Palestrina's.   So the church music at aristocratic weddings was entrusted to her, and she did not refuse to sing at noble houses, but never appeared for pay.   I know that, for she would not allow any one else to play her accompaniments.   She liked my music, and so through her I went into many aristocratic houses."

"Was she rich?"

"No, Fraulein.   She had beautiful dresses and brilliant jewels, but was compelled to economize.   Remittances of money came to her at times from Florence, but the gold pieces slipped quickly through her fingers, for though she lived plainly and eat scarcely enough for a bird, while her delicate strength required stronger food, she was lavish to imprudence if she saw poor artists in want, and she knew most of them, for she did not shrink from sitting with them over their wine in my company."

"With artists and musicians?"

"Mere artists of noble sentiments.   At times she surpassed them all in her overflowing mirth."

"At times?"

"Yes, only at times, for she had also sorrowful, pitiably sorrowful hours and days, but as sunshine and shower alternate in an April day, despair and extravagant gayety ruled her nature by turns."

"A strange character.   Do you know her end?"

"No, Fraulein.   One evening she received a letter from Milan, which must have contained bad news, and the next day vanished without any farewell."

"And you did not try to follow her?"

Wilhelm blushed, and answered in an embarrassed tone:

"I had no right to do so, and just after her departure I fell sick—dangerously sick."

"You loved her?"

"Fraulein, I must beg you—"

"You loved her! And did she return your affection?"

"We have known each other only since yesterday, Fraulein von Hoogstraten."

"Pardon me! But if you value my desire, we shall not have seen each other for the last time, though my double is undoubtedly a different person from the one I supposed. Farewell till we meet again. You hear, that calling never ends. You have aroused an interest in your strange friend, and some other time must tell me more about her. Only this one question: Can a modest maiden talk of her with you without disgrace?"

"Certainly, if you do not shrink from speaking of a noble lady who had no other protector than herself."

"And *you*, don't forget yourself!" cried Henrica, leaving the room.

The musician walked thoughtfully towards home. Was Isabella a relative of this young girl? He had told Henrica almost all he knew of her external circumstances, and this perhaps gave the former the same right to call her an adventuress, that many in Rome had assumed. The word wounded him, and Henrica's inquiry whether he loved the stranger disturbed him, and appeared intrusive and unseemly. Yes, he had felt an ardent love for her; ay, he had suffered deeply because he was no more to her than a pleasant companion

and reliable friend.   It had cost him struggles enough
to conceal his feelings, and he knew, that but for the
dread of repulse and scorn, he would have yielded and
revealed them to her.   Old wounds in his heart opened
afresh, as he recalled the time she suddenly left Rome
without a word of farewell.   After barely recovering from
a severe illness, he had returned home pale and dispirited,
and months elapsed ere he could again find genuine
pleasure in his art.   At first, the remembrance of her
contained nothing save bitterness, but now, by quiet,
persistent effort, he had succeeded, not in attaining forgetfulness, but in being able to separate painful emotions from the pure and exquisite joy of remembering
her.   To-day the old struggle sought to begin afresh,
but he was not disposed to yield, and did not cease to
summon Isabella's image, in all its beauty, before his
soul.

Henrica returned to her aunt in a deeply-agitated
mood.   Was the adventuress of whom Wilhelm had
spoken, the only creature whom she loved with all the
ardor of her passionate soul?   Was Isabella her lost sister?   Many incidents were opposed to it, yet it was possible.   She tortured herself with questions, and the less
peace her aunt gave her, the more unendurable her headache became, the more plainly she felt that the fever,
against whose relaxing power she had struggled for days,
would conquer her.

CHAPTER IX.

On the evening of the third day after Wilhelm's interview with Henrica, his way led him through Nobelstrasse past the Hoogstraten mansion.

Ere reaching it, he saw two gentlemen, preceded by a servant carrying a lantern, cross the causeway towards it.

Wilhelm's attention was attracted. The servant now seized the knocker, and the light of his lantern fell on the men's faces. Neither was unfamiliar to him.

The small, delicate old man, with the peaked hat and short black velvet cloak, was Abbé Picard, a gay Parisian, who had come to Leyden ten years before and gave French lessons in the wealthy families of the city. He had been Wilhelm's teacher too, but the musician's father, the Receiver-General, would have nothing to do with the witty abbé; for he was said to have left his beloved France on account of some questionable transactions, and Herr Cornelius scented in him a Spanish spy. The other gentleman, a grey-haired, unusually stout man, of middle height, who required a great deal of cloth for his fur-bordered cloak, was Signor Lamperi, the representative of the great Italian mercantile house of Bonvisi in Antwerp, who was in the habit of annually coming to Leyden on business for a few weeks with the storks and swallows, and was a welcome guest in every tap-room as the inexhaustible narrator of funny stories. Before these two men entered the house, they were joined by a third, preceded by two servants carrying lanterns.   A wide cloak enveloped his tall figure; he too stood on the threshold of old age and was no stranger to Wilhelm, for the Catholic Monseigneur Gloria, who often came to Leyden from Haarlem, was a patron of the noble art of music, and when the young man set out on his journey to Italy had provided him, spite of his heretical faith, with valuable letters of introduction.

Wilhelm, as the door closed behind the three gentlemen, continued his way.   Belotti had told him the day before that the young lady seemed very ill, but since her aunt was receiving guests, Henrica was doubtless better.

The first story in the Hoogstraten mansion was brightly lighted, but in the second a faint, steady glow streamed into Nobelstrasse from a single window, while she for whom the lamp burned sat beside a table, her eyes sparkling with a feverish glitter, as she pressed her forehead against the marble top.   Henrica was entirely alone in the wide, lofty room her aunt had assigned her. Behind curtains of thick faded brocade was her bedstead, a heavy structure of enormous width. The other articles of furniture were large and shabby, but had once been splendid.   Every chair, every table looked as if it had been taken from some deserted banqueting-hall. Nothing really necessary was lacking in the apartment, but it was anything but home-like and cosey, and no one would ever have supposed a young girl occupied it, had it not been for a large gilt harp that leaned against the long, hard couch beside the fireplace.

Henrica's head was burning but, though she had wrapped a shawl around her lower limbs, her feet were freezing on the uncarpeted stone floor.

A short time after the three gentlemen had entered

her aunt's house, a woman's figure ascended the stairs leading from the first to the second story. Henrica's over-excited senses perceived the light tread of the satin shoes and the rustle of the silk train, long before the approaching form had reached the room, and with quickened breathing, she sat erect.

A thin hand, without any preliminary knock, now opened the door and old Fraulein Van Hoogstraten walked up to her niece.

The elderly dame had once been beautiful, now and at this hour she presented a strange, unpleasing appearance.

The thin, bent figure was attired in a long trailing robe of heavy pink silk. The little head almost disappeared in the ruff, a large structure of immense height and width. Long chains of pearls and glittering gems hung on the sallow skin displayed by the open neck of her dress, and on the false, reddish-yellow curls rested a roll of light-blue velvet decked with ostrich plumes. A strong odor of various fragrant essences preceded her. She herself probably found them somewhat overpowering, for her large glittering fan was in constant motion and fluttered violently, when in answer to her curt: " Quick, quick," Henrica returned a resolute " no, *ma tante*."

The old lady, however, was not at all disconcerted by the refusal, but merely repeated her " Quick, quick," more positively, adding as an important reason :

" Monseigneur has come and wants to hear you."

" He does me great honor," replied the young girl, " great honor, but how often must I repeat: 1 will not come."

" Is it allowable to ask why not, my fair one ?" said the old lady.

"Because I am not fit for your society," cried Henrica vehemently, "because my head aches and my eyes burn, because I can't sing to-day, and because—because—because—I entreat you, leave me in peace."

Old Fraulein Van Hoogstraten let her fan sink by her side, and said coolly:

"Were you singing two hours ago—yes or no?"

"Yes."

"Then your headache can't be so very bad, and Denise will dress you."

"If she comes, I'll send her away. When I just took the harp, I did so to sing the pain away. It was relieved for a few minutes, but now my temples are throbbing with twofold violence."

"Excuses."

"Believe what you choose. Besides—even if I felt better at this moment than a squirrel in the woods, I wouldn't go down to see the gentlemen. I shall stay here. I have given my word, and I am a Hoogstraten as well as you."

Henrica had risen, and her eyes flashed with a gloomy fire at her oppressor. The old lady waved her fan faster, and her projecting chin trembled. Then she said curtly:

"Your word of honor! So you won't! You won't!"

"Certainly not," cried the young girl with undutiful positiveness.

"Everybody must have his way," replied the old lady, turning towards the door. "What is too wilful is too wilful. Your father won't thank you for this."

With these words Fraulein Van Hoogstraten raised her long train and approached the door. There she paused, and again glanced enquiringly at Henrica. The latter doubtless noticed her aunt's hesitation, but without heeding the implied threat intentionally turned her back.

As soon as the door closed, the young girl sank back into her chair, pressed her forehead against the marble slab and let it remain there a long time. Then she rose as suddenly and hastily as if obeying some urgent summons, raised the lid of her trunk, tossed the stockings, bodices and shoes, that came into her way, out on the floor, and did not rise until she had found a few sheets of writing-paper which she had laid, before leaving her father's castle, among the rest of her property.

As she rose from her kneeling posture, she was seized with giddiness, but still kept her feet, carried to the table first the white sheets and a portfolio, then the large inkstand that had already stood several days in her room, and seated herself beside it.

Leaning far back in her chair, she began to write. The book that served as a desk lay on her knee, the paper on the book. Creaking and pausing, the goose-quill made large, stiff letters on the white surface. Henrica was not skilled in writing, but to-day it must have been unspeakably difficult for her; her high forehead became covered with perspiration, her mouth was distorted by pain, and whenever she had finished a few lines, she closed her eyes or drank greedily from the water-pitcher that stood beside her.

The large room was perfectly still, but the peace that surrounded her was often disturbed by strange noises and tones, that rose from the dining-hall directly under her chamber. The clinking of glasses, shrill tittering, loud, deep laughter, single bars of a dissolute love-song, cheers, and then the sharp rattle of a shattered wineglass reached her in mingled sounds. She did not wish to hear it, but could not escape and clenched her white teeth indignantly. Yet meantime the pen did not wholly stop.

She wrote in broken, or long, disconnected sentences, almost incoherently involved. Sometimes there were gaps, sometimes the same word was twice or thrice repeated. The whole resembled a letter written by a lunatic, yet every line, every stroke of the pen, expressed the same desire uttered with passionate longing : " Take me away from here! Take me away from this woman and this house!"

The epistle was addressed to her father. She implored him to rescue her from this place, come or send for her. " Her uncle, Matanesse Van Wibisma," she said, " seemed to be a sluggish messenger; he had probably enjoyed the evenings at her aunt's, which filled her, Henrica, with loathing. She would go out into the world after her sister, if her father compelled her to stay here." Then she began a description of her aunt and her life. The picture of the days and nights she had now spent for weeks with the old lady, presented in vivid characters a mixture of great and petty troubles, external and mental humiliations.

Only too often the same drinking and carousing had gone on below as to-day—Henrica had always been compelled to join her aunt's guests, elderly dissolute men of French or Italian origin and easy morals. While describing these conventicles, the blood crimsoned her flushed cheeks still more deeply, and the long strokes of the pen grew heavier and heavier. What the abbé related and her aunt laughed at, what the Italian screamed and Monseigneur smilingly condemned with a slight shake of the head, was so shamelessly bold that she would have been defiled by repeating the words.

Was she a respectable girl or not? She would rather hunger and thirst, than be present at such a banquet again. If the dining-room was empty, other unprecedented demands were made upon Henrica, for then her aunt, who could not endure to be alone a moment, was sick and miserable, and she was obliged to nurse her. That she gladly and readily served the suffering, she wrote, she had sufficiently proved by her attendance on the village children when they had the small-pox, but if her aunt could not sleep she was compelled to watch beside her, hold her hand, and listen until morning as she moaned, whined and prayed, sometimes cursing herself and sometimes the treacherous world. She, Henrica, had come to the house strong and well, but so much disgust and anger, such constant struggling to control herself had robbed her of her health.

The young girl had written until midnight. The letters became more and more irregular and indistinct, the lines more crooked, and with the last words: " My head, my poor head! You will see that I am losing my senses. I beseech you, I beseech you, my dear, stern father, take me home. I have again heard something about Anna—" her eyes grew dim, her pen dropped from her hand, and she fell back in the chair unconscious.

There she lay, until the last laugh and sound of rattling glass had died away below, and her aunt's guests had left the house.

Denise, the cameriera, noticed the light in the room, entered, and after vainly endeavoring to rouse Henrica, called her mistress.

The latter followed the maid, muttering as she ascended the stairs:

" Fallen asleep, found the time hang heavy — that's all! She might have been lively and laughed with us! Stupid race! 'Men of butter,' King Philip says. That wild Lamperi was really impertinent to-night, and the abbé said things—things—"

The old lady's large eyes were sparkling vinously, and her fan waved rapidly to and fro to cool the flush on her cheeks.

She now stood opposite to Henrica, called her, shook her and sprinkled her with perfumed water from the large shell, set in gold, which hung as an essence-bottle from her belt. When her niece only muttered incoherent words, she ordered the maid to bring her medicine-chest.

Denise had gone and Fraulein Van Hoogstraten now perceived Henrica's letter, raised it close to her eyes, read page after page with increasing indignation, and at last tossed it on the floor and tried to shake her niece awake; but in vain.

Meantime Belotti had been informed of Henrica's serious illness and, as he liked the young girl, sent for a physician on his own responsibility, and instead of the family priest summoned Father Damianus. Then he went to the sick girl's chamber.

Even before he crossed the threshold, the old lady in the utmost excitement, exclaimed:

" Belotti, what do you say now, Belotti? Sickness in the house, perhaps contagious sickness, perhaps the plague."

" It seems to be only a fever," replied the Italian soothingly. " Come, Denise, we will carry the young lady to the bed. The doctor will soon be here."

"The doctor?" cried the old lady, striking her fan on the marble top of the table. "Who permitted you, Belotti—"

"We are Christians," interrupted the servant, not without dignity.

"Very well, very well," she cried. "Do what you please, call whom you choose, but Henrica can't stay here. Contagion in the house, the plague, a black tablet."

"Excellenza is disturbing herself unnecessarily. Let us first hear what the doctor says."

"I won't hear him; I can't bear the plague and the small-pox. Go down at once, Belotti, and have the sedan-chair prepared. The old chevalier's room in the rear building is empty."

"But, Excellenza, it's gloomy, and so damp that the north wall is covered with mould."

"Then let it be aired and cleaned. What does this delay mean? You have only to obey. Do you understand?"

"The chevalier's room isn't fit for my mistress's sick niece," replied Belotti civilly, but resolutely.

"Isn't it? And you know exactly?" asked his mistress scornfully. "Go down, Denise, and order the sedan-chair to be brought up. Have you anything more to say, Belotti?"

"Yes, Padrona," replied the Italian, in a trembling voice. "I beg your excellenza to dismiss me."

"Dismiss you from my service?"

"With your excellenza's permission, yes—from your service."

The old woman started, clasped her hands tightly upon her fan, and said :

" You are irritable, Belotti."

" No, Padrona, but I am old and dread the misfortune of being ill in this house."

Fraulein Van Hoogstraten shrugged her shoulders and turning to her maid, cried :

"The sedan-chair, Denise. You are dismissed, Belotti."

CHAPTER X.

THE night, on which sorrow and sickness had entered the Hoogstraten mansion, was followed by a beautiful morning. Holland again became pleasant to the storks, that with a loud, joyous clatter flew down into the meadows on which the sun was shining. It was one of those days the end of April often bestows on men, as if to show them that they render her too little, her successor too much honor. April can boast that in her house is born the spring, whose vigor is only strengthened and beauty developed by her blooming heir.

It was Sunday, and whoever on such a day, while the bells are ringing, wanders in Holland over sunny paths, through flowery meadows where countless cattle, woolly sheep, and idle horses are grazing, meeting peasants in neat garments, peasant women with shining gold ornaments under snow-white lace caps, citizens in gay attire and children released from school, can easily fancy that even nature wears a holiday garb and glitters in brighter green, more brilliant blue, and more varied ornaments of flowers than on work-days.

A joyous Sunday mood doubtless filled the minds of the burghers, who to-day were out of doors on foot, in large over-crowded wooden wagons, or gaily-painted boats on the Rhine, to enjoy the leisure hours of the day of rest, eat country bread, yellow butter, and fresh cheese, or drink milk and cool beer, with their wives and children.

The organist, Wilhelm, had long since finished playing in the church, but did not wander out into the fields with companions of his own age, for he liked to use such days for longer excursions, in which walking was out of the question.

They bore him on the wings of the wind over his native plains, through the mountains and valleys of Germany, across the Alps to Italy. A spot propitious for such forgetfulness of the present and his daily surroundings, in favor of the past and a distant land, was ready. His brothers, Ulrich and Johannes, also musicians, but who recognized Wilhelm's superior talent without envy and helped him develop it, had arranged for him, during his stay in Italy, a prettily-furnished room in the narrow side of the pointed roof of the house, from which a broad door led to a little balcony. Here stood a wooden bench on which Wilhelm liked to sit, watching the flight of his doves, gazing dreamily into the distance or, when inclined to artistic creation, listening to the melodies that echoed in his soul.

This highest part of the house afforded a beautiful prospect; the view was almost as extensive as the one from the top of the citadel, the old Roman tower situated in the midst of Leyden. Like a spider in its

web, Wilhelm's native city lay in the midst of countless
streams and canals that intersected the meadows. The
red brick masonry of the city wall, with its towers and
bastions, washed by a dark strip of water, encircled the
pretty place as a diadem surrounds a young girl's head;
and like a chaplet of loosely-bound thorns, forts and redoubts extended in wider, frequently broken circles
around the walls. The citizens' herds of cattle grazed between the defensive fortifications and the city wall, while
beside and beyond them appeared villages and hamlets.

On this clear April day, looking towards the north,
Haarlem lake was visible, and on the west, beyond the
leafy coronals of the Hague woods, must lie the downs
which nature had reared for the protection of the country
against the assaults of the waves. Their long chain of
hillocks offered a firmer and more unconquerable resistance to the pressure of the sea, than the earthworks and
redoubts of Alfen, Leyderdorp and Valkenburg, the
three forts situated close to the banks of the Rhine, presented to hostile armies. The Rhine! Wilhelm gazed
down at the shallow, sluggish river, and compared it to
a king deposed from his throne, who has lost power and
splendor and now kindly endeavors to dispense benefits
in little circles with the property that remains. The
musician was familiar with the noble, undivided German
Rhine; and often followed it in imagination towards the
south but more often still his dreams conveyed him
with a mighty leap to Lake Lugano, the pearl of the
Western Alps, and when he thought of it and the Medi-
terranean, beheld rising before his mental vision emerald
green, azure blue, and golden light; and in such hours
all his thoughts were transformed within his breast into
harmonies and exquisite music.

And his journey from Lugano to Milan ! The conveyance that bore him to Leonardo's city was plain and overcrowded, but in it he had found Isabella. And Rome, Rome, eternal, never-to-be-forgotten Rome, where so long as we dwell there, we grow out of ourselves, increase in strength and intellectual power, and which makes us wretched with longing when it lies behind us.

By the Tiber Wilhelm had first thoroughly learned what art, his glorious art was; here, near Isabella, a new world had opened to him, but a sharp frost had passed over the blossoms of his heart that had unfolded in Rome, and he knew they were blighted and could bear no fruit—yet to-day he succeeded in recalling her in her youthful beauty, and instead of the lost love, thinking of the kind friend Isabella and dreaming of a sky blue as turquoise, of slender columns and bubbling. fountains, olive groves and marble statues, cool churches and gleaming villas, sparkling eyes and fiery wine, magnificent choirs and Isabella's singing.

The doves that cooed and clucked, flew away and returned to the cote beside him, could now do as they chose, their guardian neither saw nor heard them.

Allertssohn, the fencing-master, ascended the ladder to his watch-tower, but he did not notice him until he stood on the balcony by his side, greeting him with his deep voice.

"Where have we been, Herr Wilhelm?" asked the old man. "In this cloth-weaving Leyden? No! Probably with the goddess of music on Olympus, if she has her abode there."

"Rightly guessed," replied Wilhelm, pushing the hair back from his forehead with both hands. "I have been visiting her, and she sends you a friendly greeting."

"Then offer one from me in return," replied the other, "but she usually belongs to the least familiar of my acquaintances. My throat is better suited to drinking than singing. Will you allow me?"

The fencing-master raised the jug of beer which Wilhelm's mother filled freshly every day and placed in her darling's room, and took a long pull. Then wiping his moustache, he said:

"That did me good, and I needed it. The men wanted to go out pleasuring and omit their drill, but we forced them to go through it, Junker von Warmond, Duivenvoorde and I. Who knows how soon it may be necessary to show what we can do. Roland, my fore man, such imprudence is like a cudgel, against which one can do nothing with Florentine rapiers, clever tierce and quarte. My wheat is destroyed by the hail."

"Then let it lie, and see if the barley and clover don't do better," replied Wilhelm gaily, tossing vetches and grains of wheat to a large dove that had alighted on the parapet of his tower.

"It eats, and what use is it?" cried Allertssohn, looking at the dove. "Herr von Warmond, a young man after God's own heart, has just brought me two falcons; do you want to see how I tame them?"

"No, Captain, I have enough to do with my music and my doves."

"That is your affair. The long-necked one yonder is a queer-looking fellow."

"And of what country is he probably a native? There he goes to join the others. Watch him a little while and then answer me."

"Ask King Soloman that; he was on intimate terms with birds."

"Only watch him, you'll find out presently."

"The fellow has a stiff neck, and holds his head unusually high."

"And his beak?"

"Curved, almost like a hawk's! Zounds, why does the creature strut about with its toes so far apart? Stop, bandit! He'll peck that little dove to death. As true as I live, the saucy rascal must be a Spaniard!"

"Right, it is a Spanish dove. It flew to me, but I can't endure it and drive it away; for I keep only a few pairs of the same breed and try to get the best birds possible. Whoever raises many different kinds in the same cote, will accomplish nothing."

"That gives food for thought. But I believe you haven't chosen the handsomest species."

"No, sir. What you see are a cross between the carrier and tumblers, the Antwerp breed of carrier-pigeons. Bluish, reddish, spotted birds. I don't care for the colors, but they must have small bodies and large wings, with broad quills on their flag-feathers, and above all ample muscular strength. The one yonder— stop, I'll catch him—is one of my best flyers. Try to lift his pinions."

"Heaven knows the little thing has marrow in its bones! How the tiny wing pinches; the falcons are not much stronger."

"It's a carrier-dove too, that finds its way alone."

"Why do you keep no white tumblers? I should think they could be watched farthest in their flight."

"Because doves fare like men. Whoever shines very brightly and is seen from a distance, is set upon by opponents and envious people, and birds of prey pounce upon the white doves first. I tell you, Captain, whoever has eyes in his head, can learn in a dove-cote how things come to pass among Adam and Eve's posterity on earth."

"There is quarrelling and kissing up here just as there is in Leyden."

"Yes, exactly the same, Captain. If I mate an old dove with one much younger, it rarely turns out well. When the male dove is in love, he understands how to pay his fair one as many attentions, as the most elegant gallant shows the mistress of his heart. And do you know what the kissing means? The suitor feeds his darling, that is, seeks to win her affection by beautiful gifts. Then the wedding comes, and they build a nest. If there are young birds, they feed them together in perfect harmony. The aristocratic doves brood badly, and we put their eggs under birds of more ordinary breed."

"Those are the noble ladies, who have nurses for their infants."

"Unmated doves often make mischief among the mated ones."

"Take warning, young man, and beware of being a bachelor. I'll say nothing against the girls who remain unmarried, for I have found among them many sweet, helpful souls."

"So have I, but unfortunately some bad ones too, as well as here in the dove-cote. On the whole my wards lead happy married lives, but if it comes to a separation—"

"Which of the two is to blame?"

"Nine times out of ten the little wife."

"Roland, my fore man, exactly as it is among

human beings," cried the fencing-master, clapping his hands.

"What do you mean by your Roland, Herr Allerts? You promised me a short time ago.— but who is coming up the ladder?"

"I hear your mother."

"She is bringing me a visitor. I know that voice— and yet. Wait. It's old Fraulein Van Hoogstraten's steward."

"From Nobelstrasse? Let me go, Wilhelm, for this Glipper crew—"

"Wait a little while, there is only room for one on the ladder," said the musician, holding out his hand to Belotti to guide him from the last rung into his room.

"Spaniards and the allies of Spain," muttered the fencing-master, opened the door, and called while descending the ladder: "I'll wait down below till the air is pure again."

The steward's handsome face, usually smoothly shaven with the most extreme care, was to-day covered with a stubbly beard, and the old man looked sad and worn, as he began to tell Wilhelm what had occurred in his mistress's house since the evening of the day before.

"Years may make a hot-tempered person weaker, but not calmer," said the Italian, continuing his story. "I can't look on and see the poor angel, for she isn't far from the Virgin's throne, treated like a sick dog that is flung out into the court-yard, so I got my discharge."

"That does you honor, but was rather out of place just now. And has the young lady really been carried to the damp room?"

"No, sir. Father Damianus came and made the old

excellenza understand what the holy Virgin expected of a Christian, and when the padrona still tried to carry out her will, the holy man spoke to her in words so harsh and stern that she yielded. The signorina is now lying in bed with burning cheeks, raving in delirium."

" And who is attending the patient ?"

" I came to you about the physician, my dear sir, for Doctor de Bont, who instantly obeyed my summons, was treated so badly by the old excellenza, that he turned his back upon her and told me, at the door of the house, he wouldn't come again."

Wilhelm shook his head, and the Italian continued :

" There are other doctors in Leyden, but Father Damianus says de Bont or Bontius, as they call him, is the most skilful and learned of them all, and as the old excellenza herself had an attack of illness about noon, and certainly won't leave her bed very speedily, the way is open, and Father Damianus says he'll go to Doctor Bontius himself if necessary. But as you are a native of the city and acquainted with the signorina, I wanted to spare him the rebuff he would probably meet from the foe of our holy Church. The poor man has enough to suffer from good-for-nothing boys and scoffers, when he goes through the city with the sacrament."

" You know people are strictly forbidden to disturb him in the exercise of his calling."

" Yet he can't show himself in the street without being jeered. We two cannot change the world, sir.' So long as the Church had the upper hand, she burned and quartered you, now you have the power here, our priests are persecuted and scorned."

" Against the law and the orders of the magistrates."

" You can't control the people, and Father Damianus is a lamb, who bears everything patiently, as good a Christian as many saints before whom we burn candles. Do you know the doctor?"

"A little, by sight."

"Oh, then go to him, sir, for the young lady's sake," cried the old man earnestly. "It is in your power to save a human life, a beautiful young life."

The steward's eyes glittered with tears. As Wilhelm laid his hand on his arm, saying kindly: "I will try," the fencing-master called: "Your council is lasting too long for me. I'll come another time."

"No, Meister, come up a minute. This gentleman is here on account of a poor sick girl. The poor, helpless creature is now lying without any care, for her aunt, old Fraulein Van Hoogstraten, has driven Doctor de Bont from her bed because he is a Calvinist."

"From the sick girl's bed?"

"It's abominable enough, but the old lady is now ill herself."

"Bravo, bravo!" cried the fencing-master, clapping his hands. "If the devil himself isn't afraid of her and wants to fetch her, I'll pay for his post-horses. But the girl, the sick girl?"

"Herr Belotti begs me to persuade de Bont to visit her again. Are you on friendly terms with the doctor?"

"I was, Wilhelm, I was; but—last Friday we had some sharp words about the new morions, and now the learned demi-god demands an apology from me, but to sound a retreat isn't written here—"

"Oh, my dear sir," cried Belotti, with touching earnestness. "The poor child is lying helpless in a raging fever. If Heaven has blessed you with children—"

"Be calm, old man, be calm," replied the fencing-master, stroking Belotti's grey hair kindly. My children are nothing to you, but we'll do what we can for the young girl. Farewell till we meet again, gentlemen. Roland, my fore man, what shall we live to see! Hemp is still cheap in Holland, and yet such a monster has lived amongst us to be as old as a raven."

With these words he went down the ladder. On reaching the street, he pondered over the words in which he should apologize to Doctor Bontius, with a face as sour as if he had wormwood in his mouth; but his eyes and bearded lips smiled.

His learned friend made the apology easy for him, and when Belotti came home, he found the doctor by the sick girl's bed.

CHAPTER XI.

Frau Elizabeth von Nordwyk and Frau Van Hout had each asked the burgomaster's wife to go into the country with them to enjoy the beautiful spring day, but in spite of Barbara's persuasions, Maria could not be induced to accept their invitation.

A week had elapsed since her husband's departure, a week whose days had run their course from morning to evening as slowly as the brackish water in one of the canals, intersecting the meadows of Holland, flowed towards the river.

Sleep loves the couches of youth, and had again found hers, but with the rising of the sun the dissatisfaction, anxiety and secret grief, that slumber had kindly interrupted, once more returned. She felt that it was not right, and her father would have blamed her if he had seen her thus.

There are women who are ashamed of rosy cheeks, unrestrained joy in life, to whom the emotion of sorrow affords a mournful pleasure. To this class Maria certainly did not belong. She would fain have been happy, and left untried no means of regaining the lost joy of her heart. Honestly striving to do her duty, she returned to little Bessie; but the child was rapidly recovering and called for Barbara, Adrian or Trautchen, as soon as she was left alone with her.

She tried to read, but the few books she had brought from Delft were all familiar, and her thoughts, ere becoming fixed on the old volumes, pursued their own course.

Wilhelm brought her the new motet, and she endeavored to sing it; but music demands whole hearts from those who desire to enjoy her gifts, and therefore melody and song refused comfort as well as pleasure to her, whose mind was engrossed by wholly different things. If she helped Adrian in his work, her patience failed much sooner than usual. On the first market-day, she went out with Trautchen to obey her husband's directions and make purchases and, while shopping at the various places where different wares were offered—here fish, yonder meat or vegetables, amid the motley crowd, hailed on every side by cries of: " Here, Frau Bürgermeisterin! I have what you want, Frau Bürgermeisterin!" forgot the sorrow that oppressed her.

With newly-animated self-reliance, she examined flour, pulse and dried fish, making it a point of honor to bargain carefully; Barbara should see that she knew how to buy. The crowd was very great everywhere, for the city magistrates had issued a proclamation bidding every household, in view of the threatened danger, to supply itself abundantly with provisions on all the market-days; but the purchasers made way for the burgomaster's pretty young wife, and this too pleased her.

She returned home with a bright face, happy in having done her best, and instantly went into the kitchen to see Barbara.

Peter's good-natured sister had plainly perceived how sorely her young sister-in-law's heart was troubled, and therefore gladly saw her go out to make her purchases. Choosing and bargaining would surely dispel her sorrows and bring other thoughts. True, the cautious house-keeper, who expected everything good from Maria except the capacity of showing herself an able, clever mistress of the house, had charged Trautchen to warn her mistress against being cheated. But when in market the demand is two or three times greater than the supply, prices rise, and so it happened that when Maria told the widow how much she had paid for this or that article, Barbara's "My child, that's perfectly unheard-of!" or, "It's enough to drive us to beggary," followed each other in quick succession.

These exclamations, which under the circumstances were usually entirely unjustifiable, vexed Maria; but she wished to be at peace with her sister-in-law, and though it was hard to bear injustice, it was contrary to her nature and would have caused her pain to express her indignation in violent words. So she merely said with a little excitement:

"Please ask what other ladies are paying, and then scold, if you think it right."

With these words she left the kitchen.

"My child, I'm not scolding at all," Barbara called after her, but Maria would not hear, hastily ascended the stairs and locked herself into her room. Her joyousness had again vanished.

On Sunday she went to church. After dinner she filled a canvas-bag with provisions for Adrian, who was going on a boating excursion with several friends, and then sat at the window in her chamber.

Stately men, among them many members of the council, passed by with their gaily-dressed wives and children; \young girls with flowers in their bosoms moved arm in arm, by twos and threes, along the footpath beside the canal, to dance in the village outside the Zyl-Gate. They walked quietly forward with eyes discreetly downcast, but many a cheek flushed and many an ill-suppressed smile hovered around rosy lips, when the youths, who followed the girls moving so decorously along, as gaily and swiftly as sea-gulls flutter around a ship, uttered teasing jests, or whispered into their ears words that no third party need hear. \

All who were going towards the Zyl-Gate seemed gay and careless, every face showed what joyous hours in the open air and sunny meadows were anticipated. The object that attracted them appeared beautiful and desirable to Maria also, but what should she do among the happy, how could she be alone amid strangers with her troubled heart? The shadows of the houses seemed especially dark to-day, the air of the city heavier than usual, as if the spring had come to every human being, great and small, old and young, except herself.

The buildings and the trees that bordered the Achtergracht were already casting longer shadows, and the golden mists hovering over the roofs began to be mingled with a faint rosy light, when Maria heard a horseman trotting up the street. She drew herself up rigidly and her heart throbbed violently. She would not receive Peter any differently from usual, she must be frank to him and show him how she felt, and that matters could not go on so, nay she was already trying to find fitting words for what she had to say to him. Just at that moment, the horse stopped before the door. She went to the window, saw her husband swing himself from the saddle and look joyously up to the window of her room and, though she made no sign of greeting, her heart drew her towards him. Every thought, every fancy was forgotten, and with winged steps she flew down the corridor to the stairs. Meantime he had entered, and she called his name. " Maria, child, are you there !" he shouted, rushed up the steps as nimbly as a youth, met her on one of the upper stairs and drew her with overflowing tenderness to his heart.

" At last, at last, I have you again !" he cried joyously, pressing his lips to her eyes and her fragrant hair. She had clasped her hands closely around his neck, but he released himself, held them in his, and asked : " Are Barbara and Adrian at home ? "

She shook her head.

The burgomaster laughed, stooped, lifted her up like a child, and carried her into his room. As a beautiful tree beside a burning house is seized by the neighboring flames, although immediately protected with cold water, Maria, in spite of her long-cherished resolve to receive him coolly, was overwhelmed by the warmth of her husband's feelings. She cordially rejoiced in having him once more, and willingly believed him, as he told her in loving words how painfully he had felt their separation, how sorely he had missed her, and how distinctly he, who usually lacked the ability to remember an absent person, had had her image before his eyes.

How warmly, with what convincing tones he understood how to give expression to his love to-day! She was still a happy wife, and showed him that she was without reserve.

Barbara and Adrian returned home, and there was now much to tell at the evening meal. Peter had had many a strange experience on the journey, and gained fresh hope, the boy had distinguished himself at school, and Bessie's sickness might already be called a danger happily overcome. Barbara was radiant with joy, for all seemed well between Maria and her brother.

The beautiful April night passed pleasantly away.

When Maria was braiding black velvet into her hair the next morning, she was full of grateful emotion, for she had found courage to tell Peter that she desired to have a larger share in his anxieties than before, and received a kind assent. A worthier, richer life, she hoped, would now begin. He was to tell her this very day what he had discussed and accomplished with the Prince and at Dortrecht, for hitherto no word of all this had escaped his lips.

Barbara, who was moving about in the kitchen and just on the point of catching three chickens to kill them, let them live a little longer, and even tossed half a handful of barley into their coop, as she heard her sister-in-law come singing down-stairs. The broken bars of Wilhelm's last madrigal sounded as sweet and full of promise as the first notes of the nightingale, which the gardener hears at the end of a long winter. It was spring again in the house, and her pleasant round face, in its large cap, looked as bright and unclouded as a sunflower amid its green leaves, as she called to Maria:

"This is a good day for you, child; we'll melt down the butter and salt the hams."

The words sounded as joyous as if she had offered her an invitation to Paradise, and Maria willingly helped in the work, which began at once. When the widow moved her hands, tongues could not remain silent, and the conversation that had probably taken place between Peter and his wife excited her curiosity not a little.

She turned the conversation upon him cleverly enough, and, as if accidentally, asked the question:

"Did he apologize for his departure on the anniversary of your wedding-day?"

"I know the reason; he could not stay."

"Of course not, of course not; but whoever is green the goats eat. We mustn't allow the men to go too far. Give, but take also. ·An injustice endured is a florin, for which in marriage a calf can be bought."

"I will not bargain with Peter, and if anything weighed heavily on my mind, I have willingly forgotten it after so long a separation."

"Wet hay may destroy a barn, and any one to whom the hare runs can catch him! People ought not to keep their troubles to themselves, but tell them; that's why they have tongues, and yesterday was the right time to make a clean breast of everything that grieves you."

"He was in such a joyous mood when he came home, and then: Why do you think I feel unhappy?"

"Unhappy. Who said so?"

Maria blushed, but the widow seized the knife and opened the hen-coop.

Trautchen was helping the two ladies in the kitchen, but she was frequently interrupted in her work, for this morning the knocker on the door had no rest, and those who entered must have brought the burgomaster no pleasant news, for his deep; angry voice was often audible.

His longest discussion was with Herr Van Hout, who had come to him, not only to ask questions and tell what occurred, but also to make complaints.

It was no ordinary spectacle, when these two men, who, towering far above their fellow-citizens, not only in stature, but moral earnestness and enthusiastic devotion to the cause of liberty, declared their opinions and expressed their wrath. The inflammable, restless Van Hout took the first part, the slow, steadfast Van der Werff, with mighty impressiveness, the second.

A bad disposition ruled among the fathers of the city, the rich men of old families, the great weavers and brewers, for to them property, life and consideration were more than religion and liberty, while the poor men, who laboriously supported their families by the sweat of their brows, were joyously determined to sacrifice money and blood for the good cause.

There was obstacle after obstacle to conquer. The scaffolds and barns, frames and all other wood-work that could serve to conceal a man, were to be levelled to the earth, as all the country-houses and other buildings near the city had formerly been. Much newly-erected wood-work was already removed, but the rich longest resisted having the axe put to theirs. New earthworks had been commenced at the important fort of Valkenburg; but part of the land, where the workmen were obliged to dig, belonged to a brewer, who demanded a large sum in compensation for his damaged meadow. When the siege was raised in March, paper-money was restored, round pieces of pasteboard, one side of which bore the Netherland lion, with the inscription, "*Haec libertatis ergo*," while the other had the coat-of-arms of the city and the motto "God guard Leyden." These were intended to be exchanged for coin or provisions, but rich speculators had obtained possession of many pieces, and were trying to raise their value. Demands of every kind pressed upon him, and amid all these claims the burgomaster was also compelled to think of his own affairs, for all intercourse with the outside world would soon be cut off, and it was necessary to settle many things with the representative of his business in Hamburg. Great losses were threatening, but he left no means untried to secure for his family what might yet be saved.

He rarely saw wife or children; yet thought he was fulfilling the promise Maria had obtained from him the evening after his return, when he briefly answered her questions or voluntarily gave her such sentences as: "There was warm work at the town-hall to-day!" or, "It is more difficult to circulate the paper-money than we expected!" He did not feel the kindly necessity of having a confidante and expressing his feelings, and his first wife had been perfectly contented and happy, if he sat silently beside her during quiet hours, called her his treasure, petted the children, or even praised her cracknels and Sunday roast. Business and public affairs had been his concern, the kitchen and nursery hers. What they had shared, was the consciousness of the love one felt for the other, their children, the distinction, honors and possessions of the household.

Maria asked more and he was ready to grant it, but when in the evening she pressed the wearied man with questions he was accustomed to hear only from the lips of men, he put her off for the answers till less busy times, or fell asleep in the midst of her inquiries.

She saw how many burdens oppressed him, how unweariedly he toiled—but why did he not move a portion of the load to other shoulders?

Once, during the beautiful spring weather, he went out with her into the country. She seized upon the opportunity to represent that it was his duty to himself and her to gain more rest.

He listened patiently, and when she had finished her entreaty and warnings, took her hand in his, saying:

"You have met Herr Marnix von St. Aldegonde and know what the cause of liberty owes him. Do you know his motto?"

She nodded and answered softly : "*Repos ailleurs.*"

"Where else can we rest," he repeated firmly.

A slight shiver ran through her limbs, and as she withdrew her hands, she could not help thinking: "Where else ;—so not here. Rest and happiness have no home here." She did not utter the words, but could not drive them from her mind.

CHAPTER XII.

DURING these May days the Hoogstraten mansion was the quietest of all the houses in quiet Nobelstrasse. By the orders of Doctor Bontius and the sick lady's attorney, a mixture of straw and sand lay on the causeway before it. The windows were closely curtained, and a piece of felt hung between the door and the knocker. The door was ajar, but a servant sat close behind it to answer those who sought admission.

On a morning early in May the musician, Wilhelm Corneliussohn, and Janus Dousa turned the corner of Nobelstrasse. Both men were engaged in eager conversation, but as they approached the straw and sand, their voices became lower and then ceased entirely.

"The carpet we spread under the feet of the conqueror Death," said the nobleman. "I hope he will lower the torch only once here and do honor to age, little worthy of respect as it may be. Don't stay too long in the infected house, Herr Wilhelm."

The musician gently opened the door. The servant silently greeted him and turned towards the stairs to call Belotti; for the "player-man" had already enquired more than once for the steward.

Wilhelm entered the little room where he usually waited, and for the first time found another visitor there, but in a somewhat peculiar attitude. Father Damianus sat bolt upright in an arm-chair, with his head drooping on one side, sound asleep. The face of the priest, a man approaching his fortieth year, was as pink and white as a child's, and framed by a thin light-brown beard. A narrow circle of thin light hair surrounded his large tonsure, and a heavy dark rosary of olive-wood beads hung from the sleeper's hands. A gentle, kindly smile hovered around his half-parted lips.

" This mild saint in long woman's robes doesn't look as if he could grasp anything strongly" thought Wilhelm, " yet his hands are callous and have toiled hard."

When Belotti entered the room and saw the sleeping

priest, he carefully pushed a pillow under his head and beckoned to Wilhelm to follow him into the entry.

"We won't grudge him a little rest," said the Italian. "He has sat beside the padrona's bed from yesterday noon until two hours ago. Usually she doesn't know what is going on around her, but as soon as consciousness returns she wants religious consolation. She still refuses to take the sacrament for the dying, for she won't admit that she is approaching her end. Yet often, when the disease attacks her more sharply, she asks in mortal terror if everything is ready, for she is afraid to die without extreme unction."

"And how is Fraulein Henrica?"

"A very little better."

The priest had now come out of the little room. Belotti reverently kissed his hand and Wilhelm bowed respectfully.

"I had fallen asleep," said Damianus simply and naturally, but in a voice less deep and powerful than would have been expected from his broad breast and tall figure. "I will read the mass, visit my sick, and then return. Have you thought better of it, Belotti?"

"It won't do sir, the Virgin knows it won't do. My dismissal was given for the first of May, this is the eighth, and yet I'm still here—I haven't left the house because I'm a Christian! Now the ladies have a good physician, Sister Gonzaga is doing her duty, you yourself will earn by your nursing a place among the martyrs in Paradise, so, without making myself guilty of a sin, I can tie up my bundle."

"You will *not* go, Belotti," said the priest firmly. "If you still insist on having your own way, at least do not call yourself a Christian."

" You will stay," cried Wilhelm, " if only for the sake of the young lady, to whom you still feel kindly."

Belotti shook his head, and answered quietly :

" You can add nothing, young sir, to what the holy Father represented to me yesterday. But my mind is made up, I shall go ; yet as I value the holy Father's good opinion and yours, I beg you to do me the favor to listen to me. I have passed my sixty-second birthday, and an old horse or an old servant stands a long time in the market-place before any one will buy them. There might probably be a place in Brussels for a Catholic steward, who understands his business, but this old heart longs to return to Naples—ardently, ardently, unutterably. You have seen our blue sea and our sky, young sir, and I yearn for them, but even more for other, smaller things. It now seems a joy that I can speak in my native language to you, Herr Wilhelm, and you, holy Father. But there is a country where every one uses the same tongue that I do. There is a little village at the foot of Vesuvius—merciful Heavens! Many a person would be afraid to stay there, even half an hour, when the mountain quakes, the ashes fall in showers, and the glowing lava pours out in a stream. The houses there are by no means so well built, and the window-panes are not so clean as in this country. I almost fear that there are few glass windows in Resina. but the children don't freeze, any more than they do here. What would a Leyden house-keeper say to our village streets ? Poles with vines, boughs of fig-trees, and all sorts of under-clothing on the roofs, at the windows, and the crooked, sloping balconies ; orange and lemon-trees with golden fruit grow in the little gardens, which have neither straight paths nor symmetrical beds. Everything there grows together topsy-turvy. The boys, who in rags that no tailor has darned or mended, clamber over the white vineyard walls, the little girls, whose mothers comb their hair before the doors of the houses, are not so pink and white, nor so nicely washed as the Holland children, but I should like to see again the brown-skinned, black-haired little ones with the dark eyes, and end my days amid all the clatter in the warm air, among my nephews, nieces and blood-relations."

As he uttered these words, the old man's features had flushed and his black eyes sparkled with a fire, that but a short time before the northern air and his long years of servitude seemed to have extinguished. Since neither the priest nor the musician answered immediately, he continued more quietly :

" Monseigneur Gloria is going to Italy now, and I can accompany him to Rome as courier. From thence I can easily reach Naples, and live there on the interest of my savings free from care. My future master will leave on the 15th, and on the 12th I must be in Antwerp, where I am to meet him."

The eyes of the priest and the musician met. Wilhelm lacked courage to seek to withhold the steward from carrying out his plan, but Damianus summoned up his resolution, laid his hand on the old man's shoulder, and said :

" If you wait here a few weeks more, Belotti, you will find the true rest, the peace of a good conscience. The crown of life is promised to those, who are faithful unto death. When these sad days are over, it will be easy to smooth the way to your home. We shall meet again towards noon, Belotti. If my assistance is necessary, send for me ; old Ambrosius knows where to find me. May God's blessing rest upon you, and if you will accept it from me, on you also, Meister Wilhelm."

After the priest had left the house, Belotti said, sighing :

" He'll yet force me to yield to his will. He abuses his power over souls. I'm no saint, and what he asks of me—"

" Is right," said Wilhelm firmly.

" But you don't know what it is to throw away, like a pair of worn-out shoes, the dearest hope of a long, sad life. And for whom, I ask you, for whom? Do you know my padrona? Oh! sir, I have experienced in this house things, which your youth does not dream could be possible. The young lady has wounded you. Am I right or wrong ?"

" You are mistaken, Belotti."

" Really? I am glad for your sake, you are a modest artist, but the signorina bears the Hoogstraten name, and that is saying everything. Do you know her father ?"

" No, Belotti."

" That's a race—a race ! Have you never heard anything of the story of our signorina's older sister ?"

" Has Henrica an older sister ?"

" Yes, sir, and when I think of her.—Imagine the signorina, exactly like our signorina, only taller, more stately, more beautiful."

" Isabella !" exclaimed the musician. A conjecture, which had been aroused since his conversation with Henrica, appeared to be confirmed ; he seized the steward's arm so suddenly and unexpectedly, that the latter drew back, and continued eagerly : " What do you know of her? I beseech you, Belotti, tell me all."

The servant looked up the stairs, then shaking his head, answered:

"You are probably mistaken. There has never been an Isabella in this house to my knowledge, but I will gladly place myself at your service.   Come again after sunset, but you must expect to hear no pleasant tale."

Twilight had scarcely yielded to darkness, when the musician again entered the Hoogstraten mansion. The little room was empty, but Belotti did not keep him waiting long.

The old man placed a dainty little waiter, bearing a jug of wine and a goblet, on the table beside the lamp and, after informing Wilhelm of the invalids' condition, courteously offered him a chair.   When the musician asked him why he had not brought a cup for himself too, he replied:

"I drink nothing but water, but allow me to take the liberty to sit down.   The servant who attends to the chambers has left the house, and I've done nothing but go up and down stairs all day. It tries my old legs, and we can expect no quiet night."

A single candle lighted the little room. Belotti, who had leaned far back in his chair, opened his clenched hands and slowly began:

"I spoke this morning of the Hoogstraten race. Children of the same parents, it is true, are often very un-like, but in your little country, which speaks its own language and has many things peculiar to itself—you won't deny that—every old family has its special traits. I know, for I have been in many a noble household in Holland. Every race has its own peculiar blood and ways. Even where—by your leave—there is a crack in the brain, it rarely happens to only one member of a family. My mistress has more of her French mother's nature. But I intended to speak only of the signorina, and am wandering too far from my subject."

"No, Belotti, certainly not, we have plenty of time, and I shall be glad to listen to you, but first you must answer one question."

"Why, sir, how your cheeks glow! Did you meet the signorina in Italy?"

"Perhaps so, Belotti."

"Why, of course, of course! Whoever has once seen her, doesn't easily forget. What is it you wish to know?"

"First, the lady's name."

"Anna."

"And not Isabella also?"

"No, sir, she was never called anything but Anna."

"And when did she leave Holland?"

"Wait; it was—four years ago last Easter."

"Has she dark, brown or fair hair?"

"I've said already that she looked just like Fraulein Henrica. But what lady might not have fair, brown or dark hair? I think we shall reach the goal sooner, if you will let *me* ask a question now. Had the lady you mean a large semi-circular scar just under the hair, exactly in the middle of her forehead?"

"Enough," cried Wilhelm, rising hastily. "She fell on one of her father's weapons when a child."

"On the contrary, sir, the handle of Junker Van Hoogstraten's weapon fell on the forehead of his own daughter. How horrified you look! Oh! I have witnessed worse things in this house. Now it is your turn again: In what city of my home did you meet the signorina?"

"In Rome, alone and under an assumed name. Isabella—a Holland girl! Pray go on with your story, Belotti; I won't interrupt you again. What had the child done, that her own father—"

"He is the wildest of all the wild Hoogstratens. Perhaps you may have seen men like him in Italy—in this country you might seek long for such a hurricane. You must not think him an evil-disposed man, but a word that goes against the grain, a look askance will rob him of his senses, and things are done which he repents as soon as they are over. The signorina received her scar in the same way. She was a mere child, and of course ought not to have touched fire-arms, nevertheless she did whenever she could, and once a pistol went off and the bullet struck one of the best hunting-dogs. Her father heard the report and, when he saw the animal lying on the ground and the pistol at the little girl's feet, he seized it and with the sharp-edged handle struck—"

"A child, his own daughter!" exclaimed Wilhelm indignantly.

"People are differently constituted," Belotti continued. "Some, the class to which you probably belong, cautiously consider before they speak or act; the second reflect a long time and, when they are ready, pour forth a great many words, but rarely act at all; while the third, and at their head the Hoogstraten family, heap deeds on deeds, and if they ever think, it is only after the act is accomplished. If they then find that they have committed an injustice, pride comes in and forbids them to confess, atone for, or recall it. So one misfortune follows another; but the gentlemen pay no heed and find forgetfulness in drinking and gambling, carousing and hunting. There are plenty of debts, but all anxiety concerning them is left to the creditors, and boys who receive no inheritance are supplied with a place at court or in the army; for the girls, thank God, there is no lack of convents, if they confess our holy religion, and both have expectations from rich aunts and other blood relations, who die without children."

"You paint in vivid colors."

"But they are true, and they all suit the Junker; though to be sure he need not keep his property for sons, since his wife gave him none. He met her at court in Brussels, and she came from Parma."

"Did you know her?"

"She died before I came to the padrona's house. The two young ladies grew up without a mother. You have heard that their father would even attack them, yet he doubtless loved them and would never resolve to place them in a convent. True, he often felt—at least he freely admitted it in conversations with her excellenza —that there were more suitable places for young girls than his castle, where matters went badly enough, and so he at last sent his oldest daughter to us. My mistress usually could not endure the society of young girls, but Fraulein Anna was one of her nearest relatives, and I know she invited her of her own accord. I can still see in memory the signorina at sixteen; a sweeter creature, Herr Wilhelm, my eyes have never beheld before or since, and yet she never remained the same. I have seen her as soft as Flemish velvet, but at other times she could rage like a November storm in your country. She was always beautiful as a rose and, as her mother's old cameriera—she was a native of Lugano—had brought her up, and the priest who taught her came from Pisa and was acknowledged to be an excellent musician, she spoke my language like a child of Tuscany and was perfectly familiar with music. You have doubtless heard her singing, her harp and lute-playing, but you should know that all the ladies of the Hoogstraten family, with the exception of my mistress, possess a special talent for your art. In summer we lived in the beautiful country-house, that was torn down before the seige by your friends—with little justice I think. Many a stately guest rode out to visit us. We kept open house, and where there is a good table and a beautiful young lady like our signorina, the gallants are not far off. Among them was a very aristocratic gentleman of middle age, the Marquis d'Avennes, whom her excellenza had expressly invited. We had never received any prince with so much attention; but this was a matter of course, for his mother was a relative of her excellenza. You must know that my mistress, on her mother's side, is descended from a family in Normandy. The Marquis d'Avennes was certainly an elegant cavalier, but rather dainty than manly. He was soon madly in love with Fraulein Anna, and asked in due form for her hand. Her excellenza favored the match, and the father said simply: 'You will take him.' He would listen to no opposition. Other gentlemen don't consult their daughters when a suitable lover appears. So the signorina became the marquis's betrothed wife, but the padrona said firmly that her niece was too young to be married. She induced Junker Van Hoogstraten, whom she held as firmly as a farmer holds a filly, to defer the wedding until Easter. The outfit was to be provided during the winter. The condition that he must wait six months was imposed on the marquis, and he went back to France with the ring on his finger. His betrothed bride did not shed a single tear for him, and as soon as he had gone, flung the engagement ring into the jewel-cup on her dressing-table, before the eyes of the camariera, from whom I heard the story. She did not venture to oppose her father, but did not hesitate to express her opinion of the marquis to her excellenza, and her aunt, though she had favored the Frenchman's suit, allowed it. Yet there had often been fierce quarrels between the old and young lady, and if the padrona had had reason to clip the wild falcon's wings and teach her what is fitting for noble ladies, the signorina would have been justified in complaining of many an exaction, by which the padrona had spoiled her pleasure in life. I am sorry to destroy the confidence of your youth, but whoever grows grey, with his eyes open, will meet persons who rejoice, nay to whom it is a necessity to injure others. Yet it is a consolation, that no one is wicked simply for the sake of wickedness, and I have often found—how shall I express it?—that the worst impulses arise from the perversion, or even the excess of the noblest virtues, whose reverse or caricature they become. I have seen base envy proceed from beautiful ambition, contemptible avarice from honest emulation, fierce hate from tender love. My mistress, when she was young, knew how to love truly and faithfully, but she was shamefully deceived, and now rancor, not against an individual, but against life, has taken possession of her, and her noble loyalty has become tenacious adherence to bad wishes. How this has happened you will learn, if you will continue to listen.

" When winter came, I was ordered to go to Brussels and establish the new household in splendid style. The ladies were to follow me. It was four years ago. The Duke of Alva then lived as viceroy in Brussels, and this nobleman held my mistress in high esteem, nay had even twice paid us the honor of a visit. His aristocratic officers also frequented our house, among them Don Luis d'Avila, a nobleman of ancient family, who was one of the duke's favorites. Like the Marquis d'Avennes, he was no longer in his early youth, but was a man of totally different stamp; tall, strong as if hammered from steel, a soldier of invincible strength and skill, a most dreaded seeker of quarrels, but a man whose glowing eyes and wonderful gift of song must have exerted a mysterious, bewitching power over women. Dozens of adventures, in which he was said to have taken part, were told in the servant's hall and half of them had some foundation of truth, as I afterwards learned by experience. If you suppose this heart-breaker bore any resemblance to the gay, curly-haired minions of fortune, on whom young ladies lavish their love, you are mistaken; Don Luis was a grave man with close-cut hair, who never wore anything but dark clothes, and even carried a sword, whose hilt, instead of gold and silver, consisted of blackened metal. He resembled death much more than blooming love. Perhaps this very thing made him irresistible, since we are all born for death and no suitor is so sure of victory as he.

" The padrona had not been favorably disposed to him at first, but this mood soon changed, and at New Year's he too was admitted to small evening receptions of intimate friends. He came whenever we invited him,.

but had no word, no look, scarcely a greeting for our young lady. Only when it pleased the signorina to sing, he went near her and sharply criticised anything in her execution that chanced to displease him. He often sang himself too, and then usually chose the same songs as Fraulein Anna, as if to surpass her by his superior skill.

"So things went on till the time of the carnival. On Shrove-Tuesday the padrona gave a large entertainment, and when I led the servants and stood behind the signorina and Don Luis, to whom her excellenza had long been in the habit of assigning the seat beside her niece, I noticed that their hands met under the table and rested in each other's clasp a long time. My heart was so full of anxiety, that it was very hard for me to keep the attention so necessary on that evening—and when the next morning, the padrona summoned me to settle the accounts, I thought it my duty to modestly remark that Don Luis d'Avila's wooing did not seem disagreeable to the young lady in spite of her betrothal. She let me speak, but when I ventured to repeat what people said of the Spaniard, angrily started up and showed me to the door. A faithful servant often hears and sees more than his employers suspect, and I had the confidence of the padrona's foster-sister, who is now dead; but at that time Susanna knew everything that concerned her mis-stress.

"There was a bad prospect for the expectant bride-groom in France, for whenever the padrona spoke of him, it was with a laugh we knew, and which boded no good; but she still wrote frequently to the marquis and his mother, and many a letter from Rochebrun reached our house. To be sure, her excellenza also gave Don Luis more than one secret audience.

"During Lent a messenger from Fraulein Van Hoogstraten's father arrived with the news, that at Easter he, himself, would come to Brussels from Haarlem, and the marquis from Castle Rochebrun, and on Maundy-Thursday I received orders to dress the private chapel with flowers, engage post-horses, and do several other things. On Good Friday, the day of our Lord's crucifixion—I wish I were telling lies—early in the morning of Good Friday the signorina was dressed in all her bridal finery. Don Luis appeared clad in black, proud and gloomy as usual, and by candle-light, before sunrise on a cold, damp morning—it seems to me as if it were only yesterday—the Castilian was married to our young mistress. The padrona, a Spanish officer and I were the witnesses. At seven o'clock the carriage drove up, and after it was packed Don Luis handed me a little box to put in the vehicle. It was heavy and I knew it well; the padrona was in the habit of keeping her gold coin in it. At Easter the whole city learned that Don Luis d'Avila had eloped with the beautiful Anna Van Hoogstraten, after killing her betrothed bridegroom in a duel on Maundy-Thursday at Hals on his way to Brussels—scarcely twenty-four hours before the wedding.

"I shall never forget how Junker Van Hoogstraten raged. The padrona refused to see him and pretended to be ill, but she was as well as only she could be during these last few years."

"And do you know how to interpret your mistress's mysterious conduct?" asked Wilhelm.

"Yes sir; her reasons are perfectly evident. But I must hasten, it is growing late; besides I cannot tell you minute particulars, for I was myself a child when the event happened, though Susanna has told me many things that would probably be worth relating. Her excellenza's mother was a Chevreaux, and my mistress spent the best years of her life with her mother's sister, who during the winter lived in Paris. It was in the reign of the late King Francis, and you doubtless know that this great Prince was a very gallant gentleman, who was said to have broken as many hearts as lances. My padrona, who in those days was very beautiful, belonged to the ladies of his court, and King Francis especially distinguished her. But the young lady knew how to guard her honor, for she had early found in the gallant Marquis d'Avennes a knight to whom she was loyally devoted, and for whom she had wept bitterly many a night. Like master, like servant, and though the marquis had worn the young lady's color for years and rendered her every service of an obedient knight, his eyes and heart often wandered to the right and left. Yet he always returned to his liege-lady, and when the sixth year came, the Chevreaux's urged the marquis to put an end to his trifling and think of marriage. My mistress began to make her preparations, and Susanna was a witness of her consultation with the marquis about whether she would keep or sell the Holland estates and castles. But the wedding did not take place, for the marquis was obliged to go to Italy with the army and her excellenza lived in perpetual anxiety about him; at that time the French fared ill in my country, and he often left her whole months without news. At last he returned and found in the Chevreaux's house his betrothed wife's little cousin, who had grown up into a charming young lady. You can imagine the rest. The rose-bud Hortense now pleased the marquis far better than the Holland flower

of five and twenty.   The Chevreaux's were aristocratic
but deeply in debt, and the suitor, while fighting in Italy,
had inherited the whole of his uncle's great estate, so
they did not suffer him to sue in vain.   My mistress returned to Holland.   Her father challenged the marquis,
but no blood was spilled in the duel, and Monsieur
d'Avennes led a happy wedded life with Hortense de
Chevreaux.   Her son was the signorina's hapless lover.
Do you understand, Herr Wilhelm ?   She had nursed
and fostered the old grudge for half a life time; for its
sake she had sacrificed her own kinswoman to Don
Luis, but in return she repaid by the death of the only
son of a hated mother, the sorrow she had suffered for
years on her account."

The musician had clenched the handkerchief, with
which he had wiped the perspiration from his brow,
closely in his hand, and asked :

"What more have you heard of Anna ?"

"Very little," replied Belotti.   "Her father has
torn her from his heart, and calls Henrica his only
daughter.   Happiness abandons those who are bur-
dened by a father's curse, and she certainly did not find
it.   Don Luis is said to have been degraded to the
rank of ensign on account of some wild escapades, and
who knows what has become of the poor, beautiful
signorina.   The padrona sometimes sent money to her
in Italy, by way of Florence, through Signor Lamperi—
but I have heard nothing of her during the last few
months."

" One more question, Belotti," said Wilhelm.   "How
could Henrica's father trust her to your mistress, after
what had befallen his older daughter in her house ?"

" Money—miserable money !   To keep his castle

and not lose his inheritance, he resigned his child. Yes, sir, the signorina was bargained for, like a horse, and her father didn't sell her cheap. Drink some wine, sir, you look ill."

" It is nothing serious," said Wilhelm, "but the fresh air will probably do me good. Thanks for your story, Belotti."

CHAPTER XIII.

ON the afternoon of the sixteenth of May, Burgomaster Van der Werff's wife was examining chests and boxes. Her husband was at the town-hall, but had told her that towards evening, the Prince's commissioner, Herr Dietrich Van Bronkhorst, the two Seigneurs von Nordwyk, the city clerk Van Hout, and several other heads of municipal affairs and friends of freedom would meet at his house for a confidential consultation. Maria had the charge of providing the gentlemen with a nice collation, wine, and many similar cares.

This invitation had a very cheering influence on the young wife. It pleased her to be able to play the hostess, according to the meaning of the word in her parents' house. How long she had been debarred from hearing any grave, earnest conversation. True, there had been no lack of visitors : the friends and relatives of her husband's family, who called upon her and talked with Barbara, often begged her to come to their houses; among them were many who showed themselves kindly disposed and could not help respecting her worth, but not one to whom she was attracted by any warm affection. Maria, whose life was certainly not crowded with amusements, dreaded their coming, and when they did call, endured their presence as an unavoidable evil. The worthy matrons were all much older than herself and, while sitting over their cakes, stewed fruit, and hippocras, knitting, spinning or netting, talked of the hard times during the siege, of the cares of children and servants, washing and soap-making, or subjected to a rigid scrutiny the numerous incomprehensible and reprehensible acts other women were said to have committed, to be committing, or to desire to commit, until Maria's heart grew heavy and her lonely room seemed to her a peaceful asylum.

She could find words only when the conversation turned upon the misery of the country and the sacred duty of bearing every privation a second time, if necessary for the freedom of the nation, and then she gladly listened to the sturdy women, who evidently meant what they said; but when the hours were filled with idle gossip, it caused her actual pain. Yet she dared not avoid it and was obliged to wait until the departure of the last acquaintance; for after she had ventured to retire early several times, Barbara kindly warned her against it, not concealing that she had had great difficulty in defending her against the reproach of pride and incivility.

"Such chat," said the widow, "is pleasant and strengthens the courage, and whoever leaves the visitors while they are together, can pray the Lord for a favorable report."

One lady in Leyden pleased the burgomaster's wife. This was the wife of Herr Van Hout, the city clerk, but the latter rarely appeared in company, for though a delicate, aristocratic-looking woman, she was obliged to be busy from morning till night, to keep the children and household in good order on a narrow income.

Maria felt brighter and happier than she had done for many days, as she stood before the shelf that contained the table-furniture and the cupboard where the silver was kept. All the handsome dishes belonging to the house were bright and shining, free from every grain of dust, so too were the white linen cloths, trimmed with lace. She selected what she needed, but many of the pewter, glass, and silver articles did not please her; for they did not match, and she found scratches and cracks on numerous pieces.

When her mother had begun to prepare her wedding-outfit, Peter expressed a desire that in these hard times the money should be kept and no useless things purchased. There was an abundance of household articles of every kind in his home, and he would have thought it wrong to buy even a plate. In fact there was no lack of anything on the shelves and cupboards, but she had not selected and bought them herself; they belonged to her, but not entirely, and what was worse, her eyes, accustomed to prettier things, could find no pleasure in these dull, scratched pewter plates, these pitchers, cups and tankards painted in coarse figures with glaring colors. The clumsy glass, too, did not suit her taste, and, while looking it over and selecting what was necessary, she could not help thinking of her recently-wedded friends, who, with sparkling eyes, had showed her their spick-and-span new table-furniture as proudly and happily, as if each piece had been their own work. But, even with the articles she possessed, a table could be set very prettily and daintily.

She had gone out with Adrian before dinner to cut some flowers in the garden by the city wall, and also gathered some delicate grasses in the meadow before the gate. These gifts of May were now tastefully arranged, mixed with peacock-feathers, and placed in vases, and she was delighted to see even the clumsiest dishes win a graceful aspect from the garlands she twined around them. Adrian watched her in astonishment. He would not have marvelled if, under her hands, the dark dining-room had been transformed into a hall of mother-of-pearl and crystal.

When the table was laid, Peter returned home for a moment. He was going to ride out to Valkenburg with Captain Allertssohn, Janus Dousa, and other gentlemen, to inspect the fortifications before his guests appeared. As he passed through the dining-room, he waved his hand to his wife and glancing over the table, said:

"This decoration was not necessary, least of all the flowers. We expect to hold a serious consultation, and you have arranged a wedding-banquet."

Perceiving that Maria cast down her eyes, he exclaimed kindly:

"But it can remain so for aught I care," and left the room.

Maria stood irresolutely before her work. Bitter emotions were again beginning to stir in her mind, and she was already extending her hand defiantly towards one particularly beautiful vase, when Adrian raised his large eyes to her face, exclaiming in a tone of earnest entreaty:

"No, mother, you mustn't do that, it looks quite too pretty."

Maria smiled, passed her hand over the boy's

curls, took two cakes from a dish, gave them to him, and said:

"One for you, the other for Bessie; our flowers shall stay."

Adrian hurried off with the sweet gifts, but Maria glanced over the table once more, saying:

"Peter never wants anything but what is absolutely necessary; yet that surely isn't all, or God would have made all the birds with grey feathers."

After helping Barbara in the kitchen, she went to her own room. There she arranged her hair, put a fresh, beautifully-starched ruff around her neck and carefully-plaited lace in the open bosom of her dress, but wore her every-day gown, for her husband did not wish to give the assembly at his house a festal aspect.

Just as she had put the last gold pin in her hair, and was considering whether the place of honor at the table belonged to Herr Van Bronkhorst, as representative of the Prince, or to the older Herr von Nordwyk, Trautchen knocked at the door and informed her, that Doctor Bontius wished to see the burgomaster on urgent business. The maid-servant had told the physician that her master had ridden out, but he would not be put off, and asked permission to see her mistress.

Maria instantly went to Peter's room. The doctor seemed to be in haste. His only greeting was to point with the gold head of his long staff towards the peaked black hat, that never left his head, even beside the sick-bed, and asked in a curt, hurried tone:

"When will Meister Peter come home?"

"In an hour," replied Maria. "Sit down, Doctor."

"Another time. It will keep me too long to wait for

your husband.   After all, you can come with me even without his consent."

"Certainly; but we are expecting visitors."

"Yes. If I find time, I shall come too. The gentlemen can do without me, but you are necessary to the sick person to whom I wish to take you."

"I have no idea of whom you are speaking."

"Haven't you?   Then once more, it is of some one who is suffering, and that will be enough for you at first."

"And you think I could—"

"You can do far more than you know. Barbara is attending to affairs in the kitchen, and now I tell you again : You must help a sufferer."

"But, Doctor—"

"I must beg you to hurry, for my time is limited. Do you wish to make yourself useful ; yes or no ?"

The door of the dining-room had remained open. Maria again glanced at the table, and all the pleasures she had anticipated this evening passed through her mind. But as the doctor was preparing to go, she stopped him, saying :

"I will come."

The manners of this blunt, but unselfish and clever man were familiar to Maria who, without waiting for a reply, brought her shawl, and led the way downstairs. As they passed by the kitchen, Bontius called to Barbara :

"Tell Meister Peter, I have taken his wife to see Fraulein Van Hoogstraten in Nobelstrasse."

Maria could scarcely keep up with the doctor's rapid strides and had some difficulty in understanding him, as in broken sentences he told her that all the Glipper friends of the Hoogstraten family had left the city, the old Fraulein was dead, the servants had run away from fear of the plague, which had no existence, and Henrica was now deserted. She had been very ill with a severe fever, but was much better during the past few days. "Misfortune has taken up its abode in the Glipper nest," he added. "The scythe-man did the old lady a favor when he took her. The French maid, a feeble nonentity, held out bravely, but after watching a few nights broke down entirely and was to have been carried to St. Catharine's hospital, but the Italian steward, who is not a bad fellow, objected and had her taken to a Catholic laundress. He has followed to nurse her. No one is left in the deserted house to attend to the young lady, except Sister Gonzaga, a good little nun, one of the three who were allowed to remain in the old convent near you, but early this morning, to cap the climax of misfortune, the kind old woman scalded her fingers while heating a bath. The Catholic priest has faithfully remained at his post, but what can we men do in nursing the sick girl! You doubtless now suspect why I brought you with me. You ought not and cannot become the stranger's nurse permanently; but if the young lady is not to sink after all, she must now have some face about her which she can love, and God has blessed you with one. Look at the sick girl, talk with her, and if you are what I believe you—but here we are."

The air of the dark entrance hall of the Hoogstraten residence was filled with a strong odor of musk. The old lady's death had been instantly announced at the town-hall by Doctor Bontius' representative, and an armed man was marching up and down in the hall, keeping guard, who told the physician that Herr Van

Hout had already been here with his men and put seals on all the doors.

On the staircase Maria siezed her guide's arm in terror; for through an open door-way of the second story, to which she was ascending with her companion, she saw in the dusk a shapeless figure, moving strangely hither and thither, up and down. Her tone was by no means confident as, pointing towards it with her finger, she asked the doctor:

"What is that?"

The physician had paused with her, and seeing the strange object to which the burgomaster's wife pointed, recoiled a step himself. But the cool-headed man quickly perceived the real nature of the ghostly apparition, and leading Maria forward exclaimed smiling:

"What in the world are you doing there on the . floor, Father Damianus?"

"I am scouring the boards," replied the priest quietly.

"Right is right," cried the doctor indignantly. "You are too good for maid-servant's work, Father Damianus, especially when there is plenty of money without an owner here in the house, and we can find as many scrubbing-women as we want to-morrow."

"But not to-day, doctor; and the young lady won't stay in yonder room any longer. You ordered her to go to sleep yourself, and Sister Gonzaga says she won't close her eyes so long as she is next door to the corpse."

"Then Van Hout's men ought to have carried her on her bed into the old lady's beautiful sitting-room."

"That's sealed, and so are all the other handsome chambers on this story. The men were obliging and tried to find scrub-women, but the poor things are afraid of the plague."

"Such rumors grow like wire-grass," cried the doctor. "Nobody sows it, yet who can uproot it when it is once here ? "

"Neither you nor I," replied the priest. "The young lady must be brought into this room at once; but it looked neglected, so I've just set it to rights. It will do the invalid good, and the exercise can't hurt me."

With these words Father Damianus rose, and seeing Maria, said:

"You have brought a new nurse ? That's right. I need not praise Sister Gonzaga, for you know her; but I assure you Fraulein Henrica won't allow her to remain with her long, and I shall leave this house as soon as the funeral is over."

"You have done your duty; but what does this news about the Sister mean?" cried the physician angrily. "I'd rather have your old Gonzaga with her burnt fingers than—What has happened?"

The priest approached and, hastily casting a side glance at the burgomaster's wife, exclaimed:

"She speaks through her nose, and Fraulein Henrica said just now it made her ache to hear her talk; I must keep her away."

Doctor Bontius reflected a moment, and then said:

"There are eyes that cannot endure a glare of light, and perhaps certain tones may seem unbearable to irritated ears. Frau Van der Werff, you have been kept waiting a long time, please follow me."

It had grown dark. The curtains of the sick-room were lowered and a small lamp, burning behind a screen, shed but a feeble light.

The doctor approached the bed, felt Henrica's pulse, said a few words in a low tone to prepare her for her visitor, and then took the lamp to see how the invalid looked.

Maria now beheld a pale face with regular outline, whose dark eyes, in their size and lustre, formed a striking contrast to the emaciated cheeks and sunken features of the sick girl.

After old Sister Gonzaga had restored the lamp to its former place, the physician said:

"Excellent! Now, Sister, go and change the bandage on your arm and lie down." Then he beckoned Maria to approach.

Henrica's face made a strange impression upon the burgomaster's wife. She thought her beautiful, but the large eyes and firmly-shut lips seemed peculiar, rather than attractive. Yet she instantly obeyed the physician's summons, approached the bed, said kindly that she had been glad to come to stay with her a short time, and asked what she desired.

At these words, Henrica raised herself and with a sigh of relief, exclaimed:

"That does me good! Thanks, Doctor. That's a human voice again. If you want to please me, Frau Van der Werff, keep on talking, no matter what you say. Please come and sit down here. With Sister Gonzaga's hands, your voice, and the doctor's—yes, I will say with Doctor Bontius' candor, it won't be difficult to recover entirely."

"Good, good," murmured the physician. "Kind Sister Gonzaga's injuries are not serious and she will stay with you, but when it is time for you to sleep, you will be moved elsewhere. You can remain here an hour,

Frau Van der Werff, but that will be enough for to-day.
I'll go to your house and send the servant for you
with a lantern."

When the two ladies were left alone together, Maria
said:

"You set great value on the sound of voices; so do
I, perhaps more than is desirable. True, I have never
had any serious illness—"

"This is my first one too," replied Henrica, "but I
know now what it is to be compelled to submit to everything we don't like, and feel with two-fold keenness
everything that is repulsive. It is better to die than
suffer."

"Your aunt is dead," said Maria sympathizingly.

"She died early this morning. We had little in common save the tie of blood."

"Are your parents no longer living?"

"Only my father; but what of that?"

"He will rejoice over your recovery; Doctor Bontius says you will soon be perfectly well."

"I think so too," replied Henrica confidently, and
then said softly, without heeding Maria's presence:
"There is one beautiful thing. When I am well again,
I shall once more—Do you practise music?"

"Yes, dear Fraulein."

"Not merely as a pastime, but because you feel you
cannot live without it?"

"You must keep quiet, Fraulein. Music;—yes, I
think my life would be far poorer without it than it is."

"Do you sing?"

"Very seldom here; but when a girl in Delft we
sung every day."

"Of course you were the soprano?"

" Yes, Fraulein."

" Let the Fraulein drop, and call me Henrica."

" With all my heart, if you will call me Maria, or Frau Maria."

" I'll try. Don't you think we could practise many a song together ? "

Just as these words were uttered, Sister Gonzaga entered the room, saying that the wife of Receiver General Cornelius had called to ask if she could do anything for the sick lady.

" What does that mean ? " asked Henrica angrily. " I don't know the woman."

" She is the mother of Herr Wilhelm, the musician," said the young wife.

" Oh !" exclaimed Henrica. " Shall I admit her, Maria ?"

The latter shook her head and answered firmly :

" No, Fraulein Henrica.   It is not good for you to have more than one visitor at this hour, and besides—"

" Well ?"

" She is an excellent woman, but I fear her blunt manner, heavy step, and loud voice would not benefit you just now. Let me go to her and ask what she desires."

" Receive her kindly, and tell her to remember me to her son. · I am not very delicate, but I see you understand me; such substantial fare would hardly suit me just now."

After Maria had performed her errand and talked with Henrica for a time, Frau Van Hout was announced. Her husband, who had been present when the doors of the house of death were sealed, had told her about the invalid and she came to see if the poor girl needed anything.

"You might receive her," said Maria, "for she would surely please you; but the bell is ringing again, and you have talked enough for to-day. Try to sleep now. I'll go home with Frau Van Hout and come again to-morrow, if agreeable to you."

"Come, pray come!" exclaimed the young girl. "Do you want to say anything more to me?"

"I should like to do so, Fraulein Henrica. You ought not to stay in this sad house. There is plenty of room in ours. Will you be our guest until your father—"

"Yes, take me home with you!" cried the invalid, tears sparkling in her eyes. "Take me away from here, only take me away—and I will be grateful to you all my life."

CHAPTER XIV.

MARIA had not mounted the stairs so joyously for weeks as she did to-day. She would have sung, had it been seemly, though she felt a little anxious; for perhaps her husband would not think she had done right to invite, on her own authority, a stranger, especially a sick stranger, who was a friend of Spain, to be their guest.

As she passed the dining-room, she heard the gentlemen consulting together. Then Peter began to speak. She noticed the pleasant depth of his voice, and said to herself that Henrica would like to hear it. A few minutes after she entered the apartment, to greet her husband's guests, who were also hers. Joyous excitement and the rapid walk through the air of the May

evening, which, though the day had been warm, was still
cool, had flushed her cheeks and, as she modestly
crossed the threshold with a respectful greeting, which
nevertheless plainly revealed the pleasure afforded by
the visit of such guests, she looked so winning and
lovely, that not a single person present remained un-
moved by the sight. The older Herr Van der Does
clapped Peter on the shoulder and then struck the palm
of his hand with his fist, as if to say: "I won't question that!" Janus Dousa whispered gaily to Van
Hout, who was a good Latin scholar:

"*Oculi sunt in amore duces.*"

Captain Allertssohn started up and raised his hand
to his hat with a military salute; Van Bronkhorst, the
Prince's Commissioner, gave expression to his feelings
in a courtly bow, Doctor Bontius smiled contentedly,
like a person who has successfully accomplished a haz-
ardous enterprise, and Peter proudly and happily strove
to attract his wife's attention to himself. But this was
not to be, for as soon as Maria perceived that she was
the mark for so many glances, she lowered her eyes with
a deep blush, and then said far more firmly than would
have been expected from her timid manner:

"Welcome, gentlemen! My greeting comes late, but
I would have gladly offered it earlier." .

"I can bear witness to that," cried Doctor Bontius,
rising and shaking hands with Maria more cordially than
ever before. Then he motioned towards Peter, and exclaimed to the assembled guests: "Will you excuse the
burgomaster for a moment?"

As soon as he stood apart with the husband and
wife at the door, he began:

"You have invited a new visitor to the house, Frau

Van der Werff; I won't drink another drop of Malmsey, if I'm mistaken."

"How do you know?" asked Maria gaily.

"I see it in your face."

"And the young lady shall be cordially welcome to me," added Peter.

"Then you know?" asked Maria.

"The doctor did not conceal his conjecture from me."

"Why yes, the sick girl will be glad to come to us, and to-morrow—"

"No, I'll send for her to-day," interrupted Peter.

"To-day?" But dear me! It's so late; perhaps she is asleep, the gentlemen are here, and our spare bed—" exclaimed Maria, glancing disapprovingly and irresolutely from the physician to her husband.

"Calm yourself, child," replied Peter. "The doctor has ordered a covered litter from St. Catharine's hospital, Jan and one of the city-guard will carry her, and Barbara has nothing more to do in the kitchen and is now preparing her own chamber for her."

"And," chimed in the physician, "perhaps the sick girl may find sleep here. Besides, it will be far more agreeable to her pride to be carried through the streets unseen, under cover of the darkness."

"Yes, yes," said Maria sadly, "that may be so; but I had been thinking—People ought not to do anything too hastily."

"Will you be glad to receive the young lady as a guest?" asked Peter.

"Why, certainly."

"Then we won't do things by halves, but show her

all the kindness in our power. There is Barbara beckoning; the litter has come, Doctor. Guide the nocturnal procession in God's name, but don't keep us waiting too long."

The burgomaster returned to his seat, and Bontius left the room.

Maria followed him. In the entry, he laid his hand on her arm and asked:

"Will you know next time, what I expect from you?"

"No," replied the burgomaster's wife, in a tone which sounded gay, though it revealed the disappointment she felt; "no—but you have taught me that you are a man who understands how to spoil one's best pleasures."

"I will procure you others," replied the doctor laughing and descended the stairs. He was Peter's oldest friend, and had made many objections to the burgomaster's marriage with a girl so many years his junior, in these evil times, but to-day he showed himself satisfied with Van der Werff's choice.

Maria returned to the guests, filled and offered glasses of wine to the gentlemen, and then went to her sister-in-law's room, to help her prepare everything for the sick girl as well as possible. She did not do so unwillingly, but it seemed as if she would have gone to the work with far greater pleasure early the next morning.

Barbara's spacious chamber looked out upon the court-yard. No sound could be heard there of the conversation going on between the gentlemen in the dining-room, yet it was by no means quiet among these men who, though animated by the same purpose, differed widely about the ways and means of bringing it to a successful issue.

There they sat, the brave sons of a little nation, the stately leaders of a small community, poor in numbers and means of defence, which had undertaken to bid defiance to the mightiest power and finest armies of its age. They knew that the storm-clouds, which had been threatening for weeks on the horizon, would rise faster and faster, mass together, and burst in a furious tempest over Leyden, for Herr Van der Werff had summoned them to his house because a letter addressed to himself and Commissioner Van Bronkhorst by the Prince, contained tidings, that the Governor of King Philip of Spain had ordered Señor del Campo Valdez to besiege Leyden a second time and reduce it to subjection. They were aware, that William of Orange could not raise an army to divert the hostile troops from their aim or relieve the city before the lapse of several months; they had experienced how little aid was to be expected from the Queen of England and the Protestant Princes of Germany, while the horrible fate of Haarlem, a neighboring and more powerful city, rose as a menacing example before their eyes. But they were conscious of serving a good cause, relied upon the faith, courage and statesmanship of Orange, were ready to die rather than allow themselves to be enslaved body and soul by the Spanish tyrant. Their belief in God's justice was deep and earnest, and each individual possessed a joyous confidence in his own resolute, manly strength.

In truth, the men who sat around the table, so daintily decked with flowers by a woman's hand, understood how to empty the large fluted goblets so nimbly, that jug after jug of Peter's Malmsey and Rhine

wine were brought up from the cellar, the men who
made breaches in the round pies and huge joints of
meat, juicier and more nourishing than any country except theirs can furnish—did not look as if pallid fear
had brought them together.

The hat is the sign of liberty, and the free man keeps
his hat on. So some of the burgomaster's guests sat at
the board with covered heads, and how admirably the
high plaited cap of dark-red velvet, with its rich ornaments of plumes, suited the fresh old face of the senior
Seigneur of Nordwyk and the clever countenance of his
nephew Janus Dousa; how well the broad-brimmed hat
with blue and orange ostrich-feathers—the colors of the
House of Orange—became the waving locks of the young
Seigneur of Warmond, Jan Van Duivenvoorde. How
strongly marked and healthful were the faces of the other
men assembled here! Few countenances lacked ruddy
color, and strong vitality, clear intellect, immovable will
and firm resolution flashed from many blue eyes
around the table. Even the black-robed magistrates,
whose plaited ruffs and high white collars were very becoming, did not look as if the dust of documents had
injured their health. The moustaches and beards on the
lips of each, gave them also a manly appearance. They
were all joyously ready to sacrifice themselves and their
property for a great spiritual prize, yet looked as if they
had a firm foothold in the midst of life; their hale, sensible faces showed no traces of enthusiasm; only the
young Seigneur of Warmond's eyes sparkled with a
touch of this feeling, while Janus Dousa's glance often
seemed turned within, to seek things hidden in his own
heart; and at such moments his sharply-cut, irregular
features possessed a strange charm.

The broad, stout figure of Commissioner Van Bronkhorst occupied a great deal of room. His body was by no means agile, but from the round, closely-shaven head looked forth a pair of prominent eyes, that expressed unyielding resolution.

The brightly-lighted table, around which such guests had gathered, presented a gay, magnificent spectacle. The yellow leather of the doublets worn by Junker von Warmond, Colonel Mulder, and Captain Allertssohn, the colored silk scarfs that adorned them, and the scarlet coat of brave Dirk Smaling contrasted admirably with the deep black robes of Pastor Verstroot, the burgomaster, the city clerk, and their associates! The violet of the commissioner's dress and the dark hues of the fur-bordered surcoats worn by the elder Herr Van der Does and Herr Van Montfort blended pleasantly and harmonized the light and dark shades. Everything sorrowful seemed to have been banished far from this brilliant, vigorous round table, so words flowed freely and voices sounded full and strong enough.

Danger was close at hand. The Spanish vanguard might appear before Leyden any day. Many preparations were made. English auxiliaries were to garrison the fortifications of Alfen and defend the Gouda lock. The defensive works of Valkenburg had been strengthened and entrusted to other British troops, the city soldiers, the militia and volunteers were admirably drilled. They did not wish to admit foreign troops within the walls, for during the first siege they had proved far more troublesome than useful, and there was little reason to fear that a city guarded by water, walls and trees would be taken by storm.

What most excited the gentlemen was the news Van

Hout had brought. Rich Herr Baersdorp, one of the four burgomasters, who had the largest grain business in Leyden, had undertaken to purchase considerable quantities of bread-stuffs in the name of the city. Several ship loads of wheat and rye had been delivered by him the day before, but he was still in arrears with three-quarters of what was ordered. He openly said that he had as yet given no positive orders for it, because owing to the prospect of a good harvest, a fall in the price of grain was expected in the exchanges of Rotterdam and Amsterdam, and he would still have several weeks time before the commencement of the new blockade.

Van Hout was full of indignation, especially as two out of the four burgomasters sided with their colleague Baersdorp.

The elder Herr von Nordwyk agreed with him, exclaiming:

"With all due respect to your dignity, Herr Peter, your three companions in office belong to the ranks of bad friends, who would willingly be exchanged for open enemies."

"Herr von Noyelles," said Colonel Mulder, "has written about them to the Prince, the good and truthful words, that they ought to be sent to the gallows."

"And they will suit them," cried Captain Allertssohn, "so long as hangmen's nooses and traitors' necks are made for each other."

"Traitors—no," said Van der Werff resolutely. "Call them cowards, call them selfish and base-minded —but not one of them is a Judas."

"Right, Meister Peter, that they certainly are not, and perhaps even cowardice has nothing to do with their conduct," added Herr von Nordwyk. "Whoever has eyes to see and ears to hear, knows the views of the gentlemen belonging to the old city families, who are reared from infancy as future magistrates; and I speak not only of Leyden, but the residents of Gouda and Delft, Rotterdam and Dortrecht. Among a hundred, sixty would bear the Spanish yoke, even do violence to conscience, if only their liberties and rights were guaranteed. The cities must rule and they themselves in them; that is all they desire. Whether people preach sermons or read mass in the church, whether a Spaniard or a Hollander rules, is a matter of secondary importance to them. I except the present company, for you would not be here, gentlemen, if your views were similar to those of the men of whom I speak."

"Thanks for those words," said Dirk Smaling, "but with all due honor to your opinion, you have painted matters in too dark colors. May I ask if the nobles do not also cling to their rights and liberties?"

"Certainly, Herr Dirk; but they are commonly of longer date than yours," replied Van Bronkhorst. "The nobleman *needs* a ruler. He is a lustreless star, if the sun that lends him light is lacking. I, and with me all the nobles who have sworn fealty to him, now believe that our sun must and can be no other person than the Prince of Orange, who is one of ourselves, knows, loves, and understands us; not Philip, who has no comprehension of what is passing within and around us, is a foreigner and detests us. We will uphold William with our fortunes and our lives for, as I have already said, we need a sun, that is, a monarch—but the cities think they have power to shine and wish to be admired as bright stars themselves. True, they feel that, in these troublous times, the country needs a leader, and that they can find no better, wiser and more faithful one than Orange; but if it comes to pass—and may God grant it—that the Spanish yoke is broken, the noble William's rule will seem wearisome, because they enjoy playing sovereign themselves. In short: the cities *endure* a ruler, the nobles *gather round him* and need him. No real good will be accomplished until noble, burgher and peasant cheerfully yield to him, and unite to battle under his leadership for the highest blessings of life."

"Right," said Van Hout. "The well-disposed nobility may well serve as an example to the governing classes here and in the other cities, but the people, the poor hard-working people, know what is coming and, thank God, have not yet lost a hearty love for what you call the highest blessings of life. They wish to be and remain Hollanders, curse the Spanish butchers with eloquent hatred, desire to serve God according to the yearning of their own souls, and believe what their own hearts dictate—and these men call the Prince their Father William. Wait a little! As soon as trouble oppresses us, the poor and lowly will stand firm, if the rich and great waver and deny the good cause."

"They are to be trusted," said Van der Werff, "firmly trusted."

"And because I know them," cried Van Hout, "we shall conquer, with God's assistance, come what may."

Janus Dousa had been looking into his glass. Now he raised his head and with a hasty gesture, said:

"Strange that those who toil for existence with their hands, and whose uncultured brains only move when their daily needs require it, are most ready to sacrifice the little they possess, for spiritual blessings."

"Yes," said the pastor, "the kingdom of heaven stands open to the simple-hearted. It is strange that the poor and unlearned value religion, liberty and their native land far more than the perishable gifts of this world, the golden calf around which the generations throng."

"My companions are not flattered to-day," replied Dirk Smaling; "but I beg you to remember in our favor, that we are playing a great and dangerous game, and property-holders must supply the lion's share of the stake."

"By no means," retorted Van Hout, "the highest stake for which the die will be cast is life, and this has the same value to rich and poor. Those who will hold back—I think I know them—have no plain motto or sign, but a proud escutcheon over their doors. Let us wait."

"Yes, let us wait," said Van der Werff; "but there are more important matters to be considered now. Day after to-morrow will be Ascension Day, when the bells will ring for the great fair. More than one foreign trader and traveller has passed through the gates yesterday and the day before. Shall we order the booths to be set up, or have the fair deferred until some other time? If the enemy hastens his march, there will be great confusion, and we shall perhaps throw a rich prize into his hands. Pray give me your opinion, gentlemen."

"The traders ought to be protected from loss and the fair postponed," said Dirk Smaling.

"No," replied Van Hout, "for if this prohibition is issued, we shall deprive the small merchants of considerable profit and prematurely damp their courage."

"Let them have their festival," cried Janus Dousa. "We mustn't do coming trouble the favor of spoiling the happy present on its account. If you want to act wisely, follow the advice of Horace."

"The Bible also teaches that 'sufficient unto the day is the evil thereof,'" added the pastor, and Captain Allertssohn exclaimed:

"On my life, yes! My soldiers, the city-guard and volunteers must have their parade. Marching in full uniform, with all their weapons, while beautiful eyes smile upon them, the old wave greetings, and children run before with exultant shouts, a man learns to feel himself a soldier for the first time."

So it was determined to let the fair be held. While other questions were being eagerly discussed, Henrica found a loving welcome in Barbara's pleasant room. When she had fallen asleep, Maria went back to her guests, but did not again approach the table; for the gentlemen's cheeks were flushed and they were no longer speaking in regular order, but each was talking about whatever he choose. The burgomaster was discussing with Van Hout and Van Bronkhorst the means of procuring a supply of grain for the city, Janus Dousa and Herr von Warmond were speaking of the poem the city clerk had repeated at the last meeting of the poets' club, Herr Van der Does senior and the pastor were arguing about the new rules of the church, and stout Captain Allertssohn, before whom stood a huge drinking-horn drained to the dregs, had leaned his forehead on Colonel Mulder's shoulder and, as usual when he felt particularly happy over his wine, was shedding tears.

CHAPTER XV.

THE next day after the meeting of the council, Burgomaster Van der Werff, Herr Van Hout, and a notary, attended by two constables, went to Nobelstrasse to set old Fraulein Van Hoogstraten's property in order. The fathers of the city had determined to seize the Glippers' abandoned dwellings and apply the property found in them to the benefit of the common cause.

The old lady's hostility to the patriots was known to all, and as her nearest relatives, Herr Van Hoogstraten and Matanesse Van Wibisma, had been banished from Leyden, the duty of representing the heirs fell upon the city. It was to be expected that only notorious Glippers would be remembered in the dead woman's will, and if this was the case, the revenue from the personal and real estate would fall to the city, until the deserters mended their ways, and adopted a course of conduct that would permit the magistrates to again open their gates to them. Whoever continued to cling to the Spaniards and oppose the cause of liberty, would forfeit his share of the inheritance. This was no new procedure. King Philip had taught its practice, nay not only the estates of countless innocent persons who had been executed, banished or gone into voluntary exile for the sake of the new religion, but also the property of good Catholic patriots had been confiscated for his benefit. After being anvil so many years, it is pleasant to play hammer; and if that was not always done in a proper and moderate way, people excused themselves on the ground of having experienced a hundred-fold harsher and more cruel treatment from the Spaniards. It might have been unchristian to repay in the same coin, but they dealt severe blows only in mortal conflict, and did not seek the Glippers' lives.

At the door of the house of death, the magistrates met the musician Wilhelm Corneliussohn and his mother, who had come to offer Henrica a hospitable reception in their house. The mother, who had at first refused to extend her love for her neighbor to the young Glipper girl, now found it hard to be deprived of the opportunity to do a good work, and gave expression to these feelings in the sturdy fashion peculiar to her.

Belotti was standing in the entry, no longer attired in the silk hose and satin-bordered cloth garments of the steward, but in a plain burgher dress. He told the musician and Peter, that he remained in Leyden principally because he could not bear to leave the sick maid, Denise, in the lurch; but other matters also detained him, especially, though he was reluctant to acknowledge it, the feeling, strengthened by long years of service, that he belonged to the Hoogstraten house. The dead woman's attorney had said that his account books were in good order, and willingly paid the balance due him. His savings had been well invested, and as he never touched the interest, but added to the capital, had considerably increased. Nothing detained him in Leyden, yet he could not leave it until everything was settled in the house where he had so long ruled.

He had daily inquired for the sick lady, and after her death, though Denise began to recover, still lingered in Leyden; he thought it his duty to show the last honors to the dead by attending her funeral.

The magistrates were glad to find Belotti in the house. The notary had managed his little property, and respected him as an honest man. He now asked him to act as guide to his companions and himself. The most important matter was to find the ' dead woman's will. Such a document must be in existence, for up to the day after Henrica's illness it had been in the lawyer's possession, but was then sent for by the old lady, who desired to make some changes in it. He could give no information about its contents, for his dead partner, whose business had fallen to him, had assisted in drawing it up.

The steward first conducted the visitors to the padrona's sitting-room and boudoir, but though they searched the writing-tables, chests and drawers, and discovered many letters, money and valuable jewels in boxes and caskets, the document was not found.

The gentlemen thought it was concealed in a secret drawer, and ordered one of the constables to call a locksmith. Belotti allowed this to be done, but meantime listened with special attention to the low chanting that issued from the bedroom where the old lady's body lay. He knew that the will would most probably be found there, but was anxious to have the priest complete the consecration of his mistress undisturbed. As soon as all was still in the death-chamber, he asked the gentlemen to follow him.

The lofty apartment into which he led them, was filled with the odor of incense. A large bedstead, over which a pointed canopy of heavy silk rose to the ceiling, stood at the back, the coffin in which the dead woman lay had been placed in the middle of the room. A linen cloth, trimmed with lace, covered the face. The delicate hands, still unwrinkled, were folded, and lightly clasped a well-worn rosary. The lifeless form was concealed beneath a costly coverlid, in the centre of which lay an exquisitely-carved ivory crucifix.

The visitors bowed mutely before the corpse. Belotti approached it and, as he saw the padrona's well-known hands, a convulsive sob shook the old man's breast. Then he knelt beside the coffin, pressed his lips, to the cold, slender fingers, and a warm tear, the only one shed for this dead form, fell on the hands now clasped forever.

The burgomaster and his companion did not interrupt him, even when he laid his forehead upon the wood of the coffin and uttered a brief, silent prayer. After he had risen, and an elderly priest in the sacerdotal robes had left the room, Father Damianus beckoned to the acolytes, with whom he had lingered in the background, and aided by them and Belotti put the lid on the coffin, then turned to Peter Van der Werff, saying:

"We intend to bury Fraulein Van Hoogstraten at midnight, that no offence may be given."

"Very well, sir!" replied the burgomaster. "Whatever may happen, we shall not expel you from the city. Of course, if you prefer to go to the Spaniards—"

Damianus shook his head and, interrupting the burgomaster, answered modestly:

"No, sir; I am a native of Utrecht and will gladly pray for the liberty of Holland."

"There, there!" exclaimed Van Hout. "Those were good words, admirable words! Your hand, Father."

"There it is; and, so long as you don't change the '*haec libertatis ergo*' on your coins to '*haec religionis ergo*,' not one of those words need be altered."

"A free country and in it religious liberty for each individual, even for you and your followers," said the burgomaster, "is what we desire. Doctor Bontius has spoken of you, worthy man; you have cared well for this dead woman. Bury her according to the customs of your church; we have come to arrange the earthly possessions she leaves behind. Perhaps this casket may contain the will."

"No, sir," replied the priest. "She opened the sealed paper in my presence, when she was first taken sick, and wrote a few words whenever she felt stronger. An hour before her end, she ordered the notary to be sent for, but when he came life had departed. I could not remain constantly beside the corpse, so I locked up the paper in the linen chest. There is the key."

The opened will was soon found. The burgomaster quietly unfolded it, and, while reading its contents aloud, the notary and city clerk looked over his shoulder.

The property was to be divided among various churches and convents, where masses were to be read for her soul, and her nearest blood relations. Belotti and Denise received small legacies.

"It is fortunate," exclaimed Van Hout, "that this paper is a piece of paper and nothing more."

"The document has no legal value whatever," added the notary, "for it was taken from me and opened with the explicit statement, that changes were to be made. Here is a great deal to be read on the back."

The task, that the gentlemen now undertook, was no easy one, for the sick woman had scrawled short notes above and below, hither and thither, on the blank back of the document, probably to assist her memory while composing a new will.

At the very top a crucifix was sketched with an unsteady hand, and below it the words: "Pray for us! Everything shall belong to holy Mother Church."

Farther down they read: "Nico, I like the lad. The castle on the downs. Ten thousand gold florins in money. To be secured exclusively to him. His father is not to touch it. Make the reason for disinheriting him conspicuous. Van Vliet of Haarlem was the gentleman whose daughter my cousin secretly wedded. On some pitiful pretext he deserted her, to form another marriage. If he has forgotten it, I have remembered and would fain impress it upon him. Let Nico pay heed: False love is poison. My life has been ruined by it—ruined."

The second "ruined" was followed by numerous repetitions of the same word. The last one, at the very end of the sentence, had been ornamented with numerous curves and spirals by the sick woman's pen.

On the right-hand margin of the sheet stood a series of short notes:

"Ten thousand florins to Anna. To be secured to herself. Otherwise they will fall into the clutches of that foot-pad, d'Avila.

"Three times as much to Henrica. Her father will pay her the money—from the sum he owes me. Where he gets it is his affair. Thus the account with him would be settled.

"Belotti has behaved badly. He shall be passed over.

"Denise may keep what was given her."

In the middle of the paper, written in large characters, twice and thrice underlined, was the sentence:

"The ebony casket with the Hoogstraten and

d'Avila arms on the lid is to be sent to the widow of the Marquis d'Avennes. Forward it to Château Rochebrun in Normandy."

The men, who had mutually deciphered these words, looked at each other silently, until Van Hout exclaimed:

" What a confused mixture of malice and feminine weakness. Let a woman's heart seem ever so cold; glacier flowers will always be found in it."

" I'm sorry for the young lady in your house, Herr Peter," cried the notary, "it would be easier to get sparks from rye-bread, than such a sum from the debt-laden poor devil. The daughter's portion will be curtailed by the father; that's what I call bargaining between relations."

" What can be in the casket? " asked the notary.

" There it is," cried Van Hout.

" Bring it here, Belotti."

" We must open it," said the lawyer, "perhaps she is trying to convey her most valuable property across the frontiers."

" Open it? Contrary to the dead woman's express desire?" asked Van der Werff.

" Certainly!" cried the notary. " We were sent here to ascertain the amount of the inheritance. The lid is fastened. Take the picklock, Meister. There, it is open."

The city magistrates found no valuables in the casket, merely letters of different dates. There were not many. Those at the bottom, yellow with age, contained vows of love from the Marquis d'Avennes, the more recent ones were brief and signed Don Louis d'Avila. Van Hout, who understood the Castilian language in which they were written, hastily read them. As he was approaching the end of the last one, he exclaimed with lively indignation :

"We have here the key of a rascally trick in our hands !   Do you remember the excitement aroused four years ago by the duel, in which the Marquis d'Avennes fell a victim to a Spanish brawler?   The miserable bravo writes in this letter that he has . . . . It will be worth the trouble ; I'll translate it for you.   The first part of the note is of no- importance ; but now comes the point : ' And now, after having succeeded in crossing swords with the marquis and killing him, not without personal danger, a fate he has doubtless deserved, since he aroused your displeasure to such a degree, the condition you imposed upon me is fulfilled, and to-morrow I hope through your favor to receive the sweetest reward. Tell Donna Anna, my adored betrothed, that I would fain lead her to the altar early to-morrow morning, for the d'Avennes are influential and the following day my safety will perhaps be imperilled.   As for the rest, I hope I may be permitted to rely upon the fairness and generosity of my patroness."

Van Hout flung the letter on the table, exclaiming : "See, what a dainty hand the bravo writes.   And, Jove's thunder, the lady to whom this plotted murder was to have been sent, is doubtless the mother of the unfortunate marquis, whom the Spanish assassin slew."

"Yes, Herr Van Hout," said Belotti, "I can confirm your supposition.   The marquise was the wife of the man, who broke his plighted faith to the young Fraulein Van Hoogstraten.   She, who lies there, saw many suns rise and set, ere her vengeance ripened."

"Throw the scrawl into the fire !" cried Van Hout impetuously.

"No," replied Peter. "We will not send the letters, but you must keep them in the archives. God's mills grind slowly, and who knows what good purpose these sheets may yet serve."

The city clerk nodded assent and folding the papers, said: "I think the dead woman's property will be an advantage to the city."

"The Prince will dispose of it," replied Van der Werff. "How long have you served this lady, Belotti?"

"Fifteen years."

"Then remain in Leyden for a time. I think you may expect the legacy she originally left you. I will urge your claim."

A few hours before the nocturnal burial of old Fraulein Van Hoogstraten, Herr Matanesse Van Wibisma and his son Nicolas appeared before the city, but were refused admittance by the men who guarded the gates, although both appealed to their relative's death. Henrica's father did not come, he had gone several days before to attend a tourney at Cologne.

CHAPTER XVI.

BETWEEN twelve and one o'clock on the 26th of May, Ascension-Day, the ringing of bells announced the opening of the great fair. The old circuit of the boundaries of the fields had long since given place to a church festival, but the name of "Ommegang" remained interwoven with that of the fair, and even after the new

religion had obtained the mastery, all sorts of processions took place at the commencement of the fair.

In the days of Catholic rule the cross had been
borne through the streets in a solemn procession, in
which all Leyden took part, now the banners of the
city and standards bearing the colors of the House of
Orange headed the train, followed by the nobles on
horseback, the city magistrates in festal array, the clergy
in black robes, the volunteers in magnificent uniforms,
the guilds with their emblems, and long joyous ranks of
school-children. Even the poorest people bought something new for their little ones on this day. Never
did mothers braid their young daughters' hair more
carefully, than for the procession at the opening of the
fair. Spite of the hard times, many a stiver was taken
from slender purses for fresh ribbons and new shoes,
becoming caps and bright-hued stockings. The spring
sunshine could be reflected from the 'little girls' shining,
smoothly-combed hair, and the big boys and little
children looked even gayer than the flowers in Herr
Van Montfort's garden, by which the procession was
obliged to pass. Each wore a sprig of green leaves in
his cap beside the plume, and the smaller the boy, the
larger the branch. There was no lack of loud
talk and merry shouts, for every child that passed its
home called to its mother, grandparents, and the
servants, and when one raised its voice many others instantly followed. The grown people too were not
silent, and as the procession approached the town-hall,
head-quarters of military companies, guild-halls or
residences of popular men, loud cheers arose, mingled
with the ringing of bells, the shouts of the sailors on
both arms of the Rhine and on the canals, the playing

of the city musicians at the street corners, and the rattle of guns and roar of cannon fired by the gunners and their assistants from the citadel. It was a joyous tumult in jocund spring! These merry mortals seemed to lull themselves carelessly in the secure enjoyment of peace and prosperity, and how blue the sky was, how warmly and brightly the sun shone! The only grave, anxious faces were among the magistrates; but the guilds and the children behind did not see them, so the rejoicings continued without interruption until the churches received the procession, and words so earnest and full of warning echoed from the pulpits, that many grew thoughtful.

All three phases of time belong to man, the past to the graybeard, the future to youth, and the present to childhood. What cared the little boys and girls of Leyden, released from school during the fair, for the peril close at hand? Whoever, on the first day and during the great linen-fair on Friday and the following days, received spending money from parents or god-parents, or whoever had eyes to see, ears to hear, and a nose to smell, passed through the rows of booths with his or her companions, stopped before the camels and dancing-bears, gazed into the open taverns, where not only lads and lasses, but merry old people whirled in the dance to the music of bagpipes, clarionets and violins—examined gingerbread and other dainties with the attention of an expert, or obeyed the blasts of the trumpet, by which the quack doctor's negro summoned the crowd.

Adrian, the burgomaster's son, also strolled day after day, alone or with his companions, through the splendors of the fair, often grasping with the secure sense of wealth the leather purse that hung at his belt, for it contained several stivers, which had flowed in from various sources; his father, his mother, Barbara and his godmother. Captain Van Duivenvoorde, his particular friend, on whose noble horse he had often ridden, had taken him three times into a wafer booth, where he eat till he was satisfied, and thus, even on the Tuesday after Ascension-Day, his little fortune was but slightly diminished. He intended to buy something very big and sensible : a knight's sword or a cross-bow ; perhaps even—but this thought seemed like an evil temptation—the ginger-cake covered with almonds, which was exhibited in the booth of a Delft confectioner. He and Bessie could surely nibble for weeks upon this giant cake, if they were economical, and economy is an admirable virtue. Something must at any rate be spared for "little brothers,"* the nice spiced cakes which were baked in many booths before the eyes of the passers-by.

On Tuesday afternoon his way led him past the famous Rotterdam cake-shop. Before the door of the building, made of boards lightly joined together and decked with mirrors and gay pictures, a stout, pretty woman, in the bloom of youth, sat in a high arm-chair, pouring rapidly, with remarkable skill, liquid dough into the hot iron plate, provided with numerous indentations, that stood just on a level with her comfortably outspread lap. Her assistant hastily turned with a fork the little cakes, browning rapidly in the hollows of the iron, and when baked, laid them neatly on small plates. The waiter prepared them for purchasers by putting a large piece of yellow butter on the smoking pile. A tempt-

* A kind of griddle or pancake.

ing odor, that only too vividly recalled former enjoyment, rose from the fireplace, and Adrian's fingers were already examining the contents of his purse, when the negro's trumpet sounded and the quack doctor's cart stopped directly in front of the booth.

The famous Doctor Morpurgo was a fine-looking man, dressed in bright scarlet, who had a thin, coal-black beard hanging over his breast. His movements were measured and haughty, the bows and gestures with which he saluted the assembled crowd, patronizing and affable. After a sufficient number of curious persons had gathered around his cart, which was stocked with boxes and vials, he began to address them in broken Dutch, spiced with numerous foreign words.

He praised the goodness of the Providence which had created the marvel of human organism. Everything, he said, was arranged and formed wisely and in the best possible manner, but in one respect nature fared badly in the presence of adepts.

" Do you know where the error is, ladies and gentlemen ? " he asked.

" In the purse," cried a merry barber's clerk, " it grows prematurely thin every day."

" Right, my son," answered the quack graciously. " But nature also provides it with the great door from which your answer has come. Your teeth are a bungling piece of workmanship. They appear with pain, decay with time, and so long as they last torture those who do not industriously attend to them. But art will correct nature. See this box—" and he now began to praise the tooth-powder and cure for toothache he had invented. Next he passed to the head, and described in vivid colors, its various pains. But they too were to be cured, people need only buy his arcanum. It was to be had for a trifle, and whoever bought it could sweep away every headache, even the worst, as with a broom.

Adrian listened to the famous doctor with mouth wide open. Specially sweet odors floated over to him from the hot surface of the stove before the booth, and he would have gladly allowed himself a plate of fresh cakes. The baker's stout wife even beckoned to him with a spoon, but he closed his hand around the purse and again turned his eyes towards the quack, whose cart was now surrounded by men and women buying tinctures and medicines.

Henrica lay ill in his father's house. He had been taken into her room twice, and the beautiful pale face, with its large dark eyes, had filled his heart with pity. The clear, deep voice in which she addressed a few words to him, also seemed wonderful and penetrated the inmost depths of his soul. He was told one morning that she was there, and since that time his mother rarely appeared and the house was far more quiet than usual; for everybody walked lightly, spoke in subdued tones, rapped cautiously at a window instead of using the knocker, and whenever Bessie or he laughed aloud or ran up or down-stairs, Barbara, his mother, or Trautchen appeared and whispered: "Gently, children, the young lady has a headache."

There were many bottles in the cart which were warranted to cure the ailment, and the famous Morpurgo seemed to be a very sensible man, no buffoon like the other mountebanks. The wife of the baker, Wilhelm Peterssohn, who stood beside him, a woman he knew well, said to her companion that the doctor's remedies were good, they had quickly cured her god-mother of a bad attack of erysipelas.

The words matured the boy's resolution. Fleeting visions of the sword, the cross-bow, the gingerbread and the nice little brothers once more rose before his mind, but with a powerful effort of the will he thrust them aside, held his breath that he might not smell the alluring odor of the cakes, and hastily approached the cart. Here he unfastened his purse from his belt, poured its contents into his hand, showed the coins to the doctor, who had fixed his black eyes kindly on the odd customer, and asked: " Will this be enough?"

" For what?"

" For the medicine to cure headache."

The quack separated the little coins in Adrian's hand with his forefinger, and answered gravely: " No, my son, but I am always glad to advance the cause of knowledge. ˙ There is still a great deal for you to learn at school, and the headache will prevent it. Here are the drops and, as it's you, I'll give this prescription for another arcanum into the bargain."

Adrian hastily wrapped the little vial the quack handed him in the piece of printed paper, received his dearly-bought treasure, and ran home. On the way he was stopped by Captain Allertssohn, who came towards him with the musician Wilhelm.

" Have you seen my Andreas, Master Good-for-nothing?" he asked.

" He was standing listening to the musicians," replied Adrian, released himself from the captain's grasp, and vanished among the crowd.

" A nimble lad," said the fencing-master. " My boy is standing with the musicians again. He has nothing but your art in his mind.   He would rather blow on a comb than comb his hair with it, he's always tooting on every leaf and pipe, makes triangles of broken sword-blades, and not even a kitchen pot is safe from his drumming; in short there's nothing but sing-song in the good-for-nothing fellow's head; he wants to be a musician or something of the sort."

"Right, right!" replied Wilhelm eagerly; "he has a fine ear and the best voice in the choir."

"The matter must be duly considered," replied the captain, "and you, if anybody, are the person to tell us what he can accomplish in your art.   If you have time this evening, Herr Wilhelm, come to me at the watch-house, I should like to speak to you.   To be sure, you'll hardly find me before ten o'clock.   I have a stricture in my throat again, and on such days—Roland, my fore man!"

The captain cleared his throat loudly and vehem-ently.   "I am at your service," said Wilhelm, "for the night is long, but I won't let you go now until I know what you mean by your fore man Roland."

"Very well, it's not much of a story, and perhaps you won't understand.   Come in here; I can tell it better over a mug of beer, and the legs rebel if they're de-prived of rest four nights in succession."

When the two men were seated opposite to each other in the tap-room, the fencing-master pushed his moustache away from his lips, and began: "How long ago is it—?   We'll say fifteen years, since I was riding to Haarlem with the innkeeper Aquanus, who as you know, is a learned man and has all sorts of old stuff and Latin manuscripts.   He talks well, and when the conversation turned upon our meeting with many

things in life that we fancy we have already seen, remarked that this could be easily explained, for the
human soul was an indestructible thing, a bird that
never dies.   So long as we live it remains with us, and
when we die flies away and is rewarded or punished
according to its deserts; but after centuries, which are
no more to the Lord than the minutes in which I
empty this fresh mug—one more, bar-maid—the merciful Father releases it again, and it nestles in some new-
born child.   This made me laugh; but he was not at all
disturbed and told the story of an old Pagan, a wonder-
fully wise chap, who knew positively that his soul had
formerly lodged in the body of a mighty hero.   This
same hero also remembered exactly where, during his
former life, he had hung his shield, and told his associates.   They searched and found the piece of armor,
with the initials of the Christian and surname which had
belonged to the philosopher in his life as a soldier,
centuries before.   This puzzled me, for you see—now
don't laugh—something had formerly happened to me
very much like the Pagan's experience.   I don't care
much for books, and from a child have always read the
same one.   I inherited it from my dead father and the
work is not printed, but written.   I'll show it to you
some time—it contains the history of the brave Roland.
Often, when absorbed in these beautiful and true stories,
my cheeks have grown as red as fire, and I'll confess to
you, as I did to my travelling-companion: If I'm not
mistaken, I've sat with King Charles at the board, or
I've worn Roland's chain armor in battle and in the
tourney.   I believe I have seen the Moorish king,
Marsilia, and once when reading how the dying Roland
wound his horn in the valley of the Roncesvalles, I felt

such a pain in my throat, that it seemed as if it would burst, and fancied I had felt the same pain before. When I frankly acknowledged all this, my companion exclaimed that there was no doubt my soul had once inhabited Roland's body, or in other words, that in a former life I had been the Knight Roland."

The musician looked at the fencing-master in amazement and asked: "Could you really believe that, Captain?"

"Why not," replied the other. "Nothing is impossible to the Highest. At first I laughed in the man's face, but his words followed me; and when I read the old stories—I needn't strain my eyes much, for at every line I know beforehand what the next will be—I couldn't help asking myself— In short, sir, my soul probably once inhabited Roland's body, and that's why I call him my 'fore man.' In the course of years, it has become a habit to swear by him. Folly, you will think, but I know what I know, and now I must go. We will have another talk this evening, but about other matters. Yes, everybody in this world is a little crack-brained, but at least I don't bore other people. I only show my craze to intimate friends, and strangers who ask me *once* about the fore man Roland rarely do so a second time. The score, bar-maid— There it is again. We must see whether the towers are properly garrisoned, and charge the sentinels to keep their eyes open. If you come prepared for battle, you may save yourself a walk, I'll answer for nothing to-day. You will probably pass the new Rhine. Just step into my house, and tell my wife she needn't wait supper for me. Or, no, I'll attend to that myself; there's something in the air, you'll see it, for I have the Roncesvalles throat again."

CHAPTER XVII.

In the big watch-house that had been erected beside the citadel, during the siege of the city, raised ten months before, city-guards and volunteers sat together in groups after sunset, talking over their beer or passing the time in playing cards by the feeble light of thin tallow candles.

The embrasure where the officers' table stood was somewhat better lighted. Wilhelm, who, according to his friend's advice, appeared in the uniform of an ensign of the city-guards, seated himself at the empty board just after the clock in the steeple had struck ten. While ordering the waiter to bring him a mug of beer, Captain Allertssohn appeared with Junker von Warmond, who had taken part in the consultation at Peter Van der Werff's, and bravely earned his captain's sash two years before at the capture of Brill. As this son of one of the richest and most aristocratic families in Holland, a youth whose mother had borne the name of Egmont, entered, he drew his hand, encased in a fencing-glove, from the captain's arm and said, countermanding the musician's order :

" Nothing of that sort, waiter! The little keg from the Wurzburger Stein can't be empty yet. We'll find the bottom of it this evening. What do you say, Captain ? "

" Such an arrangement will lighten the keg and not specially burden us," replied the other. " Good-evening, Herr Wilhelm, punctuality adorns the soldier. People

are beginning to understand how much depends upon
it.   I have posted the men, so that they can overlook
the country in every direction.   I shall have them
relieved from time to time, and at intervals look after
them myself.   This is good liquor, Junker.   All honor
to the man who melts his gold into such a fluid.   The
first glass must be a toast to the Prince."

The three men touched their glasses, and soon after
drank to the liberty of Holland and the prosperity of
the good city of Leyden.   Then the conversation took
a lively turn, but duty was not forgotten, for at the end
of half an hour the captain rose to survey the horizon
himself and urge the sentinels to vigilant watchfulness.

When he returned, Wilhelm and Junker von Warmond were so engaged in eager conversation, that they
did not notice his entrance.   The musician was speaking of Italy, and Allertssohn heard him exclaim impetuously:

"Whoever has once seen that country can never
forget it, and when I am sitting on the house-top with
my doves, my thoughts only too often fly far away
with them, and my eyes no longer see our broad,
monotonous plains and grey, misty sky."

"Oh! ho! Meister Wilhelm," interrupted the captain, throwing himself into the arm-chair and stretching
out his booted legs.   "Oh! ho! This time I've discovered the crack in your brain.   Italy, always Italy!
I know Italy too, for I've been in Brescia, looking for
good steel sword-blades for the Prince and other nobles,
I crossed the rugged Apennines and went to Florence.
to see fine pieces of armor.   From Livorno I went by
sea to Genoa, where I obtained chased gold and silver-
work for shoulder-belts and sheaths.   Truth is truth—

the brown-skinned rascals can do fine work. But the country — the country! Roland, my fore man — how any sensible man can prefer it to ours is more than I understand."

" Holland is our mother," replied von Warmond. " As good sons we believe her the best of women; yet we can admit, without shame, that there are more beautiful ones in the world."

" Do you blow that trumpet too?" exclaimed the fencing-master, pushing his glass angrily further upon the table. Did you ever cross the Alps?"

" No, but—"

" But you believe the color-daubers of the artist guild, whose eyes are caught by the blue of the sky and sea, or the musical gentry who allow themselves to be deluded by the soft voices and touching melodies there, but you would do well to listen to a quiet man too for once."

" Go on, Captain."

" Very well. And if anybody can get an untruthful word out of me, I'll pay his score till the Day of Judgment. I'll begin the story at the commencement. First you must cross the horrible Alps. There you see barren, dreary rocks, cold snow, wild glacier torrents on which no boat can be used. Instead of watering meadows, the mad waves fling stones on their banks. Then we reach the plains, where it is true many kinds of plants grow. I was there in June, and made my jokes about the tiny fields, where small trees stood, serving as props for the vines. It didn't look amiss, but the heat, Junker, the heat spoiled all pleasure. And the dirt in the taverns, the vermin, and the talk about bravos, who shed the blood of honest Christians in the dark for a little paltry money. If your tongue dries up in your mouth, you'll find nothing but hot wine, not a sip of cool beer. And the dust, gentlemen, the frightful dust. As for the steel in Brescia—it's worthy of all honor. But the feather was stolen from my hat in the tavern, and the landlord devoured onions as if they were white bread. May God punish me if a single piece of honest beef, such as my wife can set before me every day—and we don't live like princes—ever came between my teeth. And the butter, Junker, the butter! We burn oil in lamps, and grease door-hinges with it, when they creak, but the Italians use it to fry chickens and fish. Confound such doings!"

"Beware, Captain," cried Wilhelm, "or I shall take you at your word and you'll be obliged to pay my score for life. Olive-oil is a pure, savory seasoning."

"For a man that likes it. I commend Holland butter. Olive-oil has its value for polishing steel, but butter is the right thing for roasting and frying; so that's enough! But I beg you to hear me farther. From Lombardy I went to Bologna, and then crossed the Apennines. Sometimes the road ascended, then suddenly plunged downward again, and it's a queer pleasure, which, thank God, we are spared in this country, to sit in the saddle going down a mountain. On the right and left, lofty cliffs tower like walls. Your breathing becomes oppressed in the narrow valleys, and if you want to get a distant view—there's nothing to be seen, for everywhere some good-for-nothing mountain thrusts itself directly before your nose. I believe the Lord created those humps for a punishment to men after Adam's fall. On the sixth day of creation the earth was *level*. It was in August, and when the noon sun was reflected from the rocks, the heat was enough to kill one; it's a miracle, that I'm not sitting beside you dried up and baked. The famous blue of the Italian sky! Always the same! We have it here in this country too, but it alternates with beautiful clouds. There are few things in Holland I like better than our clouds. When the rough Apennines at last lay behind me, I reached the renowned city of Florence."

"And can you deny it your approval?" asked the musician.

"No, sir, there are many proud, stately palaces and beautiful churches and no lack of silk and velvet everywhere, the trade of cloth-weaving too is flourishing; but my health, my health was not good in your Florence, principally on account of the heat, and besides I found many things different from what I expected. In the first place, there's the river Arno! The stream is a puddle, nothing but a puddle! Do you know what the water looks like? Like the pools that stand between the broken fragments and square blocks in a stone-cutter's yard, after a heavy thunder-shower."

"The score, Captain, the score!"

"I mean the yard of a stone-cutter, who does a large business, and pools of tolerable width. Will you still contradict me if I maintain — the Arno is a shallow, narrow stream, just fit to sail a boy's bark-boat. It spreads over a wide surface of grey pebbles, very much as the gold fringe straggles over the top of Junker von Warmond's fencing-glove."

"You saw it at the end of a hot summer," replied Wilhelm, "it's very different in spring."

"Perhaps so; but I beg you to remember the Rhine, the Meuse, and our other rivers, even the Marne,

Drecht and whatever the smaller streams are called. They remain full and bear stately ships at all seasons of the year. Uniform and reliable is the custom of this country; to-day one way, to-morrow another, is the Italian habit. It's just the same with the blades in the fencing-school."

"The Italians wield dangerous weapons," said von Warmond.

"Very true, but they bend to and fro and lack firmness. I know what I'm talking about, for I lodged with my colleague Torelli, the best fencing-master in the city. I'll say nothing of the meals he set before me. To-day macaroni, to-morrow macaroni with a couple of chicken drumsticks to boot, and so on. I've often drawn my belt tighter after dinner. As for the art of fencing, Torelli is certainly no bungler, but he too has the skipping fashion in his method. You must keep your eyes open in a passado with him, but if I can once get to my quarte, tierce, and side-thrust, I have him."

"An excellent series," said Junker von Warmond. "It has been useful to me."

"I know, I know," replied the captain eagerly. "You silenced the French brawler with it at Namur. There's the catch in my throat again. Something will happen to-day, gentlemen, something will surely happen."

The fencing-master grasped the front of his ruff with his left hand and set the glass on the table with his right. He had often done so far more carelessly, but to-day the glass shattered into many fragments.

"That's nothing," cried the young nobleman. "Waiter, another glass for Captain Allertssohn."

The fencing-master pushed his chair back from the

table, and looking at the broken pieces of greenish glass, said in an altered tone, as if speaking to himself rather than his companions:

"Yes, yes, something serious will happen to-day. Shattered into a thousand pieces. As God wills! I know where my place is."

Von Warmond filled a fresh glass, saying with a slight shade of reproof in his tone: "Why, Captain, Captain, what whims are these? Before the battle of Brill I fell in jumping out of the boat and broke my sword. I soon found another, but the idea came into my head: 'you'll meet your death to-day.' Yet here I sit, and hope to empty many a beaker with you."

"It has passed already," said the fencing-master, raising his hat and wiping the perspiration from his forehead with the back of his hand. "Every one must meet his death-hour, and if mine is approaching to-day —be it as God wills! My family won't starve. The house on the new Rhine is free from mortgage, and though they don't inherit much else, I shall leave my children an honest name and trustworthy friends. I know you won't lose sight of my second boy, the musician, Wilhelm. Nobody is indispensable, and if Heaven wishes to call me from this command, Junker von Nordwyk, Jan Van der Does, can fill my place. You, Herr von Warmond, are in just the right spot, and the good cause will reach a successful end even without me."

The musician listened with surprise to the softened tone of the strange man's voice, but the young nobleman raised his drinking-cup, exclaiming:

"Such heavy thoughts for a light glass! You make too much of the matter, Captain. Take your bumper again, and pledge me: Long live the noble art of fencing, and your series: quarte, tierce and side-thrust!"

"They'll live," replied Allertssohn, "ay, they'll live. Many hundreds of noble gentlemen use the sword in this country, and the man who sits here has taught them to wield it according to the rules. My series has served many in duelling, and I, Andreas, their master, have made tierce follow quarte and side-thrust tierce thousands of times, but always with buttons on the foils and against padded doublets. Outside the walls, in the battle-field, no one, often as I have pressed upon the leaders, has ever stood against me in single combat. This Brescian sword-blade has more than once pierced a Spanish jerkin, but the art I teach, gentlemen, the art I love, to which my life has been devoted, I have never practised in earnest. That is hard to bear, gentlemen, and if Heaven is disposed, before calling him away from earth, to grant a poor man, who is no worse than his neighbors, one favor, I shall be permitted to cross blades once in a true, genuine duel, and try my series against an able champion in a mortal struggle. If God would grant Andreas this—"

Before the fencing-master had finished the last sentence, an armed man dashed the door open, shouting:

"The light is raised at Leyderdorp!"

At these words Allertssohn sprang from his chair as nimbly as a youth, drew himself up to his full height, adjusted his shoulder-belt and drew down his sash, exclaiming:

"To the citadel, Hornist, and sound the call for assembling the troops. To your volunteers, Captain Van Duivenvoorde. Post yourself with four companies at the Hohenort Gate, to be ready to take part, if the battle approaches the city-walls. The gunners must provide matches. Let the garrisons in the towers be doubled. Klaas, go to the sexton of St. Pancratius and tell him to ring the alarm-bell, to warn the people at the fair. Your hand, Junker. I know you will be at your post, and you, Meister Wilhelm."

"I'll go with you," said the musician resolutely. "Don't reject me. I have remained quiet long enough; I shall stifle here."

Wilhelm's cheeks flushed, and his eyes sparkled with a lustre so bright and angry, that Junker von Warmond looked at his phlegmatic friend in astonishment, while the captain called:

"Then station yourself in the first company beside my ensign. You don't look as if you felt like jesting, and the work will be in earnest now, bloody earnest."

Allertssohn walked out of doors with a steady step, addressed his men in a few curt, vigorous words, ordered the drummers to beat their drums, while marching through the city, to rouse the people at the fair, placed himself at the head of his trusty little band, and led them towards the new Rhine.

The moon shone brightly down into the quiet streets, was reflected from the black surface of the river, and surrounded the tall peaked gables of the narrow houses with a silvery lustre. The rapid tramp of the soldiers was echoed loudly back from the houses through the silence of the night, and the vibration of the air, shaken by the beating of the drums, made the panes rattle.

This time no merry children with paper flags and wooden swords preceded the warriors, this time no gay girls and proud mothers followed them, not even an old man, who remembered former days, when he himself bore arms.   As the silent troops reached the neighbor-hood of Allertssohn's house, the clock in the church-steeple slowly struck twelve, and directly after the alarm-bell began to sound from the tower of Pancratius.

A window in the second story of the fencing-master's house was thrown open, and his wife's face appeared. An anxious married life with her strange husband had prematurely aged pretty little Eva's countenance, but the mild moonlight transfigured her faded features.   The beat of her husband's drums was familiar to her, and when she saw him at midnight marching past to the horrible call of the alarm-bell, a terrible dread over-powered her and would scarcely allow her to call: " Husband, husband!   What is the matter, Andreas?"

He did not hear, for the roll of the drums, the tramp of the soldiers' feet on the pavement and the ringing of the alarm-bell drowned her voice; but he saw her distinctly, and a strange feeling stole over him.   Her face, framed in a white kerchief and illumined by the moonlight, seemed to him fairer than he had ever seen it since the days of his wooing, and he felt so youthful and full of chivalrous daring, on his way to the field of danger, that he drew himself up to his full height and marched by, keeping most perfect time to the beat of the drums, as in lover-like fashion he threw her a kiss with his left hand, while waving his sword in the right.

The beating of drums and waving of banners had banished every gloomy thought from his mind.   So he marched on to the Gansort.   There stood a cart, the home of travelling traders, who had been roused from sleep by the alarm-bell, and were hastily collecting their goods.   An old woman, amid bitter lamentations, was just harnessing a thin horse to the shafts, and from a tiny window a child's wailing voice was heard calling, " mother, mother," and then, " father, father."

The fencing-master heard the cry. The smile faded from his lips, and his step grew heavier. Then he turned and shouted a loud " Forward " to his men. Wilhelm was marching close behind him and at a sign from the captain approached; but Allertssohn, quickening his pace, seized the musician's arm, saying in a low tone :

" You'll take the boy to teach ? "

" Yes, Captain.".

" Good; you'll be rewarded for it some day," replied the fencing-master, and waving his sword, shouted " Liberty to Holland, death to the Spaniard, long live Orange !"

The soldiers joyously joined in the shout, and marched rapidly with him through the Hohenort Gate into the open country and towards Leyderdorp.

CHAPTER XVIII.

Adrian hurried home with his vial, and in his joy at bringing the sick lady relief, forgot her headache and struck the knocker violently against the door. Barbara received him with a by no means flattering greeting, but he was so full of the happiness of possessing the dearly-bought treasure, that he fearlessly interrupted his aunt's reproving words, by exclaiming eagerly, in the consciousness of his good cause :

" You'll see; I have something here for the young lady ; where is mother ?"

Barbara perceived that the boy was the bearer of some good tidings, which engrossed his whole attention, and the fresh happy face pleased her so much, that she forgot to scold and said smiling:

"You make me very curious; what is the need of so much hurry?"

"I've bought something; is mother up-stairs?"

"Yes, show me what you have bought."

"A remedy. Infallible, I tell you; a remedy for headache."

"A remedy for headache?" asked the widow in astonishment. "Who told you that fib?"

"Fib?" repeated the boy, laughing. "I got it below cost."

"Show it to me, boy," said Barbara authoritatively, snatching at the vial, but Adrian stepped back, hid the medicine behind him, and replied:

"No, aunt; I shall take it to mother myself."

"Did one ever hear of such a thing!" cried the widow. "Donkeys dance on ropes, school-boys dabble in doctor's business! Show me the thing at once! We want no quack wares."

"Quack wares!" replied Adrian eagerly. "It cost all my fair money, and it's good medicine."

During this little discussion Doctor Bontius came down-stairs with the burgomaster's wife. He had heard the boy's last words and asked sternly:

"Where did you get the stuff?"

With these words, he seized the hand of the lad, who did not venture to resist the stern man, took the little vial and printed directions from him and, after Adrian had curtly answered: "From Doctor Morpurgo!" continued angrily:

"The brew is good to be thrown away; only we must take care not to poison the fishes with it, and the thing cost half a florin. You're a rich young man, Meister Adrian! If you have any superfluous capital again, you can lend it to me."

These words spoiled the boy's pleasure, but did not convince him, and he defiantly turned half away from the physician. Barbara understood what was passing in his mind, and whispered compassionately to the doctor and her sister-in-law:

"All his fair money to help the young lady."

Maria instantly approached the disappointed child, drew his curly head towards her and silently kissed his forehead, while the doctor read the printed label, then without moving a muscle, said as gravely as ever:

"Morpurgo isn't the worst of quacks, the remedy he prescribes here may do the young lady good after all."

Adrian had been nearer crying than laughing. Now he uttered a sigh of relief, but still clasped Maria's hand firmly, as he again turned his face towards the doctor, listening intently while the latter continued:

"Two parts buckbeans, one part pepper-wort, and half a part valerian. The latter specially for women. Let it steep in boiling water and drink a cupful cold every morning and evening! Not bad—really not bad. You have found a good remedy, my worthy colleague. I had something else to say to you, Adrian. My boys are going to the English riders this evening, and would be glad to have you accompany them. You can begin with the decoction to-day."

The physician bowed to the ladies and went on; Barbara followed him into the street, asking:

"Are you in earnest about the prescription?"

"Of course, of course," replied the doctor, "my grandmother used this remedy for headache, and she was a sensible woman. Evening and morning, and the proper amount of sleep."

Henrica occupied a pretty, tastefully-furnished room. The windows looked out upon the quiet court-yard, planted with trees, adjoining the chamois-leather workshops. She was allowed to sit up part of the day in a cushioned arm-chair, supported by pillows. Her healthy constitution was rapidly rallying. True, she was still weak, and the headache spoiled whole days and nights. Maria's gentle and thoughtful nature exerted a beneficial influence upon her, and she cheerfully welcomed Barbara, with her fresh face and simple, careful, helpful ways.

When Maria told her about the purchase Adrian had made for her, she was moved to tears; but to the boy she concealed her grateful emotion under jesting words, and greeted him with the exclamation:

"Come nearer, my preserver, and give me your hand."

Afterwards, she always called him " my preserver " or, as she liked to mingle Italian words with her Dutch, " Salvatore " or " Signor Salvatore." She was particularly fond of giving the people, with whom she associated, names of her own, and so called Barbara, whose Christian name she thought frightful, " Babetta," and little slender, pretty Bessie, whose company she specially enjoyed, " the elf." The burgomaster's wife only remained " Frau Maria," and when the latter once jestingly asked the cause of such neglect, Henrica replied that she suited her name and her name her; had she been called Martha, she would probably have named her " Maria."

The invalid had passed a pleasant, painless day, and when towards evening Adrian went to see the English riders and the fragrance of the blooming lindens and the moonlight found their way through the open windows of her room, she begged Barbara not to bring a light, and invited Maria to sit down and talk with her.

From Adrian and Bessie the conversation turned upon their own childhood. Henrica had grown up among her father's boon companions, amid the clinking of glasses and hunting-shouts, Maria in a grave burgher household, and what they told each other seemed like tidings from a strange world.

" It was easy for you to become the tall, white lily you are now," said Henrica, "but I must thank the saints, that I came off as well as I did, for we really grew up like weeds, and if I hadn't had a taste for singing and the family priest hadn't been such an admirable musician, I might stand before you in a still worse guise. When will the doctor let me hear you sing ?"

" Next week ; but you musn't expect too much. You have too high an opinion of me. Remember the proverb about still waters. Here in the depths it often looks far less peaceful, than you probably suppose."

" But you have learned to keep the surface calm when it storms; I haven't. A strange stillness has stolen over me here. Whether I owe it to illness or to the atmosphere that pervades this house, I can't tell, but how long will it last ? My soul used to lie like the sea, when the hissing waves plunge into black gulfs, the sea-gulls scream, and the fishermen's wives pray on the shore. Now the sea is calm. Don't be too much frightened, if it begins to rage again."

At these words Maria clasped the excited girl's hands, saying beseechingly:

"Be quiet, be quiet, Henrica. You must think only of your recovery now. And shall I confess something? I believe everything hard can be more easily borne, if we can cast it impatiently forth like the sea of which you speak; with me one thing is piled on another and remains lying there, as if buried under the sand."

"Until the hurricane comes, that sweeps it away. I don't want to be an evil prophet, but you surely remember these words. What a wild, careless thing I was! Then a day came, that made a complete revolution in my whole nature."

"Did a false love wound you?" asked Maria modestly.

"No, except the false love of another," replied Henrica bitterly. "When I was a child this fluttering heart often throbbed more quickly, I don't know how often. First I felt something more than reverence for the one-eyed chaplain, our music-teacher, and every morning placed fresh flowers on his window, which he never noticed. Then—I was probably fifteen—I returned the ardent glances of Count Brederode's pretty page. Once he tried to be tender, and received a blow from my riding-whip. Next came a handsome young nobleman, who wanted to marry me when I was barely sixteen, but he was even more heavily in debt than my father, so he was sent home. I shed no tears for him, and when, two months after, at a tournament in Brussels, I saw Don Frederic, the son of the great Duke of Alva, fancied myself as much in love with him as ever any lady worshipped her Amadis, though the affair never went beyond looks. Then the storm, of which I have already

spoken, burst, and that put an end to love-making.   I
will tell you more about this at some future time ; I need
not conceal it, for it has been no secret.   Have you
ever heard of my sister ?   No ? · She was older than I,
a creature — God never created anything more perfect.
And her singing ! She came to my dead aunt's, and
there — But I won't excite myself uselessly — in short,
the man whom she loved with all the strength of her
heart thrust her into misery, and my father cursed and
would not stretch out a finger to aid her.   I never knew
my mother, but through Anna I never missed her.   My
sister's fate opened my eyes to men.   During the last
few years many have wanted me, but I lacked confidence and, still more, love, for I shall never have
anything to do with that."

"Until it finds you," replied Maria.   "It was wrong
to speak of such things with you, it excites you, and that
is bad."

"Never mind ; it will do me good to relieve my
heart.   Did you love no one before your husband ?"

"Love ?   No, Henrica, I never really loved any
one except him."

"And your heart waited for the burgomaster, ere it
beat faster ?"

"No, it had not always remained quiet before ; I
grew up among social people, old and young, and of
course liked some better than others."

"And surely one best of all."

"I won't deny it.   At my sister's wedding, my
brother-in-law's friend, a young nobleman, came from
Germany and remained several weeks with us.   I liked
him, and remember him kindly even now."

"Have you never heard from him again ?"

"No; who knows what has become of him. My brother-in-law expected great things from him, and he possessed many rare gifts, but was reckless, fool-hardy, and a source of constant anxiety to his mother."

"You must tell me more about him."

"What is the use, Henrica?"

"I don't want to talk any more, but I should like to lie still, inhale the fragrance of the lindens, and listen, only listen."

"No, you must go to bed now. I'll help you undress and, when you have been alone an hour, come back again."

"One learns obedience in your house, but when my preserver comes home, bring him here. He must tell me about the English riders. There comes Frau Babetta with his decoction. You shall see that I take it punctually."

The boy returned home late, for he had enjoyed all the glories of the fair with the doctor's children. He was permitted to pay only a short visit to Henrica, and did not see his father at all, the latter having gone to a night council at Herr Van Bronkhorst's.

The next morning the fair holidays were to end, school would begin and Adrian had intended to finish his tasks this evening; but the visit to the English riders had interfered, and he could not possibly appear before the rector without his exercise. He frankly told Maria so, and she cleared a place for him at the table where she was sewing, and helped the young scholar with many a word and rule she had learned with her dead brother.

When it lacked only half an hour of midnight, Barbara entered, saying:

"That's enough now.   You can finish the rest early to-morrow morning before school."

Without waiting for Maria's reply, she closed the boy's books and pushed them together.

While thus occupied, the room shook with rude blows on the door of the house.   Maria threw down her sewing and started from her seat, while Barbara exclaimed:

"For Heaven's sake, what is it?"   Adrian rushed into his father's room and opened the window.

The ladies had hurried after him, and before they could question the disturber of the peace, a deep voice called:

"Open, I must come in."

"What is it?" asked Barbara, who recognized a soldier in the moonlight.   "We can't hear our own voices; stop that knocking."

"Call the burgomaster!" shouted the messenger, who had been constantly using the knocker.   "Quick, woman; the Spaniards are coming."

Barbara shrieked aloud and beat her hands.   Maria turned pale, but without losing her composure, replied:

"The burgomaster is not at home, but I'll send for him.   Quick, Adrian, call your father."

The boy rushed down-stairs, meeting in the entry the man-servant and Trautchen, who had jumped hastily out of bed, throwing on an under-petticoat, and was now trying, with trembling hands, to unlock the door. The man pushed her aside, and as soon as the door creaked on its hinges, Adrian darted out and ran, as if in a race, down the street to the commissioner's. Arriving before any other messenger, he pressed through the open door into the dining-hall and called breathlessly to the men, who were holding a council over their wine :

" The Spaniards are here ! "

The gentlemen hastily rose from their seats. One wanted to rush to the citadel, another to the town-hall and, in the excitement of the moment, no sensible reflection was made. Peter Van der Werff alone maintained his composure and, after Allertssohn's messenger had appeared and reported that the captain and his men were on the way to Leyderdorp, the burgomaster pointed out that the leaders' care should now be devoted to the people who had come to the fair. He and Van Hout undertook to provide for them, and Adrian was soon standing with his father and the city clerk among the crowds of people, who had been roused from sleep by the wailing iron voice from the Tower of Pancratius.

CHAPTER XIX.

ADRIAN's activity for this night was not yet over, for his father did not prevent his accompanying him to the town-hall. There he directed him to tell his mother, that he should be busy until morning and the servant might send all persons, who desired to speak to him after one o'clock, to the timber-market on the Rhine. Maria sent the boy back to the town-hall, to ask his father if he did not want his cloak, wine, a lunch or anything of the sort.

The boy fulfilled this commission with great zeal, for he never had felt so important as while forcing his way through the crowds that had gathered in the narrower streets; he had a duty to perform, and at night, the time when other boys were asleep, especially his school-mates, who certainly would not be allowed to leave the house now. Besides, an eventful period, full of the beating of drums, the blare of trumpets, the rattle of musketry and roar of cannon might be expected. It seemed as if the game " Holland against Spain " was to be continued in earnest, and on a grand scale. All the vivacity of his years seized upon him, and when he had forced a way with his elbows to less crowded places, he dashed hurriedly along, shouting as merrily as if spreading some joyful news in the darkness:

" They are coming!" "the Spaniards!" or "*Hannibal ante portas.*"

After learning on his return to the town-hall, that his father wanted nothing and would send a constable if there was need of anything, he considered his errand done and felt entitled to satisfy his curiosity.

This drew him first to the English riders. The tent where they had given their performances had disappeared from the earth, and screaming men and women were rolling up large pieces of canvas, fastening packs, and swearing while they harnessed horses. The gloomy light of torches mingled with the moonbeams and showed him on the narrow steps, that led to a large four-wheeled cart, a little girl in shabby clothes, weeping bitterly. Could this be the rosy-cheeked angel who, floating along on the snow-white pony, had seemed to him like a happy creature from more beautiful worlds ? A scolding old woman now lifted the child into the cart, but he followed the crowd and saw Doctor Morpurgo, no longer clad in scarlet, but in plain dark cloth, mounted on a lean horse, riding beside his cart. The negro was furiously urging the mule forward, but his master seemed to have remained in full possession of the calmness peculiar to him. His wares were of small value, and the Spaniards had no reason to take his head and tongue, by which he gained more than he needed.

Adrian followed him to the long row of booths in the wide street, and there saw things, which put an end to his thoughtlessness and made him realize, that the point in question now concerned serious, heart-rending matters. He had still been able to laugh as he saw the ginger-bread bakers and cotton-sellers fighting hand to hand, because in the first fright they had tossed their packages of wares hap-hazard into each other's open chests, and were now unable to separate their property; but he felt sincerely sorry for the Delft crockery-dealer on the corner, whose light booth had been demolished by a large wagon from Gouda, loaded with bales, and who now stood beside her broken wares, by means of which she supported herself and children, wringing her hands, while the driver, taking no notice of her, urged on his horses with loud cracks of his whip. A little girl, who had lost her parents and was being carried away by a compassionate burgher woman, was weeping piteously. A poor rope-dancer, who had been robbed by a thief in the crowd, of the little tin box containing the pennies he had collected, was running about, wringing his hands and looking for the watchman. A shoemaker was pounding riding-boots and women's shoes in motley confusion into a wooden chest with rope handles, while his wife, instead of helping him, tore her hair and shrieked: " I told you so, you fool, you simpleton, you blockhead! They'll come and rob us of everything."

At the entrance of the street that led past the Assendelft house to the Leibfrau Bridge, several loaded wagons had become entangled, and the drivers, instead of getting down and procuring help, struck at each other in their terror, hitting the women and children seated among the bales. Their cries and shrieks echoed a long distance, but were destined to be drowned, for a dancing-bear had broken loose and was putting every one near him to flight. The people, who were frightened by the beast, rushed down the street, screaming and yelling, dragging with them others who did not know the cause of the alarm, and misled by the most imminent fear, roared: "The Spaniards! The Spaniards!" Whatever came in the way of the terrified throngs was overthrown. A sieve-dealer's child, standing beside its father's upset cart, fell beneath the mob close beside Adrian, who had stationed himself in the door-way of a house. But the lad was crowded so closely into his hiding-place, that he could not spring to the little one's aid, and his attention was attracted to a new sight, as Janus Dousa appeared on horseback. In answer to the cry of "The Spaniards! The Spaniards!" he shouted loudly: "Quiet, people, quiet! The enemy hasn't come yet! To the Rhine! Vessels are waiting there for all strangers. To the Rhine! There are *no* Spaniards there, do you hear, *no* Spaniards!"

The nobleman stopped just before Adrian, for his horse could go no farther and stood snorting and trembling under his rider. The advice bore little fruit, and not until hundreds had rushed past him, did the frightened crowd diminish. The bear, from which they fled, had been caught by a brewer's apprentice and taken back to its owner long before. The city constables now appeared, led by Adrian's father, and the boy followed them unobserved to the timber-market on the southern bank of the Rhine. There another crowd met him, for many dealers had hurried thither to save their property in the ships. Men and women pressed past bales and wares, that were being rolled down the narrow wooden bridges to the véssels. A woman, a child, and a rope-maker's cart had been pushed into the water, and the wildest confusion prevailed around the spot. But the burgomaster reached the place just at the right time, gave directions for rescuing the drowning people, and then made every exertion to bring order out of the confusion.

The constables were commanded to admit fugitives only on board the vessels bound for the places where they belonged; two planks were laid to every ship, one for goods, the other for passengers; the constables loudly shouted that—as the law directed when the alarm-bell rang—all citizens of Leyden must enter their houses and the streets be cleared, on pain of a heavy penalty. All the city gates were opened for the passage of wheeled vehicles, except the Hohenort Gate, which led to Leyderdorp, where egress was refused. Thus the crowd in the streets was lessened, order appeared amid the tumult, and when, in the dawn of morning, Adrian turned his steps towards home, there was little more bustle in the streets than on ordinary nights.

His mother and Barbara had been anxious, but he told thém about his father and in what manner he had put a stop to the confusion.

While talking, the rattle of musketry was heard in the distance, awaking such excitement in Adrian's mind, that he wanted to rush out again; but his mother stopped him and he was obliged to mount the stairs to his room. He did not go to sleep, but climbed to the upper loft in the gable of the rear building and gazed through the window, to which the bales of leather were raised by pulleys, towards the east, from whence the sound of firing was still audible. But he saw nothing except the dawn and light clouds of smoke, that assumed a rosy hue as they floated upward. As nothing new appeared, his eyes closed, and he fell asleep beside the open window where he dreamed of a bloody battle and the English riders. His slumber was so sound, that he did not hear the rumble of wheels in the quiet court-yard below him. The carts from which the noise proceeded belonged to traders from neighboring cities, who preferred to leave their goods in the threatened town, rather than carry them towards the advancing Spaniards. Meister Peter had allowed some of them to store their property with him. The carts were obliged to pass through the back-building with the workshops, and the goods liable to be injured by the weather, were to be placed in the course of the day in the large garrets of his house.

The burgomaster's wife had gone to Henrica at midnight to soothe her fears, but the sick girl seemed free from all anxiety, and when she heard that the Spaniards were on the march, her eyes sparkled joyously. Maria noticed it and turned away from her guest, but she repressed the harsh words that sprang to her lips, wished her good-night, and left the chamber.

Henrica gazed thoughtfully after her and then rose,

for no sleep was possible that night. The alarm-bell in the Tower of Pancratius rang incessantly, and more than once doors opened, voices and shots were heard. Many tones and noises, whose origin and nature she could not understand, reached her ears, and when morning dawned, the court-yard under her windows, usually so quiet, was full of bustle. Carts rattled, loud tones mingled excitedly, and a deep masculine voice seemed to be directing what was going on. Her curiosity and restlessness increased every moment. She listened so intently that her head began to ache again, but could hear only separate words and those very indistinctly. Had the city been surrendered to the Spaniards, had King Philip's soldiers found quarters in the burgomaster's house? Her blood boiled indignantly, when she thought of the Castilians' triumph and the humiliation of her native land, but soon her former joyous excitement again filled her mind, as she beheld in imagination art re-enter the bare walls of the Leyden churches, now robbed of all their ornaments, chanting processions move through the streets, and priests in rich robes celebrating mass in the newly-decorated tabernacles, amid beautiful music, the odor of incense, and the ringing of bells. She expected to receive from the Spaniards a place where she could pray and free her soul by confession. Amid her former surroundings nothing had afforded her any support, except her religion. A worthy priest, who was also her instructor, had zealously striven to prove to her, that the new religion threatened to destroy the mystical consecration of life, the yearning for the beautiful, every ideal emotion of the human soul, and with them art also; so Henrica preferred to see her native land Spanish and Catholic, rather than free from the foreigners whom she hated and Calvinistical.

The court-yard gradually became less noisy, but when the first rays of morning light streamed into her windows, the bustle again commenced and grew louder. Heavy soles tramped upon the pavement, and amid the voices that now mingled with those she had formerly heard, she fancied she distinguished Maria's and Barbara's. Yes, she was not mistaken. That cry of terror must proceed from her friend's mouth, and was followed by exclamations of grief from bearded lips and loud sobs.

Evil tidings must have reached her host's house, and the woman weeping so impetuously below was probably kind " Babetta."

Anxiety drove her from her bed. On the little table beside it, amid several bottles and glasses, the lamp and the box of matches, stood the tiny bell, at whose faint sound one of her nurses invariably hastened in. Henrica rang it three times, then again and again, but nobody appeared. Then her hot blood boiled, and half from impatience and vexation, half from curiosity and sympathy, she slipped into her shoes, threw on a morning dress, went to the chair which stood on the platform in the niche, opened the window, and looked down at the groups gathered below.

No one noticed her, for the men who stood there sorrowing, and the weeping women, among whom were Maria and Barbara, were listening with many tokens of sympathy to the eager words of a young man, and had eyes and ears for him alone. Henrica recognized in the speaker the musician Wilhelm, but only by his voice, for the morion on his curls and the blood-stained coat

of mail gave the unassuming artist a martial, nay heroic
air.

He had advanced a long way in his story, when
Henrica unseen became a listener.

"Yes, sir," he replied, in answer to a question from
the burgomaster, "we followed them, but they disappeared in the village and all remained still. To risk
storming the houses, would have been madness. So we
kept quiet, but towards two o'clock heard firing in the
neighborhood of Leyderdorp. 'Junker von Warmond
has made a sally,' said the captain, leading us in the
direction of the firing. This was what the Spaniards
had wanted, for long before we reached the goal, a company of Castilians, with white sheets over their armor,
climbed out of a ditch in the dim light, threw themselves
on their knees, murmured a ' Pater-noster,' shouted their
San Jago and pressed forward upon us. We had seen
them in time for the halberdiers to extend their pikes,.
and the musketeers to lie down amid the grass. So the
Spaniards had a warm reception, and four of them fell
in this attack. We were superior in numbers, and their
captain led them back to the ditch in good order. There
they halted, for their duty was probably to detain us and
then have us cut down by a larger body. We were too
weak to drive them from their position, but when the
east began to brighten and they still did not come forward, the captain advanced towards them with the
drummer, bearing a white flag, and shouted to them in
Italian, which he had learned to speak a little in Italy,
that he wished the Castilian gentlemen good-morning,
and if there was any officer with a sense of honor among
them, let him come forth and meet a captain who wished
to cross swords with him. He pledged his word, that

his men would look on at the duel without taking any share in it, no matter what the result might be. Just at that moment two shots were fired from the ditch and the bullets whizzed close by the poor captain. We called to him to save his life, but he did not stir, and shouted that they were cowards and assassins, like their king.

"Meantime it had grown tolerably light—we heard them calling to and fro from the ditch, and just as Allertssohn was turning away, an officer sprang into the meadow, exclaiming: 'Stand, braggart, and draw your blade.'

"The captain drew his Brescian sword, bowed to his enemy as if he were in the fencing-school, bent the steel and closed with the Castilian. The latter was a thin man of stately figure and aristocratic bearing, and as it soon appeared, a dangerous foe. He circled like a whirlwind, round the captain with bounds, thrusts and feints, but Allertssohn maintained his composure, and at first confined himself to skilful parrying. Then he dealt a magnificent quarte, and when the other parried it, followed with the tierce, and this being warded off, gave with the speed of lightning a side-thrust such as only *he* can deal. The Castilian fell on his knees, for the Brescian blade had pierced his lungs. His death was speedy.

"As soon as he lay on the turf, the Spaniards again rushed upon us, but we repulsed them and took the officer's body in our midst. Never have I seen the captain so proud and happy. You, Junker von Warmond, can easily guess the cause. He had now done honor to his series in a genuine duel against an enemy of equal rank, and told me this was the happiest morning of his life. Then he ordered us to march round the ditch and attack the enemy on the flank. But scarcely had we begun to move, when the expected troops from Leyderdorp pressed forward, their loud San Jago resounding far and wide, while at the same time the old enemy rose from the ditch and attacked us. Allertssohn rushed forward, but did not reach them—oh, gentlemen! I shall never forget it, a bullet struck him down at my side. It probably pierced his heart, for he said nothing but: 'Remember the boy!' stretched out his powerful frame and died. We wanted to bear his body away with us, but were pressed by superior numbers, and it was hard enough to come within range of Junker von Warmond's volunteers. The Spaniards did not venture so far. Here we are. The Castilian's body is lying in the tower at the Hohenort Gate. These are the papers we found in the dead man's doublet, and this is his ring; he has a proud escutcheon."

Peter Van der Werff took the dead man's letter-case in his hand, looked through it and said: "His name was Don Luis d'Avila."

He said no more, for his wife had seen Henrica's head stretched far out of the window, and cried loudly in terror: "Fraulein, for Heaven's sake, Fraulein— what are you doing?"

CHAPTER XX.

THE burgomaster's wife had been anxious about Henrica, but the latter greeted her with special cheerfulness and met her gentle reproaches with the assurance that this morning had done her good. Fate, she said, was just, and if it were true that confidence of recovery helped the physician, Doctor Bontius would have an easy task with her.   The dead Castilian must be the wretch, who had plunged her sister Anna into misery.   Maria, surprised, but entirely relieved, left her and sought her husband to tell him how she had found the invalid, and in what relation the Spanish officer, slain by Allertssohn, seemed to have stood to Henrica and her sister.   Peter only half listened to her, and when Barbara brought him a freshly-ironed ruff, interrupted his wife in the middle of her story, gave her the dead man's letter-case, and said:

"There, let her satisfy herself, and bring it to me again in the evening, I shall hardly be able to come to dinner; I suppose you'll see poor Allertssohn's widow in the course of the day."

"Certainly," she answered eagerly.   "Whom will you appoint in his place?"

"That is for the Prince to decide."

"Have you thought of any means of keeping the communication with Delft free from the enemy?"

"On your mother's account?"

"Not solely.   Rotterdam also lies to the south.   We can expect nothing from Haarlem and Amsterdam, that is, from the north, for everything there is in the hands of the Spaniards."

"I'll get you a place in the council of war.   Where do you learn your wisdom?"

"We have our thoughts, and isn't it natural that I should rather follow you into the future with my eyes open, than blindly?   Has the English troop been used to secure the fortifications on the old canal?   Kaak too is an important point."

Peter gazed at his wife in amazement, and the sense

of discomfort experienced by an unskilful writer, when some one looks over his shoulder, stole over him. She had pointed out a bad, momentous error, which, it is true, did not burden him alone, and as he certainly did not wish to defend it to her, and moreover might have found justification difficult, he made no reply, saying nothing but: "Men's affairs! Good-bye until evening." With these words he walked past Barbara, towards the door.

Maria did not know how it happened, but before he laid his hand on the latch she gained sufficient self-command to call after him:

"Are you going so, Peter! Is that right? What did you promise me on your return from the journey to the Prince?"

"I know, I know," he answered impatiently. "We cannot serve two masters, and in these times I beg you not to trouble me with questions and matters that don't concern you. To direct the business of the city is my affair; you have your invalid, the children, the poor; let that suffice."

Without waiting for her reply he left the room, while she stood motionless, gazing after him.

Barbara watched her anxiously for several minutes, then busied herself with the papers on her brother's writing-table, saying as if to herself, though turning slightly towards her sister-in-law:

"Evil times! Let every one, who is not oppressed with such burdens as Peter, thank the Lord. He has to bear the responsibility of everything, and people can't dance lightly with hundred-pound weights on their legs. Nobody has a better heart, and nobody means more honestly. How the traders at the fair praised his caution! In the storm people know the pilot, and Peter was always greatest, when things were going worst. He knows what he is undertaking, but the last few weeks have aged him years."

Maria nodded. Barbara left the room, but returning after a few minutes, said beseechingly:

"You look ill, child, come and lie down. An hour's sleep is better than three meals. At your age, such a night as this last one doesn't pass without leaving traces. The sun is shining so brightly, that I've drawn your window-curtains. I've made your bed, too. Be sensible and come."

While uttering the last words, she took Maria's hand and drew her away. The young wife made no resistance, and though her eyes did not remain dry when she was alone, sleep soon overpowered her.

Towards noon, refreshed by slumber, and newly dressed, she went to the captain's house. Her own heart was heavy, and compassion for herself and her own fate again had the mastery. Eva Peterstochter, the fencing-master's widow, a quiet, modest woman, whom she scarcely knew by sight, did not appear. She was sitting alone in her room, weeping, but Maria found in her house the musician, Wilhelm, who had spoken comforting words to his old friend's son, and promised to take charge of him and make him a good performer.

The burgomaster's wife sent a message to the widow, begging to see her the next day, and then went out into the street with Wilhelm. Everywhere groups of citizens, women, and journeymen were standing together, talking about what had happened and the coming trouble. While Maria was telling the musician who the dead Castilian was, and that Henrica desired to speak with him, Wilhelm, as soon as possible, she was interrupted more than once; for sometimes a company of volunteers or city guards, relieved from duty in the towers and on the walls, sometimes a cannon barred their way. Was it the anticipation of coming events, or the beat of drums and blare of trumpets, which so excited her companion, that he often pressed his hand to his forehead and she was obliged to request him to slacken his pace. There was a strange, constrained tone in his voice as, in accordance with her request, he told her that the Spaniards had come by ship up the Amstel, the Drecht, and the Brasem See to the Rhine and landed at Leyderdorp.

A mounted messenger wearing the Prince's colors, and followed not only by children, but by grown persons, who ran after him eager to reach the town-hall at the same time, interrupted Wilhelm, and as soon as the crowd had passed, the burgomaster's wife asked her companion one question after another. The noise of war, the firing audible in the distance, the gay military costumes everywhere to be seen in place of the darker citizens' dress, also aroused her eager interest, and what she learned from Wilhelm was little calculated to diminish it. The main body of the Spanish troops was on the way to the Hague. The environment of the city had commenced, but the enemy could hardly succeed in his purpose; for the English auxiliaries, who were to defend the new fortifications of Valkenburg, the village of Alfen, and the Gouda sluice might be trusted. Wilhelm had seen the British soldiers, their commander, Colonel Chester, and Captain Gensfort, and praised their superb equipments and stately bearing.

On reaching her own house, Maria attempted to

take leave of her companion, but the latter earnestly
entreated permission to have an interview with Henrica
at once, and could scarcely be convinced that he must
have patience until the doctor had given his consent.

At dinner Adrian, who when his father was not
present, talked freely enough, related all sorts of things
he had seen himself, as well as news and rumors heard
at school and in the street, his eloquence being no little
encouraged by his step-mother's eager questions.

Intense anxiety had taken possession of the burgomaster's wife.   Her enthusiasm for the cause of liberty,
to which her most beloved relatives had fallen victims,
blazed brightly, and wrath against the oppressors of her
native land seethed passionately in her breast.   The
delicate, maidenly, reserved woman, who was utterly
incapable of any loud or rude expression of feeling in
ordinary life, would now have rushed to the walls, like
Kanau Hasselaer of Haarlem, to fight the foe among
the men.

Offended pride, and everything that an hour ago
had oppressed her heart, yielded to sympathy for her
country's cause.   Animated with fresh courage, she went
to Henrica and, as evening had closed in, sat down by
the lamp to write to her mother; for she had neglected
to do so since the invalid's arrival, and communication
with Delft might soon be interrupted.

When she read over the completed letter, she was
satisfied with it and herself, for it breathed firm confidence in the victory of the good cause, and also
distinctly and unconstrainedly expressed her cheerful
willingness to bear the worst.

Barbara had retired when Peter at last appeared, so
weary that he could scarcely touch the meal that had

been kept ready for him. While raising the food to his lips, he confirmed the news Maria had already heard from the musician, and was gentle and kind, but his appearance saddened her, for it recalled Barbara's allusion to the heavy burden he had assumed. To-day, for the first time, she noticed two deep lines that anxiety had furrowed between his eyes and lips, and full of tender compassion, went behind him, laid her hands on his cheeks and kissed him on the forehead. He trembled slightly, seized her slender right hand so impetuously that she shrank back, raised it first to his lips, then to his eyes, and held it there for several minutes.

At last he rose, passed before her into his sleeping-room, bade her an affectionate good-night, and lay down to rest. When she too sought her bed, he was breathing heavily. Extreme fatigue had quickly overpowered him. The slumber of both was destined to be frequently interrupted during this night, and whenever Maria woke, she heard her husband sigh and moan. She did not stir, that she might not disturb the sleep he sought and needed, and twice held her breath, for he was talking to himself. First he murmured softly: "Heavy, too heavy," and then: "If I can only bear it."

When she awoke next morning, he had already left the room and gone to the town-hall. At noon he returned home, saying that the Spaniards had taken the Hague and been hailed with delight by the pitiful adherents of the king. Fortunately, the well-disposed citizens and Beggars had had time to escape to Delft, for brave Nicolas Ruichhaver had held the foe in check for a time at Geestburg. The west was still open, and the newly-fortified fort of Valkenburg, garrisoned by the English soldiers, would not be so easy to storm. On the east, other British auxiliaries were posted at Alfen in the Spaniards' rear.

The burgomaster told all this unasked, but did not speak as freely and naturally as when conversing with men. While talking, he often looked into his plate and hesitated. It seemed as if he were obliged to impose a certain restraint upon himself, in order to speak before women, servants, and children, of matters he was in the habit of discussing only with men of his own position. Maria listened attentively, but maintained a modest reserve, urging him only by loving looks and sympathizing exclamations, while Barbara boldly asked one question after another.

The meal was approaching an end, when Junker von Warmond entered unannounced, and requested the burgomaster to accompany him at once, for Colonel Chester was standing before the White Gate with a portion of his troops, asking admittance to the city.

At these tidings, Peter dashed his mug of beer angrily on the table, sprang from his seat, and left the room before the nobleman.

During the late hours of the afternoon, the Van der Werff house was crowded with people. The gossips came to talk over with Barbara the events occurring at the White Gate. Burgomaster Van Swieten's wife had heard from her own husband, that the Englishmen, without making any resistance, had surrendered the beautiful new fort of Valkenburg and taken to their heels, at the mere sight of the Spaniards. The enemy had marched out from Haarlem through the downs above Nordwyk, and it would have been an easy matter for the Britons to hold the strong position.

" Fine aid such helpers give !" cried Barbara indignantly. "Let Queen Elizabeth keep the men on her island for herself, and send us the women."

"Yet they are real sons of Anak, and bear themselves like trim soldiers," said the wife of the magistrate Heemskerk. "High boots, doublets of fine leather, gay plumes in their morions and hats, large coats of mail, halberds that would kill half a dozen—and all like new."

"They probably didn't want to spoil them, and so found a place of safety as soon as possible, the windy cowards," cried the wife of Church-warden de Haes, whose sharp tongue was well known. "You seem to have looked at them very closely, Frau Margret."

"From the wind-mill at the gate," replied the other. "The envoy stopped on the bridge directly under us. A handsome man on a stately horse. His trumpeter too was mounted, and the velvet cloth on his trumpet bristled with beautful embroidery in gold thread and jewels. They earnestly entreated admittance, but the gate remained closed."

"Right, right!" cried Frau Heemskerk. "I don't like the Prince's commissioner, Van Bronkhorst. What does he care for us, if only the Queen doesn't get angry and withdraw the subsidies? I've heard he wants to accommodate Chester and grant him admission."

"He would like to do so," added Frau Van Hout. "But your husband, Frau Maria, and mine—I was talking with him on the way here—will make every effort to prevent it. The two Seigneurs of Nordwyk are of their opinion, so perhaps the commissioner will be out-voted."

"May God grant it!" cried the resolute voice of Wilhelm's mother. "By to-morrow or the day after, not even a cat will be allowed to leave the gates, and my husband says we must begin to save provisions at once."

"Five hundred more consumers in the city, to lessen our children's morsels; that would be fine business!" cried Frau de Haes, throwing herself back in her chair so violently, that it creaked, and beating her knees with her hands.

"And they are Englishmen, Frau Margret, Englishmen," said the Receiver-General's wife. "They don't eat, they don't consume, they devour. We supply our troops; but Herr von Nordwyk — I mean the younger one, who has been at the Queen's court as the Prince's ambassador, told my Wilhelm what a British glutton can gobble. They'll clear off your beef like cheese, and our beer is dish-water compared with their black malt brew."

"All that might be borne," replied Barbara, "if they were stout soldiers. We needn't mind a hundred head of cattle more or less, and the glutton becomes temperate, when a niggard rules the house. But I wouldn't take one of our Adrian's grey rabbits for these runaways."

"It would be a pity," said Frau de Haes. "I shall go home now, and if I find my husband, he'll learn what sensible people think of the Englishmen."

"Gently, my friend, gently," said Burgomaster Van Swieten's wife, who had hitherto been playing quietly with the cat. "Believe me, it will be just the same on the whole, whether we admit the auxiliaries or not, for before the gooseberries in our gardens are ripe, all resistance will be over."

Maria, who was passing cakes and hippocras, set her waiter on the table and asked:

" Do you wish that, Frau Magtelt ? "

" I do," replied the latter positively, " and many sensible people wish it too. No resistance is possible against such superior force, and the sooner we appeal to the King's mercy, the more surely it will be granted."

The other women listened to the bold speaker in silence, but Maria approached and answered indignantly :

" Whoever says *that*, can go to the Spaniards at once; whoever says that, desires the disgrace of the city and country; whoever says that — "

Frau Magtelt interrupted Maria with a forced laugh, saying :

" Do you want to school experienced women, Madam Early-Wise ? Is it customary to attack a visitor ? "

" Customary or not," replied the other, " I will never permit such words in our house, and if they crossed the lips of my own sister I would say to her : Go, you are my friend no longer ! "

Maria's voice trembled, and she pointed with outstretched arm towards the door.

Frau Magtelt struggled for composure, but as she left the room found nothing to say, except : " Don't be troubled, don't be troubled — you won't see me again."

Barbara followed the offended woman, and while those who remained fixed their eyes in embarrassment upon their laps, Wilhelm's mother exclaimed :

" Well said, little woman, well said ! "

Herr Van Hout's kind wife threw her arm around Maria, kissed her forehead, and whispered :

" Turn away from the other women and dry your eyes."

CHAPTER XXI.

A STORY is told of a condemned man, whom his cruel executioner cast into a prison of ingenious structure. Each day the walls of this cage grew narrower and narrower, each day they pressed nearer and nearer to the unfortunate prisoner, until in despair he died and the dungeon became his coffin. Even so, league by league, the iron barriers of the Spanish regiments drew nearer and nearer Leyden, and, if they succeeded in destroying the resistance of their victim, the latter was threatened with a still more cruel and pitiless end than that of the unhappy prisoner. The girdle Valdez, King Philip's commander, and his skilful lieutenant, Don Ayala, had drawn around the city in less than two days, was already nearly closed, the fort of Valkenburg, strengthened with the utmost care, belonged to the enemy, and the danger had advanced more rapidly and with far more irresistible strength, than even the most timid citizens had feared. If Leyden fell, its houses would be delivered to fire and pillage, its men to death, its women to disgrace—this was guaranteed by the fate of other conquered cities and the Spanish nature.

Who could imagine the guardian angel of the busy city, except under a sullen sky, with clouded brow and anxious eyes, and yet it looked as gay and bright at the White Gate as if a spring festival was drawing to a close with a brilliant exhibition. Wherever the walls, as far as Catherine's Tower, afforded a foothold, they were crowded with men, women, and children. The old masonry looked like the spectators' seats in an arena, and the buzzing of the many-headed, curious crowd was heard for a long distance in the city.

It is a kind dispensation of Providence, that enables men to enjoy a brief glimpse of sunshine amid terrible storms, and thus the journeymen and apprentices, women and children, forgot the impending danger and feasted their eyes on the beautifully-dressed English soldiers, who were looking up at them, nodding and laughing saucily to the young girls, though part of them, it is true, were awaiting with thoughtful faces the results of the negotiations going on within the walls.

The doors of the White Gate now opened; Commissioner Van Bronkhorst, Van der Werff, Van Hout and other leaders of the community accompanied the British colonel and his trumpeter to the bridge. The former seemed to be filled with passionate indignation and several times struck his hand on the hilt of his sword, the Leyden magistrates were talking to him, and at last took leave with low bows, which he answered only with a haughty wave of the hand. The citizens returned, the portals of the gate closed, the old lock creaked, the iron-shod beams fell back into their places, the chains of the drawbridge rattled audibly, and the assembled throng now knew that the Englishmen had been refused admittance to the city.

Loud cheers, mingled with many an expression of displeasure, were heard. "Long live Orange!" shouted the boys, among whom were Adrian and the son of the dead fencing-master Allertssohn; the women waved their handkerchiefs, and all eyes were fixed on the Britons. A loud flourish of trumpets was heard, the

English mounted officers dashed towards the colonel and held a short council of war with him, interrupted by hasty words from several individuals, and soon after a signal was sounded. The soldiers hurriedly, formed in marching array, many of them shaking their fists at the city. Halberds and muskets, which had been stacked, were seized by their owners and, amid the beating of drums and blare of trumpets, order arose out of the confusion. Individuals fell into ranks, ranks into companies, gay flags were unfurled and flung to the evening breeze, and with loud hurrahs the troops marched along the Rhine towards the south-west, where the Spanish outposts were stationed.

The Leyden boys joined loudly in the Englishmen's cheer.

Even Andreas, the fencing-master's son, had begun to shout with them; but when he saw a tall captain marching proudly before his company, his voice failed and, covering his eyes with his hands, he ran home to his mother.

The other lads did not notice him, for the setting sun flashed so brightly on the coats of mail and helmets of the soldiers, the trumpets sounded so merrily, the officers' steeds caracoled so proudly under their riders, the gay plumes and banners and the smoke of the glimmering matches gained such beautiful hues in the roseate light of sunset, that eyes and ears seemed spellbound by the spectacle. But a fresh incident now attracted the attention of great and small.

Thirty-six Englishmen, among them several officers, lingered behind the others and approached the gate. Again the lock creaked and the chains rattled. The little band was admitted to the city and welcomed at the first houses of the northern end by Herr Van Bronk-horst and the burgomaster.

Every one on the walls had expected, that a skirmish between the retreating Englishmen and Castilians would now take place before their eyes. But they were greatly mistaken. Before the first ranks reached the enemy, the matches for lighting the cannon flew through the air, the banners were lowered, and when darkness came and the curious spectators dispersed, they knew that the Englishmen had deserted the good cause and gone over to the Spaniards.

The thirty-six men, who had been admitted through the gates, were the only ones who refused to be accessory to this treason.

The task of providing quarters for Captain Cromwell and the other Englishmen and Netherlanders, who had remained faithful, was assigned to Van Hout. Burgomaster Van der Werff went home with Commissioner Van Bronkhorst. Many a low-voiced but violent word had been exchanged between them. The commissioner protested that the Prince would be highly incensed at the refusal to admit the Englishmen, for with good reason he set great value on Queen Elizabeth's favorable disposition to the cause of freedom, to which the burgomaster and his friends had rendered bad service that day. Van der Werff denied this, for everything depended upon holding Leyden. After the fall of this city, Delft, Rotterdam and Gouda would also be lost, and all farther efforts to battle for the liberty of Holland useless. Five hundred consumers would prematurely exhaust the already insufficient stock of provisions. Everything had been done to soften their refusal to admit the Englishmen, nay they had had free choice to encamp beneath the protection of the walls under the cannon of the city.

When the two men parted, neither had convinced the other, but each felt sure of his comrade's loyalty.

As Peter took leave, he said:

" Van Hout shall explain the reasons for our conduct to the Prince, in a letter as clear and convincing as only he can make it, and his excellency will finally approve of it.   Rely upon that."

" We will wait," replied the commissioner, "but don't forget that we shall soon be shut within these walls behind bolts and bars, like prisoners, and perhaps day after to-morrow no messenger will be able to get to him."

" Van Hout is swift with his pen."

" And let a proclamation be read aloud, early to-morrow morning, advising the women, old men and children, in short, all who will diminish the stock of provisions and add no strength to the defence, to leave the city.   They can reach Delft without danger, for the roads leading to it are still open."

" Very well," replied Peter.   " It's said that many girls and women have gone to-day in advance of the others."

" That's right," cried the commissioner.   " We are driving in a fragile vessel on the high seas.   If I had a daughter in the house, I know what I should do.   Farewell till we meet again, Meister.   How are matters at Alfen?   The firing is no longer heard."

·' Darkness has probably interrupted the battle."

" We'll hope for the best news to-morrow, and even if all the men outside succumb, we within the walls will not flinch or yield."

"We will hold out firmly to the end," replied Peter resolutely.

"To the end, and, if God so wills it, a successful end."

"Amen," cried Peter, pressed the commissioner's hand and pursued his way home.

Barbara met him on the steps and wanted to call Maria, who was with Henrica; but he forbade it and paced thoughtfully to and fro, his lips often quivering as if he were suffering great pain. When, after some time, he heard his wife's voice in the dining-room, he controlled himself by a violent effort, went to the door, and slowly opened it.

"You are at home already, and I sitting quietly here spinning!" she exclaimed in surprise.

"Yes, child. Please come in here, I have something to say to you."

"For Heaven's sake! Peter, tell me what has happened. How your voice sounds, and how pale you look!"

"I'm not ill, but matters are serious, terribly serious, Maria."

"Then it is true that the enemy—"

"They gained great advantage to-day and yesterday, but I beg you, if you love me, don't interrupt me now; what I have to say is no easy thing, it is hard to force the lips to utter it. Where shall I begin? How shall I speak, that you may not misunderstand me? You know, child, I took you into my house from a warm nest. What we could offer was very little, and you had doubtless expected to find more. I know you have not been happy."

"But it would be so easy for you to make me so."

"You are mistaken, Maria. In these troublous times but one thing claims my thoughts, and whatever diverts them from it is evil. But just now one thing paralyzes my courage and will—anxiety about your fate; for who knows what is impending over us, and therefore it must be said, I must take my heart to the shambles and express a wish.— A wish? Oh, merciful Heaven, is there no other word for what I mean!"

"Speak, Peter, speak, and do not torture me!" cried Maria, gazing anxiously into her husband's face. It could be no small matter, that induced the clear-headed, resolute man to utter such confused language.

The burgomaster summoned up his courage and began again:

"You are right, it is useless to keep back what must be said. We have determined at the town-hall to-day, to request the women and girls to leave the city. The road to Delft is still open; day after to-morrow it may no longer be so, afterwards—who can predict what will happen afterwards? If no relief comes and the provisions are consumed, we shall be forced to open the gates to the enemy, and then, Maria, imagine what will happen! The Rhine and the canals will grow crimson, for much blood will flow into them and they will mirror an unequalled conflagration. Woe betide the men, tenfold woe betide the women, against whom the conqueror's fury will then be directed. And you, you— the wife of the man who has induced thousands to desert King Philip, the wife of the exile, who directs the resistance within these walls."

At the last words Maria had opened her large eyes wider and wider, and now interrupted her husband with the question: "Do you wish to try how high my courage will rise?"

"No, Maria. I know you will hold out loyally, and would look death in the face as fearlessly as your sister did in Haarlem; but I, I cannot endure the thought of seeing you fall into the hands of our butchers. Fear for you, terrible fear, will destroy my vigorous strength in the decisive hours, so the words must be uttered—"

Maria had hitherto listened to her husband quietly; she knew what he desired. Now she advanced nearer and interrupted him by exclaiming firmly, nay imperiously:

"No more, no more, do you hear! I will not endure another word!"

"Maria!"

"Silence! It is my turn now. To escape *fear*, you will thrust your wife from the house; *fear*, you say, would undermine your strength. But will *longing* strengthen it? If you love me, it will not fail to come—"

"If I love you, Maria!"

"Well, well! But you have forgotten to consider how *I* shall feel in exile, if I also love you. I am your wife. We vowed at the altar, that nothing save death should part us. Have you forgotten it? Have your children become mine? Have I taught them, rejoiced to call myself their mother? Yes, or no?"

"Yes, Maria, yes, yes, a hundred times yes!"

"And you have the heart to throw me into the arms of this wasting longing! You wish to prevent me from keeping the most sacred of vows? You can bring yourself to tear me from the children? You think me too shallow and feeble, to endure suffering and death for the sacred cause, which is mine as well as yours! You are fond of calling me your child, but I can be strong, and whatever may come, will not weep. You are the husband and have the right to command, I am only the wife and shall obey. Shall I go? Shall I stay? I await your answer."

She had uttered the last words in a trembling voice, but the burgomaster exclaimed with deep emotion:

"Stay, stay, Maria! Come, come, and forgive me!"

Peter seized her hand, exclaiming again:

"Come, come!"

But the young wife released herself, retreated a step and said beseechingly:

"Let me go, Peter, I cannot; I need time to overcome this."

He let his arms fall and gazed mournfully into her face, but she turned away and silently left the room.

Peter Van der Werff did not follow her, but went quietly into his study and strove to reflect upon many things, that concerned his office, but his thoughts constantly reverted to Maria. His love oppressed him as if it were a crime, and he seemed to himself like a courier, who gathers flowers by the way-side and in this idling squanders time and forgets the object of his mission. His heart felt unspeakably heavy and sad, and it seemed almost like a deliverance when, just before midnight, the bell in the Tower of Pancratius raised its evil-boding voice. In danger, he knew, he would feel and think of nothing except what duty required of him, so with renewed strength he took his hat from the hook and left the house with a steady step.

In the street he met Junker Van Duivenvoorde, who

summoned him to the Hohenort Gate, before which a body of Englishmen had again appeared; a few brave soldiers who, in a fierce, bloody combat, had held Alfen and the Gouda sluice against the Spaniards until their powder was exhausted and necessity compelled them to yield or seek safety in flight. The burgomaster followed the officer and ordered the gates to be opened to the brave soldiers. They were twenty in number, among them the Netherland Captain Van der Laen, and a young German officer. Peter commanded, that they should have shelter for the night in the town-hall and the guard-house at the gate. The next morning suitable quarters would be found for them in the houses of the citizens. Janus Dousa invited the captain to lodge with him, the German went to Aquanus's tavern. All were ordered to report to the burgomaster at noon the next day, to be assigned to quarters and enrolled among the volunteer troops.

The ringing of the alarm-bell in the tower also disturbed the night's rest of the ladies in the Van der Werff household. Barbara sought Maria, and neither returned to their rooms until they had learned the cause of the ringing and soothed Henrica.

Maria could not sleep. Her husband's purpose of separating from her during the impending danger, had stirred her whole soul, wounded her to the inmost depths of her heart. She felt humiliated, and, if not misunderstood, at least unappreciated by the man for whose sake she rejoiced, whenever she perceived a lofty aspiration or noble emotion in her own soul. What avail is personal loveliness to the beautiful wife of a blind man; of what avail to Maria was the rich treasure buried in her bosom, if her husband would not see and bring it to the surface!   "Show him, tell him how lofty are your feelings," urged love; but womanly pride exclaimed: "Do not force upon him what he disdains to seek."

So the hours passed, bringing her neither sleep, peace, nor the desire to forget the humiliation inflicted upon her.

At last Peter entered the room, stepping lightly and cautiously, in order not to wake her. She pretended to be asleep, but with half-closed eyes could see him distinctly. The lamp-light fell upon his face, and the lines she had formerly perceived looked like deep shadows between his eyes and mouth. They impressed upon his features the stamp of heavy, sorrowful anxiety, and reminded Maria of the "too hard" and "if I can only bear it," he had murmured in his sleep the night before. Then he approached her bed and stood there a long time; she no longer saw him, for she kept her eyes tightly closed, but the first loving glance, with which he gazed down upon her, had not escaped her notice. It continued to beam before her mental vision, and she thought she felt that he was watching and praying for her as if she were a child.

Sleep had long since overpowered her husband, while Maria lay gazing at the glimmering dawn, as wakeful as if it were broad day. For the sake of his love she would forgive much, but she could not forget the humiliation she had experienced. "A toy," she said to herself, " a work of art which we enjoy, is placed in security when danger threatens the house; the axe and the bread, the sword and the talisman that protects us, in short whatever we cannot dispense with while we live, we do not release from our hands till death comes.

She was not necessary, indispensable to him. If she had obeyed his wish and left him, then—yes, then—"

Here the current of her thoughts was checked, for the first time she asked herself the question: "Would he have really missed your helping hand, your cheering word?"

She turned restlessly, and her heart throbbed anxiously, as she told herself that she had done little to smooth his rugged pathway. The vague feeling, that he had not been entirely to blame, if she had not found perfect happiness by his side, alarmed her. Did not her former conduct justify him in expecting hindrance rather than support and help in impending days of severest peril?

Filled with deep longing to obtain a clear view of her own heart, she raised herself on her pillows and reviewed her whole former life.

Her mother had been a Catholic in her youth, and had often told her how free and light-hearted she had felt, when she confided everything that can trouble a woman's heart to a silent third person, and received from the lips of God's servant the assurance that she might now begin a new life, secure of forgiveness. "It is harder for us now," her mother said before her first communion, "for we of the Reformed religion are referred to ourselves and our God, and must be wholly at peace with ourselves before we approach the Lord's table. True, that is enough, for if we frankly and honestly confess to the judge within our own breasts all that troubles our consciences, whether in thought or deed, and sincerely repent, we shall be sure of forgiveness for the sake of the Saviour's wounds."

Maria now prepared for this silent confession, and

sternly and pitilessly examined her conduct. Yes, she had fixed her gaze far too steadily upon herself, asked much and given little. The fault was recognized, and now the amendment should begin.

After this self-inspection, her heart grew lighter, and when she at last turned away from the morning light to seek sleep, she looked forward with pleasure to the affectionate greeting she meant to offer Peter in the morning; but she soon fell asleep and when she woke, her husband had long since left the house.

As usual, she set Peter's study in order before proceeding to any other task, and while doing so, cast a friendly glance at the dead Eva's picture. On the writing-table lay the bible, the only book not connected with his business affairs, that her husband ever read. Barbara sometimes drew comfort and support from the volume, but also used it as an oracle, for when undecided how to act she opened it and pointed with her finger to a certain passage. This usually had a definite meaning and she generally, though not always, acted as it directed. To-day she had been disobedient, for in response to her question whether she might venture to send a bag of all sorts of dainties to her son, a Beggar of the Sea, in spite of the Spaniards encircling the city, she had received the words of Jeremiah: "Their tents and their flocks shall they take away: they shall take to themselves their curtains and all their vessels and their camels," and yet the bag had been entrusted early that morning to a widow, who intended to make her escape to Delft with her young daughter, according to the request of the magistrates. The gift might perhaps reach Rotterdam; a mother always hopes for a miracle in behalf of her child.

Before Maria restored the bible to its old place, she opened it at the thirteenth chapter of the first Epistle of Paul to the Corinthians, which speaks of love, and was specially dear to her. There were the words: "Charity suffereth long and is kind, charity is not easily provoked;" and "Charity beareth all things, believeth all things, hopeth all things, endureth all things."

To be kind and patient, to hope and endure all things, was the duty love imposed upon her.

When she had closed the bible and was preparing to go to Henrica, Barbara ushered Janus Dousa into the room. The young nobleman to-day wore armor and gorget, and looked far more like a soldier than a scientist or poet. He had sought Peter in vain at the town-hall, and hoped to find him at home. One of the messengers sent to the Prince had returned from Dortrecht with a letter, which conferred on Dousa the office made vacant by Allertssohn's death. He was to command not only the city-guard, but all the armed force. . He had accepted the appointment with cheerful alacrity, and requested Maria to inform her husband.

"Accept my congratulations," said the burgomaster's wife. "But what will now become of your motto: '*Ante omnia Musae?*'"

"I shall change the words a little and say: *Omnia ante Musas.*"

"Do you understand that jargon, child?" asked Barbara.

"A passport will be given the Muses," replied Maria gaily.

Janus was pleased with the ready repartee and exclaimed: "How bright and happy you look! Faces free from care are rare birds in these days."

Maria blushed, for she did not know how to interpret the words of the nobleman, who understood how to reprove with subtle mockery, and answered naively: "Don't think me frivolous, Junker. I know the seriousness of the times, but I have just finished a silent confession and discovered many bad traits in my character, but also the desire to replace them with more praiseworthy ones."

"There, there," replied Janus. "I knew long ago that you had formed a friendship in the Delft school with my old sage. 'Know thyself,' was the Greek's principal lesson, and you wisely obey it. Every silent confession, every desire for inward purification, must begin with the purpose of knowing ourselves and, if in so doing we unexpectedly encounter things which tend to make our beloved selves uncomely, and have the courage to find them just as hideous in ourselves as in others— "

"Abhorrence will come, and we shall have taken the first step towards improvement."

"No, dear lady, we shall then stand on one of the higher steps. After hours of long, deep thought, Socrates perceived—do you know what?"

"That he knew nothing at all. I shall arrive at this perception more speedily."

"And the Christian learns it at school," said Barbara, to join in the conversation. "All knowledge is botchwork."

"And we are all sinners," added Janus. "That's easily said, dear madam, and easily understood, when others are concerned. '*He* is a sinner' is quickly uttered, but '*I* am a sinner' escapes the lips with more difficulty, and whoever does exclaim it with sorrow, in the stillness of his own quiet room, mingles the white feathers of angels' wings with the black pinions of the devil. Pardon me! In these times everything thought and said is transformed into solemn earnest. Mars is here, and the cheerful Muses are silent. Remember me to your husband, and tell him, that Captain Allertssohn's body has been brought in and to-morrow is appointed for the funeral.

The nobleman took his leave, and Maria, after visiting her patient and finding her well and bright, sent Adrian and Bessie into the garden outside the city-wall to gather flowers and foliage, which she intended to help them weave into wreaths for the coffin of the brave soldier. She herself went to the captain's widow.

CHAPTER XXII.

THE burgomaster's wife returned home just before dinner, and found a motley throng of bearded warriors assembled in front of the house, They were trying to make themselves intelligible in the English language to some of the constables, and when the latter respectfully saluted Maria, raised their hands to their morions also.

She pleasantly returned the greeting and passed into the entry, where the full light of noon streamed in through the open door.

Peter had assigned quarters to the English soldiers outside, and after a consultation with the new commandant, Jan Van der Does, gave them officers. They were probably waiting for their comrades, for when the young wife had ascended the first steps of the staircase

and looked upward, she found the top of the narrow
flight barred by the tall figure of a soldier. The latter
had his back towards her and was showing Bessie
his dark velvet cap, surrounded by rectangular teeth,
above which floated a beautiful light-blue ostrich-plume.
The child seemed to have formed a close friendship with
the soldier, for, although the latter was refusing her
something, the little girl laughed gaily.

Maria paused irresolutely a moment; but when the
child snatched the gay cap and put it on her own
curls, she thought she must check her and exclaimed
warningly: "Why, Bessie, that is no plaything for
children."

The soldier turned, stood still a moment in astonishment, raised his hand to his forehead, and then, with
a few hurried bounds, sprang down the stairs and
rushed up to the burgomaster's wife. Maria had started
back in surprise; but he gave her no time to think, for
stretching out both hands he exclaimed in an eager,
joyous tone, with sparkling eyes: "Maria! Jungfrau
Maria! You here! This is what I call a lucky day!"

The young wife had instantly recognized the soldier
and willingly laid her right hand in his, though not
without a shade of embarrassment.

The officer's clear, blue eyes sought hers, but she
fixed her gaze on the floor, saying: "I am no longer
what I was, the young girl has become a housewife."

"A housewife!" he exclaimed. "How dignified
that sounds! And yet! Yet! You are still Jungfrau
Maria! You haven't changed a hair. That's just the
way you bent your head at the wedding in Delft, the
way you raised your hands, lowered your eyes—you
blushed too, just as prettily."

There was a rare melody in the voice which uttered these words with joyous, almost childlike freedom, which pleased Maria no less than the officer's familiar manner annoyed her. With a hasty movement she raised her head, looked steadily into the young man's handsome face and said with dignity:

"You see only the exterior, Junker von Dornburg; three years have made many changes within."

"Junker von Dornburg," he repeated, shaking his waving locks. "I was Junker Georg in Delft. Very different things have happened to us, dear lady, very different things. You see I have grown a tolerable, though not huge moustache, am stouter, and the sun has bronzed my pink and white boyish face—in short: my outer man has changed for the worse, but within I am just the same as I was three years ago."

Maria felt the blood again mounting into her cheeks, but she did not wish to blush and answered hastily:

"Standing still is retrograding, so you have lost three beautiful years, Herr von Dornburg."

The officer looked at Maria in perplexity, and then said more gravely than before:

"Your jest is more opportune, than you probably suppose; I had hoped to find you again in Delft, but powder was short in Alfen, so the Spaniard will probably reach your native city sooner than we. Now a kind fate brings me to you here; but let me be honest— What I hope and desire stands clearly before my eyes, echoes in my soul, and when I thought of our meeting, I dreamed you would lay both hands in mine and, instead of greeting me with witty words, ask the old companion of happy hours, your brother Leonhard's best friend: 'Do you still remember our dead?' And when I had told you: 'Yes, yes, yes, I have never forgotten him,' then I thought the mild lustre of your eyes—Oh, oh, how I thank you! The dear orbs are floating in a mist of tears. You are not so wholly changed as you supposed, Frau Maria, and if I loyally remember the past, will you blame me for it?"

"Certainly not," she answered cordially. "And now that you speak to me so, I will with pleasure again call you Junker Georg, and as Leonhard's friend and mine, invite you to our house."

"That will be delightful," he cried cordially. "I have so much to ask you and, as for myself—alas, I wish I had less to tell."

"Have you seen my husband?" asked Maria.

"I know nobody in Leyden," he replied, "except my learned, hospitable host, and the doge of this miniature Venice, so rich in water and bridges."

Georg pointed up the stair-case. Maria blushed again as she said:

"Burgomaster Van der Werff is my husband."

The nobleman was silent for a short time, then he said quickly:

"He received me kindly. And the pretty elf up yonder?"

"His child by his first marriage, but now mine also. How do you happen to call her the elf?"

"Because she looks as if she had been born among white flowers in the moonlight, and because the afterglow of the sunrise, from which the elves flee, crimsoned her cheeks when I caught her."

"She has already received the name once," said Maria. "May I take you to my husband?"

"Not now, Frau Van der Werff, for I must attend

to my men outside, but to-morrow, if you will allow me."

Maria found the dishes smoking on the dining-table. Her family had waited for her, and, heated by the rapid walk at noon, excited by her unexpected meeting with the young German, she opened the door of the study and called to her husband:

"Excuse me! I was detained. It is very late."

"We were very willing to wait," he answered kindly, approaching her. Then all she had resolved to do returned to her memory and, for the first time since her marriage, she raised her husband's hand to her lips. He smilingly withdrew it, kissed her on the forehead, and said:

"It is delightful to have you here."

"Isn't it?" she asked, gently shaking her finger at him.

"But we are all here now, and dinner is waiting."

"Come then," she answered gaily. "Do you know whom I met on the stairs?"

"English soldiers."

"Of course, but among them Junker von Dornburg."

"He called on me. A handsome fellow, whose gayety is very attractive, a German from the evangelical countries."

"Leonhard's best friend. Don't you know? Surely I've told you about him. Our guest at Jacoba's wedding."

"Oh! yes. Junker Georg. He tamed the chestnut horse for the Prince's equerry."

"That was a daring act," said Maria, drawing a long breath.

"The chestnut is still an excellent horse," replied

Peter. " Leonhard thought the Junker, with his gifts and talents, would lift the world out of its grooves; I remember it well, and now the poor fellow must remain quietly here and be fed by us. How did he happen to join the Englishmen and take part in the war ?"

" I don't know; he only told me that he had had many experiences."

" I can easily believe it. He is living at the tavern; but perhaps we can find a room for him in the side wing, looking out upon the court-yard."

" No, Peter," cried the young wife eagerly. " There is no room in order there."

" That can be arranged later. At any rate we'll invite him to dinner to-morrow, he may have something to tell us. There is good marrow in the young man. He begged me not to let him remain idle, but make him of use in the service. Jan Van der Does has already put him in the right place, the new commandant looks into people's hearts."

Barbara mingled in the conversation, Peter, though it was a week-day, ordered a jug of wine to be brought instead of the beer, and an event that had not occurred for weeks happened : the master of the house sat at least fifteen minutes with his family after the food had been removed, and told them of the rapid advance of the Spaniards, the sad fate of the fugitive Englishmen, who had been disarmed and led away in sections, the brave defence the Britons, to whose corps Georg belonged, had made at Alfen, and of another hot combat in which Don Gaytan, the right-hand and best officer of Valdez, was said to have fallen. Messengers still went and came on the roads leading to Delft, but · to-morrow these also would probably be blocked by the enemy.

He always addressed everything he said to Maria, unless Barbara expressly questioned him, and when he at last rose from the table, ordered a good roast to be prepared the next day for the guest he intended to invite. Scarcely had the door of his room closed behind him, when little Bessie ran up to Maria, threw her arms around her and asked:

"Mother, isn't Junker Georg the tall captain with the blue feather, who ran down-stairs so fast to meet you?"

"Yes, child."

"And he's coming to dinner to-morrow! He's coming, Adrian."

The child clapped her hands in delight and then ran to Barbara to exclaim once more:

"Aunt Bärbel, did you hear? He's coming!"

"With the blue feather," replied the widow.

"And he has curls, curls as long as Assendelft's little Clara. May I go with you to see Cousin Henrica?"

"Afterwards, perhaps," replied Maria. "Go now, children, get the flowers and separate them carefully from the leaves. Trautchen will bring some hoops and strings, and then we'll bind the wreaths."

Junker Georg's remark, that this was a lucky day, seemed to be verified; for the young wife found Henrica bright and free from pain. With the doctor's permission, she had walked up and down her room several times, sat a longer time at the open window, relished her chicken, and when Maria entered, was seated in the softly-cushioned arm-chair, rejoicing in the consciousness of increasing strength.

Maria was delighted at her improved appearance, and told her how well she looked that day.

"I can return the compliment," replied Henrica. "You look very happy. What has happened to you?"

"To me? Oh! my husband was more cheerful than usual, and there was a great deal to tell at dinner. I've only come to enquire for your health. I will see you later. Now I must go with the children to a sorrowful task."

"With the children? What have the little elf and Signor Salvatore to do with sorrow?"

"Captain Allertssohn will be buried to-morrow, and we are going to make some wreaths for the coffin."

"Make wreaths!" cried Henrica, "I can teach you that! There, Trautchen, take the plate and call the little ones."

The servant went away, but Maria said anxiously:

"You will exert yourself too much again, Henrica."

"I? I shall be singing again to-morrow. My preserver's potion does wonders, I assure you. Have you flowers and oak-leaves enough?"

"I should think so."

At the last words the door opened and Bessie cautiously entered the room, walking on tiptoe as she had been told, went up to Henrica, received a kiss from her, and then asked eagerly:

"Cousin Henrica, do you know? Junker Georg, with the blue feather, is coming again to-morrow and will dine with us."

"Junker Georg?" asked the young lady.

Maria interrupted the child's reply, and answered in an embarrassed tone:

"Herr von Dornburg, an officer who came to the city with the Englishmen, of whom I spoke to you—a German—an old acquaintance. Go and arrange the flowers with Adrian, Bessie, then I'll come and help you."

"Here, with Cousin Henrica," pleaded the child.

"Yes, little elf, here; and we'll both make the loveliest wreath you ever saw."

The child ran out, and this time, in her delight, forgot to shut the door gently.

The young wife gazed out of the window. Henrica watched her silently for a time and then exclaimed:

"One word, Frau Maria. What is going on in the court-yard? Nothing? And what has become of the happy light in your eyes? Your house isn't swarming with guests; why did you wait for Bessie to tell me about Junker Georg, the German, the old acquaintance?"

"Let that subject drop, Henrica."

"No, no! Do you know what I think? The storm of war has blown to your house the young madcap, with whom you spent such happy hours at your sister's wedding. Am I right or wrong? You needn't blush so deeply."

"It is he," replied Maria gravely. "But if you love me, forget what I told you about him, or deny yourself the idle amusement of alluding to it, for if you should still do so, it would offend me."

"Why should I! You are the wife of another."

"Of another whom I honor and love, who trusts me and himself invited the Junker to his house. I have liked the young man, admired his talents, been anxious when he trifled with his life as if it were a paltry leaf, which is flung into the river."

"And now that you have seen him again, Maria?"

" Now I know, what my duty is.   Do *you* see, that my peace here is not disturbed by idle gossip."

" Certainly not, Maria ; yet I am still curious about this Chevalier Georg and his singing.   Unfortunately we shan't be long together.   I want to go home."

" The doctor will not allow you to travel yet."

" No matter.   I shall go as soon as I feel well enough.   My father is refused admittance, but your husband can do much, and I must speak with him."

" Will you receive him to-morrow ?"

" The sooner the better, for he is your husband and, I repeat, the ground is burning under my feet."

" Oh !" exclaimed Maria.

" That sounds very sad," cried Henrica.   " Do you want to hear, that I shall find it hard to leave you ?   I shouldn't go yet; but my sister Anna, she is now a widow—   Thank God, I should like to say, but she is suffering want and utterly deserted.   I must speak to my father about her, and go forth from the quiet haven into the storm once more."

" My husband will come to you," said Maria.

" That's right, that's right !   Come in, children ! Put the flowers on the table yonder.   You, little elf, sit down on the stool and you, Salvatore, shall give me the flowers.   What does this mean ?   I really believe the scamp has been putting perfumed oil on his curly head. In honor of me, Salvatore ?   Thank you !—   We shall need the hoops later.   First we'll make bouquets, and then bind them with the leaves to the wood.   Sing me a song while we are working, Maria.   The first one !   I can bear it to-day."

CHAPTER XXIII.

HALF Leyden had followed the brave captain's coffin, and among the other soldiers, who rendered the last honors to the departed, was Georg von Dornburg. After the funeral, the musician Wilhelm led the son of the kind comrade, whom so many mourned, to his house. Van der Werff found many things to be done after the burial, but reserved the noon hour; for he expected the German to dine.

The burgomaster, as usual, sat at the head of the table; the Junker had taken his place between him and Maria, opposite to Barbara and the children.

The widow never wearied of gazing at the young man's fresh, bright face, for although her son could not compare with him in beauty, there was an honest expression in the Junker's eyes, which reminded her of her Wilhelm.

Many a question and answer had already been exchanged between those assembled round the board, many a pleasant memory recalled, when Peter, after the dishes had been removed and a new jug with better wine placed on the table, filled the young nobleman's glass again, and raised his own.

"Let us drink this bumper," he cried, gazing at Georg with sincere pleasure in his eyes, "let us drink to the victory of the good cause, for which you too voluntarily draw your sword. Thanks for the vigorous pledge. Drinking is also an art, and the Germans are masters of it."

"We learn it in various places, and not worst at the University of Jena."

"All honor to the doctors and professors, who bring their pupils up to the standard of my dead brother-in-law, and judging from this sample drink, you also."

"Leonhard was my teacher in the *ars bibendi*. How long ago it is!"

"Youth is not usually content," replied Peter, "but when the point in question concerns years, readily calls 'much,' what seems to older people 'little.' True, many experiences may have been crowded into the last few years of your life. I can still spare an hour, and as we are all sitting so cosily together here, you can tell us, unless you wish to keep silence on the subject, how you chanced to leave your distant home for Holland, and your German and Latin books to enlist under the English standard."

"Yes," added Maria, without any trace of embarrassment. "You still owe me the story. Give thanks, children, and then go."

Adrian gazed beseechingly first at his mother and then at his father, and as neither forbade him to stay, moved his chair close to his sister, and both leaned their heads together and listened with wide open eyes, while the Junker first quietly, then with increasing vivacity, related the following story:

"You know that I am a native of Thuringia, a mountainous country in the heart of Germany. Our castle is situated in a pleasant valley, through which a clear river flows in countless windings. Wooded mountains, not so high as the giants in Switzerland, yet by no means contemptible, border the narrow boundaries of the valley. At their feet lie fields and meadows, at a greater height rise pine forests, which, like the huntsman, wear green robes at all seasons of the year. In winter, it is true, the snow cover them with a glimmering white sheet. When spring comes, the pines put forth new shoots, as fresh and full of sap as the budding foliage of your oaks and beeches, and in the meadows by the river it begins to snow in the warm breezes, for then one fruit-tree blooms beside another, and when the wind rises, the delicate white petals flutter through the air and fall among the bright blossoms in the grass, and on the clear surface of the river. There are also numerous barren cliffs on the higher portions of the mountains, and where they towered in the most rugged, inaccessible ridges, our ancestors built their fastnesses, to secure themselves from the attacks of their enemies. Our castle stands on a mountain-ridge in the midst of the valley of the Saale. There I was born, there I sported through the years of my boyhood, learned to read and guide the pen. There was plenty of hunting in the forests, we had spirited horses in the stable, and, wild lad that I was, I rarely went voluntarily into the school-room, the grey-haired teacher, Lorenz, had to catch me, if he wanted to get possession of me. My sisters and Hans, our youngest child, the boy was only three years younger than I, kept quiet—I had an older brother too, yet did not have him. When his beard was first beginning to grow, he was given by our gracious Duke to Chevalier von Brand as his esquire, and sent to Spain, to buy Andalusian horses. John Frederick's father had learned their value in Madrid after the battle of Mühlburg. Louis was a merry fellow when he went away, and knew how to tame the wildest stallion. It was hard for our parents to believe him dead, but years elapsed, and as neither he nor Chevalier von Brand appeared, we were obliged to give him up for lost. My mother alone could not do this, and constantly expected his return. My father called me the future heir and lord of the castle. When I had passed beyond boyhood and understood Cicero tolerably well, I was sent to the University of Jena to study law, as my uncle, the chancellor, wished me to become a counsellor of state.

"Oh Jena, beloved Jena! There are blissful days in May and June, when only light clouds float in the sky, and all the leaves and flowers are so fresh and green, that one would think—they probably think so themselves—that they could never fade and wither; such days in human existence are the period of joyous German student life. You can believe it. Leonhard has told you enough of Jena. He understood how to unite work and pleasure; I, on the contrary, learned little on the wooden benches, for I rarely occupied them, and the dust of books certainly didn't spoil my lungs. But I read Ariosto again and again, devoted myself to singing, and when a storm of feeling seethed within my breast, composed many songs for my own pleasure. We learned to wield the sword too in Jena, and I would gladly have crossed blades with the sturdy fencing-master Allertssohn, of whom you have just told me. Leonhard was older than I, and when he graduated with honor, I was still very weak in the pandects. But we were always one in heart and soul, so I went to Holland with him to attend his wedding. Ah, those were days! The theologians in Jena have actively disputed about the part of the earth, in which the little garden of Paradise should be sought. I considered them all fools, and thought: ' There is only one Eden, and that lies in Holland, and the fairest roses the dew waked on the first sunny morning, bloom in Delft!'"

At these words Georg shook back his waving locks and hesitated in great embarrassment, but as no one interrupted him and he saw Barbara's eager face and the children's glowing cheeks, quietly continued:

"So I came home, and was to learn for the first time, that in life also beautiful sunny days often end with storms. I found my father ill, and a few days after my return he closed his eyes in death. I had never seen any human being die, and the first, the very first, was he, my father."

Georg paused, and deeply moved, passed his hand over his eyes.

"Your father!" cried Barbara, in a tone of cordial sympathy, breaking the silence. "If we can judge the tree by the apple, he was surely a splendid man."

The Junker again raised his head, exclaiming with sparkling eyes:

"Unite every good and noble quality, and embody them in the form of a tall, handsome man, then you will have the image of my father;—and I might tell you of my mother—"

"Is she still alive?" asked Peter.

"God grant it!" exclaimed the young man. "I have heard nothing from my family for two months. That is hard. Pleasures smile along every path, and I like my profession of soldier, but it often grieves me sorely to hear so little from home. Oh! if one were only a bird, a sunbeam, or a shooting-star, one might, if only for the twinkling of an eye, learn how matters go at home and fill the soul with fresh gratitude, or, if it must be—but I will not think of that. In the valley of the Saale, the trees are blossoming and a thousand flowers deck all the meadows, just as they do here, and did there two years ago, when I left home for the second time.

" After my father's death I was the heir, but neither hunting nor riding to court, neither singing nor the clinking of beakers could please me. I went about like a sleep-walker, and it seemed as if I had no right to live without my father. Then — it is now just two years ago—a messenger brought from Weimar a letter which had come from Italy with several others, addressed to our most gracious sovereign; it contained the news that our lost brother was still alive, lying sick and wretched in the hospital at Bergamo. A kind nun had written for him, and we now learned that on the journey from Valencia to Livorno Louis had been captured by corsairs and dragged to Tunis. How much suffering he endured there, with what danger he at last succeeded in obtaining his liberty, you shall learn later. He escaped to Italy on a Genoese galley. His feet carried him as far as Bergamo, but he could go no farther, and now lay ill, perhaps dying, among sympathizing strangers. I set out at once and did not spare horseflesh on the way to Bergamo, but though there were many strange and beautiful things to be seen on my way, they afforded me little pleasure, the thought of Louis, so dangerously ill, saddened my joyous spirits. Every running brook urged me to hasten, and the lofty mountains seemed like jealous barriers. When once beyond St. Gotthard I felt less anxious, and as I rode down from Bellinzona to Lake Lugano, and the sparkling surface of the water beyond the city smiled at me like a blue eye, forgot my grief for a time, waved my hat, and sung a song.   In Bergamo I found my brother, alive, but enfeebled in mind and body, weak, and without any desire to take up the burden of life again.   He had been in good hands, and after a few weeks we were able to travel homeward—this time I went through beautiful Tyrol.   Louis's strength daily increased, but the wings of his soul had been paralyzed by suffering.   Alas, for long years he had dug and carried heavy loads, with chains on his feet, beneath a broiling sun.   Chevalier von Brand could not long endure this hard fate, but Louis, while in Tunis, forgot both how to laugh and weep, and which of the two can be most easily spared?

" Even when he saw my mother again, he could not shed a tear, yet his whole body—and surely his heart also—trembled with emotion.   Now he lives quietly at the castle.   In the prime of manhood he is an old man, but he is beginning to accommodate himself to life, only he can't bear the sight of a strange face.   I had a hard battle with him, for as the eldest son, the castle and estate, according to the law, belong to him, but he wanted to resign his rights and put me in his place. Even when he had brought my mother over to his side, and my uncle and brothers and sisters tried to persuade me to yield to his wish, I remained resolute.   I would not touch what did not belong to me, and our youngest boy, Wolfgang, has grown up, and can fill my place wherever it is necessary.   When the entreaties and persuasions became too strong for me, I saddled my horse and went away again.   It was hard for my mother to let me go, but I had tasted the delight of travelling, and rode off as if to a wedding.   If I must be perfectly frank, I'll confess that I resigned castle and estates like a troublesome restraint. Free as the wind and clouds, I followed the same road over which I had ridden with Leonhard, for in your country a war after my own heart was going on, and my future fortune was to be based upon my sword. In Cologne I enlisted under the banner of Louis of Nassau, and fought with him at Mook Heath till every one retreated. My horse had fallen, my doublet was torn, there was little left save good spirits and the hope of better days. These were soon found, for Captain Gensfort asked me to join the English troops. I became his ensign, and at Alfen held out beside him till the last grain of powder was exhausted. What happened there, you know."

"And Captain Van der Laen told us," said Peter, "that he owes his life to you. You fought like a lion."

"It was wild work enough at the fortifications, yet neither I nor my horse had a hair ruffled, and this time I even saved my knapsack and a full purse. Fate, like mothers, loves troublesome children best, and therefore led me to you and your family, Herr Burgomaster."

"And I beg you to consider yourself one of them," replied Peter. "We have two pleasant rooms looking out upon the court-yard; they shall be put in order for you, if you would like to occupy them."

"With pleasure," replied the Junker, and Peter, offering him his hand, said:

"The duties of my office call me away, but you can tell the ladies what you need, and when you mean to move in. The sooner, the better we shall be pleased. Shall we not, Maria?"

"You will be welcome, Junker Georg. Now I must look after the invalid we are nursing here. Barbara will ascertain your wishes."

The young wife took her husband's hand and left the room with him.

The widow was left alone with the young nobleman and tried to learn everything he desired. Then she followed her sister-in-law, and finding her in Henrica's room, clapped her hands, exclaiming:

"That *is* a man! Fraulein, I assure you that, though I'm an old woman, I never met so fine a young fellow in all my life. So much heart, and so handsome too! 'To whom fortune gives once, it gives by bushels, and unto him that hath, shall be given!' Those are precious words!"

CHAPTER XXIV.

PETER had promised Henrica, to request the council to give her permission to leave the city.

It was hard for her to part from the burgomaster's household. Maria's frank nature exerted a beneficial influence; it seemed as if her respect for her own sex increased in her society. The day before she had heard her sing. The young wife's voice was like her character. Every note flawless and clear as a bell, and Henrica grieved that she should be forbidden to mingle her own voice with her hostess's. She was very sorry to leave the children too. Yet she was obliged to go, on Anna's account, for her father could not be persuaded by letters to do anything. Had she appealed to him in writing to forgive his rejected child, he would hardly have read the epistle to the end. Something might more easily be won from him through words, by taking advantage of a favorable moment. She must have speech with him, yet she dreaded the life in his castle, especially as she was forced to acknowledge, that she too was by no means necessary to her father. To secure the inheritance, he had sent her to a terrible existence with her aunt; while she lay dangerously ill, he had gone to a tournament, and the letter received from him the day before, contained nothing but the information that he was refused admittance to the city, and a summons for her to go to Junker de Heuter's house at the Hague. Enclosed was a pass from Valdez, enjoining all King Philip's soldiers to provide for her safety.

The burgomaster had intended to have her conveyed in a litter, accompanied by a flag of truce, as far as the Spanish lines, and the doctor no longer opposed her wish to travel. She hoped to leave that day.

Lost in thought, she stationed herself in the bay-window and gazed out into the court-yard. Several windows in the building on the eastern side stood open. Trautchen must have risen early, for she came out of the rooms arranged for Georg's occupation, followed by a young assistant carrying various scrubbing utensils. Next Jan appeared with a large arm-chair on his head. Bessie ran after the Frieselander, calling:

"Aunt Bärbel's grandfather's chair; where will she take her afternoon nap?"

Henrica had heard the words, and thought first of good old "Babetta," who could also feel tenderly, then of Maria and the man who was to lodge in the rooms opposite. Were there not some loose threads still remaining of the old tie, that had united the burgomaster's wife to the handsome nobleman? A feeling of dread overpowered her. Poor Meister Peter, poor Maria!

Was it right to abandon the young wife, who had held out a saving hand in her distress? Yet how much nearer was her own sister than this stranger! Each day that she allowed herself to linger in this peaceful asylum, seemed like a theft from Anna—since she had read in a letter from her to her husband, the only one the dead man's pouch contained, that she was ill and sunk in poverty with her child.

Help was needed here, and no one save herself could offer it.

With aid from Barbara and Maria, she packed her clothes. At noon everything was ready for her departure, and she would not be withheld from eating in the dining-room with the family. Peter was prevented from coming to dinner, Henrica took his seat and, under the mask of loud, forced mirth, concealed the grief and anxieties that filled her heart. At twilight Maria and the children followed her into her room, and she now had the harp brought and sang. At first her voice failed to reach many a note, but as the snow falling from the mountain peaks to the plains at first slides slowly, then rapidly increases in bulk and power, her tones gradually gained fulness and irresistible might and, when at last she rested the harp against the wall and walked to the chair exhausted, Maria clasped her hand and said with deep emotion:

"Stay with us, Henrica."

"I ought not," replied the girl. "You are enough for each other. Shall I take you with me, children?"

Adrian lowered his eyes in embarrassment, but Bessie jumped into her lap, exclaiming.

"Where are you going? Stay with us.

Just at that moment some one knocked at the door,

and Peter entered. It was evident that he brought no good tidings. His request had been refused. The council had almost unanimously voted an assent to Van Bronkhorst's proposition, that the young lady, as a relation of prominent friends of Spain among the Netherland nobility, should be kept in the city. Peter's representations were unheeded; he now frankly told Henrica what a conflict he had had, and entreated her to have patience and be content to remain in his house as a welcome guest.

The young girl interrupted him with many a passionate exclamation of indignation, and when she grew calmer, cried:

"Oh, you men, you men! I would gladly stay with you, but you know from what this base deed of violence detains me. And then: to be a prisoner, to live weeks, months, without mass and without confession. Yet first and last—merciful Heavens, what will become of my unfortunate sister?"

Maria gazed beseechingly at Peter, and the latter said:

"If you desire the consolations of your religion, I will send Father Damianus to you, and you can hear mass with the Grey Sisters, who live beside us, as often as you desire. We are not fighting against your religion, but for the free exercise of every faith, and the whole city stands open to you. My wife will help you bear your anxiety about your sister far better than I could do, but let me say this: wherever and however I can help you, it shall be done, and not merely in words."

So saying, he held out his hand to Henrica. She gave him hers, exclaiming:

"I have cause to thank you, I know, but please

leave me now and give me time to think until to-morrow."

" Is there no way of changing the decision of the council ? " Maria asked her husband.

" No, certainly not."

" Well, then," said the young wife earnestly, " you must remain our guest. Anxiety for your sister does not cloud your pleasure alone, but saddens me too. Let us first of all provide for her. How are the roads to Delft ?"

" They are cut, and no one will be able to pass after to-morrow or the day after."

" Then calm yourself, Henrica, and let us consider what is to be done."

The questions and counter-questions began, and Henrica gazed in astonishment at the delicate young wife, for with unerring resolution and keenness, she held the first voice in the consultation. The surest means of gaining information was to seek that very day a reliable messenger, by whom to send Anna d'Avila money, and if possible bring her to Holland. The burgomaster declared himself ready to advance from his own pro-perty, a portion of the legacy bequeathed Henrica's sister by Fraulein Van Hoogstraten, and accepted his guest's thanks without constraint.

" But whom could they send ? "

Henrica thought of Wilhelm; he was her sister's friend.

" But he is in the military service," replied the burgomaster. " I know him. He will not desert the city in these times of trouble, not even for his mother."

" But I know the right messenger," said Maria. " We'll send Junker Georg."

"That's a good suggestion," said Peter. "We shall find him in his lodgings. I must go to Van Hout, who lives close by, and will send the German to you. But my time is limited, and with such gentlemen, fair women can accomplish more than bearded men. Farewell, dear Fraulein, once more—we rejoice to have you for our guest."

When the burgomaster had left the room, Henrica said:

"How quickly, and how differently from what I expected, all this has happened. I love you. I am under obligations to you, but to be imprisoned, imprisoned.— The walls will press upon me, the ceiling will seem like a weight. I don't know whether I ought to rejoice or despair. You have great influence with the Junker. Tell him about Anna, touch his heart, and if he would go, it would really be best for us both."

"You mean for you and your sister," replied Maria with a repellent gesture of the hand. "There is the lamp. When the Junker comes, we shall see each other again."

Maria went to her room and threw herself on the couch, but soon rose and paced restlessly to and fro. Then stretching out her clasped hands, she exclaimed:

"Oh, if he would only go, if he would only go! Merciful God! Kind, gracious Father in Heaven, grant him every happiness, every blessing, but save my peace of mind; let him go, and lead him far, far away from here."

CHAPTER XXV.

THE tavern where Georg von Dornburg lodged stood on the "broad street," and was a fine building with a large court-yard, in which were numerous vehicles. On the left of the entrance was a large open room entered through a lofty archway. Here the drivers and other folk sat over their beer and wine, suffering the innkeeper's hens to fly on the benches and even sometimes on the table, here vegetables were cleaned, boiled and fried, here the stout landlady was frequently obliged to call her sturdy maid and men servants to her aid, when her guests came to actual fighting, or some one drank more than was good for him. Here the new custom of tobacco-smoking was practised, though only by a few sailors who had served on Spanish ships—but Frau Van Aken could not endure the acrid smoke and opened the windows, which were filled with blooming pinks, slender stalks of balsam, and cages containing bright-plumaged goldfinches. On the side opposite to the entrance were two closed rooms. Above the door of one, neatly carved in wood, were the lines from Horace:

> " Ille terrarum mihi praeter omnes.
> Angulus ridet." *

Only a few chosen guests found admittance into this long, narrow apartment. It was completely wainscoted with wood, and from the centre of the richly-carved

---

* Of all the corners of the world,
There is none that so charms me.

ceiling a strange picture gleamed in brilliant hues. This represented the landlord. The worthy man with the smooth face, firmly-closed lips, and long nose, which offered an excellent straight line to its owner's burin, sat on a throne in the costume of a Roman general, while Vulcan and Bacchus, Minerva and Pomona, offered him gifts. Klaus Van Aken, or as he preferred to be called, Nicolaus Aquanus, was a singular man, who had received good gifts from more than one of the Olympians; for besides his business he zealously devoted himself to science and several of the arts. He was an excellent silver-smith, a die-cutter and engraver of great skill, had a remarkable knowledge of coins, was an industrious student and collector of antiquities. His little tap-room was also a museum; for on the shelves, that surrounded it, stood rare objects of every description, in rich abundance and regular order; old jugs and tankards, large and small coins, gems in carefully-sealed glass-cases, antique lamps of clay and bronze, stones with ancient Roman inscriptions, Roman and Greek terra-cotta, polished fragments of marble which he had found in Italy among the ruins, the head of a faun, an arm, a foot and other bits of Pagan works of art, a beautifully-enamelled casket of Byzantine work, and another with enamelled ornamentation from Limoges. Even half a Roman coat of mail and a bit of mosaic from a Roman bath were to be seen here. Amid these antiquities, stood beautiful Venetian glasses, pine-cones and ostrich-eggs. Such another tap-room could scarcely be found in Holland, and even the liquor, which a neatly-dressed maid poured for the guests from oddly-shaped tankards into exquisitely-wrought goblets, was exceptionally fine. In this room Herr Aquanus himself was in the habit of appearing among his guests; in the other, opposite to the entrance, his wife held sway.

On this day, the "Angulus," as the beautiful tap-room was called, was but thinly occupied, for the sun had just set, though the lamps were already lighted. These rested in three-branched iron chandeliers, every portion of which, from the slender central shaft to the intricately-carved and twisted ornaments, had been carefully wrought by Aquanus with his own hand.

Several elderly gentlemen were at one table enjoying their wine, while at another were Captain Van der Laen, a brave Hollander, who was receiving English pay and had come to the city with the other defenders of Alfen, the musician Wilhelm, Junker Georg, and the landlord.

"It's a pleasure to meet people like you, Junker," said Aquanus. "You've travelled with your eyes open, and what you tell me about Brescia excites my curiosity. I should have liked to see the inscription."

"I'll get it for you," replied the young man; "for if the Spaniards don't send me into another world, I shall certainly cross the Alps again. Did you find any of these Roman antiquities in your own country?"

"Yes. At the Roomburg Canal, perhaps the site of the old Praetorium, and at Katwyk. The forum Hadriani was probably located near Voorburg. The coat of mail, I showed you, came from there."

"An old, green, half-corroded thing," cried Georg. "And yet! What memories the sight of it awakens! Did not some Roman armorer forge it for the wandering emperor? When I look at this coat of mail, Rome and her legions appear before my eyes. Who would not, like you, Herr Wilhelm, go to the Tiber to increase

the short span of the present by the long centuries of
the past!"

"I should be glad to go to Italy once more with
you," replied Wilhelm.

"And I with you."

"Let us first secure our liberty," said the musician.
"When that is accomplished, each individual will
belong to himself, and then: why should I conceal it,
nothing will keep me in Leyden."

"And the organ?   Your father?" asked Aquanus.

"My brothers will remain here, snug in their own
nest," answered Wilhelm.   "But something urges, im-
pels me—"

· "There are still waters and rivers on earth," interrupted Georg, "and in the sky the fixed stars remain
quiet and the planets cannot cease from wandering. So
among human beings, there are contented persons, who
like their own places, and birds of passage like us.   To
be sure, you needn't go to Italy to hear fine singing. I
just heard a voice, a voice—"

"Where?   You make me eager."

"In the court-yard of Herr Van der Werff's house."

"That was his wife."

"Oh, no!   *Her* voice sounds differently."

During this conversation, Captain Van der Laen had
risen and examined the landlord's singular treasures.
He was now standing before a board, on which the
head of an ox was sketched in charcoal, freely, boldly
and with perfect fidelity to nature.

"What magnificent piece of beef is this?" he asked
the landlord.

"No less a personage than Frank Floris sketched
it," replied Aquanus.   "He once came here from Brus-

sels and called on Meister Artjen. The old man had gone out, so Floris took a bit of charcoal and drew these lines with it. When Artjen came home and found the ox's head, he stood before it a long time and finally exclaimed: 'Frank Floris, or the devil!' This story— But there comes the burgomaster. Welcome, Meister Peter. A rare honor."

All the guests rose and respectfully greated Van der Werff; Georg started up to offer him his chair. Peter sat down for a short time and drank a glass of wine, but soon beckoned to the Junker and went out with him into the street.

There he briefly requested him to go to his house, for they had an important communication to make, and then went to Van Hout's residence, which was close beside the inn.

Georg walked thoughtfully towards the burgomaster's.

The "they" could scarcely have referred to any one except Maria. What could she want of him at so late an hour? Had his friend regretted having offered him lodgings in her own house? He was to move into his new quarters early next morning; perhaps she wished to inform him of this change of mind, before it was too late. Maria treated him differently from before, there was no doubt of that, but surely this was natural! He had dreamed of a different, far different meeting! He had come to Holland to support the good cause of Orange, yet he would certainly have turned his steed towards his beloved Italy, where a good sword was always in demand, instead of to the north, had he not hoped to find in Holland her, whom he had never forgotten, for whom he had never ceased to long— Now she was the wife of another, a man who had shown him kindness, given him his confidence. To tear his love from his heart was impossible; but he owed it to her husband and his own honor to be strong, to resolutely repress every thought of possessing her, and only rejoice in seeing her; and this he must try to accomplish.

He had told himself all these things more than once, but realized that he was walking with unsteady steps, upon a narrow pathway, when she met him outside the dining-room and he felt how cold and tremulous was the hand she laid in his. ·

Maria led the way, and he silently followed her into Henrica's room. The latter greeted him with a friendly gesture, but both ladies hesitated to utter the first word. The young man turned hastily, noticed that he was in the room overlooking the court-yard, and said, eagerly :

" I was down below just before twilight, to look at my new quarters, and heard singing from this room, and such singing ! At first I didn't know what was coming, for the tones were husky, weak, and broken, but after-wards—afterwards the melody burst forth like a stream of lava through the ashes. We ought to wish many sorrows to one, who can lament thus."

" You shall make the singer's acquaintance," said Maria, motioning towards the young girl.   " Fraulein Henrica Van Hoogstraten, a beloved guest in our house."

" Were you the songstress ?" asked Georg.

" Does that surprise you ?" replied Henrica. ."My voice has certainly retained its strength better than my body, wasted by long continued suffering.   I feel how deeply my eyes are sunken and how pale I must be. Singing certainly lightens pain, and I have been deprived of the comforter long enough. Not a note has passed my lips for weeks, and now my heart aches so, that I would far rather weep than sing. 'What troubles me?' you will ask, and yet Maria gives me courage to request a chivalrous service, almost without parallel, at your hands."

"Speak, speak," Georg eagerly exclaimed. "If Frau Maria summons me and I can serve you, dear lady: here I am, dispose of me."

Henrica did not avoid his frank glance, as she replied:

"First hear what a great service we ask of you. You must prepare yourself to hear a short story. I am still weak and have put my strength to a severe test to-day, Maria must speak for me."

The young wife fulfilled this task quietly and clearly, closing with the words:

"The messenger we need, I have found myself. You must be he, Junker Georg."

Henrica had not interrupted the burgomaster's wife; but now said warmly:

"I have only made your acquaintance to-day, but I trust you entirely. A few hours ago, black would have been my color, but if you will be my knight, I'll choose cheerful green, for I now begin to hope again. Will you venture to take the ride for me?"

Hitherto Georg had gazed silently at the floor. Now he raised his head, saying:

"If I can obtain leave of absence, I will place my-self at your disposal;—but my lady's color is blue, and I am permitted to wear no other."

Henrica's lips quivered slightly, but the young noble-man continued:

"Captain Van der Laen is my superior officer. I'll speak to him at once."

"And if he says no?" asked Maria.

Henrica interrupted her and answered haughtily:

"Then I beg you to send me Herr Wilhelm, the musician."

Georg bowed and went to the tavern.

As soon as the ladies were alone, the young girl asked:

"Do you know Herr von Dornburg's lady?"

"How should I?" replied Maria. "Give yourself a little rest, Fraulein. As soon as the Junker comes back, I'll bring him to you."

The young wife left the room and seated herself at the spinning-wheel with Barbara. Georg kept them waiting a long time, but at midnight again appeared, accompanied by two companions. It was not within the limits of the captain's authority to grant him a leave of absence for several weeks — the journey to Italy would have required that length of time — but the Junker had consulted the musician, and the latter had found the right man, with whom Wilhelm speedily made the necessary arrangements, and brought him without delay: it was the old steward, Belotti.

CHAPTER XXVI.

On the morning of the following day the spacious shooting-grounds, situated not far from the White Gate, between the Rapenburg and the city-wall, presented a busy scene, for by a decree of the council the citizens and inhabitants, without exception, no matter whether they were poor or rich, of noble or plebeian birth, were to take a solemn oath to be loyal to the Prince and the good cause.

Commissioner Van Bronkhorst, Burgomaster Van der Werff, and two other magistrates, clad in festal attire, stood under a group of beautiful linden-trees to receive the oaths of the men and youths, who flocked to the spot. The solemn ceremonial had not yet commenced. Janus Dousa, in full uniform, a coat of mail over his doublet and a helmet on his head, arm-in-arm with Van Hout, approached Meister Peter and the commissioner, saying: " Here it is again! Not one of the humbler citizens and workmen is absent, but the gentlemen in velvet and fur are but thinly represented."

" They shall come yet!" cried the city clerk menacingly.

" What will formal vows avail ?" replied the burgomaster. " Whoever desires liberty, must grant it. Besides, this hour will teach us on whom we can depend."

" Not a single man of the militia is absent," said the commissioner.

" There is comfort in that. What is stirring yonder in the linden ?"

The men looked up and perceived Adrian, who was swaying in the top of the tree, as a concealed listener.

" The boy must be everywhere," exclaimed Peter. " Come down, saucy lad. You appear at a convenient time."

The boy clung to a limb with his hands, let himself drop to the ground and stood before his father with a penitent face, which he knew how to assume when occasion required. The burgomaster uttered no further words of reproof, but bade him go home and tell his mother, that he saw no possibility of getting Belotti through the Spanish lines in safety, and also that Father Damianus had promised to call on the young lady in the course of the day.

"Hurry, Adrian, and you, constables, keep all unbidden persons away from these trees, for any place where an oath is taken becomes sacred ground— The clergymen have seated themselves yonder near the target. They have the precedence. Have the kindness to summon them, Herr Van Hout. Dominie Verstroot wishes to make an address, and then I would like to utter a few words of admonition to the citizens myself."

Van Hout withdrew, but before he had reached the preachers Junker von Warmond appeared, and reported that a messenger, a handsome young lad, had come as an envoy. He was standing before the White Gate and had a letter.

"From Valdez?"

"I don't know; but the young fellow is a Hollander and his face is familiar to me."

"Conduct him here; but don't interrupt us until the ceremony of taking the oath is over. The messenger can tell Valdez what he has seen and heard here. It will do the Castilian good, to know in advance what we intend."

The Junker withdrew, and when he returned with Nicolas Van Wibisma, who was the messenger, Dominie Verstroot had finished his stirring speech. Van der Werff was still speaking. The sacred fire of enthusiasm sparkled in his eyes, and though the few words he addressed to his fellow-combatants in the deepest chest tones of his powerful voice were plain and unadorned, they found their way to the souls of his auditors.

Nicolas also followed the speech with a throbbing heart; it seemed as if the tall, earnest man under the linden were speaking directly to him and to him alone, when at the close he raised his voice once more and exclaimed enthusiastically:

"And now let what will, come! A brave man from your midst has said to-day: 'We will not yield, so long as an arm is left on our bodies, to raise food to our lips and wield a sword!' If we all think thus, twenty Spanish armies will find their graves before these walls. On Leyden depends the liberty of Holland. If we waver and fall, to escape the misery that only threatens us to-day, but will pitilessly oppress and torture us later, our children will say: 'The men of Leyden were blind cowards; it is their fault, that the name of Hollander is held in no higher esteem, than that of a useless slave.' But if we faithfully hold out and resist the gloomy foreigner to the last man and the last mouthful of bread, they will remember us with tears and joyfully exclaim: 'We owe it to them, that our noble, industrious, happy people is permitted to place itself proudly beside the other nations, and need no longer tolerate the miserable cuckoo in its own nest. Let whoever loves honor, whoever is no degenerate wretch, that betrays his parents' house, whoever would rather be a free man than a slave, ere raising his hand before God to take the oath, exclaim with me: 'Long live our shield, Orange, and a free Holland!'"

"They shall live!" shouted hundreds of powerful voices, five, ten, twenty times. The gunner discharged the cannon planted near the target, drums beat, one flourish of trumpets after another filled the air, the ringing of bells from all the towers of the city echoed over the heads of the enthusiastic crowd, and the cheering continued until the commissioner waved his hand and the swearing fealty began.

'The guilds and the armed defenders of the city pressed forward in bands under the linden. Now impetuously, now with dignified calmness, now with devout exaltation, hands were raised to take the oath, and whoever clasped hands did so with fervent warmth. Two hours elapsed before all had sworn loyalty, and many a group that had passed under the linden together, warmly grasped each other's hands on the grounds in pledge of a second silent vow.

Nicolas Van Wibisma sat silently, with his letter in his lap, beside a target opposite the spot where the oath was taken, but sorrowful, bitter emotions were seething in his breast. How gladly he would have wept aloud and torn his father's letter ! How gladly, when he saw the venerable Herr Van Montfort come hand in hand with the grey-haired Van der Does to be sworn, he would have rushed to their side to take the oath, and call to the earnest man beneath the linden :

" I am no degenerate wretch, who betrays his parents' house ; I desire to be no slave, no Spaniard ; I am a Netherlander, like yourself."

But he did not go, did not speak, he remained sitting motionless till the ceremony was over and Junker von Warmond conducted him under the linden. Van Hout and both the Van der Does had joined the magistrates who had administered the oath. Bowing silently, Nicolas delivered his father's letter to the burgomaster.

Van der Werff broke the seal, and after reading it, handed it to the other gentlemen, then turning to Nicolas, said :

"Wait here, Junker. Your father counsels us to yield the city to the Spaniards, and promises a pardon from the King. You cannot doubt the answer, after what you have heard in this place."

"There is but one," cried Van Hout, in the midst of reading the letter. "Tear the thing up and make no reply."

"Ride home, in God's name," added Janus Dousa. "But wait, I'll give you something more for Valdez."

"Then you will vouchsafe no reply to my father's letter?" asked Nicolas.

"No, Junker. We wish to hold no intercourse with Baron Matanesse," replied the commissioner. "As for you, you can return home or wait here; just as you choose."

"Go to your cousin, Junker," said Janus Dousa kindly; "it will probably be an hour before I can find paper, pen and sealing wax. Fraulein Van Hoogstraten will be glad to hear, through you, from her father."

"If agreeable to you, young sir," added the burgomaster; "my house stands open to you."

Nicolas hesitated a moment, then said quickly:

"Yes, take me to her."

When the youth had reached the north end of the city with Herr von Warmond, who had undertaken to accompany him, he asked the latter:

"Are you Junker Van Duivenvoorde, Herr von Warmond ?"

"I am."

" And you captured Brill, with the Beggars, from the Spaniards ?"

" I had that good fortune."

" And yet, you are of a good old family. And were there not other noblemen with the Beggars also ?"

" Certainly. Do you suppose it ill-beseems us, to have a heart for our ancestors' home ? My forefathers, as well as yours, were noble before a Spaniard ever entered the land."

" But King Philip rules us as the lawful sovereign."

" Unhappily. And therefore we obey his Stadtholder, the Prince, who reigns in his name. The perjured hangman needs a guardian. Ask on; I'll answer willingly."

Nicolas did not heed the request, but walked silently beside his companion until they reached the Achtergracht. There he stood still, seized the captain's arm in great excitement, and said hastily in low, broken sentences :

" It weighs on my heart. I must tell *some one*. I want to be Dutch. I hate the Castilians. I have learned to know them in Leyderdorp and at the Hague. They don't heed me, because I am young, and they are not aware that I understand their language. So my eyes were opened. When they speak of us, it is with contempt and scorn. I know all that has been done by Alva and Vargas. I have heard from the Spaniards' own lips, that they would like to root us out, exterminate us. If I could only do as I pleased, and were it not for my father, I know what I would do. My head is so confused. The burgomaster's speech is driving me out of my wits. Tell him, Junker, I beseech you, tell him I hate the Spaniards and it would be my pride to be a Netherlander."

Both had continued their walk, and as they approached the burgomaster's house, the captain, who had listened to the youth with joyful surprise, said:

"You're cut from good timber, Junker, and on the way to the right goal. Only keep Herr Peter's speech in your mind, and remember what you have learned in history. To whom belong the shining purple pages in the great book of national history? To the tyrants, their slaves and eye-servants, or the men who lived and died for liberty? Hold up your head. This conflict will perhaps outlast both our lives, and you still have a long time to put yourself on the right side. The nobleman must serve his Prince, but he need be no slave of a ruler, least of all a foreigner, an enemy of his nation. Here we are; I'll come for you again in an hour. Give me your hand. I should like to call you by your Christian name in future, my brave Nico."

"Call me so," exclaimed the youth, "and—you'll send no one else? I should like to talk with you again."

The Junker was received in the burgomaster's house by Barbara. Henrica could not see him immediately, Father Damianus was with her, so he was obliged to wait in the dining-room until the priest appeared. Nicolas knew him well, and had even confessed to him once the year before. After greeting the estimable man and answering his inquiry how he had come there, he said frankly and hastily:

"Forgive me, Father, but something weighs upon my heart. You are a holy man, and must know. Is it a crime, if a Hollander fights against the Spaniards, is it a sin, if a Hollander wishes to be and remain what God made him?   I can't believe it."

"Nor do I," replied Damianus in his simple manner. "Whoever clings firmly to our holy church, whoever loves his neighbor and strives to do right, may confidently favor the Dutch, and pray and fight for the freedom of his native land."

"Ah!" exclaimed Nicolas, with sparkling eyes.

"For," continued Damianus more eagerly, "for you see, before the Spaniards came into the country, they were good Catholics here and led devout lives, pleasing in the sight of God. Why should it not be so again? The most High has separated men into nations, because He wills, that they should lead their own lives and shape them for their salvation and His honor; but not to give the stronger nation the right to torture and oppress another. Suppose your father went out to walk and a Spanish grandee should jump on his shoulders and make him taste whip and spur, as if he were a horse. It would be bad for the Castilian. Now substitute Holland for Herr Matanesse, and Spain for the grandee, and you will know what I mean. There is nothing left for us to do, except cast off the oppressor. Our holy church will sustain no loss. God appointed it, and it will stand whether King Philip or another rules. Now you know my opinion. Do I err or not, in thinking that the name of Glipper no longer pleases you, dear Junker?"

"No, Father Damianus!—You are right, a thousand times right. It is no sin, to desire a free Holland."

"Who told you it was one?"

"Canon Bermont and our chaplain."

"Then we are of a different opinion concerning this temporal matter. Give to God the things that are

God's, and remain where the Lord placed you. When your beard grows, if you wish to fight for the liberty of Holland, do so confidently. That is a sin for which I will gladly grant you absolution."

Henrica was greatly delighted to see the fresh, happy-looking youth again. Nicolas was obliged to tell her about her father and his, and inform her how he had come to Leyden. When she heard that he intended to return in an hour, a bright idea entered her mind, which was wholly engrossed by Belotti's mission. She told Nicolas what she meant to do, and begged him to take the steward through the Spanish army to the Hague. The Junker was not only ready to fulfil her request, but promised that, if the old man wanted to return, he would apprize her of it in some way.

At the end of an hour she bade the boy farewell, and when again walking towards the Achtergracht with Herr von Warmond, he asked joyously:

"How shall I get to the Beggars?"

"You?" asked the captain in astonishment.

"Yes, I!" replied the Junker eagerly. "I shall soon be seventeen, and when I am—Wait, just wait—you'll hear of me yet."

"Right, Nicolas, right," replied the other. "Let us be Holland nobles and noble Hollanders."

Three hours later, Junker Matanesse Van Wibisma rode into the Hague with Belotti, whom he had loved from childhood. He brought his father nothing but a carefully-folded and sealed letter, which Janus Dousa, with a mischievous smile, had given him on behalf of the citizens of Leyden for General Valdez, and which contained, daintily inscribed on a large sheet, the following lines from Dionysius Cato:

"*Fistula dulce canit volucrem dum decipit auceps.*"

"Sweet are the notes of the flute, when the fowler lures the bird to his nest."

CHAPTER XXVII.

THE first week in June and half the second had passed, the beautiful sunny days had drawn to a close, and numerous guests sought the "Angulus" in Aquanus's tavern during the evening hours. It was so cosy there when the sea-breeze whistled, the rain poured, and the water fell plashing on the pavements. The Spanish besieging army encompassed the city like an iron wall. Each individual felt that he was a fellow-prisoner of his neighbor, and drew closer to companions of his own rank and opinions. Business was stagnant, idleness and anxiety weighed like lead on the minds of all, and whoever wished to make time pass rapidly and relieve his oppressed soul, went to the tavern to give utterance to his own hopes and fears, and hear what others were thinking and feeling in the common distress.

All the tables in the Angulus were occupied, and whoever wanted to be understood by a distant neighbor was forced to raise his voice very loud, for special conversations were being carried on at every table. Here, there, and everywhere, people were shouting to the busy bar-maid, glasses clinked together, and pewter lids fell on the tops of hard stone-ware jugs.

The talk at a round table in the end of the long room was louder than anywhere else. Six officers had seated themselves at it, among them Georg von Dorn-

burg. Captain Van der Laen, his superior officer, whose
past career had been a truly heroic one, was loudly relating in his deep voice, strange and amusing tales of
his travels by sea and land, Colonel Mulder often interrupted him, and at every somewhat incredible story,
smilingly told a similar, but perfectly impossible adven-
ture of his own. Captain Van Duivenvoorde soothingly
interposed, when Van der Laen, who was conscious of
never deviating far from the truth, angrily repelled the
old man's jesting insinuations. Captain Cromwell, a
grave man with a round head and smooth long hair,
who had come to Holland to fight for the faith, rarely
mingled in the conversation, and then only with a few
words of scarcely intelligible Dutch. Georg, leaning
far back in his chair, stretched his feet out before him
and stared silently into vacancy.

Herr Aquanus, the host, walked from one table to
another, and when he at last reached the one where
the officers sat, paused opposite to the Thuringian,
saying:

"Where are your thoughts, Junker? One would
scarcely know you during the last few days. What
has come over you?"

Georg hastily sat erect, stretched himself like a
person roused from sleep, and answered pleasantly:

"Dreams come in idleness."

"The cage is getting too narrow for him," said Captain Van der Laen. "If this state of things lasts long,
we shall all get dizzy like the sheep."

"And as stiff as the brazen Pagan god on the shelf
yonder," added Colonel Mulder.

"There was the same complaint during the first
siege," replied the host, "but Herr von Noyelles drowned

his discontent and emptied many a cask of my best liquor."

"Tell the gentlemen how he paid you," cried Colonel Mulder.

"There hangs the paper framed," laughed Aquanus. " Instead of sending money, he wrote this:

> ' Full many a favor, dear friend, hast thou done me,
>   For which good hard coin glad wouldst thou be to see
>   There's none in my pockets ; so for the debt
>   In place of dirty coin,
>   This written sheet so fine ;
>   Paper money in Leyden is easy to get.' "

"Excellent!" cried Junker von Warmond, "and besides you made the die for the pasteboard coins yourself."

"Of course! Herr von Noyelles' sitting still, cost me dear. You have already made two expeditions."

"Hush, hush, for God's sake say nothing about the first sally!" cried the captain. "A well-planned enterprise, which was shamefully frustrated, because the leader lay down like a mole to sleep! Where has such a thing happened a second time ?"

"But the other ended more fortunately," said the host. "Three hundred hams, one hundred casks of beer, butter, ammunition, and the most worthless of all spies into the bargain ; always an excellent prize."

"And yet a failure !" cried Captain Van der Laen, " We ought to have captured and brought in all the provision ships on the Leyden Lake! And the Kaag! To think that this fort on the island should be in the hands of the enemy."

"But the people have held out bravely," said von Warmond.

" There are real devils among them," replied Van der Laen, laughing. "One struck a Spaniard down and, in the midst of the battle, took off his red breeches and pulled them on his own legs."

" I know the man," added the landlord, " his name is Van Keulen; there he sits yonder over his beer, telling the people all sorts of queer stories. A fellow with a face like a satyr. We have no lack of comfort yet! Remember Chevraux' defeat, and the Beggars' victory at Vlissingen on the Scheldt."

"To brave Admiral Boisot and the gallant Beggar troops!" cried Captain Van der Laen, touching glasses with Colonel Mulder. The latter turned with upraised beaker towards the Thuringian and, as the Junker who had relapsed into his reverie, did not notice the movement, irritably exclaimed:

" Well, Herr Dornburg, you require a long time to pledge a man."

Georg started and answered hastily:

"Pledge? Oh! yes. Pledge. I pledge you, Colonel!" With these words he raised the goblet, drained it at a single draught, made the nail test and replaced it on the table.

"Well done!" cried the old man; and Herr Aquanus said:

" He learned that at the University; studying makes people thirsty."

As he uttered the words, he cast a friendly glance of anxiety at the young German, and then looked towards the door, through which Wilhelm had just entered the Angulus. The landlord went to meet him and whispered:

" I don't like the German nobleman's appearance.

The singing lark has become a mousing night-bird. What ails him ?"

" Home-sickness, no news from his family, and the snare into which the war has drawn him in his pursuit of glory and honor. He'll soon be his old self again."

. " I hope so," replied the host. " Such a succulent little tree will quickly rebound, when it is pressed to the earth; help the fine young fellow."

A guest summoned the landlord, but the musician joined the officers and began a low conversation with Georg, which was drowned by the confused mingling of loud voices.

Wilhelm came from the Van der Werff house, where he had learned that the next day but one, June fourteenth, would be the burgomaster's birthday. Adrian had told Henrica, and the latter informed him. The master of the house was to be surprised with a song on the morning of his birthday festival.

" Excellent," said Georg, interrupting his friend, " she will manage the matter admirably."

" Not she alone; we can depend upon Frau Van der Werff too. At first she wanted to decline, but when I proposed a pretty madrigal, yielded and took the soprano."

" The soprano ?" asked the Junker excitedly. " Of course I'm at your service. Let us go; have you the notes at home ?"

" No, Herr von Dornburg, I have just taken them to the ladies; but early to-morrow morning—"

" There will be a rehearsal early to-morrow morning ! The jug is for me, Jungfer Dortchen ! Your health, Colonel Mulder ! Captain Duivenvoorde, I drain this goblet to your new standard and hope to have many a jolly ride by your side."

The German's eyes again sparkled with an eager light, and when Captain Van der Laen, continuing his conversation, cried enthusiastically: "The Beggars of the Sea will yet sink the Spanish power. The sea, gentlemen. the sea! To base one's cause on nothing, is the best way! To exult, leap and grapple in the storm! To fight and struggle man to man and breast to breast on the deck of the enemy's ship! To fight and conquer, or perish with the foe!"

"To your health, Junker!" exclaimed the colonel. "Zounds, we need such youths!"

"Now you are your old self again," said Wilhelm, turning to his friend. "Touch glasses to your dear ones at home."

"Two glasses for one," cried Georg. "To the dear ones at home—to the joys and sorrows of the heart, to the fair woman we love! War is rapture, love is life! Let the wounds bleed, let the heart break into a thousand pieces. Laurels grow green on the battle-field, love twines garlands of roses—roses with thorns, yet beautiful roses! Go, beaker! No other lips shall drink from you."

Georg's cheeks glowed as he flung the glass goblet into a corner of the room, where it shattered into fragments. His comrades at the table cheered loudly, but Captain Cromwell rose quietly to leave the room, and the landlord shook his wise head doubtfully.

It seemed as if fire had poured into Georg's soul and his spirit had gained wings. The thick waving locks curled in dishevelled masses around his handsome head, as leaning far back in his chair with unfastened collar, he mingled clever sallies and brilliant similes with the quiet conversation of the others. Wilhelm listened to his words sometimes with admiration, sometimes with anxiety. It was long past midnight, when the musician left the tavern with his friend. Colonel Mulder looked after him and exclaimed to those left behind:

"The fellow is possessed with a devil."

The next morning the madrigal was practised at the burgomaster's house, while its master was presiding over a meeting at the town-hall. Georg stood between Henrica and Maria. So long as the musician found it necessary to correct errors and order repetitions, a cheerful mood pervaded the little choir, and Barbara, in the adjoining room, often heard the sound of innocent laughter; but when each had mastered his or her part and the madrigal was faultlessly executed, the ladies grew more and more grave. Maria gazed fixedly at the sheet of music, and rarely had her voice sounded so faultlessly pure, so full of feeling. Georg adapted his singing to hers and his eyes, whenever they were raised from the notes, rested on her face. Henrica sought to meet the Junker's glance, but always in vain, yet she wished to divert his attention from the young wife, and it tortured her to remain unnoticed. Some impulse urged her to surpass Maria, and the whole passionate wealth of her nature rang out in her singing. Her fervor swept the others along. Maria's treble rose exultantly above the German's musical voice, and Henrica's tones blended angrily yet triumphantly in the strain. The delighted and inspired musician beat the time and, borne away by the liquid melody of Henrica's voice, revelled in sweet recollections of her sister.

When the serenade was finished, he eagerly cried:

"Again!" The rivalry between the singers commenced with fresh vigor, and this time the Junker's beaming gaze met the young wife's eyes. She hastily lowered the notes, stepped out of the semicircle, and said:

"We know the madrigal. Early to-morrow morning, Meister Wilhelm; my time is limited."

"Oh, oh!" cried the musician regretfully. "It was going on so splendidly, and there were only a few bars more." But Maria was already standing at the door and made no reply, except:

"To-morrow."

The musician enthusiastically thanked Henrica for her singing; Georg courteously expressed his gratitude. When both had taken leave, Henrica paced rapidly to and fro, passionately striking her clenched fist in the palm of her other hand.

The singers were ready early on the birthday morning, but Peter had risen before sunrise, for there was a proposition to be arranged with the city clerk, which must be completed before the meeting of the council. Nothing was farther from his thoughts than his birthday, and when the singers in the dining-room commenced their madrigal, he rapped on the door, exclaiming:

"We are busy; find another place for your singing."

The melody was interrupted for a moment, and Barbara said:

"People picking apples don't think of fishing-nets. He has no idea it is his birthday. Let the children go in first."

Maria now entered the study with Adrian and Bessie. They carried bouquets in their hands, and the young wife had dressed the little girl so prettily that, in her white frock, she really looked like a dainty fairy.

Peter now knew the meaning of the singing, warmly embraced the three well-wishers, and when the madrigal began again, stood opposite to the performers to listen. True, the execution was not nearly so good as at the rehearsal, for Maria sang in a low and somewhat muffled voice, while, spite of Wilhelm's vehement beating of time, the warmth and verve of the day before would not return.

"Admirable, admirable," cried Peter, when the singers ceased. "Well planned and executed, a beautiful birthday surprise." Then he shook hands with each, saying a few cordial words and, as he grasped the Junker's right hand, remarked warmly: "You have dropped down on us from the skies during these bad days, just at the right time. It is always something to have a home in a foreign land, and you have found one with us."

Georg had bent his eyes on the floor, but at the last words raised them and met the burgomaster's. How honestly, how kindly and frankly they looked at him! Deep emotion overpowered him, and without knowing what he was doing, he laid his hands on Peter's arms and hid his face on his shoulder.

Van der Werff suffered him to do so, stroked the youth's hair, and said smiling:

"Like Leonhard, wife, just like our Leonhard. We will dine together to-day. You, too, Van Hout; and don't forget your wife."

Maria assigned the seats at the table, so that she was not obliged to look at Georg. His place was beside Frau Van Hout and opposite Henrica and the musician. At first he was silent and embarrassed, but Henrica gave him no rest, and when he had once begun to answer her questions he was soon carried away by her glowing vivacity, and gave free, joyous play to his wit. Henrica did not remain in his debt, her eyes sparkled, and in the increasing pleasure of trying the power of her intellect against his, she sought to surpass every jest and repartée made by the Junker. She drank no wine, but was intoxicated by her own flow of language and so completely engrossed Georg's attention, that he found no time to address a word to the other guests. If he attempted to do so, she quickly interrupted him and compelled him to turn to her again. This constraint annoyed the young man; while struggling against it his spirit of wantonness awoke, and he began to irritate Henrica into making unprecedented assertions, which he opposed with equally unwarrantable ones of his own.

Maria sometimes listened to the young lady in surprise, and there was something in Georg's manner that vexed her. Peter took little notice of Henrica; he was talking with Van Hout about the letters from the Glippers asking a surrender, three of which had already been brought into the city, of the uncertain disposition of some members of the council and the execution of the captured spy.

Wilhelm, who had scarcely vouchsafed his neighbor an answer, was now following the conversation of the older men and remarked, that he had known the traitor. He was a tavern-keeper, in whose inn he had once met Herr Matanesse Van Wibisma.

"There we have it," said Van Hout. "A note was found in Quatgelat's pouch, and the writing bore a mysterious resemblance to the baron's hand. Quatgelat was to enquire about the quantity of provisions in Leyden."

"All alike!" exclaimed the burgomaster. "Unhappily he could have brought tidings only too welcome to Valdez. Little that is cheering has resulted from the investigation; though the exact amount has not yet been ascertained."

"We must place it during the next few days in charge of the ladies."

"Give it to the women?" asked Peter in astonishment.

"Yes, to us!" cried Van Hout's wife. "Why should we sit idle, when we might be of use."

"Give us the work!" exclaimed Maria. "We are as eager as you, to render the great cause some service."

"And believe me," added Frau Van Hout, "we shall find admittance to store-rooms and cellars much more quickly than constables and guards, whom the housewives fear."

"Women in the service of the city," said Peter thoughtfully. "To be honest—but your proposal shall be considered.—The young lady is in good spirits to-day."

Maria glanced indignantly at Henrica, who had leaned far across the table. She was showing Georg a ring, and laughingly exclaimed:

"Don't you wish to know what the device means? Look, a serpent biting its own tail."

"Aha!" replied the Junker, "the symbol of self-torment."

"Good, good! But it has another meaning, which you would do well to notice, Sir Knight. Do you know the signification of eternity and eternal faith?"

"No, Fraulein, I wasn't taught to think so deeply at Jena."

"Of course. Your teachers were men. Men and faith, eternal faith!"

"Was Delilah, who betrayed Samson to the Philistines, a man or a woman?" asked Van Hout.

"She was a woman. The exception, that proves the rule. Isn't that so, Maria?"

The burgomaster's wife made no reply except a silent nod; then indignantly pushed back her chair, and the meal was over.

CHAPTER XXVIII.

Days and weeks had passed, July was followed by a sultry August, and that, too, was drawing to a close. The Spaniards still surrounded Leyden, and the city now completely resembled a prison. The soldiers and armed citizens did their duty wearily and sullenly, there was business enough at the town-hall, but the magistrates' work was sad and disagreeable; for no message of hope came from the Prince or the Estates, and everything to be considered referred to the increasing distress and the terrible follower of war, the plague, which had made its entry into Leyden with the famine. Moreover the number of malcontents weekly increased. The friends of the old order of affairs now raised their voices more and more loudly, and many a friend of liberty, who saw his family sickening, joined the Spanish sympathizers and demanded the surrender of the city. The children went to school and met in the playgrounds as before, but there was rarely a flash of the merry pertness of former days, and what had become of the boys' red cheeks and the round arms of the little girls ? The poor drew their belts tighter, and the morsel of bread, distributed by the city to each individual, was no longer enough to quiet hunger and support life.

Junker Georg had long been living in Burgomaster Van der Werff's house.

On the morning of August 29th he returned home from an expedition, carrying a cross-bow in his hand, while a pouch hung over his shoulder. This time he did not go up-stairs, but sought Barbara in the kitchen. The widow received him with a friendly nod; her grey eyes sparkled as brightly as ever, but her round face had grown narrower and there was a sorrowful quiver about the sunken mouth.

"What do you bring to-day?" she asked the Junker.

Georg thrust his hand into his game-bag and answered, smiling: "A fat snipe and four larks; you know."

"Poor sparrows! But what sort of a creature can this be? Headless, legless, and carefully plucked! Junker, Junker, that's suspicious."

"It will do for the pan, and the name is of no consequence."

"Yet, yet; true, nobody knows on what he fattens, but the Lord didn't create every animal for the human stomach."

"That's just what I said. It's a short-billed snipe, a corvus, a real corvus."

"Corvus! Nonsense, I'm afraid of the thing—the little feathers under the wings. Good heavens! surely it isn't a raven?"

"It's a corvus, as I said. Put the bird in vinegar,

roast it with seasoning and it will taste like a real snipe. Wild ducks are not to be found every day, as they were a short time ago, and sparrows are getting as scarce as roses in winter. Every boy is standing about with a cross-bow, and in the court-yards people are trying to catch them under sieves and with lime-twigs. They are going to be exterminated, but one or another is still spared. How is the little elf?"

"Don't call her that!" exclaimed the widow. "Give her her Christian name. She looks like this cloth, and since yesterday has refused to take the milk we daily procure for her at a heavy cost. Heaven knows what the end will be. Look at that cabbage-stalk. Half a stiver! and that miserable piece of bone! Once I should have thought it too poor for the dogs—and now! The whole household must be satisfied with it. For supper I shall boil ham-rind with wine and add a little porridge to it. And this for a giant like Peter! God only knows where he gets his strength; but he looks like his own shadow. Maria doesn't need anything more than a bird, but Adrian, poor fellow, often leaves the table with tears in his eyes, yet I know he has broken many a bit of bread from his thin slice for Bessie. It is pitiable. Yet the proverb says: 'Stretch yourself towards the ceiling, or your feet will freeze—' 'Necessity knows no law,' and 'Reserve to preserve.' Day before yesterday, like the rest, we again gave of the little we still possessed. To-morrow, everything beyond what is needed for the next fortnight, must be delivered up, and Peter won't allow us to keep even a bag of flour, but what will come then—merciful Heaven!—"

The widow sobbed aloud as she uttered the last words and continued, weeping: "Where do you get your strength ? At your age this miserable scrap of meat is a mere drop of water on a red-hot stone."

" Herr Van Aken gives me what he can, in addition to my ration. I shall get through ; but I witnessed a terrible sight to-day at the tailor's, who mends my clothes."

" Well ?"

" Two of his children have starved to death."

" And the weaver's family opposite," added Barbara, weeping. " Such nice people! The young wife was confined four days ago, and this morning mother and child expired of weakness, expired, I tell you, like a lamp that has consumed its oil and must go out. At the cloth-maker Peterssohn's, the father and all five children have died of the plague. If that isn't pitiful!"

" Stop, stop!" said Georg, shuddering. " I must go to the court-yard to drill."

" What's the use of that! The Spaniards don't attack; they leave the work to the skeleton death. Your fencing gives an appetite, and the poor hollow herrings can scarcely stir their own limbs."

" Wrong, Frau Barbara, wrong," replied the young man. " The exercise and motion sustains them. Herr von Nordwyk knew what he was doing, when he asked me to drill them in the dead fencing-master's place."

" You're thinking of the ploughshare that doesn't rust. Perhaps you are right; but before you go to work, take a sip of this. Our wine is still the best. When people have something to do, at least they don't mutiny, like those poor fellows among the volunteers day before yesterday. Thank God, they are gone !"

While the widow was filling a glass, Wilhelm's mother came into the kitchen and greeted Barbara and the young nobleman. She carried under her shawl a small package clasped tightly to her bosom. Her breadth was still considerable, but the flesh, with which she had moved about so briskly a few months ago, now seemed to have become an oppressive burden.

She took the little bundle in her right hand, saying:

"I have something for your Bessie. My Wilhelm, good fellow—"

Here she paused and restored her gift to its old place. She had seen the Junker's plucked present, and continued in an altered tone: "So you already have a pigeon—so much the better! The city clerk's little girl is beginning to droop too. I'll see you to-morrow, if God wills."

She was about to go, but Georg stopped her, saying: "You are mistaken, my good lady. I shot that bird to-day, I'll confess now, Frau Barbara; my corvus is a wretched crow."

"I thought so," cried the widow. "Such an abomination!"

Yet she thrust her finger into the bird's breast, saying: "But there's meat on the creature."

"A crow!" cried Wilhelm's mother, clasping her hands. "True, dogs and cats are already hanging on many a spit and have wandered into many a pan. There is the pigeon."

Barbara unwrapped the bird as carefully, as if it might crumble under her fingers, gazing tenderly at it as she weighed it carefully in her hand; but the musician's mother said:

"It's the fourth one Wilhelm has killed, and he said it would have been a good flier. He intended it specially for your Bessie. Stuff it nicely with yellow paste, not too solid and a little sweetened. That is what children like, and it will agree with her, for it is cheerfully given. Put the little thing away. When we have known any creature, we feel sorry to see it dead."

"May God reward you!" cried Barbara, pressing the kind old hand. "Oh! these terrible times!"

"Yet there is still something to be thankful for."

"Of course, for it will be even worse in hell," replied the widow.

"Don't fall into sin," said the aged matron: "You have only *one* sick person in the house. Can I see Frau Maria?"

"She is in the workshops, taking the people a little meat from our store. Are you too so short of flour? Cows are still to be seen in the pastures, but the grain seems to have been actually swept away; there wasn't a peck in the market. Will you take a sip of wine too? Shall I call my sister-in-law?"

"I will seek her myself. The usury in the market is no longer to be endured We can do nothing more there, but she is already bringing people to reason."

"The traders in the market?" asked Georg.

"Yes, Herr von Dornburg, yes. One wouldn't believe how much that delicate woman can accomplish. Day before yesterday, when we went about to learn how large a stock of provisions every house contains, people treated me and the others very rudely, many even turned us out of doors. But she went to the roughest, and the cellars and store-rooms opened before her, as the waves of the sea divided before the people of Israel. How she does it, Heaven knows, but the people can't refuse her."

Georg drew a long breath and left the kitchen. In the court-yard he found several city soldiers, volunteers and militia-men, with whom he went through exercises in fencing. Van der Werff placed it at his disposal for this purpose, and there certainly was no man in Leyden more capable than the German of supplying worthy Allertssohn's place.

Barbara was not wrong. His pupils looked emaciated and miserable enough, but many of them had learned, in the dead man's school, to wield the sword well, and were heartily devoted to the profession.

In the centre of the court-yard stood a human figure, stuffed with tow and covered with leather, which bore on the left breast a bit of red paper in the shape of a heart. The more unskilful were obliged to thrust at this figure to train the hand and eye; the others stood face to face in pairs and fought under Georg's direction with blunt foils.

The Junker had felt very weak when he entered the kitchen, for the larger half of his ration of bread had been left at the unfortunate tailor's; but Barbara's wine had revived him and, rousing himself, he stepped briskly forth to meet his fencers. His doublet was quickly flung on a bench, his belt drawn tighter, and he soon stood in his white shirt-sleeves before the soldiers.

As soon as his first word of command was heard, Henrica's window closed with a bang. Formerly it had often been opened when the fencing drill began, and she had not even shrunk from occasionally clapping her hands and calling " bravo." This time had long since passed, it was weeks since she had bestowed a word or glance on the young noble. She had never made such advances to any man, would not have striven so hard to win a prince's favor! And he? At first he had been distant, then more and more assiduously avoided her. Her pride was deeply wounded. Her purpose of diverting his attention from Maria had long been forgotten, and moreover something—she knew not what—had come between her and the young wife. Not a day elapsed in which he did not meet her, and this was a source of pleasure to Henrica, because she could show him that his presence was a matter of indifference, nay even unpleasant. Her imprisonment greatly depressed her, and she longed unutterably for the open country, the fields and the forest. Yet she never expressed a wish to leave the city, for—Georg was in Leyden, and every waking and dreaming thought was associated with him. She loved him to-day, loathed him to-morrow, and did both with all the ardor of her passionate heart. She often thought of her sister too, and uttered many prayers for her. To win the favor of Heaven by good works and escape *ennui*, she helped the Grey Sisters, who lived in a little old convent next to Herr Van der Werff's house, nurse the sick whom they had lovingly received, and even went with Sister Gonzaga to the houses of the Catholic citizens, to collect alms for the little hospital. But all this was done without joyous self-devotion, sometimes with extravagant zeal, sometimes lazily, and for days not at all. She had become excessively irritable, but after being unbearably arrogant one day, would seem sorrowful and ill at ease the next, though without asking the offended person's pardon.

The young girl now stood behind the closed window, watching Georg, who with a bold spring dashed at the leathern figure and ran the sword in his right hand through the phantom's red heart.

The soldiers loudly expressed their admiration.

Henrica's eyes also sparkled approvingly, but suddenly they lost their light, and she stepped farther back into the room, for Maria came out of the workshops in the court-yard and, with her gaze fixed on the ground, walked past the fencers.

The young wife had grown paler, but her clear blue eyes had gained a more confident, resolute expression. She had learned to go her own way, and sought and found arduous duties in the service of the city and the poor. She had remained conqueror in many a severe conflict of the heart, but the struggle was not yet over; she felt this whenever Georg's path crossed hers. As far as possible she avoided him, for she did not conceal from herself, that the attempt to live with him on the footing of a friend and brother, would mean nothing but the first step on the road to ruin for him and herself. That he was honestly aiding her by a strong effort at self-control, she gratefully felt, for she stood heart to heart with her husband on the ship of life. She wished no other guide; nay the thought of going to destruction with Peter had no terror to her. And yet, yet! Georg was like the magnetic mountain, that attracted her, and which she must avoid to save the vessel from sinking.

To-day she had been asking the different workmen how they fared, and witnessed scenes of the deepest misery.

The brave men knew that the surrender of the city might put an end to their distress, but wished to hold out for the sake of liberty and their religion, and endured their suffering as an inevitable misfortune.

In the entry of the house Maria met Wilhelm's mother, and promised her she would consult with Frau Van Hout that very day, concerning the extortion practised by the market-men. Then she went to poor Bessie, who sat, pale and weak, in a little chair. Her prettiest doll had been lying an hour in the same position on her lap. The child's little hands and will were too feeble to move the toy. Trautchen brought in a cup of new milk. The citizens were not yet wholly destitute of this, for a goodly number of cows still grazed outside the city walls under the protection of the cannon, but the child refused to drink and could only be induced, amid tears, to swallow a few drops.

While Maria was affectionately coaxing the little one, Peter entered the room. The tall man, the very model of a stately burgher, who paid careful heed to his outward appearance, now looked careless of his person. His brown hair hung over his forehead, his thick, closely-trimmed moustache straggled in thin lines over his cheeks, his doublet had grown too large, and his stockings did not fit snugly as usual, but hung in wrinkles on his powerful legs.

Greeting his wife with a careless wave of the hand, he approached the child and gazed silently at it a long time with tender affection. Bessie turned her pretty little face towards him and tried to welcome him, but the smile died on her lips, and she again gazed listlessly at her doll. Peter stooped, raised her in his arms, called her by name and pressed his lips to her pale cheeks. The child gently stroked his beard and then said feebly:

" Put me down, dear father, I feel dizzy up here."

The burgomaster, with tears in his eyes, put his darling carefully back in her little chair, then left the room and went to his study. Maria followed him and asked: " Is there no message yet from the Prince or the estates ?"

He silently shrugged his shoulders.

"But they will not, dare not forget us?" cried the young wife eagerly.

"We are perishing and they leave us to die," he answered in a hollow tone.

"No, no, they have pierced the dykes; I know they will help us."

"When it is too late. One thing follows another, misfortune is heaped on misfortune, and on whom do the curses of the starving people fall? On me, me, me alone."

"You are acting with the Prince's commissioner."

Peter smiled bitterly, saying: "He took to his bed yesterday. Bontius says it is the plague. I, I alone bear everything."

"We bear it with you," cried Maria. "First poverty, then hunger, as we promised."

"Better than that. The last grain was baked to-day. The bread is exhausted."

"We still have oxen and horses."

"We shall come to them day after to-morrow. It was determined: Two pounds with the bones to every four persons. Bread gone, cows gone, milk gone. And what will happen then? Mothers, infants, sick people! And our Bessie!"

The burgomaster pressed his hands on his temples and groaned aloud. But Maria said: "Courage, Peter, courage. Hold fast to one thing, don't let one thing go —hope."

"Hope, hope," he answered scornfully.

"To hope no longer," cried Maria, "means to despair. To despair means in our case to open the gates, to open the gates means—"

"Who is thinking of opening the gates? Who talks of surrender?" he vehemently interrupted. "We will still hold firm, still, still— There is the portfolio, take it to the messenger."

CHAPTER XXIX.

BESSIE had eaten a piece of roast pigeon, the first morsel for several days, and there was as much rejoicing over it in the Van der Werff household, as if some great piece of good fortune had befallen the family. Adrian ran to the workshops and told the men, Peter went to the town-hall with a more upright bearing, and Maria, who was obliged to go out, undertook to tell Wilhelm's mother of the good results produced by her son's gift.

Tears ran down the old lady's flabby cheeks at the story and, kissing the burgomaster's wife, she exclaimed:

"Yes, Wilhelm, Wilhelm! If he were only at home now. But I'll call his father. Dear me, he is probably at the town-hall too. Hark, Frau Maria, hark—what's that?"

The ringing of bells and firing of cannon had interrupted her words; she hastily threw open the window, crying:

"From the Tower of Pancratius! No alarm-bell, firing and merry-ringing. Some joyful tidings have come. We need them! Ulrich, Ulrich! Come back at once and bring us the news. Dear Father in Heaven! Merciful God! Send the relief. If it were only that!"

The two women waited in great suspense. At last

Wilhelm's brother Ulrich returned, saying that the messengers sent to Delft had succeeded in passing the enemy's ranks and brought with them a letter from the estates, which the city-clerk had read from the window of the town-hall. The representatives of the country praised the conduct and endurance of the citizens, and informed them that, in spite of the damage done to thousands of people, the dykes would be cut.

In fact, the water was already pouring over the land, and the messengers had seen the vessels appointed to bring relief. The country surrounding Leyden must soon be inundated, and the rising flood would force the Spanish army to retreat, "Better a drowned land than a lost land," was a saying that had been decisive in the execution of the violent measure proposed, and those who had risked so much might be expected to shrink from no sacrifice to save Leyden.

The two women joyously shook hands with each other; the bells continued to ring merrily, and report after report of cannon made the window-panes rattle.

As twilight approached, Maria turned her steps towards home. It was long since her heart had been so light. The black tablets on the houses containing cases of plague did not look so sorrowful to-day, the emaciated faces seemed less pitiful than usual, for to them also help was approaching. The faithful endurance was to be rewarded, the cause of freedom would conquer.

She entered the "broad street" with winged steps. Thousands of citizens had flocked into it to see, hear, and learn what might be hoped, or what still gave cause for fear. Musicians had been stationed at the corners to play lively airs; the Beggars' song mingled with the pipes and trumpets and the cheers of enthusiastic men. But there were also throngs of well-dressed citizens and women, who loudly and fearlessly mocked at the gay music and exulting simpletons, who allowed themselves to be cajoled by empty promises. Where was the relief? What could the handful of Beggars—which at the utmost were all the troops the Prince could bring— do against King Philip's terrible military power, that surrounded Leyden? And the inundation of the country? The ground on which the city stood was too high for the water ever to reach it. The peasants had been injured, without benefiting the citizens. There was only one means of escape—to trust to the King's mercy.

"What is liberty to us?" shouted a brewer, who, like all his companions in business, had long since been deprived of his grain and forbidden to manufacture any fresh beer. "What will liberty be to us, when we're cold in death? Let whoever means well go the town-hall, and demand a surrender before it is too late."

"Surrender! The mercy of the King!" shouted the citizens.

"Life comes first, and then the question whether it shall be free or under Spanish rule, Calvanistical or Popish!" screamed a master-weaver. "I'll march to the town-hall with you."

"You are right, good people," said Burgomaster Baersdorp, who, clad in his costly fur-bordered cloak, was coming from the town-hall and had heard the last speaker's words. "But let me set you right. To-day the credulous are beginning to hope again, and the time for pressing your just desire is ill-chosen. Wait a few days and then, if the relief does not appear, urge your views. I'll speak for you, and with me many a good man in the magistracy. We have nothing to expect from Valdez, but gentleness and kindness. To rise against the King was from the first a wicked deed—to fight against famine, the plague and death is sin and madness. May God be with you, men!"

"The burgomaster is sensible," cried a cloth-dyer.

"Van Swieten and Norden think as he does, but Meister Peter rules through the Prince's favor. If the Spaniards rescue us, his neck will be in danger, when they make their entrance into the city. So no matter who dies; he and his are living on the fat of the land and have plenty."

"There goes his wife," said a master-weaver, pointing to Maria. "How happy she looks! The leather business must be doing well. Holloa—Frau Van der Werff! Holloa! Remember me to your husband and tell him, his life may be valuable; but ours are not wisps of straw."

"Tell him, too," cried a cattle-dealer, who did not yet seem to have been specially injured by the general distress, "tell him oxen can be slaughtered, the more the better; but Leyden citizens—"

The cattle-dealer did not finish his sentence, for Herr Aquanus had seen from the Angulus what was happening to the burgomaster's wife, came out of the tavern into the street, and stepped into the midst of the malcontents.

"For shame!" he cried. "To assail a respectable lady in the street! Are these Leyden manners? Give me your hand, Frau Maria, and if I hear a single reviling word, I'll call the constables. I know you. The gallows Herr Van Bronkhorst had erected for men like you, is still standing by the Blue Stone. Which of you wants to inaugurate them ?"

The men, to whom these words were addressed, were not the bravest of mortals, and not a syllable was heard, as Aquanus led the young wife into the tavern. The landlord's wife and daughter received her in their own rooms, which were separated from those occupied by guests of the inn, and begged her to make herself comfortable there until the crowd had dispersed. But Maria longed to reach home, and when she said she must go, Aquanus offered his company.

Georg von Dornburg was standing in the entry and stepped back with a respectful bow, but the innkeeper called to him, saying:

" There is much to be done to-day, for many a man will doubtless indulge himself in a glass of liquor after the good news. No offence, Frau Van der Werff, but the Junker will escort you home as safely as I—and you, Herr von Dornburg—"

" I am at your service," replied Georg, and went out into the street with the young wife.

For a time both walked side by side in silence, each fancying he or she could hear the beating of the other's heart. At last Georg, drawing a long breath, said:

" Three long, long months have passed since my arrival here. Have I been brave, Maria ?"

" Yes, Georg."

" But you cannot imagine what it has cost me to fetter this poor heart, stifle my words, and blind my eyes. Maria, it must once be said—"

"Never, never," she interrupted in a tone of earnest entreaty. " I know that you have struggled honestly, do not rob yourself of the victory now."

"Oh! hear me, Maria, this once hear me."

"What will it avail, if you oppress my soul with ardent words? I must not hear from any man that he loves me, and what I must not hear, you must not speak."

"Must not?" he asked in a tone of gentle reproach, then in a gloomy, bitter mood, continued: "You are right, perfectly right. Even speech is denied me. So life may run on like a leaden stream, and everything that grows and blossoms on its banks remain scentless and grey. The golden sunshine has hidden itself behind a mist, joy lies fainting in my heart, and all that once pleased me has grown stale and charmless. Do you recognize the happy youth of former days?"

"Seek cheerfulness again, seek it for my sake."

"Gone, gone," he murmured sadly. "You saw me in Delft, but you did not know me thoroughly. These eyes were like two mirrors of fortune in which every object was charmingly transfigured, and they were rewarded; for wherever they looked they met only friendly glances. This heart then embraced the whole world, and beat so quickly and joyously! I often did not know what to do with myself from sheer mirth and vivacity, and it seemed as if I must burst into a thousand pieces like an over-loaded firelock, only instead of scattering far and wide, mount straight up to Heaven. Those days were so happy, and yet so sad—I felt it ten times as much in Delft, when you were kind to me. And now, now? I still have wings, I still might fly, but here I creep like a snail—because it is your will."

"It is not my wish," replied Maria. "You are dear to me, that I may be permitted to confess—and to see you thus fills me with grief. But now—if I am dear to you, and I know you care for me—cease to torture me so cruelly. You are dear to me. I have said it, and it must be spoken, that everything may be clearly understood between us. You are dear to me, like the beautiful by-gone days of my youth, like pleasant dreams, like a noble song, in which we take delight, and which refreshes our souls, whenever we hear or remember it—but more you are not, more you can never be. You are dear to me, and I wish you to remain so, but that you can only do by not breaking the oath you have sworn."

"Sworn ?" asked Georg. "Sworn ?"

"Yes, sworn," interrupted Maria, checking her steps. "On Peter's breast, on the morning of his birthday— after the singing. You remember it well. At the time you took a solemn vow; I know it, know it no less surely, than that I myself swore faith to my husband at the altar. If you can give me the lie, do so."

Georg shook his head, and answered with increasing warmth :

"You read my soul. Our hearts know each other like two faithful friends, as the earth knows her moon, the moon her earth. What is one without the other ? Why must they be separated ? Did you ever walk along a forest path ? The tracks of two wheels run side by side and never touch. The axle holds them asunder, as our oath parts us."

"Say rather—our honor."

"As our honor parts us. But often in the woods we find a place where the road ends in a field or hill, and there the tracks cross and intersect each other, and in this hour I feel that my path has come to an end. I can go no farther, I cannot, or the horses will plunge into the thicket and the vehicle be shattered on the roots and stones."

"And honor with it. Not a word more. Let us walk faster. See the lights in the windows. Everyone wants to show that he rejoices in the good news. Our house mustn't remain dark either."

"Don't hurry so. Barbara will attend to it, and how soon we must part! Yet you said that I was dear to you."

"Don't torture me," cried the young wife, with pathetic entreaty.

"I will not torture you, Maria, but you must hear me. I was in earnest, terrible earnest in the mute vow I swore, and have sought to release myself from it by death. You have heard how I rushed like a madman among the Spaniards, at the storming of the Boschhuizen fortification in July. Your bow, the blue bow from Delft, the knot of ribbons the color of the sky, fluttered on my left shoulder as I dashed upon swords and lances. I was not to die, and came out of the confusion uninjured. Oh! Maria, for the sake of this oath I have suffered unequalled torments. Release me from it, Maria, let me once, only once, freely confess—"

"Stop, Georg, stop," pleaded the young wife. "I will not, must not hear you—neither to-day, nor to-morrow, never, never, to all eternity!"

"Once, only once, I will, I must say to you, that I love you, that life and happiness, peace and honor—"

"Not one word more, Junker von Dornburg. There is our house. You are our guest, and if you address a single word like the last ones to your friend's wife—"

"Maria, Maria — oh, don't touch the knocker.

How can you so unfeelingly destroy the whole happiness of a human being—"

The door had opened, and the burgomaster's wife crossed the threshold. Georg stood opposite to her, held out his hand as if beseeching aid, and murmured in a hollow tone:

"Cast forth to death and despair! Maria, Maria, why do you treat me thus?"

She laid her right hand in his, saying:

"That we may remain worthy of each other, Georg."

She forcibly withdrew her icy hand and entered the house; but he wandered for hours through the lighted streets like a drunken man, and at last threw himself, with a burning brain, upon his couch. A small volume, lightly stitched together, lay on a little table beside the bed. He seized it, and with trembling fingers wrote on its pages. The pencil often paused, and he frequently drew a long breath and gazed with dilated eyes into vacancy. At last he threw the book aside and watched anxiously for the morning.

CHAPTER XXX.

Just before sunrise Georg sprang from his couch, drew out his knapsack, and filled it with his few possessions; but this time the little book found no place with the other articles.

The musician Wilhelm also entered the court-yard at a very early hour, just as the first workmen were going to the shops. The Junker saw him coming, and met him at the door.

The artist's face revealed few traces of the want he had endured, but his whole frame was trembling with excitement and his face changed color every moment, as he instantly, and in the utmost haste, told Georg the purpose of his early visit.

Shortly after the arrival of the city messengers, a Spanish envoy had brought Burgomaster Van der Werff a letter written by Junker Nicolas Matanesse, containing nothing but the tidings, that Henrica's sister had reached Leyderdorp with Belotti and found shelter in the elder Baron Matanesse's farm-house. She was very ill, and longed to see her sister. The burgomaster had given this letter to the young lady, and Henrica hastened to the musician without delay, to entreat him to help her escape from the city and guide her to the Spanish lines. Wilhelm was undergoing a severe struggle. No sacrifice seemed too great to see Anna again, and what the messenger had accomplished, he too might succeed in doing. But ought he to aid the flight of the young girl detained as hostage by the council, deceive the sentinels at the gate, desert his post?

Since Henrica's request that Georg would escort her sister from Lugano to Holland, the young man had known everything that concerned the latter, and was also aware of the state of the musician's heart.

"I must, and yet I ought not," cried Wilhelm. "I have passed a terrible night; imagine yourself in my place, in the young lady's."

"Get a leave of absence until to-morrow," said Georg resolutely. "When it grows dark, I'll accompany Henrica with you. She must swear to return to the city in case of a surrender. As for me, I am no longer bound by any oath to serve the English flag. A month ago we received permission to enter the service of the Netherlands. It will only cost me a word with Captain Van der Laen, to be my own master."

"Thanks, thanks; but the young lady forbade me to ask your assistance."

"Folly, I shall go with you, and when our goal is reached, fight my way through to the Beggars.' Our departure will not trouble the council, for, when Henrica and I are outside, there will be two eaters less in Leyden. The sky is grey; I hope we shall have a dark night. Captain Van Duivenvoorde commands the guard at the Hohenort Gate. He knows us both, and will let us pass. I'll speak to him. Is the farm-house far inside the village?"

"No, outside on the road to Leyden."

"Well then, we'll meet at Aquanus's tavern at four o'clock."

"But the young lady—"

"It will be time enough, if she learns at the gate who is to accompany her."

When Georg came to the tavern at the appointed hour, he learned that Henrica had received another letter from Nicolas. It had been given to the outposts by the Junker himself, and contained only the words: "Until midnight, the Spanish watch-word is '*Lepanto.*' Your father shall know to-day, that Anna is here."

After the departure from the Hohenort Gate had been fixed for nine o'clock in the evening, Georg went to Captain Van der Laen and the commandant Van der Does, received from the former the discharge he requested, and from Janus a letter to his friend, Admiral

Boisot. When he informed his men, that he intended to leave the city and make his way to the Beggars, they declared they would follow, and live or die with him. It was with difficulty that he succeeded in restraining them. Before the town-hall he slackened his pace. The burgomaster was always to be found there at this hour. Should he quit the city without taking leave of him? No, no! And yet—since yesterday he had forfeited the right to look frankly into his eyes. He was afraid to meet him, it seemed as if he were completely estranged from him. So Georg rushed past the town-hall, and said defiantly: "Even if I leave him without a farewell, I owe him nothing; for I must pay for his kindness with cruel suffering, perhaps death. Maria loved me first, and what she is, and was, and ever will be to me, she shall know before I go."

He returned to his room at twilight, asked the manservant to carry his knapsack to Captain Van Duivenvoorde at the Hohenort Gate, and then went, with his little book in his doublet, to the main building to take leave of Maria. He ascended the staircase slowly and paused in the upper entry.

The beating of his heart almost stopped his breath. He did not know at which door to knock, and a torturing dread overpowered him, so that he stood for several minutes as if paralyzed. Then he summoned up his courage, shook himself, and muttered: "Have I become a coward!" With these words he opened the door leading into the dining-room and entered. Adrian was sitting at the empty table, beside a burning torch, with some books. Georg asked for his mother.

"She is probably spinning in her room," replied the boy.

"Call her, I have something important to tell her."

Adrian went away, returning with the answer that the Junker might wait in his father's study.

"Where is Barbara?" asked Georg.

"With Bessie."

The German nodded, and while pacing up and down beside the dining-room, thought, "I can't go so. It must come from the heart; once, once more I will hear her say, that she loves me, I will—I will—· Let it be dishonorable, let it be worthy of execration, I will atone for it; I will atone for it with my life!"

While Georg was pacing up and down the room, Adrian gathered his books together, saying: "B-r-r-r, Junker, how you look to-day! One might be afraid of you. Mother is in there already. The tinder-box is rattling; she is probably lighting the lamp."

"Are you busy?" asked Georg.

"I've finished."

"Then run over to Wilhelm Corneliussohn and tell him it is settled: we'll meet at nine, punctually at nine."

"At Aquanus's tavern?" asked the boy.

"No, no, he knows; make haste, my lad."

Adrian was going, but Georg beckoned to him, and said in a low tone: "Can you be silent?" ·

"As a fried sole."

"I shall slip out of the city to-day, and perhaps may never return." ·

"You, Junker? To-day?" asked the boy.

"Yes, dear lad. Come here, give me a farewell kiss. You must keep this little ring to remember me."

The boy submitted to the kiss, put the ring on his finger, and said with tearful eyes: "Are you in earnest? Yes, the famine! God knows I'd run after you, if it

were not for Bessie and mother. When will you come
back again ?"

"Who knows, my lad! Remember me kindly, do
you hear? Kindly! And now run."

Adrian rushed down the stairs, and a few minutes
after the Junker was standing in Peter's study, face to
face with Maria. The shutters were closed, and the
sconce on the table had two lighted candles.

"Thanks, a thousand thanks for coming," said
Georg. "You pronounced my sentence yesterday, and
to-day—"

"I know what brings you to me," she answered gently. "Henrica has bidden me farewell, and I must not
keep her. She doesn't wish to have you accompany
her, but Meister Wilhelm betrayed the secret to me.
You have come to say farewell."

"Yes, Maria, farewell forever."

"If it is God's will, we shall see each other again. I
know what is driving you away from here. You are
good and noble, Georg, and if there is one thing that
lightens the parting, it is this: We can now think of
each other without sorrow and anger. You will not forget us, and—you know that the remembrance of you
will be cherished here by old and young—in the hearts
of all—"

"And in yours also, Maria?"

"In mine also."

"Hold it firmly. And when the storm has blown
out of your path the poor dust, which to-day lives and
breathes, loves and despairs, grant it a place in your
memory."

Maria shuddered, for deep despair looked forth with
a sullen glow from the eyes that met hers. Seized with

an anxious foreboding, she exclaimed: "What are you thinking of, Georg? for Christ's sake! tell me what is in your mind."

"Nothing wrong, Maria, nothing wrong. We birds now sing differently. Whoever can saunter, with luke-warm blood and lukewarm pleasures, from one decade to another in peace and honor, is fortunate. My blood flows in a swifter course, and what my eager soul has once clasped with its polyp arms, it will never release until the death-hour comes. I am going, never to re-turn; but I shall take you and my love with me to bat-tle, to the grave.—I go, I go—"

"Not so, Georg, you must not part from me thus."

"Then cry: 'Stay!' Then say: 'I am here and pity you!' But don't expect the miserable wretch, whom you have blinded, to open his eyes, behold and enjoy the beauties of the world. There you stand, trembling and shaking, without a word for him who loves you, for him —him—"

The youth's voice faltered with emotion and sighing heavily, he pressed his hand to his brow. Then he seemed to recollect himself and continued in a low, sad tone: "Here I stand, to tell you for the last time the state of my heart. You should hear sweet words, but grief and pain will pour bitter drops into everything I say. I have uttered in the language of poetry, when my heart impelled me, that for which dry prose possesses no power of expression. Read these pages, Maria, and if they wake an echo in your soul, oh! treasure it. The honeysuckle in your garden needs a support, that it may grow and put forth flowers; let these poor songs be the espalier around which your memory of the absent one can twine its tendrils and cling lovingly. Read, oh!

read, and then say once more: 'You are dear to me,' or send me from you."

"Give it to me," said Maria, opening the volume with a throbbing heart.

He stepped back from her, but his breath came quickly and his eyes followed hers while she was reading.

She began with the last poem but one. It had been written just after Georg's return the day before, and ran as follows:

> "Joyously they march along,
> Lights are flashing through the panes,
> In the streets a busy throng
> Curiosity enchains.
> Oh! the merry festal night;
> Would that it might last for aye!
> For aye! Alas! Love, splendor, light,
> All, all have passed away."

The last lines Georg had written with a rapid pen the night before. In them he bewailed his hard fate. She must hear him once, then he would sing her a peerless song. Maria had followed the first verses silently with her eyes, but now her lips began to move and in a low, rapid tone, but audibly she read:

> "Sometimes it echoes like the thunder's peal,
> Then soft and low through the May night doth steal;
> Sometimes, on joyous wing, to Heaven it soars,
> Sometimes, like Philomel, its woes deplores.
> For, oh! this a song that ne'er can die,
> It seeks the heart of all humanity.
> In the deep cavern and the darksome lair,
> The sea of ether o'er the realm of air,
> In every nook my song shall still be heard,
> And all creation, with sad yearning stirred,
> United in a full, exultant choir,
> Pray thee to grant the singer's fond desire.

E'en when the ivy o'er my grave hath grown,
Still will ring on each sweet, enchanting tone,
Through the whole world and every earthly zone,
Resounding on in æons yet to come."

Maria read on, her heart beating more and more violently, her breath coming quicker and quicker, and when she had reached the last verse, tears burst from her eyes, and she raised the book with both hands to hurl it from her and throw her arms around the writer's neck.

He had been standing opposite to her, as if spell-bound, listening blissfully to the lofty flight of his own words. Trembling with passionate emotion, he yet restrained himself until she had raised her eyes from his lines and lifted the book, then his power of resistance flew to the winds and, fairly beside himself, he exclaimed: "Maria, my sweet wife!"

"Wife?" echoed in her breast like a cry of warning, and it seemed as if an icy hand clutched her heart. The intoxication passed away, and as she saw him standing before her with out-stretched arms and sparkling eyes, she shrank back, a feeling of intense loathing of him and her own weakness seized upon her and, instead of throwing the book aside and rushing to meet him, she tore it in halves, saying proudly: "Here are your verses, Junker von Dornburg; take them with you." Then, maintaining her dignity by a strong effort, she continued in a lower, more gentle tone, "I shall remember you without this book. We have both dreamed; let us now wake. Farewell! I will pray that God may guard you. Give me your hand, Georg, and when you return, we will bid you welcome to our house as a friend."

With these words Maria turned away from the

Junker and only nodded silently, when he exclaimed: "Past! All past!"

CHAPTER XXXI.

GEORG descended the stairs in a state of bewilderment. Both halves of the book, in which ever since the wedding at Delft he had written a succession of verses to Maria, lay in his hand.

The light of the kitchen-fire streamed into the entry. He followed it, and before answering Barbara's kind greeting, went to the hearth and flung into the fire the sheets, which contained the pure, sweet fragrance of a beautiful flower of youth.

"Oho! Junker!" cried the widow. "A quick fire doesn't suit every kind of food. What is burning there?"

"Foolish paper!" he answered. "Have no fear. At the utmost it might weep and put out the flames. It will be ashes directly. There go the sparks, flying in regular rows through the black, charred pages. How pretty it looks! They appear, leap forth and vanish — like a funeral procession with torches in a pitch-dark night. Good-night, poor children — good-night, dear songs! Look, Frau Barbara! They are rolling themselves up tightly, convulsively, as if it hurt them to burn."

"What sort of talk is that?" replied Barbara, thrusting the charred book deeper into the fire with the tongs. Then pointing to her own forehead, she continued: "One often feels anxious about you. High-sounding words. such as we find in the Psalms, are not meant for every-day life and our kitchen. If you were my own son, you'd often have something to listen to. People who travel at a steady pace reach their goal soonest."

"That's good advice for a journey," replied Georg, holding out his hand to the widow. "Farewell, dear mother. I can't bear it here any longer. In half an hour I shall turn my back on this good city."

"Go then—just as you choose—Or is the young lady taking you in tow? Nobleman's son and nobleman's daughter! Like to like—Yet, no; there has been nothing between you. Her heart is good, but I should wish you another wife than that Popish Everyday-different."

"So Henrica has told you—"

"She has just gone. Dear me—she has her relatives outside; and we—it's hard to divide a plum into twelve pieces. I said farewell to her cheerfully; but you, Georg, you—"

"I shall take her out of the city, and then—you won't blame me for it—then I shall make my way through to the Beggars."

"The Beggars! That's a different matter, that's right. You'll be in your proper place there! Cheer up, Junker, and go forth boldly? Give me your hand, and if you meet my boy—he commands a ship of his own.—Dear me, I remember something.. You can wait a moment longer. Come here, Trautchen. The woollen stockings I knit for him are up in the painted chest. Make haste and fetch them. He may need them on the water in the damp autumn weather. You'll take them with you?"

"Willingly, most willingly; and now let me thank you for all your kindness. You have been like an own mother to me." Georg clasped the widow's hand, and neither attempted to conceal how dear each had become to the other and how hard it was to part. Trautchen had given Barbara the stockings, and many tears fell upon them, while the widow was bidding the Junker farewell. When she noticed they were actually wet, she waved them in the air and handed them to the young man.

The night was dark but still, even sultry. The travellers were received at the Hohenort Gate by Captain Van Duivenvoorde, preceded by an old sergeant, carrying a lantern, who opened the gate. The captain embraced his brave, beloved comrade, Dornburg; a few farewell words and god-speeds echoed softly from the fortification walls, and the trio stepped forth into the open country.

For a time they walked silently through the darkness. Wilhelm knew the way and strode in front of Henrica; the Junker kept close at her side.

All was still, except from time to time they heard a word of command from the walls, the striking of a clock, or the barking of a dog.

Henrica had recognized Georg by the light of the lantern, and when Wilhelm stopped to ascertain whether there was any water in the ditch over which he intended to guide his companions, she said, under her breath:

"I did not expect your escort, Junker."

"I know it, but I, too, desired to leave the city."

"And wish to avail yourself of our knowledge of the watchword. Then stay with us."

"Until I know you are safe, Fraulein."

"The walls of Leyden already lie between you and the peril from which you fly."

"I don't understand you."

"So much the better."

Wilhelm turned and, in a muffled voice, requested his companions to keep silence. They now walked noiselessly on, until just outside the camp they reached the broad road around which they had made a circuit.

A Spanish sentinel challenged them.

"*Lepanto!*" was the answer, and they passed on through the camp unmolested. A coach drawn by four horses, a mere box hung between two tiny fore-wheels and a pair of gigantic hind-wheels, drove slowly past them. It was conveying Magdalena Moons, the daughter of an aristocratic Holland family, distinguished among the magistracy, back to the Hague from a visit to her lover and future husband, Valdez. No one noticed Henrica, for there were plenty of women in the camp. Several poorly-clad ones sat before the tents, mending the soldiers' clothes. Some gaily-bedizened wenches were drinking wine and throwing dice with their male companions in front of an officer's tent. A brighter light glowed from behind the general's quarters, where, under a sort of shed, several confessionals and an altar had been erected. Upon this altar candles were burning, and over it hung a silver lamp; a dark, motionless stream pressed towards it; Castilian soldiers, among whom individuals could be recognized only when the candle-light flashed upon a helmet or coat of mail.

The loud singing of carousing German mercenaries, the neighing and stamping of the horses, and the laughter of the officers and girls, drowned the low chanting of the priests and the murmur of the penitents, but the shrill sounding of the bell calling to mass from time to time pierced, with its swift vibrations, through the noise

of the camp. Just outside the village the watch-word
was again used, and they reached the first house unmolested.

"Here we are," said Wilhelm, with a sigh of relief.
"Profit by the darkness, Junker, and keep on till you
have the Spaniards behind you."

"No, my friend; you will remain here. I wish to
share your danger. I shall return with you to Leyden
and from thence try to reach Delft; meantime I'll keep
watch and give you warning, if necessary."

"Let us bid each other farewell now, Georg; hours
may pass before I return."

"I have time, a horrible amount of time. I'll wait.
There goes the door."

The Junker grasped his sword, but soon removed
his hand from the hilt, for it was Belotti, who came out
and greeted the signorina.

Henrica followed him into the house and there
talked with him in a low tone, until Georg called her,
saying:

"Fraulein Van Hoogstraten, may I ask for a word
of farewell?"

"Farewell, Herr von Dornburg!" she answered distantly, but advanced a step towards him.

Georg had also approached, and now held out his
hand. She hesitated a moment, then placed hers in it,
and said so softly, that only he could hear:

"Do you love Maria?"

"So I am to confess?"

"Don't refuse my last request, as you did the first.
If you can be generous, answer me fearlessly. I'll not
betray your secret to any one. Do you love Frau Van
der Werff?"

" Yes, Fraulein."

Henrica drew a long breath, then continued: " And now you are rushing out into the world to forget her ?"

" No, Fraulein."

" Then tell me why you have fled from Leyden ?"

" To find an end that becomes a soldier."

Henrica advanced close to his side, exclaiming so scornfully, that it cut Georg to the heart:

" So it has grasped you too! It seizes all: Knights, maidens, wives and widows; not one is spared. Never-ending sorrow! Farewell, Georg! We can laugh at or pity each other, just as we choose. A heart pierced with seven swords: what an exquisite picture! Let us wear blood-red knots of ribbon, instead of green and blue ones. Give me your hand once more, now farewell."

Henrica beckoned to the musician and both followed Belotti up the steep, narrow stairs. Wilhelm remained behind in a little room, adjoining a second one, where a beautiful boy, about three years old, was being tended by an Italian woman. In a third chamber, which like all the other rooms in the farm-house, was so low that a tall man could scarcely stand erect, Henrica's sister lay on a wide bedstead, over which a screen, supported by four columns, spread like a canopy. Links dimly lighted the long narrow room. The reddish-yellow rays of their broad flames were darkened by the canopy, and scarcely revealed the invalid's face.

Henrica had given the Italian woman and the child in the second room but a hasty greeting, and now impetuously pressed forward into the third, rushed to the bed, threw herself on her knees, clasped her arms passionately around her sister, and covered her face with glowing kisses.

She said nothing but "Anna," and the sick woman found no other word than "Henrica." Minutes elapsed, then the young girl started up, seized one of the torches and cast its light on her regained sister's face. How pale, how emaciated it looked! But it was still beautiful, still the same as before. Strangely-blended emotions of joy and grief took possession of Henrica's soul. Her cold hard feelings grew warm and melted, and in this hour the comfort of tears, of which she had been so long deprived, once more became hers.

Gradually the flood tide of emotion began to ebb, and the confusion of loving exclamations and incoherent words gained some order and separated into question and answer. When Anna learned that the musician had accompanied her sister, she wished to see him, and when he entered, held out both hands, exclaiming:

" Meister, Meister, in what a condition you find me again! Henrica, this is the best of men; the only unselfish friend I have found on earth."

The succeeding hours were full of sorrowful agitation.

Belotti and the old Italian woman often undertook to speak for the invalid, and gradually the image of a basely-destroyed life, that had been worthy of a better fate, appeared before Henrica and Wilhelm. Fear, anxiety and torturing doubt had from the first saddened Anna's existence with the unprincipled adventurer and gambler, who had succeeded in beguiling her young, inexperienced heart. A short period of intoxication was followed by an unexampled awakening. She was clasping her first child to her breast, when the unprecedented outrage occurred—Don Luis demanded that she should move with him into the house of a notorious Marchesa, in whose ill-famed gambling-rooms he had spent his evenings and nights for months. She indignantly refused, but he coldly and threateningly persisted in having his will. Then the Hoogstraten blood asserted itself, and without a word of farewell she fled with her child to Lugano. There the boy was received by his mother's former waiting-maid, while she herself went to Rome, not as an adventuress, but with a fixed, praiseworthy object in view. She intended to fully perfect her musical talents in the new schools of Palestrina and Nanini, and thus obtain the ability, by means of her art, to support her child independently of his father and hers. She risked much, but very definite hopes hovered before her eyes, for a distinguished prelate and lover of music, to whom she had letters of introduction from Brussels, and who knew her voice, had promised that after her return from her musical studies he would give her the place of singing-mistress to a young girl of noble birth, who had been educated in a convent at Milan. She was under his guardianship, and the worthy man took care to provide Anna, before her departure, with letters to his friends in the eternal city.

Her hasty flight from Rome had been caused by the news, that Don Luis had found and abducted his son. She could not lose her child, and when she did not find the boy in Milan, followed and at last discovered him in Naples. There d'Avila restored the child, after she had declared her willingness to make over to him the income she still received from her aunt. The long journey, so full of excitement and fatigue, exhausted her strength, and she returned to Milan feeble and broken in health.

Her patron had been anxious to keep the place of singing-mistress open for her, but she could only fulfil for a short time the duties to which the superior of the convent kindly summoned her, for her sickness was increasing and a terrible cough spoiled her voice. She now returned to Lugano, and there sought to compensate her poor honest friend by the sale of her ornaments, but the time soon came when the generous artist was forced to submit to be supported by the charity of a servant. Until the last six months she had not suffered actual want, but when her maid's husband died, anxiety about the means of procuring daily bread arose, and now maternal love broke down Anna's pride: she wrote to her father as a repentant daughter, bowed down by misfortune, but received no reply. At last, reduced to starvation with her child, she undertook the hardest possible task, and besought the man, of whom she could only think with contempt and loathing, not to let his son grow up like a beggar's child. The letter, which contained this cry of distress, had reached Don Luis just before his death. No help was to come to her from him. But Belotti appeared, and now she was once more at home, her friend and sister were standing beside her bed, and Henrica encouraged her to hope for her father's forgiveness.

It was past midnight, yet Georg still awaited his friend's return. The noise and bustle of the camp began to die away and the lantern, which at first had but feebly lighted the spacious lower-room of the farmhouse, burned still more dimly. The German shared this apartment with agricultural implements, harnesses, and many kinds of grain and vegetables heaped in piles

against the walls, but he lacked inclination to cast even
a glance at his motley surroundings. There was nothing
pleasant to him in the present or future. He felt
humiliated, guilty, weary of life. His self-respect was
trampled under foot, love and happiness were forfeited,
there was naught before him save a colorless, charmless
future, full of bitterness and mental anguish. Nothing
seemed desirable save a speedy death. At times the
fair image of his home rose before his memory—but it
vanished as soon as he recalled the burgomaster's
dignified figure, his own miserable weakness and the
repulse he had experienced. He was full of fierce indignation against himself, and longed with passionate
impatience for the clash of swords and roar of cannon,
the savage struggle man to man.

Time passed without his perceiving it, but a torturing desire for food began to torment the starving man.
There were plenty of turnips piled against the wall, and
he eat one after another, until he experienced the feeling
of satiety he had so long lacked. Then he sat down on
a kneading-trough and considered how he could best
get to the Beggars. He did not know his way, but woe
betide those who ventured to oppose him. His arm and
sword were good, and there were Spaniards enough at
hand whom he could make feel the weight of both. His
impatience began to rise, and it seemed like a welcome
diversion, when he heard steps approaching and a man's
figure entered the house. He had stationed himself by
the wall with his sword between his folded arms, and
now shouted a loud "halt" to the new-comer.

The latter instantly drew his sword, and when Georg
imperiously demanded what he wanted, replied in a boyish voice, but a proud, resolute tone:

"I ask you that question! I am in my father's house."

"Indeed!" replied the German smiling, for he had now recognized the speaker's figure by the dim light. "Put up your sword. If you are young Matanesse Van Wibisma, you have nothing to fear from me."

"I am. But what are you doing on our premises at night, sword in hand?"

"I'm warming the wall to my own satisfaction, or, if you want to know the truth, mounting guard."

"In our house?"

"Yes, Junker. There is some one up-stairs with your cousins, who wouldn't like to be surprised by the Spaniards. Go up. I know from Captain Van Duivenvoorde what a gallant young fellow you are."

"From Herr von Warmond?" asked Nicolas eagerly. "Tell me! what brings you here, and who are you?"

"One who is fighting for your liberty, a German, Georg von Dornburg."

"Oh, wait here, I entreat you. I'll come back directly. Do you know whether Fraulein Van Hoogstraten—"

"Up there," replied Georg, pointing towards the ceiling.

Nicolas sprang up the stairs in two or three bounds, called his cousin, and hastily told her that her father had had a severe fall from his horse while hunting, and was lying dangerously ill. When Nicolas spoke of Anna he had at first burst into a furious passion, but afterwards voluntarily requested him to tell him about her, and attempted to leave his bed to accompany him. He succeeded in doing so, but fell back fainting. When his father came early the next morning, she might tell him that he, Nicolas, begged his forgiveness; he was about to do what he believed to be his duty.

He evaded Henrica's questions, and merely hastily enquired about Anna's health and the Leyden citizen, whom Georg had mentioned.

When he heard the name of the musician Wilhelm, he begged her to warn him to depart in good time, and if possible in his company, then bade her a hurried farewell and ran down-stairs.

Wilhelm soon followed.   Henrica accompanied him to the stairs to see Georg once more, but as soon as she heard his voice, turned defiantly away and went back to her sister.

The musician found Junker von Dornburg engaged in an eager conversation with Nicolas.

"No, no, my boy," said the German cordially, "my way cannot be yours."

"I am seventeen years old."

"That's not it; you've just confronted me bravely, and you have a man's strength of will—but life ought still to bear flowers for you, if such is God's will—you are going forth to fight sword-in-hand to win a worthy destiny of peace and prosperity, for yourself and your native land, in freedom—but I, I—give me your hand and promise—"

"My hand?   There it is; but I must refuse the promise.   With or without you—I shall go to the Beggars!"

Georg gazed at the brave boy in delight, and asked gently:

"Is your mother living?"

"No."

"Then come. We shall probably both find what we seek with the Beggars."

Nicolas clasped the hand Georg offered, but Wilhelm approached the Junker, saying:

"I expected this from you, after what I saw at St. Peter's church and Quatgelat's tavern."

"You first opened my eyes," replied Nicolas. "Now come, we'll go directly through the camp; they all know me."

In the road the boy pressed close to Georg, and in answer to his remark that he would be in a hard position towards his father, replied:

"I know it, and it causes me such pain—such pain. —But I can't help it. I won't suffer the word 'traitor' to cling to our name."

"Your cousin Matanesse, Herr von Rivière, is also devoted to the good cause."

"But my father thinks differently. He has the courage to expect good deeds from the Spaniards. From the Spaniards! I've learned to know them during the last few months. A brave lad from Leyden, you knew him probably by his nickname, Löwing, which he really deserved, was captured by them in fair fight, and then—it makes me shudder even now when I think of it—they hung him up head downward, and tortured him to death. I was present, and not one word of theirs escaped my ears. Such ought to be the fate of all Holland, country and people, that was what they wanted. And remarks like these can be heard every day. No abuse of us is too bad for them, and the King thinks like his soldiers. Let some one else endure to be the slave of a master, who tortures and despises us! My holy religion is eternal and indestructible. Even if it is hateful to many of the Beggars, that shall not trouble me—if only they will help break the Spanish chains."

Amid such conversation they walked through the Castilian camp, where all lay buried in sleep. Then they reached that of the German troops, and here gay carousing was going on under many a tent. At the end of the encampment a sutler and his wife were collecting together the wares that remained unsold.

Wilhelm had walked silently behind the other two, for his heart was deeply stirred, joy and sorrow were striving for the mastery. He felt intoxicated with lofty, pure emotions, but suddenly checked his steps before the sutler's stand and pointed to the pastry gradually disappearing in a chest.

Hunger had become a serious, nay only too serious and mighty power, in the city beyond, and it was not at all surprising that Wilhelm approached the venders, and with sparkling eyes bought their last ham and as much bread as they had left.

Nicolas laughed at the bundle he carried under his arm, but Georg said:

"You haven't yet looked want in the face, Junker. This bread is a remedy for the most terrible disease."

At the Hohenort Gate Georg ordered Captain von Warmond to be waked, and introduced Nicolas to him as a future Beggar. The captain congratulated the boy and offered him money to supply himself in Delft with whatever he needed, and defray his expenses during the first few weeks; but Nicolas rejected his wealthy friend's offer, for a purse filled with gold coins hung at his girdle. A jeweller in the Hague had given them to him yesterday in payment for Fraulein Van Hoogstraten's emerald ring.

Nicolas showed the captain his treasure, and then exclaimed:

"Now forward, Junker von Dornburg, I know where we shall find them; and you, Captain Van Duivenvoorde, tell the burgomaster and Janus Dousa what has become of me."

CHAPTER XXXII.

A WEEK had elapsed since Henrica's flight, and with it a series of days of severe privation. Maria knew from the musician, that young Matanesse had accompanied Georg, and that the latter was on his way to the Beggars. This was the right plan. The bubbling brook belonged to the wild, rushing, mighty river. She wished him happiness, life and pleasure; but—strange— since the hour that she tore his verses, the remembrance of him had receeded as far as in the days before the approach of the Spaniards. Nay, after her hard-won conquest of herself and his departure, a rare sense of happiness, amid all her cares and troubles, had taken possession of the young wife's heart. She had been cruel to herself, and the inner light of the clear diamond first gleams forth with the right brilliancy, after it has endured the torture of polishing. She now felt with joyous gratitude, that she could look Peter frankly in the eye, grant him love, and ask love in return. He scarcely seemed to notice her and her management under the burden of his cares, but she felt, that many things she said and could do for him pleased him. The young wife did not suffer specially from the long famine, while

it caused Barbara pain and unstrung her vigorous frame.
Amid so much suffering, she often sunk into despair before the cold hearth and empty pots, and no longer
thought it worth while to plait her large cap and ruffs.
It was now Maria's turn to speak words of comfort, and
remind her of her son, the Beggar captain, who would
soon enter Leyden.

On the sixth of September the burgomaster's wife
was returning home from an early walk. Autumn mists
darkened the air, and the sea-breeze drove a fine, driz-
zling spray through the streets. The dripping trees had
long since been robbed of their leaves, not by wind and
storm, but by children and adults, who had carried the
caterpillars' food to their kitchens as precious vegetables.

At the Schagensteg Maria saw Adrian, and overtook
him. The boy was sauntering idly along, counting aloud.
The burgomaster's wife called to him, and asked why
he was not at school and what he was doing there.

"I'm counting," was the reply. "Now there are
nine."

"Nine?"

"I've met nine dead bodies so far; the rector sent
us home. Master Dirks is dead, and there were only
thirteen of us to-day. There are some people bringing
another one."

Maria drew her kerchief tighter and walked on. At
her left hand stood a tall, narrow house, in which lived a
cobbler, a jovial man, over whose door were two inscriptions. One ran as follows:

> "Here are shoes for sale,
>   Round above and flat below;
>   If David's foot they will not fit,
>   Goliath's sure they'll suit, I know."

The other was:

> "When through the desert roved the Jews,
> Their shoes for forty years they wore,
> Were the same custom now in use,
> 'Prentice would ne'er seek cobbler's door."

On the ridge of the lofty house was the stork's nest, now empty. The red-billed guests did not usually set out on their journey to the south so early, and some were still in Leyden, standing on the roofs as if lost in thought. What could have become of the cobbler's beloved lodgers? At noon the day before, their host, who in March usually fastened the luck-bringing nest firmly with his own hands, had stolen up to the roof, and with his cross-bow shot first the little wife and then the husband. It was a hard task, and his wife sat weeping in the kitchen while the evil deed was done, but whoever is tormented by the fierce pangs of hunger and sees his dear ones dying of want, doesn't think of old affection and future good fortune, but seeks deliverance at the present time.

The storks had been sacrificed too late, for the cobbler's son, his growing apprentice, had closed his eyes the night before for his eternal sleep. Loud lamentations reached Maria's ear from the open door of the shop, and Adrian said: "Jacob is dead, and Mabel is very sick. This morning their father cursed me on father's account, saying it was his fault that everything was going to destruction. Will there be no bread again to-day, mother? Barbara has some biscuit, and I feel so sick. I can't swallow the everlasting meal any longer."

"Perhaps there will be a slice. We must save the baked food, child."

In the entry of her house Maria found a man-servant,

clad in black. He had come to announce the death of Commissioner Dietrich Van Bronkhorst. The plague had ended the strong man's life on the evening of the day before, Sunday.

Maria already knew of this heavy loss, which threw the whole responsibility of everything, that now happened, upon her husband's shoulders. She had also learned that a letter had been received from Valdez, in which he had pledged his word of honor as a nobleman, to spare the city, if it would surrender itself to the king's "mercy," and especially to grant Burgomaster Van der Werff, Herr Van der Does, and the other supporters of the rebellion, free passage through the Spanish lines. The Castilians would retire and Leyden should be garrisoned only by a few German troops. He invited Van der Werff and Herr von Nordwyk to come to Leyderdorp as ambassadors, and in any case, even if the negotiations failed, agreed to send them home uninjured under a safe escort. Maria knew that her husband had appointed that day for a great assembly of the council, the magistrates, and all the principal men in the city, as well as the captains of the city-guard—but not a word of all this had reached her ears from Peter. She had heard the news from Frau Van Hout and the wives of other citizens.

During the last few days a great change had taken place in her husband. He went out and returned with a pallid, gloomy face. Taciturn and wasting away with anxiety, he withdrew from the members of his family even when at home, repelling his wife curtly and impatiently when, yielding to the impulse of her heart, she approached him with encouraging words. Night brought him no sleep, and he left his couch before morning dawned, to pace restlessly to and fro, or gaze at Bessie, who to him alone still tried to show recognition by a faint smile.

When Maria returned home, she instantly went to the child and found Doctor Bontius with her. The physician shook his head at her appearance, and said the delicate little creature's life would soon be over. Her stomach had been injured during the first months of want; now it refused to do its office, and to hope for recovery would be folly.

"She must live, she must not die!" cried Maria, frantic with grief and yet full of hope, like a true mother, who cannot grasp the thought that she is condemned to lose her child, even when the little heart is already ceasing to beat and the bright eyes are growing dim and closing. "Bessie, Bessie, look at me! Bessie, take this nice milk. Only a few drops! Bessie, Bessie, you must not die."

Peter had entered the room unobserved and heard the last words. Holding his breath, he gazed down at his darling, his broad shoulders shook, and in a stifled, faltering voice he asked the physician: "Must she die?"

"Yes, old friend; I think so! Hold up your head! You have much still left you. All five of Van Loo's children have died of the plague."

Peter shuddered, and without taking any notice of Maria, passed from the room with drooping head.

Bontius followed him into his study, laid his hand on his arm, and said:

"Our little remnant of life is made bitter to us, Peter. Barbara says a corpse was laid before your door early this morning."

"Yes. When I went out, the livid face offered me a morning greeting. It was a young person. All whom death mows down, the people lay to my charge. Wherever one looks—corpses! Whatever one hears—curses! Have I authority over so many lives? Day and night nothing but sorrow and death before my eyes;—and yet, yet, yet—oh God! save me from madness!"

Peter clasped both hands over his brow; but Bontius found no word of comfort, and merely exclaimed:

"And I, and I? My wife and child ill with a fever, day and night on my feet, not to cure, but to see people die. What has been learned by hard study becomes childish folly in these days, and yet the poor creatures utter a sigh of hope when I feel their pulses. But this can't go on, this can't go on. Day before yesterday seventy, yesterday eighty-six deaths, and among them two of my colleagues."

"And no prospect of improvement?"

"To-morrow the ninety will become a hundred—the one hundred will become two, three, four, five, until at last one individual will be left, for whom there will be no grave-digger."

"The pest-houses are closed, and we still have cattle and horses."

"But the pestilence creeps through the joints, and since the last loaf of bread and the last malt-cake have been divided, and there is nothing for the people to eat except meat, meat, and nothing else—one tiny piece for the whole day—disease is piled on disease in forms utterly unprecedented, of which no book speaks, for which no remedy has yet been discovered. This drawing water with a bottomless pitcher is beginning to be too much for me. My brain is no stronger than yours. Farewell until to-morrow."

"To-day, to-day! You are coming to the meeting at the town-hall?"

"Certainly not! Do what you can justify; I shall practise my profession, which now means the same thing as saying: 'I shall continue to close eyes and hold coroner's inquests.' If things go on so, there will soon be an end to practice."

"Once for all: if you were in my place, you would treat with Valdez?"

"In *your* place? I am not *you*; I am a physician, one who has nothing to do except to take the field against suffering and death. You, since Bronkhorst's death, are the providence of the city. Supply a bit of bread, if only as large as my hand, in addition to the meat, or—I love my native land and liberty as well as any one—or—"

"Or?"

"Or—leave Death to reap his narvest, you are no physician."

Bontius bade his friend farewell and left him, but Peter thrust his hand through his hair and stood gazing out of the window, until Barbara entered, laid his official costume on a chair and asked with feigned carelessness:

"May I give Adrain some of the last biscuit? Meat is repulsive to him. He's lying on the bed, writhing in pain."

Peter turned pale, and said in a hollow tone:

"Give it to him and call the doctor."

"Maria and Bontius are already with him."

The burgomaster changed his clothing, feeling a

thrill of fierce indignation against every article he put on. To-day the superb costume was as hateful to him as the office, which gave him the right to wear it, and which, until a few weeks ago, he had occupied with a joyous sense of confidence in himself.

Before leaving the house, he sought Adrian. The boy was lying in Barbara's room, complaining of violent pains, and asking if he must die too.

Peter shook his head, but Maria kissed him, exclaiming :

" No, certainly not."

The burgomaster's time was limited. His wife stopped him in the entry, but he hurried down-stairs without hearing what she called after him.

The young wife returned to Adrian's bedside, thinking anxiously of the speedy death of many comrades of the dear boy, whose damp hand rested in hers. She thought of Bessie, followed Peter in imagination to the town-hall, and heard his powerful voice contending for resistance to the last man and the last pound of meat; nay, she could place herself by his side, for she knew what was to come : To stand fast, stand fast for liberty, and if God so willed, die a martyr's death for it like Jacoba, Leonhard, and Peter's noble father.

One anxious hour followed another.

When Adrian began to feel better, she went to Bessie, who pale and inanimate, seemed to be gently fading away, and only now and then raised her little finger to play with her dry lips.

Oh, the pretty, withering human flower! How closely the little girl had grown into her heart, how impossible it seemed to give her up ! With tearful eyes, she pressed her forehead on her clasped hands, which rested on the head-board of the little bed, and fervently implored God to spare and save this child. Again and again she repeated the prayer, but when Bessie's dim eyes no longer met hers and her hands fell into her lap, she could not help thinking of Peter, the assembly, the fate of the city, and the words: "Leyden saved, Holland saved! Leyden lost, all is lost!"

So the hours passed until the gloomy day wore away into twilight, and twilight was followed by evening. Trautchen brought in the lamp, and at last Peter's step was heard on the stairs.

It must be he, and yet it was not, for he never came up with such slow and dragging feet.

Then the study door opened.

It was he!

What could have happened, what had the citizens determined?

With an anxious heart, she told Trautchen to stay with the child, and then went to her husband.

Peter sat at the writing-table in full official uniform, with his hat still on his head. His face lay buried on his folded arms, beside the sconce.

He saw nothing, heard nothing, and when she at last called him, started, sprang up and flung his hat violently on the table. His hair was dishevelled, his glance restless, and in the faint light of the glimmering candles his cheeks looked deadly pale.

"What do you want?" he asked curtly, in a harsh voice; but for a time Maria made no reply, fear paralyzed her tongue.

At last she found words, and deep anxiety was apparent in her question:

"What has happened?"

"The beginning of the end," he answered in a hollow tone.

"They have out-voted you?" cried the young wife. "Baersdorp and the other cowards want to negotiate?"

Peter drew himself up to his full height, and exclaimed in a loud, threatening tone:

"Guard your tongue! He who remains steadfast until his children die and corpses bar the way in front of his own house, he who bears the responsibility of a thousand deaths, endures curses and imprecations through long weeks, and has vainly hoped for deliverance during more than a third of a year—he who, wherever he looks, sees nothing save unprecedented, constantly increasing misery and then no longer repels the saving hand of the foe—"

"Is a coward, a traitor, who breaks the sacred oath he has sworn."

"Maria," cried Peter angrily, approaching with a threatening gesture.

She drew her slender figure up to its full height and with quickened breath awaited him, pointing her finger at him, as she exclaimed with a sharp tone perceptible through the slight tremor in her voice:

"You, you have voted with the Baersdorps, *you*, Peter Van der Werff! *You* have done this thing, you, the friend of the Prince, the shield and providence of this brave city, *you*, the man who received the oaths of the citizens, the martyr's son, the servant of liberty —"

"No more!" he interrupted, trembling with shame and rage. "Do you know what it is to bear the guilt of this most terrible suffering before God and men?"

"Yes, yes, thrice yes; it is laying one's heart on the rack, to save Holland and liberty. That is what it means! Oh, God, my God! You are lost! You intend to negotiate with Valdez!"

"And suppose I do?" asked the burgomaster, with an angry gesture.

Maria looked him sternly in the eye, and exclaimed in a loud, resolute tone:

"Then it will be my turn to say: Go to Delft; we need different men here."

The burgomaster turned pale and bent his eyes on the floor, while she fearlessly confronted him with a steady glance.

The light fell full upon her glowing face, and when Peter again raised his eyes, it seemed as if the same Maria stood before him, who as a bride had vowed to share trouble and peril with him, remain steadfast in the struggle for liberty to the end; he felt that his "child" Maria had grown to his own height and above him, recognized for the first time in the proud woman before him his companion in conflict, his high-hearted helper in distress and danger. An overmastering yearning, mightier than any emotion ever experienced before, surged through his soul, impelled him towards her, and found utterance in the words:

"Maria, Maria, my wife, my guardian angel! We have written to Valdez, but there is still time, nothing binds me yet, and with you, with you I will stand firm to the end."

Then, in the midst of these days of woe, she threw herself on his breast, crying aloud in the abundance of this new, unexpected, unutterable happiness:

"With you, one with you—forever, unto death, in conflict and in love!"

CHAPTER XXXIII.

PETER felt animated with new life. A fresh store of courage and enthusiasm filled his breast, for he constantly received a new supply from the stout-hearted woman by his side.

Under the pressure of the terrible responsibility he endured, and urged by his fellow-magistrates, he had consented, at the meeting of the council, to write to Valdez and ask him to give free passage to embassadors, who were to entreat the estates and the Prince of Orange to release the tortured city from her oath.

Valdez made every effort to induce the burgomaster to enter into farther negotiations, but the latter remained firm, and no petition for release from the sacred duty of resistance left the city. The two Van der Does, Van Hout, Junker von Warmond, and other resolute men, who had already, in the great assembly, denounced any intercourse with the enemy, now valiantly supported him against his fellow-magistrates and the council, that with the exception of seven of its members, persistently and vehemently urged the commencement of negotiations.

Adrian rapidly recovered, but Doctor Bontius's prediction was terribly fulfilled, for famine and pestilence vied with each other in horrible fury, and destroyed almost half of all the inhabitants of the flourishing city. Intense was the gloom, dark the sky, yet even amidst the cruel woe there was many an hour in which bright sunshine illumined souls, and hope unfurled her green banner. The citizens of Leyden rose from their couches more joyously, than a bride roused by the singing of her companions on her wedding-day, when on the morning of September eleventh loud and long-continued cannonading was heard from the distance, and the sky became suffused with a crimson glow. The villages southwest of the city were burning. Every house, every barn that sunk into ashes, burying the property of honest men, was a bonfire to the despairing citizens.

The Beggars were approaching !

Yonder, where the cannon thundered and the horizon glowed, lay the Land-scheiding, the bulwark which for centuries had guarded the plains surrounding Leyden from the assaults of the waves, and now barred the way of the fleet bringing assistance.

" Fall, protecting walls, rise, tempest, swallow thy prey, raging sea, destroy the property of the husbandman, ruin our fields and meadows, but drown the foe or drive him hence." So sang Janus Dousa, so rang a voice in Peter's soul, so prayed Maria, and with her thousands of men and women.

But the glow in the horizon died away, the firing ceased. A second day elapsed, a third and fourth, but no messenger arrived, no Beggar ship appeared, and the sea seemed to lie calm; but another terrible power increased, moving with mysterious, stealthy, irresistible might; Death, with his pale companions, Despair and Famine.

The dead were borne secretly to their graves under cover of the darkness of night, to save their scanty ration for the survivors, in the division of food. The angel of death flew from house to house, touched pretty little

Bessie's heart, and kissed her closed eyes while she slumbered in the quiet night.

The faint-hearted and the Spanish sympathizers raised their heads and assembled in bands, one of which forced a passage into the council-chamber and demanded bread. But not a crumb remained, and the magistrates had nothing more to distribute except a small portion of cow and horse-flesh, and boiled and salted hides.

During this period of the sorest distress, Van der Werff was passing down the "broad street." He did not notice that a throng of desperate men and women were pursuing him with threats; but as he turned to enter Van Hout's house, suddenly found himself surrounded. A pallid woman, with her dying child in her arms, threw herself before him, held out the expiring infant, and cried in hollow tones: "Let this be enough, let this be enough—see here, see this; it is the third. Let this be enough!"

"Enough, enough! Bread, bread! Give us bread!" was shrieked and shouted around him, and threatening weapons and stones were raised; but a carpenter, whom he knew, and who had hitherto faithfully upheld the good cause, advanced saying in measured accents, in his deep voice: "This can go on no longer. We have patiently borne hunger and distress in fighting against the Spaniards and for our Bible, but to struggle against certain death is madness."

Peter, pale and agitated, gazed at the mother, the child, the sturdy workman and the threatening, shrieking mob. The common distress, which afflicted them and so many starving people, oppressed his soul with a thousand-fold greater power. He would fain have drawn them all to his heart, as brothers in misfortune, companions of a future, worthier existence. With deep emotion, he looked from one to the other, then pressed his hand upon his breast and called to the crowd, which thronged around him:

"Here I stand. I have sworn to faithfully endure to the end; and you did so with me. I will not break my oath, but I can die. If my life will serve you, here I am! I have no bread, but here, here is my body. Take it, lay hands on me, tear me to pieces. Here I stand, here I stand. I will keep my oath."

The carpenter bent his head, and said in a hollow tone: "Come, people, let God's will be done; we have sworn."

The burgomaster quietly entered his friend's house. Frau Van Hout had seen and heard all this, and on the very same day told the story to Maria, her eyes sparkling brightly as she exclaimed: "Never did I see any man so noble as he was in that hour! It is well for us, that he rules within these walls. Never will our children and children's children forget this deed."

They have treasured it in their memories, and during the night succeeding the day on which the burgomaster acted so manly a part, a letter arrived from the Prince, full of joyous and encouraging news. The noble man had recovered, and was striving with all his power to rescue brave Leyden. The Beggars had cut the Landscheiding, their vessels were pressing onward—help was approaching, and the faithful citizen who brought the letter, had seen with his own eyes the fleet bringing relief and the champions of freedom, glowing with martial ardor. The two Van der Does, by the same letter, were appointed the Prince's commissioners in place of the late Herr Van Bronkhorst. Van der Werff no longer stood alone, and when the next morning "Father William's" letter was read aloud and the messenger's news spread abroad, the courage and confidence of the tortured citizens rose like withering. grass after a refreshing rain.

But they were still condemned to long weeks of anxiety and suffering.

During the last days of September they were forced to slaughter the cows hitherto spared for the infants and young mothers, and then, then ?

Help was close at hand, for the sky often reddened, and the air was shaken by the roar of distant cannon ; but the east wind continued to prevail, driving back the water let in upon the land, and the vessels needed a rising flood to approach the city.

Not one of all the messengers, who had been sent out, returned; there was nothing certain, save the cruelly increasing unendurable suffering. Even Barbara had succumbed, and complained of weakness and loathing of the ordinary food.

Maria thought of the roast-pigeon, which had agreed with Bessie so well, and went to the musician, to ask if he could sacrifice another of his pets for her sister-in-law.

Wilhelm's mother received the burgomaster's wife. The old lady was sitting wearily in an arm-chair; she could still walk, but amid her anxiety and distress a strange twitching had affected her hands. When Maria made her request, she shook her head, saying: " Ask him yourself.   He's obliged to keep the little creatures shut up, for whenever they appear, the poor starving people shoot at them.   There are only three left.   The messengers took the others, and they haven't returned.

Thank God for it; the little food he still has, will do more good in dishes, than in their crops. Would you believe it? A fortnight ago he paid fifty florins out of his savings for half a sack of peas, and Heaven knows where he found them. Ulrich, Ulrich! Take Frau Van der Werff up to Wilhelm. I'd willingly spare you the climb, but he's watching for the carrier-pigeons that have been sent out, and won't even come down to his meals. To be sure, they would hardly be worth the trouble!"

It was a clear, sunny day. Wilhelm was standing in his look-out, gazing over the green, watery plain, that lay out-spread below him, towards the south. Behind him sat Andreas, the fencing-master's fatherless boy, writing notes, but his attention was not fixed on his work; for as soon as he had finished a line he too gazed towards the horizon, watching for the pigeon his teacher expected. He did not look particularly emaciated, for many a grain of the doves' food had been secretly added to his scanty ration of meat.

Wilhelm showed that he felt both surprised and honored by Frau Van der Werff's visit, and even promised to grant her request, though it was evident that the "saying yes" was by no means easy for him.

The young wife went out on the balcony with him, and he showed her in the south, where usually nothing but a green plain met the eye, a wide expanse over which a light mist was hovering. The noon sun seemed to steep the white vapor with light, and lure it upward by its ardent rays. This was the water streaming through the broken dyke, and the black oblong specks moving along its edges were the Spanish troops and herds of cattle, that had retreated before the advancing flood from the outer fortifications, villages and hamlets. The Land-scheiding itself was not visible, but the Beggars had already passed it. If the fleet succeeded in reaching the Zoetermere Lake and from thence.—

Wilhelm suddenly interrupted his explanation, for Andreas had suddenly started up, upsetting his stool, and exclaimed:

"It's coming! The dove! Roland, my fore man, there it comes!"

For the first time Wilhelm heard the boy's lips utter his father's exclamation. Some great emotion must have stirred his heart, and in truth he was not mistaken; the speck piercing the air, which his keen eye had discovered, was no longer a mere spot, but an oblong something—a bird, the pigeon!

Wilhelm seized the flag on the balcony, and waved it as joyously as ever conqueror unfurled his banner after a hard-won fight. The dove came nearer— alighted, slipped into the cote, and a few minutes after the musician appeared with a tiny letter.

"To the magistrates!" cried Wilhelm. "Take it to your husband at once. Oh! dear lady, dear lady, finish what the dove has begun. Thank God! thank God! they are already at North-Aa. This will save the poor people from despair! And now one thing more! You shall have the roasted bird, but take this grain too; a barley-porridge is the best medicine for Barbara's condition; I've tried it!"

When evening came, and the musician had told his parents the joyful news, he ordered the blue dove with the white breast to be caught. "Kill it outside the house," said he, "I can't bear to see it."

Andreas soon came back with the beheaded pigeon.

His lips were bloody, Wilhelm knew from what, yet he did not reprove the hungry boy, but merely said:

"Fie, you pole-cat!"

Early the next morning a second dove returned. The letters the winged messengers had brought were read aloud from the windows of the town-hall, and the courage of the populace, pressed to the extremest limits of endurance, flickered up anew and helped them bear their misery. One of the letters were addressed to the magistrates, the other to Janus Dousa; they sounded confident and hopeful, and the Prince, the faithful shield of liberty, the friend and guide of the people, had recovered from his sickness and visited the vessels and troops intended for the relief of Leyden. Rescue was so near, but the north-east wind would not change, and the water did not rise. Great numbers of citizens, soldiers, magistrates and women stood on the citadel and other elevated places, gazing into the distance.

A thousand hands were clasped in fervent prayer, and the eyes of all were turned in feverish expectation and eager yearning towards the south, but the boundary line of the waves did not move; and the sun, as if in mockery, burst cheerily through the mists of the autumn morning, imparted a pleasant warmth to the keen air, and in the evening sank towards the west in the midst of radiant light, diffusing its golden rays far and wide. The cloudless blue sky arched pitilessly over the city, and at night glittered with thousands of twinkling stars. Early on the morning of the twenty-ninth the mists grew denser, the grass remained dry, the fogs lifted, the cool air changed to a sultry atmosphere, the grey clouds piled in masses on each other, and grew black and threatening. A light breeze rose, stirring the leafless branches of the trees, then a sudden gust of wind swept over the heads of the throngs watching the distant horizon. A second and third followed, then a howling tempest roared and hissed without cessation through the city, wrenching tiles from the roofs, twisting the fruit-trees in the gardens and the young elms and lindens in many a street, tearing away the flags the boys had fastened on the walls in defiance of the Spaniards, lashing the still waters of the city moat and quiet canals, and—the Lord does not abandon His own—and the vanes turned, the storm came from the north-west. No one saw the result, but the sailors shouted the tidings, and each individual caught up the words and bore them exultantly on—the hurricane drove the sea into the mouth of the Meuse, forcing back the waves of the river by its fierce assault, driving them over its banks through the gaps opened in the dykes, and the gates of the sluices, and bearing forward on their towering crests the vessels bringing deliverance.

Roar, roar, thou storm, stream, stream, rushing rain, rage, waves, and destroy the meadows, swallow up houses and villages! Thousands and thousands of people on the walls and towers of Leyden hail your approach, behold in you the terrible armies of the avenging God, exult and shout a joyous welcome!

For two successive days the burgomaster, Maria and Adrian, the Van der Does and Van Houts stood with brief intervals of rest among the throng on the citadel or the tower at the Cow-Gate; even Barbara, far more strengthened by hope than by the barley-porridge or the lean carrier-pigeon, would not stay at home, but dragged herself to the musician's look-out, for every one wanted to see the rising water, the earth softening, the moisture creeping between the blades of grass, then spreading into pools and ponds, until at last there was a wide expanse of water, on which bubbles rose, burst under the descending rain, and formed ever-widening circles. Every one wanted to watch the Spaniards, hurrying hither and thither like sheep pursued by a wolf. Every one wanted to hear the thunder of the Beggars' cannon, the rattle of their arquebuses and muskets; men and women thought the tempest that threatened to sweep them away, pleasanter than the softest breeze, and the pouring rain, which drenched them, preferable to spring dew-drops mirroring the sunshine.

Behind the strong fort of Lammen, defended by several hundred Spanish soldiers, and the Castle of Cronenstein, a keen eye could distinguish the Beggars' vessels.

During Thursday and Friday Wilhelm watched in vain for a dove, but on Saturday his best flier returned, bringing a letter from Admiral Boisot, who called upon the armed forces of the city to sally out on Friday and attack Lammen.

The storm had blown the pigeon away. It had reached the city too late, but on Saturday evening Janus Dousa and Captain Van der Laen were actively engaged, summoning every one capable of bearing arms to appear early Sunday morning. Poor, pale, emaciated troops were those who obeyed the leaders' call, but not a man was absent, and each stood ready to give his life for the deliverance of the city and his family.

The tempest had moderated, the firing had ceased, and the night was dark and sultry. No eyes wished to sleep, and those whom slumber overpowered for a short time, were startled and terrified by strange, mysterious noises. Wilhelm sat in his look-out, gazing towards the south and listening intently. Sometimes a light gust of wind whistled around the lofty house, sometimes a shout, a scream, or the blast of a trumpet echoed through the stillness of the night; then a crashing noise, as if an earthquake had shaken part of the city to its foundations, arose near the Cow-Gate. Not a star was visible in the sky, but bright spots, like will-o'-the-wisps, moved through the dense gloom in regular order near Lammen. It was a horrible, anxious night.

Early next morning the citizens saw that a part of the city-wall near the Cow-Gate had fallen, and then unexampled rejoicing arose at the breach, no longer dangerous; exultant cries echoed through every street and alley, drawing from the houses men and women, grey-beards and children, the sick and the well, one after another thronging to the Cow-Gate, where the Beggars' fleet was seen approaching. The city-carpenter, Thomassohn, and other men, tore out of the water the posts by which the Spaniards had attempted to bar the vessels' advance, then the first ship, followed by a second and third, arrived at the walls. Stern, bearded men, with fierce, scarred, weather-beaten faces, whose cheeks for years had been touched by no salt moisture, save the sea-spray, smiled kindly at the citizens, flung them one loaf of bread after another, and many other good things of which they had long been deprived, weeping and sobbing with emotion like children, while the poor people eat and eat, unable to utter a word of thanks. Then the leaders came, Admiral Boisot embraced the Van der Does and Burgomaster Van der Werff, the Beggar captain Van Duijkenburg was clasped in the arms of his mother, Barbara, and many a Leyden man hugged a liberator, on whom his eyes now rested for the first time. Many, many tears fell, thousands of hearts overflowed, and the Sunday bells, sounding so much clearer and gayer than usual, summoned rescuers and rescued to the churches to pray. The spacious sanctuary was too small for the worshippers, and when the pastor, Corneliussohn, who filled the place of the good Verstroot, now ill from caring for so many sufferers, called upon the congregation to give thanks, his exhortation had long since been anticipated; from the first notes of the organ, the thousands who poured into the church had been filled with the same eager longing, to utter thanks, thanks, fervent thanks.

In the Grey Sisters' chapel Father Damianus also thanked the Lord, and with him Nicolas Van Wibisma and other Catholics, who loved their native land and liberty.

After church Adrian, holding a piece of bread in one hand and his shoes in the other, waded at the head of his school-mates through the higher meadows to Leyderdorp, to see the Spaniards' deserted camp. There stood the superb tent of General Valdez, in which, over the bed, hung a map of the Rhine country, drawn by the Netherlander Beeldsnijder to injure his own nation. The boys looked at it, and a Beggar, who had formerly been in a writing-school and now looked like a sea-bear, said:

"Look here, my lads. There is the Land-scheiding. We first pierced that, but more was to be done. The green path had many obstacles, and here at the third. dyke—they call it the Front-way—there were hard nuts to crack, and farther progress was impossible. We now returned, made a wide circuit across the Segwaert-way, and through this canal here, where there was hard fighting, to North-Aa. The Zoetermeer Lake now lay behind us, but the water became too shallow and we could get no farther. Have you seen the great Ark of Delft? It's a huge vessel, moved by wheels, by which the water is thrust aside. You'll be delighted with it. At last the Lord gave us the storm and the spring-tide. Then the vessels had the right depth of water. There was warm work again at the Kirk-way, but the day before yesterday we reached Lammen. Many a brave man has fallen on both sides, but at Lammen every one expected the worst struggle to take place. We were going to attack it early this morning, but when day dawned everything was unnaturally quiet in the den, and moreover, a strange stillness prevailed. Then we thought: Leyden has surrendered; starvation conquered her. But it was nothing of the sort! You are people of the right stamp, and soon after a lad about as large as one of you, came to our vessel and told us he had seen a long procession of lights move out of the fort during the night and march away. At first we wouldn't believe him, but the boy was right. The water had grown too hot for the crabs, and the lights the lad saw were the Spaniards' lunts. Look, children, there is Lammen—"

Adrian had gone close to the map with his companions and now interrupted the Beggar by laughing loudly.

"What is it, curly-head?" asked the latter.

"Look, look!" cried the boy, " the great General Valdez has immortalized himself here, and there is his name too. Listen, listen! The rector would hang a placard with the word donkey round his neck, for he has written : '*Castelli parvi! Vale civitas, valete castelli parvi ; relicti estis propter aquam et non per vim inimicorum !*' Oh! the donkey ' *Castelli parvi !*'"

"What does it mean ?" asked the Beggar.

"Farewell, Leyden, farewell, ye little ' *Castelli*;' ye are abandoned on account of the waves, and not of the power of the enemy. ' *Parvi Castelli !*' I must tell mother that !"

On Monday, William of Orange entered Leyden, and went to Herr von Montfort's house. The people received their Father William with joy, and the unwearied champion of liberty, in the midst of the exultation and rejoicing that surrounded him, labored for the future prosperity of the city. At a later period he rewarded the faithful endurance of the people with a peerless memorial : the University of Leyden. This awakened and kept alive in the busy city and the country bleeding for years in severe conflicts, that lofty aspiration and effort, which is its own reward, and places eternal welfare far above mere temporal prosperity. The tree, whose seed was planted amid the deepest misery, conflict and calamity, has borne the noblest fruits for humanity, still bears them, and if it is the will of God will continue to bear them for centuries.

On the twenty-sixth of July, 1581, seven years after the rescue of Leyden, Holland and Zealand, whose political independence had already been established for six years, proclaimed themselves at the Hague free from Spain. Hitherto, William of Orange had ruled as King

Philip's "stadtholder," and even the war against the monarch had been carried on in his name. Nay, the document establishing the University, a paper, which with all the earnestness that dictated it, deserves to be called an unsurpassed masterpiece of the subtlest political irony, purported to issue from King Philip's mouth, and it sounds amusing enough to read in this paper, that the gloomy dunce in the Escurial, after mature deliberation with his dear and faithful cousin, William of Orange, has determined to found a free-school and university, from motives, which could not fail to seem abominable to the King.

On the twenty-fourth of July this game ceased, allegiance to Philip was renounced, and the Prince assumed sovereign authority.

Three days after, these joyful events were celebrated by a splendid banquet at Herr Van der Werff's house.

The windows of the dining-room were thrown wide open, and the fresh breeze of the summer night fanned the brows of the guests, who had assembled around the burgomaster's table. They were the most intimate friends of the family: Janus Dousa, Van Hout, the learned Doctor Grotius of Delft, who to Maria's delight had been invited to Leyden as a professor, and this very year filled the office of President of the new University, the learned tavern-keeper Aquanus, Doctor Bontius, now professor of medicine at the University, and many others.

The musician Wilhelm was also present, but no longer alone; beside him sat his beautiful, delicate wife, Anna d'Avila, with whom he had recently returned from Italy. He had borne for several years the name of Van Duivenbode (messenger-dove), which the city had bestowed on him, together with a coat of arms bearing three blue doves on a silver field and two crossed keys.

With the Prince's consent the legacies bequeathed by old Fraulein Van Hoogstraten to her relatives and servants, had been paid, and Wilhelm now occupied with his wife a beautiful new house, that did not lack a dovecote, and where Maria, though her four children gave her little time, took part in many a madrigal. The musician had much to say about Rome and his beautiful sister-in-law Henrica, to Adrian, now a fine young man, who had graduated at the University and was soon to be admitted to the council. Belotti, after the death of the young girl's father, who had seen and blessed Anna again, went to Italy with her, where she lived as superior of a secular institution, where music was cultivated with special devotion.

Barbara did not appear among the guests. She had plenty to do in the kitchen. Her white caps were now plaited with almost coquettish skill and care, and the firm, contented manner in which she ruled Trautchen and the two under maid-servants, showed that everything was going on well in Peter's house and business. It was worth while to do a great deal for the guests upstairs. Junker von Warmond was among them, and had been given the seat of honor between Doctor Grotius and Janus Dousa, the first trustee of the University, for he had become a great nobleman and influential statesman, who found much difficulty in getting time to leave the Hague and attend the banquet with his young assistant, Nicolas Van Wibisma. He drank to Meister Aquanus as eagerly and gaily as ever, exclaiming:

"To old times and our friend, Georg von Dornburg."

"With all my heart," replied the landlord. "We haven't heard of his bold deeds and expeditions for a long time."

"Of course! The fermenting wine is now clear. Dornburg is in the English service, and four weeks ago I met him as a member of her British Majesty's navy in London. His squadron is now on the way to Venice. He still cherishes an affectionate memory of Leyden, and sends kind remembrances to you, but you would never recognize in the dignified commander and quiet, cheerful man, our favorite in former days. How often his enthusiastic temperament carried him far beyond us all, and how it would make the heart ache to see him brooding mournfully over his secret grief."

"I met the Junker in Delft," said Doctor Grotius. "Such enthusiastic natures easily soar too high and then get a fall, but when they yoke themselves to the chariot of work and duty, their strength moves vast burdens, and with cheerful superiority conquers the hardest obstacles."

Meantime Adrian, at a sign from his father, had risen and filled the glasses with the best wine. The "hurrah," led by the Burgomaster, was given to the Prince, and Janus Dousa followed it by a toast to the independence and liberty of their native land.

Van Hout devoted a glass to the memory of the days of trouble, and the city's marvellous deliverance.

All joined in the toast, and after the cheers had died away, Aquanus said :

"Who would not gladly recall the exquisite Sunday of October third; but when I think of the misery that preceded it, my heart contracts, even at the present day."

At these words Peter clasped Maria's hand, pressed it tenderly, and whispered:

"And yet, on the saddest day of my life, I found my best treasure."

"So did I!" she replied, gazing gratefully into his faithful eyes.

THE END.